Arise

Book Two of the Henchmen Saga

by

Eric Lahti

Dedication

Dedicated to my wife and son.
And everyone who ever wanted to get in a running shootout with a bunch
of immortals.

Also by Eric Lahti:

Henchmen
Join a small organization of loveable bad guys: a supervillain and her henchmen. Eve, the seven-foot-tall, bulletproof blonde is their leader. Frank and Jean are a couple that can get into any computer or building unseen. Jacob is a rough-around-the-edges biker type that has a deep and abiding love of guns and explosives. And Steven? Well, he's really good at manipulating people and pretty handy to have around in a fight. As supervillainy goes, they're just starting out. They don't have much of a secret base. They don't have matching uniforms. Not a one of them owns a single pair of tights. What they do have is an interest in tearing down the country and watching it burn.

There's just one little problem, though. No matter how tough and smart a small group may be, tearing down a country is almost impossible for five people to pull off, so they while away their time pulling small jobs and putting together as much advanced technology as they can.

A chance encounter at a sushi bar has led them to a young woman with a terrifying secret she doesn't even know she possesses. The Yakuza wants to use her to put pressure on a missing father. No one's entirely certain exactly what the secret is, but it smells like a weapon and it might be just the sort of thing to help topple a nation.

They're done pulling small jobs. Now they're aiming for the top – because why bother robbing jewelry stores when you can topple governments?
Yakuza gang fights.
Incursions into high-security, top-secret government buildings.
Picking fake fights with losers in bars.
A psycho ex-coworker who has some strange friends.
And a well-dressed older gentleman who haunts dreams.
It's all in a day's work for Steven…one of the world's most dedicated and dangerous…
HENCHMEN

Contents

01 | I Hate Visitors 1
02 | The Best Part of Waking Up 6
03 | Because Fuck 'Em All, That's Why 11
04 | Viva Mexico 15
05 | Boom 20
06 | Raze the Bar 25
07 | Bordering on Sanity 34
08 | New Friends and Old 39
09 | Sheesh, How Many of These Guys Are There? 45
10 | First Class, Motherfuckers 48
11 | The Shadow Knows 56
12 | The Land of Enchantment 59
13 | Burgers! 63
14 | Dance Hall Days 74
16 | Dreamtime 81
17 | Could Be A Good Day 104
18 | Reprioritize Your Actionable Items Matrix 108
19 | Money Money Money Money Money 119
20 | Date Night 126
21 | Not These Guys Again 135
22 | We Are So Boned 140
23 | Smith, Mr. Smith 149
24 | My Idea of Roughing It… 157
25 | …Is No Room Service 163
26 | Hi, Can We Tell You About Our Lord And Savior, Cthulhu? 170
27 | HIPAA Violations Galore 175
28 | Going Down 180
29 | Finally Some Answers 186
30 | Hell Breaks Loose 192
31 | The Master Race 196
32 | Underground. Again. 203
33 | When Dreams Have Come 209
34 | Eve 215
35 | Feeling Stabby 223
36 | Dreamer. Again. 230

37 | Bad to Worse...235
38 | Tyson vs. Holyfield...240
39 | Meet the New Boss...244
40 | What I Don't Know About Being A God Could Fill A Warehouse....................249
41 | Like Moths to a Flame...255
42 | Time To Go..258
43 | With Great Power Comes Great Responsibility To Abuse That Power 262
Acknowledgments and Final Thoughts 270

01 | I Hate Visitors

Where were you when *it* happened?

This is the current question of the day from almost anyone you meet. No one needs to ask "when what happened?" because we all know what the asker is talking about.

It's used as an ice breaker, like asking what someone's major was or their sign is. It can be a challenge: Where were *you* when it happened? It can also be a straightforward question, a way to find out about someone.

People still remember exactly where they were, kind of like a lot of people still remember exactly where they were when they found out Elvis was dead (I was six, riding in a car with my mom and asking who is Elvis?) or when the towers came crashing down.

Your answer gives you a certain amount of street cred. If you say you were in Albuquerque, people act you're a returning war hero and ask you if you're OK. I actually met someone who was in the building when it all went down and barely escaped before the building collapsed. He was telling the story to people in some bar in Durango and was getting a lot of mileage, and drinks, out of it. I had to leave before I laughed out loud when he told everyone how he had the beast cornered and would have been able to stop the whole thing if those damned government agents hadn't screwed the whole thing up.

If you say you were in D.C., people treat you like a refugee from some genocide in Africa. If you were in Colorado, you're less of a hero, but all those southwestern states are, like, right next to each other, right? If you were in Texas you get to act like you could have stopped the whole thing with your trusty six shooter. Albuquerque gives you the best props, D.C. is a close second. You lose more and more cred the further away you were from either of those places. If you say you were in Minneapolis no one gives a rat's ass.

I was at ground zero, riding up an elevator with a demigoddess on one side and Dreamer on the other, hoping to hell I didn't get shot when the doors opened.

I don't bring this up.

Most people shed nary a tear over the death of everyone in Congress. Someone went so far, probably someone on 4chan, to put up a picture of everyone in the House dead and dismembered with the caption "You can't spell slaughter without laughter." The idea of killing Congress still brings a smile to a lot of faces, but the actuality of killing Congress still terrifies and enrages.

I still get a chuckle out of it, but I'm kind of a dick that way.

* * * *

Sometimes, I can feel Dreamer in my head. I'm beginning to wonder if it was a mistake to let him in. He's not exactly there there, but he's definitely there. That probably doesn't make much sense. Oh, well. I don't know if I can explain it more succinctly than this: I had a God in my head and my thoughts are still kind of tainted by his thoughts. My dreams are extremely vivid. For about a month after we let him out, I felt like I wasn't sleeping. It felt more like I would go to sleep and immediately wake up somewhere else as someone else.

Yeah. Pretty disorienting.

It took a while, but I finally realized I was jumping in and out of other people's dreams. Once I got that, it made more sense and I could relax into the situation. The end result was I got to get some meaningful sleep because I started shutting off my brain and treating the whole process as a movie, even if it was someone else's reality I was watching. In time, I learned to control the dream. That was always something I'd wanted to learn to do, anyway, and the results were pretty awesome. I found I could jump between people's dreams and ride along or change them to suit my own needs. It was a total rush, even if I couldn't control whose dreams I was watching.

Most of the time people's dreams are pretty bland: sitting at a desk working, fantasizing about the new secretary, driving a fast car, whatever. Every now and then I'd hit a nightmare. There are people out there who can dream up some pretty tweaked shit. I once came across someone who spent the night dreaming about dismembering prostitutes while she (the dreamer, not the prostitute) was dressed in an SS uniform. I slipped into someone dreaming in North Korea and woke up devastated. This kid was dreaming of finding ways to rat out his fellow prisoners so he could eat some more food. You know you're fucked when you're dreaming about getting other people killed so you can eat a bit more gruel. We should nuke that hermit kingdom and be done with it. It would be an act of pity for the people stuck living there and an act of revenge for their leaders.

Of course, there is the philosophy that holds that all reality is someone else's dream, so maybe my sleep and wake times are really just someone else's dreams.

* * * *

Hesperus, Colorado was gorgeous this winter. We got the kind of snow that buries all the evil in the world and makes you think there's nothing wrong. It was the perfect place to dream.

It's spring now, so the worst of the snow has melted off, but there's still plenty on the ground. The snow isn't so deep that you can't travel, but it's deep enough that the tourists stay away. The air is crisp and clear in the mornings. It's so quiet I can hear someone breathing from across the room so I don't even have to open my eyes to know I'm not alone and it doesn't surprise me in the slightest when a familiar voice says, "Good morning, sunshine."

"Fuck you, asshole," I reply. "I need some coffee before I deal with you."

Wilford Saxton is sitting across the room from me, holding my gun. He's wearing his traditional business casual attire: suit, no tie, semi-dress shoes. The last time I saw this man in the flesh he was lying in a pool of someone else's blood with a whole whack of tiny arrows in his head. That was the second time I'd shot him in the face. It was also the second time someone had dropped a building on him. Yet, here he is, not a scar on him. Not a hair out of place or a wrinkle in sight, either.

"What makes you think I'm not here to kill you or arrest you?" he asks.

"If you wanted me dead, you would've shot me while I was still sleeping. If you were going to arrest me, you wouldn't wait patiently for me to wake up. You're alone in here and not wearing your ID badge. You want something. Let me get some coffee and we'll talk." I tell him.

"Well, well, well," he says and then sighs. "You're still a regular Sherlock Holmes, aren't you?"

"Can you go somewhere else? Really, anywhere would do."

I slide out of my nice warm bed. It's not freezing all the time anymore, but it's still damned chilly in the mornings. When my feet hit the tile floor it's like sticking them in a freezer. Damn. I need to invest in heated floors one of these days.

"So, Captain Willard, why aren't you dead?" I ask.

"How many times do I have to tell you? I'm not a captain and my name's not Willard."

I sigh and look around for some socks and a warmer shirt. I find some socks that don't match – left is red, right is gray - and a sweatshirt with a three-eyed smiley face and "Mutants for a Nuclear America" written on it.

"That looks like a hell of a party you had last night." Saxton says.

"What party?" I ask.

"Really, Steven, I'm not an idiot. You're a neat-freak and there are beer cans all over the floor in your living room."

"You're the neat freak. I'm organized." I say. "What beer cans?"

"The ones all over the floor downstairs. I always thought you were one of those snooty bastards who only drank small batch beers made by hippies. I may have to adjust my opinion of you up a few notches. That was no small amount of MGD you put down last night. What was it, almost a case?"

For the record, life is too short to drink mass produced beer. It doesn't necessarily need to be made by hippies, but good beer needs to be made by people who care about beer. I don't think Miller Genuine Draft counts, and I've never cared for or bought the stuff.

Also for the record, Wilford Saxton is an ass.

"Can I have my gun back?" I ask him.

He tosses it to me and I check and make sure it's still loaded. My little buddy the .45 Detonics Combat Master still has rounds.

"What's going on, Steven?" He can sense that I'm nervous and he's got his own gun out now. We may not always get along, and I did once swear to take his head, but we worked together for a long time and have learned to read other. To be fair, I was peckish when

I swore to cut off his head and I get pretty grumpy when I get hungry. Also to be fair, I'm going to take his head.

"I don't know, but I do know I don't drink Miller. Someone else is in here." I tell him.

When I hear the toilet down the hall flush and the sink come on I relax a bit. People may be crazy and violent, but they usually don't waste time flushing the toilet and washing their hands when they break into your house to kill you.

A seven foot tall woman saunters down the hall and stops to stare at us. She's wearing a pair of men's sweats that barely make it to her calves and a Ministry T-Shirt. The opposite pair of my socks cover her feet; red on the right, gray on the left.

"Two questions: why are you guys holding guns and where's the coffee?"

Eve's eyes are red rimmed and her hair is mussed up. Apparently a case of MGD has the same effect on demi goddesses that it does on everyone else. It may taste like ass going down, but the hangover is spectacular.

"Hi, Eve," I say, lowering my gun. "You remember Wilford Saxton, you slammed his face into jail cell and I shot him in the head. We dropped a couple of buildings on him."

Eve peers at Saxton and recognition slowly penetrates her stupor. "Oh. Hi," she says and punches him.

02 | The Best Part of Waking Up

When Saxton comes to half an hour later we've got the espresso flowing like wine and Eve is in a much better mood. I hand him an espresso and an ice pack.

"Why the fuck did you hit me?" Saxton asks Eve.

"You were between me and coffee. Never get between me and coffee," she says. "Also, you're an ass and I don't trust you."

Wilford glares at her for a moment and then thinks better of pushing his luck. He sips his espresso and pushes the ice pack on the side of his face.

"So," Wilford finally asks Eve, "and don't take this the wrong way, what the hell are you?"

"Why aren't you dead?" She responds.

"For that matter," I chime in, "why are either of you here?"

Eve finishes her espresso and slides the cup over to me; the universal sign for more. "I had a case of beer and was in the area. You were already asleep like some old guy, though, and I had to drink it by myself."

"You were 'in the area?'" I say. "Eve, the area is miles from any place people go wandering around."

I look at Wilford, sipping his espresso and trying to look innocent. "And you. What the hell are you doing here if you're not trying to either kill me or arrest me?"

Eve points at her empty cup and coughs politely. Wilford acts like he's thinking.

I didn't think my security was so bad that anyone could simply wander in. Of course, there aren't a whole lot of doors that can keep Eve out and Wilford has snuck into places more fortified than this. All in all, I guess it's not an insult to my securing skills. I mean, it's not like I woke up and there was a cadre of teenagers in my living room.

"Guys. What the fuck is going on?" I ask my uninvited guests

Wilford crunches his face like he's about to admit he's into My Little Pony porn. "I got fired. Because of you."

"So," I say. "How is that my problem?"

"Well, I know you were involved in the late unpleasantness, but I can't prove it since you shot me before I could actually see anything. I wanted to know what you did and why," He says. "Then I was thinking about maybe shooting you. Then she showed up and punched me and here we are."

Eve smiles warmly at him. It's warm like the smile you get from a bear right before you get eaten. It's nice to have friends in high places. She waves her hand at me and points to her empty cup again. I'd better get a good tip out of this.

While I'm getting her third cappuccino of the morning ready, Wilford looks at Eve and says, "So that's why I'm here. Why are you here?" I swear he flinches slightly when he says it. Dude may be able to take a building falling on him, but I doubt it feels good.

"I'd really rather not discuss it with you here," she responds.

"Why?" he asks her. "What's wrong with me?"

"Jesus, you are dense," she responds. "You tortured him, tried to shoot a couple of my employees, killed one of them and cut off his head and hands and ordered your lackeys to shoot me. There's probably a bunch of other shit you've done that I wouldn't like and, frankly, I still think you're an ass."

Wilford looks a little hurt. "You guys broke into not one, but two, secret installations. Killed a bunch of my men, shot me in the face twice, blew up a DHS facility, detonated the Simms building, and unleashed some damned thing that killed almost everyone in Congress."

At least he hasn't figured out about Vegas.

Before we started in on all the stuff he knows about, we also robbed an R&D facility outside of Vegas. No one died, but we did manage to steal a lot of a very special material that goes rigid when it gets hit hard. It makes for very nice body armor.

It was in Vegas that we found Jessica and she's filled my dreams nearly every night since then, yet I can't quite make myself go find her. It's like a part of me feels she's safest where she is and my presence would put her in grave danger.

We were celebrating the successful heist at a sushi restaurant in

Las Vegas when we ran afoul of some Yakuza. There was some shooting and a fair bit of torturing and the gangsters got killed.

Not like it would make things much worse in the eyes of the law.

"Your people were trying to kill us," Eve says.

"Because you were breaking the law!" Wilford responds.

"Screw your laws and screw you," Eve says. "Try to stop me."

Wilford is getting pissed. He doesn't realize this will end badly for him if he lets his temper get the better of him. Amazingly, though, he manages to pull it together. He closes his eyes and takes a couple of deep breaths. "I don't want to stop you. I'd rather join you," he finally says.

Eve eyes him. "Join us in what? I wanted Congress dead and got my wish. I'm done."

"Technically speaking, there's still a few of them left," Wilford responds.

"So fucking what? Technically speaking there's a few Congress critters left. Realistically speaking the vast majority of them are dead," she responds.

"Then why are you here?" Wilford asks.

Her cappuccino finally finishes brewing and she gives me the two-handed gimme gimme gimme show. She takes it half steamed milk, half espresso, no sugar. Easy enough to do, but I never could stand coffee with no sugar.

She grasps the giant mug in both hands, sips it, and sighs like she just drank the nectar of the gods. Which, frankly, my cappuccino is.

"Well?" asks Wilford.

"Well what?" Eve responds. "Oh. Sorry. The cappuccino is great, thank you. This is probably the best thing the Italians ever gave the world."

I nod to her and toast her with my half-full cup.

"No. Why are you here?" Wilford asks again. "Seriously, who are you?"

I'd like to warn him to tread lightly, but I know he won't listen.

"I'm here because one of my friends is in a Mexican prison and I thought Steven here would enjoy helping me break him out. What I am is none of your fucking business. Ask me again and I'll rip your spine out through your nose. You may be able to take a face full of bullets and buildings, but I'd love to see you survive that."

I don't doubt that she would do it.

Wilford blanches, but maintains his cool. "Okay, okay. Why show up when you could have called?"

Eve shrugs and says, "I believe in the personal touch. Call it old-school, but I like to discuss things in person. Now, all that earlier bullshit about being fired aside, why are you here?"

"Yeah," I chime in, "it's not like you were fired because you couldn't find me, because, like, here you are. What's really going on?"

Wilford stares at his cup and sighs. "I really was fired. I could have turned you in any time I wanted. I knew exactly where you were, but I started seeing strange behaviors in DHS. People were moving around like they were in a dream and no one, and I mean no one, seemed interested in the case. I got my ass chewed when I went on the news and put up the pictures of you guys. Whatever you guys let slip infiltrated everything and it seems to want you left alone."

I look at Eve. I have absolutely no problem wiping out Congress critters, in fact I think it should happen more frequently. This seems different, though, and not necessarily good.

"You think he's taking over everything?" I ask.

She shrugs. "Possible. I don't really care. Let him have it."

"What's going on, Eve?"

"Nothing. Let it go," she replies.

"Not this time. What the hell is going on and why are you here?" I ask again.

"There are rumblings that you and everyone else is in danger. Certain…individuals…want you eliminated," she says.

"Well, that's nothing new. There's a guy in my kitchen right now that wants me eliminated. Is that why you're here?" I ask.

"Yeah. I … Kind of. I was sent to take care of you. As a kind of retribution."

OK, that's kind of scary. Wilford I can handle. Eve would break me into tiny pieces and there's not a damned thing I can do about it. It's not the death I'm worried about so much, everyone dies. It hurts to think Eve might do it. Still, there are rules about this kind of situation and they decree that you must keep your cool.

"Alright. There are two people in my kitchen right now that

want me dead. It must be a Tuesday," I say.

"I don't want to kill you, but they'll send others after both of us now. And the others. Jacob, Frank, Jessica, they're all targeted." I feel a stab when she mentions Jessica. Unlike the rest of us, Jessica didn't have much of a choice, she was dropped in the middle of this mess when her father sent her a postcard.

She points at Wilford, "They'll probably send someone after him, too."

"Who will send someone after me?" Wilford asks.

"You know what, it's best you don't know. The less you know, the better off you are," she responds.

"Better off? Someone's coming to kill me and you won't tell me because it might make it worse for me?" I say. Eve's cageyness has always been frustrating, but this is getting ridiculous. It's not like I can force the information out of her.

She tries to give me the innocent look, but fails miserably.

"You know what? Fuck you both." I point at Eve. "I worked some fucking magic for you and kept my mouth shut about it." Then I point at Wilford. "I kept your secrets and you kept your precious job. And this is how you guys pay me back?"

I leave them sitting there sipping their coffee and head out back to smoke.

03 | Because Fuck 'Em All, That's Why

The back of my house faces east toward the mountains and away from the road. I can stand out here and pretend there's no one left on Earth. I have a perfect view of nothing but nature. There's not even a fence in sight, just aspens up the mountains and evergreens going up the side of the mountain. Both sides have a lot of windows to capture the passive solar heat. It gets cold up here and every little bit helps. If I turn around, I could see straight through my house.

I can see Wilford get up and grab some milk out of the fridge. Who the fuck does he think he is? What gives him the right to get my milk out of my fridge? I've got half a mind to grab a kukri out of my arsenal and cut that fucker to pieces. If he survives, so much the better. Teach him to take my milk.

I stop myself before I can go through with it. *Take a deep breath, Steven, and relax. It's only milk.*

I've been finding myself getting more and more enraged over trivial things lately. Granted, my two problems inside are not trivial, but Wilford getting some milk almost drove me to murder him. So far, I've managed to keep it from overcoming me, but one of these days something bad is going to happen if I don't get it all sorted out.

It gets worse when I think about Jessica. Every time her face crosses my mind I feel an incredible pull to go find her and bring her back.

I need someone to talk to and neither of those two honyocks inside will do. Wilford's a dick. We got along alright and worked together well, but he's still a dick and I don't entirely trust him. Eve, for all intents and purposes, is some kind of demigoddess. You don't seek out goddesses for advice. They're too far removed from

11

humanity. I need Frank or Jessica.

The cigarette and the cold clear my senses and let me focus on the problem. In my car, a Subaru Impreza Sti if you must know, is a button hidden in under the driver's seat. That button is my escape plan. Push it and the twenty pounds of C4 I have hidden around the walls of my place will detonate. If I was smart, I'd push that button and send both Eve and Wilford straight to hell.

Oh, who the fuck am I kidding? I could nuke my house and all that would happen is Wilford would be out of commission for a week or so, Eve would need to get some new clothes and I'd be out the A-frame house in the mountains I always wanted. Shit.

In every situation there's a point when it becomes more and more obvious that the only way out is through. You can't run from it, you can't avoid it, you have to power through it and hope for the best. If you make it through, you're that much better off for it. If you fail, fail spectacularly and take out as many of the bastards as you can before you go down.

I put out my cigarette and go back inside.

"So," I say. "We go find Dreamer, right? I mean, he's infiltrating DHS and God only knows what else, and he's pissed off your people, whoever the hell they are, right? Am I missing anything here?"

Wilford shakes his head. "That would appear to sum it up."

"Eve?" I ask.

She shakes her head and slides her cappuccino cup toward me.

"Make your own damned coffee," I tell her and her face falls a notch.

I shouldn't be too harsh on her. She didn't kill me, and did warn me that bad things were coming. I grab her mug and head over to the machine. While I'm refilling it I ponder the situation. D.C. is impenetrable right now. We need backup. We need guns. We need someone who can get in and out places.

I hand Eve her cup and she smiles a sad "Thank you" at me.

"We need everyone back," I say. "Who's in prison in Mexico?"

"Jacob. He got grabbed by the Federales for moving unlicensed firearms around," Eve tells me.

Jacob is a former and future member of our little cabal. He was a biker once, not that long ago, and his MC (don't call it a biker gang, call it an MC – Motorcycle Club) got into a shootout with the

FBI. The FBI took umbrage at Jacob's former MC selling weapons to anyone with cash. There was some gun play, some dead bikers, some dead Feds, and we found Jacob at a rest stop. He's a hell of a resource when it comes to finding guns and an expert at blowing things up.

"Better the Federales than one of the cartels," Wilford says. I've got to agree with him. The Mexican Federales might be corrupt - like all law-enforcement agencies - but I'd rather hang out with them than the crazy bastards in the cartels. The Feds might rough you up. The cartels will put you in barrel and set your ass on fire.

"OK. We'll need to get him out. Wilford, did you perchance keep your badge when you left DHS?"

He nods. "They're so whacked out over there right now that no one even thought to ask for it."

"Good. It might come in handy. We'll need to scrounge up some paperwork to make it look official. Frank's in Seattle. If I give him a call he can probably meet us in Albuquerque or Las Cruces."

Frank was our expert at getting into places. He's a master at breaking and entering and one Hell of a planner. We'll need him if we're going to get into anything more difficult than a Tuff Shed.

"Jessica's running a bar somewhere in Mexico," I add, "We'll need to find her, too."

They both look at me.

"Who?" Wilford asks.

"Jessica," I say.

"Jessica? The girl at the Simms building?" Wilford asks.

"Yeah, why?" I ask.

"What do you need with her?" Wilford asks. "The other two, I get. Guns and infiltration. What does the girl bring?"

What indeed? I'm not 100% positive why I need to get to her, I just know I do.

"Backup," I improvise, "I trust both of you about as far as I can throw you right now. Unfortunately, I can't kill you two and pretend I've never heard of you. I need someone else I can trust. I need a fighter."

"Sure. A fighter with a nice rack," Wilford smirks.

"I can't kill you, fuck-nuts, but I can make you hurt," I spit at him. "Speaking of which, why can't I kill you?"

"I didn't get fired only for failing to bring you two in. When I woke up after you'd shot me in the face I thought it was only a dream. Until I found one of those flechette darts stuck in my shirt. I started digging into my own file and hacked through the encrypted parts," he says.

"What was in the encrypted part?" Eve asks him.

"They did something to me. I don't know what it was, but they did it without asking and won't tell me what it was," he replies. "Even the classified file I found was heavily redacted. The original might have more, but that's locked in a safe at HQ."

"In D.C.?," I ask.

"Yup."

Typical government bullshit. I'm not trying to imply that all government agencies experiment on random workers, but it's definitely not unheard of for an agency to experiment on its own people. From spraying people with DDT or Agent Orange to letting employees watch atomic blasts without warning them of the danger, it's a time-honored tradition in government circles to run some experiments and not tell anyone about it.

"That's why you want to come with us, right? Not because of any misplaced sense of honor, you want to know what they did to you," Eve says.

Wilford nods.

"Alright," I say. "Let's get started. I'll get hold of Frank. Wilford, there's a computer in the office, see if you can find some official-looking prisoner transfer request forms. Eve, see if you can get hold of Jessica. Her number's on the wall there."

"Would that be the number under the picture of her in a bikini?" Eve smirks.

04 | Viva Mexico

Jacob is currently being held in a state prison in Ciudad Juarez, Mexico, immediately across the border from El Paso, Texas. From all accounts, it's not a nice place. The prison, I mean. Juarez is simply another town with an exceptionally high murder rate, but with generally nice people. Think Detroit but with better food and cheaper beer. If you don't cross paths with the murderous thugs running the drug rings, you'll be fine.

I'll be meeting with Frank at the San Diego airport tomorrow afternoon. It's a short timeline, but doable. Either our plan to pull Jacob out of prison will work within a few hours or it won't work at all. Eve is still being cagey about exactly who is after us but it's plainly obvious that she's scared of them. Anyone that can scare that woman is worth being scared of, so we decided to get everyone back together and in one place sooner rather than later. There is strength in numbers, after all.

Frank would have met us in El Paso, but apparently his new beau balked at him leaving so I offered to meet the guy. I have no idea what I'm going to say to Frank's new guy. I'm terrible at easing people's worries or generally lightening their load. My idea of easing worries is remember Mencius's famous saying: "I dislike death, however, there are some things I dislike more than death. Therefore, there are times when I will not avoid danger."

It usually doesn't make people feel better.

No one could get hold of Jessica, which scares me, but we did find out her bar is on the beach in Tijuana. I spent a couple of days calling, but no one answered. My heart says she's okay, but my mind is terrified she's in serious trouble. Hopefully I'll be able to find her safe and sound and we can both meet up with Frank.

Since Jacob is actually incarcerated, though, he's our first target. Americans have this vision of Mexico that's completely incompatible with the truth. Sure, it's a poor country, but Americans seem to envision Mexico as nothing but mud huts and people in huge sombreros sleeping off tequila benders under saguaro cacti. The truth is Juarez looks an awful lot like every other human city on the planet. Roads, libraries, banks, businesses, bars. Pick any given town in the U.S., change the language on all the signs, and you've got Juarez.

There is one notable difference, though, between Juarez and most U.S. cities: the walls of pictures of missing girls. This is not a good a place to be a pretty girl in. Most of these missing girls are abducted, hooked on drugs and forced into prostitution. The desert is filled with their corpses and the problem is so epidemic the local police have largely given up trying to sort it all out. They have larger problems trying to keep people alive in a city overrun with drug cartels. Like I said, think Detroit.

The state prison in Juarez looks like almost every other prison on the planet. It's blocky, surrounded by razor wire and full of locked doors. There was a riot here a while back that killed twenty or so people and required the Mexican Army and police forces to put down.

It's quiet here today. Well, quiet for a prison, which actually means pretty loud. When prisons go quiet, that's when you need to beat a path for the door with the speed of a thousand horses. It's quiet in the sense that it doesn't feel like it's about to explode.

Wilford and I have our best federal-looking suits on, dark gray with crisp white shirts, shiny black shoes, and IDs on lanyards. His ID is real, if not exactly legit at the moment; mine we had to make up and hope no one looks at too closely. Normally it would require the FBI to request a prison transfer from a foreign country, but we're hoping no one here realizes this. We've also got a tidy sum of cash on hand if need be.

We check our guns at the office and are escorted through security.

The prison warden is a guy named Ruben Galbán and he is a real pig of a man. His suit is trashy, even by prison warden standards. To say it looks like his suit was made from hotel curtains would be an insult to hotel curtains. His beady little eyes scream cruelty. Fortunately, he's also got the stink of greed on him, so this may go our way after all.

His office is spartan, a solid metal desk that's seen better days, an aging computer, a potted plant that could use some water, and a book shelf with surprisingly few books on it. My Spanish is pretty shaky, but they all look to be about psychology and prison operations.

Galbán peruses our paperwork, acting like he's looking it over with a fine-toothed comb. In reality he's trying to show how powerful he is by making us wait. Saxton explained to us on the way over that all field agents have to attend a class on dealing with foreign officials. Among other things, the class explained that it is extremely common for foreign officials to be put off and nervous around U.S. agents. We, as a country, have something of a reputation out in the world, and some of these small functionaries feel the need to show us that they're not afraid of us. This display of power usually comes in the form of some pathetic show like making you wait a long time or finding every damned little thing that's wrong with a form and making you fix it in front of them. It's pathetic, but U.S. agents are trained to smile and take it.

"This man you're looking for, Jacob Skelton, he's wanted for drug smuggling. It won't be easy to get him out," Galbán finally says. "My government is trying to crack down on the drug cartels."

"I certainly understand that, sir," Wilford says putting the perfect about of emphasis on the *sir*. "Our government is dedicated to doing exactly the same thing. Drugs are a blight and we'd like to see them eradicated."

Galbán nods. "*Sí*, drugs have ruined my country. Every day people in my city are murdered by these running dogs."

"Sir, I completely agree with you, they are running dogs and are ruining everything they touch," Wilford responds.

"This man, this Jacob Skelton, has worked for the cartels. We caught him and his gang trying to smuggle guns to the Aztecas. Your country floods my country with guns to fuel the violence."

"That's why we want Skelton back in U.S. custody," Wilford says. "We think he's a mid-level runner and we want to find out where he's getting his weapons."

"Because people in your country keep buying the drugs these cartel dogs make, the cartels have more power than my government."

This is another power tactic. No matter what the problem with your country is, it's America's fault.

"Believe me, sir, we are doing everything in our power to arrest those responsible for these crimes," Wilford responds.

Another tactic. Never tell these guys that they're wrong.

"Yes, I know. I've seen your commercials and your incarceration rates. Still, the problem continues, no?" Galbán says with a sigh. His sigh says it all, he's fighting the good fight and it's all America's fault that he has to carry this burden.

"It is a problem we're committed to eradicating."

"This man committed crimes against Mexico on Mexican soil. He should pay for his crimes here."

This is getting tiresome. I never had the patience to deal with these people. If I were up to me, I would've simply thumped this guy and made him carry Jacob out.

"We completely understand your reticence to hand him over. If our roles were reversed I would certainly hold that position," Wilford tells him, buttering him up.

Galbán glances at the paperwork on his desk. Shuffling through the sheaf of papers in front of him, he says, "I'm not sure this paperwork is completely in order. Some of these are in blue pen, but we specifically require transfer requests to be in black ink to make it easier to read."

"I have to apologize, sir, my trainee here is still learning the ropes."

Wilford looks at me, a not so subtle encouragement to apologize for my *faux pas*.

"My apologies, sir. I'm hoping to learn to ropes," I say with a smile. Jesus, I'd like to strangle this bastard.

Galbán's face softens. He's gotten a concession and his ego has pumped up a notch. "*Señor*, everybody has to start somewhere. I'll personally make sure the form processor understands that this is OK. Just this time, though."

Asshole.

"Thank you, sir," I tell him acting like I'm sighing in relief.

He eats it up. It's not every day you get American agents thanking you. Tonight, he'll be a stallion with whatever young girl he pays to have sex with. Luckily for her it will probably be over pretty quickly.

"Well," Galbán says, leaning back in his chair, "That settles that. Now, all that's left is the matter of the transfer fee."

And there it is. The transfer fee is actually nothing more than a bribe, or a *mordida* as it's more colloquially known.

"Of course, sir," Wilford says, smiling, "We understand and appreciate the amount of effort it takes for you to release a prisoner into our custody." Wilford pulls an envelope from inside his suit and sets it in front of Galbán. "Thank very much for allowing us to take up some of your important time and please don't hesitate to ask if you need anything from either agent Smith or me in the future."

We shake hands and Galbán tells us he'll have Jacob out in the reception area within the hour. Unfortunately, he explains to us, it takes time to locate prisoners and bring them out.

It winds up taking slightly over three hours. Yet another little power play from Galbán.

Jacob is escorted to us by two armed guards. He looks like he's been whacked about with a stick a few times and is in a pretty foul mood when they bring him in. His countenance lightens significantly when he sees us. Fortunately, he's smart enough to hide it.

The guards uncuff him and shove him toward us. I manage to catch Jacob before he falls and Wilford slaps some cuffs on him. Jacob fights him and starts yelling about the "fucking fascists that railroaded him" until one of the Federales slams him in the kidney with a baton. Jacob falls to his knees and the guard asks Wilford, "You sure you don't want one of us to come with you, *pendejo?*"

His buddies get quite a laugh out of that. Jacob will be pissing blood for a week from the blow.

Wilford and I pull Jacob up and march him out of the building and into the waiting car. As soon as we turn the corner Eve unlocks his cuffs and we head the hell out of Juarez.

That right there is the beauty of corruption; we just busted a guy out of prison without firing a shot or picking a lock. We didn't have to wade through sewers or dig a tunnel. The bribe was only $3,000 and, had we felt like pushing our luck, could probably have gotten Jacob out for $500.

God, I love corrupt functionaries.

05 | Boom

Borders between nations are rarely as cut and dried as we like to think. Sure, there's a physical line between countries, and when you cross that line you have technically crossed into a different country. The actual border between countries is usually a nebulous affair and, like all nebulous affairs, it's rarely a pretty picture. Well, except for the border between Canada and the U.S., but that's only because the Canadians are so damned nice.

The border between the United States and Mexico is pretty porous and has been used as political capital by both major parties for years. It's been used as a source of more boogeymen than the actual gates of Hell. Like everything else those idiots scream about, the truth is pretty tame. Most people crossing the border only want to make a few bucks and send some money home to their families. I've heard people, for years now, screaming "They're taking our jobs!" and I've never been able to fathom exactly how this is. I've never been passed over for a job because the company found some semi-literate itinerant worker to take my place.

Anyway, the border between the U.S. and Mexico is an industrialized wasteland. The crime rate is phenomenal, the police presence is minimal and it's the perfect place to stage a surprise attack.

We rolled across the bridge in Saxton's official Suburban. It's black with tinted windows and all but screams Government. The only thing that could make it a more obvious government vehicle would be a flashing neon sign on the hood that read "Your tax dollars at work."

We're out of sight of the border when the first shooter opens up. We never see him, the windshield erupts in spider webs and the whole truck rocks back and forth like we've got an orgy going on in here. It's over in a few seconds, but a few seconds of lead flying at you feels like an eternity. Then, as suddenly as it started, the attack is over and the sudden silence feels stifling.

No one moves for a beat.

The first voice to break the silence is Wilford's. "I guess they didn't realize these things are bullet-proof."

"They knew," Eve says. "This was just a warning."

I turn around to look at her. She's mad.

"Who knew?" I ask her.

"The shooters," she says, "and the people that sent them. These guys were hired guns, if they really wanted us dead, they would have sent their real hitters."

"Who are the *real hitters*?" Wilford asks.

"Modified assassins, bodies rebuilt into nearly indestructible tanks. Shoot them and they'll fall down and get right back up. Cut them and they won't bleed. They're true believers who have no qualms with losing their humanity in favor of becoming walking weapons," Eve says.

I get a vision of Wilford lying on the ground with a face full of flechettes and no blood. I've personally shot him twice and seen a couple of buildings dropped on him. The DHS office in Albuquerque was detonated while he was in it and then the Simms building fell on him. Yet, here he is, smiling and driving a purloined Suburban.

"What kind of walking weapons?" I ask.

"A lot like him, but more powerful," Eve says pointing at Wilford. "Almost indestructible. Not entirely bullet-proof, but they heal extremely rapidly."

"And they use assault rifles?" Wilford asks. "Seems kind of lazy, you know? Why make things like that and then give them AKs?"

"The guys that shot us up were nothing more than regular thugs, probably hired cartel members who didn't even know who they were working for. The real hitters are more like the people they work for and their weapons are far more dangerous."

"Eve, who are we really up against?" I ask.

Eve sighs and rubs the bridge of her nose. I know she doesn't want to talk about this, but it's high time we got a better of idea of the enemy. I fix her with my best serious stare and motion to Wilford to keep the Suburban stopped.

She stares back at me and you can see the gears whirring. She almost starts trying to tell us the same old line about we're better off not knowing but thinks better of it.

"You would probably call them gods, but that's kind of an oversimplification. They're powerful, to be sure, but they're basically personifications of various forces. Or the forces are force versions of them. What you see may look mostly human, but what you can see is the tip of the iceberg. They're much, much deeper than you can imagine."

"Like Dreamer?"

"Exactly, but representative of different things. Fear, hope, anger, dreams. Hell, the land itself has its own power and its own gods."

"How do you know all this?" Wilford asks.

"Because I've tangled with them before," Eve replies. "Believe me, they're not to be trifled with."

"If they're so powerful, why send hired guns? Why not show up and screw with us in person?" Wilford asks.

"They think humans are beneath them and regular interaction with you is distasteful, almost like a taboo," Eve says, staring out the window at the broken down world around us. "This is just the first volley, there will be more."

"So, we're kind of stuck between the proverbial rock and hard place, right? We don't have anything that can take out one god and if we don't take him out the rest of the gods are coming after us?" I ask.

"Basically, yeah," Eve sighs. "Can we get moving again? I don't like sitting here. One of those assholes might have a rocket launcher."

Wilford gets the big Suburban moving again and the thing acts like it wasn't peppered with lead a few minutes ago. Say what you will about government Suburbans, they're tough.

You'd think someone would have noticed a couple of guys opening up with AKs in the middle of El Paso, but this is the border area; it doesn't happen all the time, but people around here are smart enough to keep their heads down when the lead starts flying.

"We're boned, aren't we?" Jacob says as we pull away from the corner. "You guys busted me out of prison just in time for something to whack me on the outside."

"You're welcome," Wilford says with a huge grin.

"We need to get everyone back together," I say. "If we keep running we're well and truly fucked. Maybe if we go on the offensive, we'll have a shot."

"You want to march into D.C., a place that's been surrounded by a fog? A place that no one has come back out of? I knew people who were stationed around that place, they said you could hear screaming twenty four hours a day. Some guy got too close to the fog and something ripped him in half and chucked the pieces at a tank. You want to go into that and take this guy on in his own turf?" Wilford says incredulously.

"Got a better idea?" I ask.

"Yeah, steal a nuke from Kirtland and drop in on D.C.," Wilford says.

"What makes you think that will work?" Eve asks.

"It's a nuke. That's what makes me think it will work. Fry that whole place and kill all the monsters," Wilford responds.

I have to admit, that's a thought. The only problem is breaking into Kirtland Air Force Base isn't an easy task, and locating the nukes is even harder. They're probably stuffed into the side of the mountain somewhere and surrounded by serious people with serious guns.

The other problem I keep bumping into is I'm not entirely certain I want to take out Dreamer. I think it may be possible to join up with him. I'm not sure now is the best time to bring it up, though.

"You want to break into an Air Force Base?" Jacob asks. "That seems pretty reckless."

"Worse than trying to get through whatever's in that fog?" Wilford asks.

"Do you know how to set off a nuke?" I ask. "Because I wouldn't have the first fucking clue about how to do that. It's not like there's a button you can push that detonates one."

"No, but I'm sure someone on the Internet knows how to."

"We'd have to get it off base, too, and find a way to deliver it to DC," Eve says.

"FedEx has strict prohibitions about delivering explosives," Jacob adds. "And they actually do check. Trust me, I've tried."

Everyone stops and stares at him for a moment. Even after someone has shot at us. Even after we found out gods are gunning for us. Even after all the shit we've been through today everything is thinking the exact same thing I am.

"Why were you FedExing explosives?" I ask.

"I was running late and needed them delivered the next day," Jacob says with a sly grin. "I paid for extra insurance."

"Oh. My. God," is all Wilford can come up with. "How are you not cooling your heels in Cuba?"

"Used a fake name, fake address. I'm not an idiot, you know," Jacob growls.

"You are going to have to tell me the whole story about that someday," Eve says. "In the interim, we need to get everyone back together and get the base back in order. Once we're settled and secured, we can continue planning."

"You got it boss," Jacob says, happy to be doing something.

"Can't wait to see the mythical evil lair," Wilford says.

"Great. Jacob, Wilford, you're with me. Steven, get Frank and your girl and bring them back."

"Wait a minute, now she's my girl?" I say.

"I'm not the one who had a picture of her in a bikini on my fridge," Eve says.

Okay, so she's got me there.

"Drop me at the airport," I say. "I can catch a flight from here to San Diego and walk across the border."

06 | Raze the Bar

If Ciudad Juarez is Mexico's Detroit, Tijuana is their San Diego. Tijuana has its seedy parts, but it's mostly plain and safe. The city has a vested interest in keeping itself safe. The place is a tourist trap and tourists don't go to scary places.

Jessica's bar is on the beach in Tijuana, right up next to the U.S. border, in what looks like an old car repair shop. The main bar is built into the repair floor and the old garage-type doors are still there. She probably opens them up when the weather's nice, but it's still too chilly to keep them open. The place is designed to look a bit seedy and tough and caters to the tourists who want to feel like they're in an authentic Mexican dive bar without having to worry about getting gutted in the bathroom. The place looks a bit beat up. The tables and chairs have chips in them, but everything's been sanded smooth and lacquered. The walls are covered with pictures of Mexican wrestlers, with a giant poster of Mil Mascaras right over the bar.

The place is fairly quiet with only a few patrons. It's still off-season in Tijuana, but I'm sure during tourist season this place would be jam packed with college students trying to have sex with each other.

Jessica is behind the bar, laughing at some patron's joke while she hands him a beer. Her black hair is pulled back into a pony tail. She's wearing a red lace-topped camisole under a black leather motorcycle jacket. When she turns around to get the guy another beer, I see the back of her jacket features a cartoon cow holding a shotgun with "Janitors of Anarchy Motorcycle Club Albuquerque Original" written in a roundel around the cow. She had Jacob's art work transferred to the back of a jacket that actually fits her. Jacob's old jacket is in a glass frame behind the bar. Jessica looks radiant. After she hands the guy his second beer, she leans on her elbows on the bar while the guy wildly gestures about something. She listens for a minute, jots something on bar napkin and slides it to him, pointing to the south.

The guy at the bar thanks her, says something that makes her laugh and heads back to his seat where his girlfriend is looking less than happy at him for flirting with the hot bartender. They'll have their drinks, maybe a small argument, and get over it. It's Tijuana: they'll be screwing each other's brains out on some secluded beach within an hour.

Jessica leans back against the rack of booze behind the bar, brushes a stray lock of hair from her face, crosses her arms and looks around the bar. Whatever veneer of happiness she had with the guy has faded and she looks sad and bored. Her eyes slide across me and keep going. About half way past me recognition kicks in and she does a double take, staring at me wide-eyed. A little smile plays across her lips. She turns around, grabs a bottle of scotch and sets two shot glasses on the bar. She walks around the bar and motions me over.

There's an awkward moment when I get there. You know how it is when you see someone for the first time for a long time and neither of you is sure of what to do? We can't decide whether to shake hands or hug and wind up doing a little dance before settling on both. She grabs my shoulders, pushes me back at arm's length and looks at me. I must pass muster because she smiles, hugs me again, and then pushes me into a bar stool.

That stray lock of hair is back in her face and she pushes it away while she pours two shots. Without saying a word, she takes one, hands me the other and toasts. We both drain the shots and she pours two more and sits down next to me.

"I wondered if you'd ever come see me," she says.

"Sorry for the delay," I tell her. "I was snowed in."

"How is ... where was it? Somewhere in Colorado?"

"Hesperus," I tell her. "Well, La Plata canyon to be more specific."

"How is Hesperus?" she asks.

"Tiny, quiet and quite chilly right now," I say. "We still have snow on the ground. I like your bar. Never figured you for a Lucha Libre fan, though."

She rolls her eyes and laughs. "I always thought it would be cool to own a bar on the beach. It actually kind of sucks. It's a lot of damned work and the tourists are so damned pushy. I always heard about ugly Americans in foreign countries, but, damn, these people are annoying as shit."

We look at each other for a while, not sure what to say, and then down our shots.

"Jessica," I say. It feels right to see her again, but I also feel like I'm dragging her back into something she didn't really want be a part of in the first place. Something about how I say her name or the look on my face must sound strange to her.

"Uh, oh. That doesn't sound like happy," she says.

"I'm happy to see you, don't get me wrong, but we've got a problem, and I think you might be in danger."

"I'm in danger every time I drink the water down here," she says.

I chuckle. I've had Montezuma's Revenge, it's no fun.

"Eve screwed up," I say. "Her penance was to kill me. Since she won't do it, the people she pissed off are gunning for all of us."

Her smile falls. "Who does she work for that would go after us for killing Congress?"

"I don't know who she pissed off and she's being evasive about it.. Gods or spirits or something. I do know that whoever they are, they couldn't give a damn about Congress. They're pissed that we released Dreamer. Apparently that wasn't supposed to happen."

"So, because she won't kill you, the rest of us are fucked?" she asks. "Seems like I could shoot you and save everyone a lot of time."

When I turn a little white, she laughs at me. "I wouldn't kill you. I might shoot Eve, but I doubt it would do any good."

She pours two more shots and we down them. I'm beginning to feel like I'm in a bar in Mongolia. I'm not a lightweight, but three shots in five minutes are starting to take their toll.

"So, what's the plan?" she asks.

"We're going into D.C. Since the bad guys are pissed about us releasing Dreamer, it seems like the best bet would be to go ask him why. Wilford says Dreamer's slowly infiltrated DHS, and I imagine everything else, too," I tell her. "Well, either that or we're going nuke D.C. Frankly, the plan is kind of up in the air right now."

I can see she's confused. She's got that cute little furrow on her brow. Yep, I'm getting a bit tipsy.

"Who's Wilford?"

"The guy who tortured me and held you and Jacob at gunpoint in the Simms building."

"The guy you shot in the face twice?" she asks. "How is he still alive?"

"I don't know and he doesn't know."

"I trust you beat the shit out of him regularly. He seemed like a dick," she says.

"He's kind of working with us," I tell her.

"What? Are you nuts?"

"Yeah, but that's beside the point," I tell her. "He got fired when he was trying to figure out how he survived. He came to me for help."

"You know you can't trust him, right?"

"Yeah, I know. He's a duplicitous bastard under the best of circumstances," I tell her. "We have similar goals and could use his help, though."

"Just so you know I'm going to knock that guy on his ass if I see him."

"Eve already did," I say. "Knocked him out cold for half an hour."

She laughs. "Good. I still want to kick him in the nuts, though."

"Can't blame you."

"So, where is everyone else?" she asks me.

"Setting up shop in Albuquerque. Apparently no one ever discovered our old hideout. Rather than clean up six months of dirt and rotting food, I volunteered to come find you and Frank," I say.

"Is that the only reason you came?" she asks.

How do I handle this? I've daydreamed of this woman for nearly six months. I'm too damned old to have a crush.

"No," I say. "It's not." *Please don't push it,* I think to myself.

She smiles and looks into my eyes for a minute.

"Good," she says, simply. "Is Frank here in Mexico?"

Whew.

"No, he's supposed to meet us tonight in San Diego. We can fly back to Albuquerque from there."

"What would you have done if I said 'No'?"

"I would have respected your wishes and warned you to keep your head low for a week or so." I tell her.

She pours another couple of shots and turns to face the beach before slamming hers down.

While we were talking her bar emptied out. It's just the two of us in here now.

"Are you coming?" I ask her.

"Wouldn't miss it for the world," she says. She looks around at her bar and frowns wistfully. "I thought owning a bar would be fun, but it's so tedious. And you would not believe the bribes I have to pay out. Every two-bit functionary needs a bribe to get anything done. I swear this whole damned country is corrupt."

"It's not so much that they're corrupt as they really like money," I tell her. "Do you need anything? Should we lock up?"

"I've got a bag behind the bar that I need and then we can hit the road. Don't worry about locking up; let the tourists drink themselves into oblivion. I'm not planning on coming back."

She starts to get up and notices two guys walking in. They're both wearing black suits and black wrap sunglasses. Both of them stop right inside the bar and look around.

"Help yourself to the bar," she calls to them. "I quit."

Neither responds and I get a cold chill up my spine. The one on the right nods to his buddy and both of them focus right on us. They both reach into their jacket and pull out some kind of gun. Before I can figure out what's going on, Jessica tackles me and both wind up on the floor in front of the bar.

There's a sound like thumping and twin explosions rip the bar apart.

I'm covered in Jessica and we're both covered in debris. My ears are ringing from the explosion and she's trying to tell me something.

"What?" I yell.

She shakes her head, gives me a quick kiss on the cheek and crawls over the top of me. For a moment I think maybe I died in the explosion and this is heaven and then she's gone around what's left of the bar.

My senses come back and I snap back to reality. Two men want to kill me. That's enough to wake you up. It's time to let old painless out of the bag. After El Paso I decided it was probably a good idea to arm up, so I manage to get my right arm behind my back and pull out my own little Mjolnir.

The gun is my personal best friend, a sawed-off, double-barreled shotgun with etchings of Norse mythology covering the frame. Right now it's loaded with straight heavy gauge steel shot in both barrels. There's nothing overly special about the shot, but at close range it will make big holes in things. I manage to swing it up in time to see one of the guys heading straight toward me. I pull the trigger twice in rapid succession, each barrel spitting fire and steel at him. Both shots hit him square and he flies backward.

Getting to my feet I find the second guy to my right. He's trying to get his gun into position. There's no time to reload so I crack him in the face with Mjolnir and he staggers back. It gives me just enough time to slide the gun back behind my back and pull out a shiny tanto knife.

The second hit man aims at my head and I dodge to the right before he can fire. There's another thumping sound and something behind me explodes. I really hope it's not Jessica.

I grab the gun by the top of the frame with my left hand and cut up inside his forearm with the tanto, severing the tendons that move his fingers. Before he can react, I draw the knife across the right side of his throat. Holding onto his gun, I kick him in the stomach and he staggers back.

I've never seen one of these guns and have a sneaking suspicion it will be important. I don't have much room behind my back, but I manage to wedge it into place and keep my knife out in front of me.

The thing about knife fighting is you expect it to be bloody. I've been in a couple where there was so much blood it was hard to hold onto the knife. That's why knives have rough handles and some knife fighters swear by wrist lanyards.

The guy in front of me is unfazed and there's not a drop of blood on him. I can see the deep cut on his throat. It's spread wide, but there's no blood whatsoever. He's also still standing, which is kind of freaking me out.

He reaches into the other side of his jacket and pulls a knife of his own. Before he can get to me someone grabs my shoulder and spins me out of the way. Jessica is holding a shotgun of her own and fires it point blank into the guy's chest. He goes down and slides across the floor, knocking over a couple of chairs in the process.

Jessica's shotgun is a SPAS-12, a beast of an assault shotgun. It's a two mode military shotgun, meaning it can work in pump action or semi-automatic. A semi-automatic shotgun, how cool is that? She racks it and the spent shell ejects. Sure, semi-auto is cool, but there's nothing as terrifying as the sound of a shotgun racking another shell.

She's got a yellow backpack slung over her shoulder and a bit of blood running off her cheek. That stray lock of hair is back in her face. Her brown eyes are fierce and there's a look of determination on her face.

The first guy, the one I gave both barrels to, is getting to his feet when she turns and blasts him, too.

This is bad. It was bad enough when Wilford could take a shot and live. These guys have probably been trained to exploit this advantage and they certainly seem to recover a lot quicker. A solid shot to the chest would put Wilford down for at least several minutes, but these guys barely even notice they've been shot. It knocks them down, but they pop right back up like some kind of damned Weeble Wobbles.

Jessica grabs my hand and pulls me to the back of the bar. My hearing must be getting better because I can hear her yell, "This way!"

We run through a door in the back, slipping a bit on debris soaked in alcohol and find a door leading outside. There's a sign on it reading *"Salida De Emergencia"*. I stop in front of the door, something worrying at me. My brain may be slow but it hasn't entirely stopped and it's shouting at me that I'm missing something here.

Then it hits me: we saw two guys out front. Who sends two people? A two-person fire team has mobility but it lacks firepower and the ability to surround a target. There's got to be a third around here somewhere.

Jessica slams into me from behind, not expecting my sudden stop.

"What the fuck?" she says.

"I'll lay you dollars to donuts there's a third guy around here somewhere," I tell her.

She pauses for a moment and then nods.

"I'll kick open the door, you get ready to shoot whatever's out there," I say. "After I kick it open, stay behind the wall for a minute. If he's expecting us, he'll fire as soon as he sees us."

"OK," she gulps. "Let's do it." She gets next to the wall to the left of the door, shotgun at the ready.

I kick open the door and dodge to the right of the door. I was right. The third guy was right outside. I hear a thumping sound and the wall across from us explodes.

Jessica spins, drops to one knee and brings her gun to bear. The third shooter sees her but doesn't react. He knows it may hurt but it won't kill him. Her shot hits him dead in the chest and he goes down, but probably not for long.

She sprints to a waiting motorcycle, a real nice Harley with a custom paint job. Jacob must have rubbed off on her. She tosses me the keys and says, "Start it up, I'll give us cover."

"I don't know how to ride a motorcycle," I tell her.

"Are you fucking shitting me?" she asks.

"Nope. Never learned how to ride one."

She shakes her head and grabs the keys from me. Handing me the gun and her bag she swings a leg over the bike and says, "Get on."

I sling the bag over my shoulder, check the gun and climb on the back.

"Hold on," she tells me.

I wrap an arm around her waist and she peels out, peppering the guy on the ground with dirt and rocks. We roar out of the alley behind her bar and find one of the other guys waiting for us. As Jessica puts the bike into a drift, I hold on for dear life with one hand and shoot the guy with the other hand. Lucky break for me; I manage to hit him. That's the nice thing about a shotgun, you don't need to do a whole lot of aiming when the target's right next to you. They suck for range, but you can't beat a shotgun for close in firepower.

The kick nearly ripped the damned thing out of my hand, though. Have to be careful of that in the future.

We're roaring down the street, Jessica's got the throttle full open. The bike is so loud I don't hear the tell-tale thump, but I do feel it when the car on the other side of the street explodes. Jessica weaves and almost drops the bike getting us past. She manages to recover it and we, fortunately, don't get peppered with sharp, flaming debris. I guess the third guy is back up again.

Another car further down explodes in a glorious fireball. This one was closer and Jessica doesn't quite dodge the explosion. Ever ridden a motorcycle through a fireball? It's an amazing and terrifying experience. It's also extremely hot and filled with all manner of fast-moving pointy things.

One of those pointy things lodges itself in my forearm and my hand spasms open in a flash, dropping the shotgun. I almost let go of Jessica's waist but manage to hold tight with my good arm.

In a heartbeat, we're through the blast. We're slightly singed, but otherwise okay. Like I said: amazing and terrifying.

The ritzy beachside street is now filled with debris and black smoke. Windows are shattered, people are screaming, but I can't hear them. They're blurs with open mouths. The only sound is the roar of the big Harley engine.

The next thing I know, the street is filled with automatic weapon fire, aiming back at Jessica's bar. Guys with Kalashnikovs materialize on the streets. Looking back over my shoulder I see them open fire on the hit man in front of Jessica's bar. I guess one of the cars that got toasted belonged to some local cartel members. I've got no love for those guys, but they'll keep the assassins at bay long enough for us to clear out of Mexico. With any luck, the cartel guys and the hit men will kill each other off.

I lean in close to Jessica and we head for the border like the bike has a jalapeno stuffed up its ass.

07 | Bordering on Sanity

We ditch the bike in an alley and walk the rest of the way to the border post, just a couple of American tourists enjoying the day in Mexico. I'm a little nervous about my shotgun, but they almost never check for that kind of thing. We found a 7-11 in Tijuana and cleaned ourselves up a bit before walking across the border, hand in hand, looking totally innocent, even though our clothes were singed and torn up and there was a pretty big bandage around my arm.

The border guard asks us the standard, cursory question: "Where were you born?"

"Mesa, Arizona," I say.

"Los Angeles, California," Jessica says.

The bored border guard waves us through and just like that, we're back on U.S. soil.

Yes, getting across the border works just like that. Of course, we're a couple of white folks so it may be more difficult if you look Hispanic.

"Hungry?" I ask.

"Starving," she responds.

We catch a bus and head for the airport, keeping our eyes peeled for something that looks edible. About two miles from the airport we find a Waffle House and signal a stop. There's always a Waffle House near an airport. It's like some kind of unwritten rule. It's also an unwritten rule that you can walk into a Waffle House any time day or night and there will always be someone in there eating waffles.

We collapse into the worn booth and order waffles and coffee. Feet up on each other's bench seats, we sip our coffee and enjoy the brief respite for a bit.

"Where are you supposed to meet Frank?" she finally asks.

"At the airport," I say. "Our flight is scheduled to leave in about five hours."

"So, we've got plenty of time," she says, leaning back in the booth.

"Yeah," I respond. "Let's enjoy our food."

She rolls her eyes and shakes her head.

"What have you been doing the last six months?" she asks me.

"I spent some time researching Dreamer, but couldn't find out much. I did manage to scrounge up an old book written by a Navajo guy that may or may not have mentioned him. It was kind of vague, but it said he wasn't to be trusted. Other than that, I spent my time decorating my house, watching movies and playing in the snow," I tell her. "What about you?"

"I visited Mexico to spend some time on the beach and sort of decided to stay there. After a while, I got bored and decided to try running a bar. The rest, as they say, is history," she says.

"Don't take this the wrong way," I tell her, "but you seem different. More relaxed or something."

For a moment, I think I may have said the wrong thing. She closes her eyes and breathes deeply. "I was pretty angry for a lot of my life. Dad gone, mother drank herself to death, gangsters threatening to gang rape me. I was in a pretty bad way when our paths crossed."

I nod. I think we were all in a bad way at that time.

"When you guys showed up and actually helped me, I thought I'd found another family," she continues.

"A dysfunctional and crazy family," I interject.

She nods. "Sure, but you guys took care of each other and you accepted me. It's pretty fucked up in hindsight, but as shocked as I was, it felt more normal than anything else. That probably doesn't make much sense."

I wish I had something flippant to say here. I've never been comfortable talking about anything, uh, touchy, so I nod instead.

"When we were done and everyone split, I was kind of hurt that I was alone again," she says.

"I'm sorry," I tell her.

"No, it's all good," she continues. "I made my way to Mexico and sat on the beach and drank margaritas and learned to surf and kind of came to the conclusion that I could handle life on my own terms and could do whatever I wanted to do."

"So you bought a bar," I say.

"I bought a bar. It was fun for a while, but it gold old pretty quickly." After a brief pause, she adds, "You guys spoiled me. Too much excitement over such a short period of time. Everything seems boring now."

Another pause, while she sips her coffee. She lowers her eyes and says, "I missed you."

Before I can respond, our waitress shows up and fills the table with greasy food. "Are you folks having a nice morning?" she asks us.

"Fine so far," I say, "Visiting Mexico before our flight."

Jessica stretches out and puts her feet on the seat next to me. "You know, the usual," she tells the waitress with a smile, "drinking on the beach, looking for pottery, blowing up bars."

The waitress laughs and says, "Sweetie, if you need anything, you or your man here whistle and I'll come running."

Our waitress saunters off to fill up someone else's coffee and Jessica giggles. "Hey," she says, kicking my leg with her shoes, "you're my man."

I smile and say, "You have poor taste in men."

She looks at me and says, "I don't think so," and takes a bite of waffle. "How many other guys would come running down to Mexico to save me?"

I smile and eat my waffle.

"Have you had any strange dreams lately," I finally ask her.

She shakes her head no. "Why, have you?" she asks me.

"That guy that we came up the elevator with, the one who recognized you was essentially a god of some kind. While we were down in the cavern he wanted to see how I got rid of that senator, so he ... got into my head somehow. Ever since he was in my head, my dreams have been really vivid. I can see places I've never been in intricate detail. I feel like I know my way around the White House like I've lived there for months," I tell her.

"Well, it does show up in a lot of movies, maybe you're remembering seeing something in a movie sometime."

"A few nights ago I dreamed of walking down a hallway eating cookies. I had to do something, I don't remember what, that I needed both hands for so I put a cookie in pocket. When I woke up, there was a cookie in my pocket," I say.

"What kind of cookie?" she asks me.

"Peanut butter chocolate chip."

"How was it?"

I have to smile that she would know I actually ate the damn thing. "It was great."

"See, you're still alive. It's all good," she says.

I don't tell her she was in the dream later on and we were dancing in some ballroom, twirling and smiling on a floor made of stars. Or that when I dipped her I could see into her dreams.

"It still makes me nervous," I tell her.

She frowns and says, "You need a hobby."

"I have a hobby," I tell her. "I collect enemies."

Jessica shrugs and says, "There are worse things to collect. When I was a little girl I collected rocks I found in our neighbors' yards."

"Find anything nice?"

"I thought they were nice when I was seven," she laughs.

"I always wanted to collect fast cars, but then I found out they're, like, really expensive."

"They tend to break down a lot, too."

"I know, right?" I say, "If I pay a quarter of million dollars for a car it had damned well not have to be in the shop every other weekend."

"Chicks tend to dig them, though, so they've got that going for them."

"Yeah, but the kind of chicks that dig them are like the cars themselves: hot, fast and prone to catastrophic breakdown at the worst possible moment," I tell her.

"I like supercars," she grins.

I flag the waitress down. "Is there a Lamborghini dealership around here, somewhere?" I ask her.

Jessica laughs and steals a piece of bacon off my plate. Our waitress looks at me like I just took off my pants in the middle of the restaurant. "I'm," she stammers, "not entirely certain. Maybe?"

"It's OK," Jessica tells her, "he's had too much coffee."

I act like I'm vibrating. "I'm fine fine fine," I say, twitching. "Actually, is there a Pak N Mail or something like that around here? I've got a shotgun and some kind of super weapon I need to mail to someone." I give her my best fake grin and our waitress gives me a solid guffaw.

Over the years I've found you can say almost anything you want to people if you're smiling when you say it. I used to work with this woman who everyone in the office hated. Problem was she thought everyone loved her. Why, yes, she was blonde, why do you ask? Anyway, I was talking to her one day and she said people were mean to her. I smiled a giant grin and told her it was because everyone in the office hated her. She laughed her ass off and went home with a huge grin on her face. Everyone actually did hate her. She also thought we were best buddies from then on. Well, until she got fired, anyway.

When our waitress stops laughing she points to the north and says, "There's a little place down the road. Can I get you fine folks anything else?"

"No, thank you," Jessica says, "Just the check, please."

I leave a fifty on the table and call it good. On the way out Jessica asks me, "What do we need a mail place for?"

"I need to send someone a shotgun."

"Who do you need to send a shotgun to?" she asks me.

"Me. You can actually check a gun in your luggage if you declare it, but I don't trust those idiots in the TSA to not steal or impound it," I tell her. "Plus I've got that other little toy I stole from one of those guys. That thing would definitely raise eyebrows."

"Didn't you work for the TSA?" she asks me.

"No. I worked for the Department of Homeland Security. They're the parent organization. DHS may be a bit squirrely sometimes, but the TSA was like our crazy cousin that we kept in the basement because he was always flinging shit at visitors."

"Huh," Jessica says, "I didn't know you could even mail a gun."

"I hope so. No one's ever said anything, so I guess it's cool."

08 | New Friends and Old

After we drop my shotgun and the bizarre pistol off with the fine folks at FedEx we grab a cab to the airport where we find Frank and a guy holding hands in front of the Southwest entrance. Whoever the guy is, he looks very serious and very disturbed. When I grab Jessica's bag out of the trunk and set it on the sidewalk and tip the cabbie, the guy with Frank straightens himself up and stalks over to me. Frank tries to stop him, but he pulls his hand out of Frank's and comes straight at me.

Pointing his finger at me he says, "I don't know who you are and I don't trust you."

You know, I was about to say it was cute that he flew down here from Seattle with Frank just to have a bit more time together, but I think he only flew down to start shit with me.

Damn, if I had nickel every time someone flew twelve hundred miles to start a fight with me, I'd be rich.

"Welcome to the club," I say. "You and the other billion members should have lots to talk about. Bring lots of dip."

Frank steps up between us, embarrassed and muttering something to this guy. "Hi, this is Chet. Chet and I are together," he tells me. "Hi, Jessica. Long time no see."

She gives him a big hug and shakes Chet's hand.

"Chet," I say, holding my hand out to him. "It's nice to meet you. I'm Steven."

Chet puts his hand on my chest and I see Frank in the background waving his hands and shaking his head at me. I sigh and resist the urge to break his wrist. I must be tired because it's obvious Chet's only worried.

"Okay," I tell him, "what can I do for you."

The big guy relaxes and says, "I'm sorry. I'm terrified. I'm sorry."

"Dude, I'm sorry I'm taking him away, but I promise you I'll keep an eye on him. I can't promise you he'll be safe because that would be a lie and I don't want to lie to you. You seem like a nice guy, so I'm going to give you a bit of truth. The truth is we could all fall out of the sky in a couple of hours. The truth is there could be a Liberian Ebola case on the plane and we'll all bleed to death in a few days. I'll do my best to keep him alive. I'm good, she's good, the rest of the people we're meeting are good. We'll keep an eye on him."

"Why do you have to take him anyway?" he asks me.

"It's best I don't tell you," I tell him.

"Why?"

"The less you know, the better off you'll be," I say.

Now I know how Eve must feel when she won't answer my questions. I guess I'll have to buy her a beer and apologize later.

The guy looks like he's going to explode. I know how he feels.

"Look, I promise I'll do my best to bring Frank back to you in one piece. Personally."

He doesn't look happy, but he nods and goes back to Frank. They hug, kiss, and say their goodbyes.

With that, we all head into the airport. The gang's back together and it's time to get to work.

* * * *

We make it through security easily. Our bored TSA agent barely noticed our ID or boarding passes, he was too focused on Jessica's breasts. She was singled out to go through the imaging scanner. Officially, I'm sure, it was a random screening and had absolutely nothing to do with wanting to see what's under her clothes.

No one wanted anything to do with me or Frank so we breezed through. For some reason, though, I'm absolutely convinced Jessica's picture from the scanner is going to wind up on the Internet. For another odd reason, this makes me extremely angry so I get my shoes on and head over the scanner operator.

A tiny part of my brain is screaming at me that this feeling doesn't make a damned bit of sense, but the larger portion of my brain is incensed that someone would dare take her picture, dare question her, dare question me.

"What are you doing with the pictures you take?" I ask him.

He rolls his eyes and tells me, "You can't be back here, sir, you need to leave."

"I need to speak to your supervisor," I tell him.

"Well, you can't," he responds.

"Listen, man," I tell him, "I get it. The job sucks. I'm with DHS, too, the organization sucks. The whole damn thing sucks. I only want to know what you're doing with the pictures you take."

"It's TSA policy that we delete them," he tells me.

That's not answering my question.

"I know policy dictates you delete the pictures, but I want to know what you do with them," I say.

"Sir, you cannot be back here," he tells me, getting frustrated. "If you won't leave, I'll be forced to arrest you."

"Do I need to pull rank, here?" I ask him, hoping he won't ask for ID.

"I need to see your ID," he tells me.

Asshole. God, I hate these guys. They're dumb as stumps but with just enough power to think they're important.

Before I can rip into him Jessica grabs my arm and pulls me back. "I'm so sorry," she tells agent Asshole. "He's been sick and his medicine is making him paranoid."

"It's OK, ma'am. Please take care of him before he gets himself into trouble."

As she's pulling me away she hisses in my ear, "What are you thinking?"

"I wanted to know what he was doing with the pictures he took of you," I tell her.

"That's sweet, but if I cared I would have asked him on my own," she says. "In case you haven't noticed I can take care of myself."

"I worked with these idiots and I don't trust them."

"Yes, worked. Past tense. Have you forgotten that people think you're a terrorist?" she asks me.

"I'm not a terrorist," I snap. Quietly. You don't say the T word out loud in an airport, just like you don't say bomb in an airport if you like your freedom. Don't even say something was "the bomb," or a movie "bombed at the box office."

"I know. They think I'm a terrorist, also, remember? Come on, buy me a drink." She grabs my hand and pulls me out into the main part of the concourse.

Frank is waiting for us right outside of security.

"Are you out of your goddamned mind?" he asks me. "You're going to blow this thing before we even get out of California."

He's right. I used to be able to hide in plain sight. There was a time when I would have made it through that line without raising a single eyebrow. Now, I'm doing my best to completely torpedo everything. Shit.

I think I've spent too much time on my own. It's never a good idea to spend too much time with your thoughts. It tends to warp your reality when reality doesn't have any external inputs. Up until a few days ago, I hadn't actually spoken to anyone in weeks and hadn't had a meaningful conversation in months. I need to get my edge back if I'm going to survive.

I stop in my tracks and look up at Frank. "You're right. I almost totally fucked that up."

I look over at Jessica and say, "Thank you. If you hadn't pulled me away from that guy I would have ruined everything. I was almost enraged when I thought he had a picture of you. It doesn't make any sense."

She puts a hand on my shoulder and says, "You'll be fine. We're here. We're together. It will be fine."

Her face looks worried.

Frank puts his arm around my shoulder. "Listen, Carlos Danger, you need some drink and some rest." He flashes a toothy grin.

Together they steer me to the first brewery we come across. There we proceed to consume a lot of beer and peanuts and get to know each other all over again.

It turns out Frank has been knocking off every pawn shop in Portland, OR. He doesn't take money or jewelry, but he's gotten himself quite the Swatch collection. He met Chet (seriously, that's his name) at some Swatch convention and they hit it off. Swatch: bringing people together since 1983.

Chet doesn't know about Frank's involvement in the Dreamer business, and that's perfectly fine with Frank. I solemnly swear to him that I will not tell Chet about Frank's darker past. Chet thinks Frank's money was inherited and has never bothered to question it or dig too deep. Gotta love that. I've never dated a guy, but I've dated plenty of women that would happily dig into every aspect of my life and find it wanting.

"Have either of you guys been to one of those Dream Churches?" Frank asks us.

I shake my head no and explain that I've been largely isolated in Hesperus. Jessica tells him she didn't come across any of those in Mexico.

"They must be an American thing," he says. "They started springing up in New Mexico and spread out like a virus. We got one in Portland last month. On a lark, I checked it out. Scary shit. The pastor was claiming he was a Prophet of Dreams and the people ate it up. Some guy stood up and started shaking a Bible at the pastor and these shadows came out of nowhere and covered him. He was completely engulfed and screaming. When they left, the guy threw down his Bible and walked away. Have you ever heard of anything like that?"

Actually, I have. I've seen the results of Dreamer's shadows sprawled on the floor under the Simms building with their eyes clawed out. I've been covered by his shadows and shared my brain with him.

"I've seen worse," I say.

I pick up my beer and drain it. They're both looking at me. Jessica says simply, "Oh, my God."

"Yeah. He's a God. Or something like it," I say.

"Is that what we let out?" Frank asks.

I'm kind of drunk. Just like everyone else, I do stupid things when I'm drunk. Sometimes I do stupid things when I'm not drunk.

"In my defense, he seemed like a nice guy," I say.

Frank looks horrified. Jessica seems torn.

"I had no idea he would do that," she says. "It felt like we were just letting someone out of prison."

"We were," I say.

"So, what you're saying is we let loose some biological weapon and it got out of hand?" Frank asks me.

"Yup," I say without a care. "He's like sentient Anthrax."

I hold up my hand to order another drink when Jessica pulls my hand down and says, "I think we need to get to our flight."

I give her my best unsteady glare and put my hand right back up. I'm getting a drink and nuts to her.

When my beer finally comes Frank and Jessica are getting up. I slam it down and follow them, leaving some cash on the table.

I stop to go to the bathroom and finally catch up with them at the gate, where they're talking to some Native American guy. When I walk up, he stops talking mid-sentence, looks me in the eye and says, "It's about damned time you showed up. The plane's about to leave."

09 | Sheesh, How Many of These Guys Are There?

"Sorry," I tell him. "I was confounded by the hand dryers."

"Oh, *Bilagáana*, always with the clever, never with the serious," the man responds.

"Are you going to call him kemosabe now?" some random asshole asks. Why do people feel the need to say every little damned thing that floats through their head?

"I don't need made-up words," the Native American guy tells the asshole. "I'm *Diné*. We have a real language. Saved your punk asses in World War II."

"*Diné*? I've never heard of that." Jessica says.

"He's Navajo," I say. "*Diné* means 'The People.'"

"Well, it's good to know that even though you're drunk and reeking of dreams, you're not completely lost to the world," the Native American man says, extending his hand to shake mine. "I'm John Begay, and I'm here to help you."

His hand is strong and rough, the kind of hand you get from living and working in the desert all your life. I can match his physical strength, but there's a toughness to him that comes through in his eyes and his easy smile. He's not the least bit concerned about anything going on around him.

"If you guys will excuse me, I need to find the bathroom," Jessica says.

I watch her go for a minute and turn my attention back to John Begay. "What can we do for you Mr. Begay?"

He's watching Jessica walk away and again I feel a blast of jealousy.

"For starters," Begay says, "You can call me John. For another you can be nicer to her. You need her more than she needs you."

"She's fine," I say.

"Just in case you're blind as well as stupid and drunk, that girl has a serious thing for you," Frank says.

"She's too young," I reply.

"Too young? She's what, 24, 25? She's had to take care of herself for years. She knows what she's doing," Frank says. "Besides, why do you care how old she is? What is this? Some kind of ethics you're suddenly developing? It doesn't suit you."

"You've been angry a lot lately, haven't you?" Begay asks me. "Feeling possessive of her, short tempered when it comes to her, haven't you?"

You know, yes. Yes I have. What the fuck is up with that?

"I've got a short temper about most things. More so than ever. But about her, yeah, it's worse. What's going on?"

"You reek of him. Did you let him into your head?" Begay asks me.

"Yeah, I did. In my defense, it seemed like a good idea at the time," I reply.

"*Bilagáana*," Begay says. "You people have lost all connection to reality."

"Huh?" I say, before something occurs to me. "Why are you here, John?"

"I'm here to help you," he says. "I never did get on with those assholes."

"What assholes?" Frank asks.

"The assholes that put out the hit on you," Begay responds.

"Who are they?" I ask.

"I'll tell you on the plane," he says.

An announcement plays warning us all that boarding will start shortly. I feel a pang of panic when I realize Jessica isn't back yet. Begay notices and says, "She's fine. Relax."

I nearly hit him before he holds up his hand and says, "*Na'iidzeeł* is making you crazy. Those are his feelings, not yours. He's got his eye on her, too."

"Why?" I ask.

"I've no idea," Begay responds.

I get a feeling, more like I brushed up against some information that Begay is lying. I can't put my finger on exactly why I feel that way, but I can sense he knows more than he's telling me. That coupled with her absence makes me tense up. I feel like hitting something.

There, that guy over there. Did he pop his gum at me?

Frank puts his hand on my shoulder and assures me, "We're on your side, man."

When Jessica finally shows back up, I hold my hand out to her. She looks at me kind of confused for a moment before she finally takes my hand and stands next to me. I finally feel relaxed. What the hell is going on with me?

10 | First Class, Motherfuckers

We're flying first class, which is a new experience for me. I'm used to sitting in coach and getting sneered at by flight attendants. First class is a totally different experience. For starters, there's actual leg room. For another, no one has sneered at me. Sure, it costs four times as much to fly first class as coach, but what's the point of having a bunch of stolen money if you don't use it?

We got one of those cool arrangements where there are four seats facing each other. Unlike in coach, our knees aren't even rubbing each other. Amazing! Ok, I'll stop ranting about first class seating, now. Honestly, though, you should totally try it. If you have to rob a rich widow to get the cash, go for it. It's totally worth it.

Once the plane has settled I ask John, "Ok, so what's your angle on this?"

"My angle?"

"Yeah, your angle. Why are you here? Who are you?" I ask him. I was willing to accept Eve with little question because she showed up at the right time and was planning on doing something I get could get on board with. Who hasn't dreamed of killing Congress? John Begay showed up out of the blue and knew far more than he should have.

"I told you, I don't get on with the things that want you dead," he says. "*Bilagáana*, you're dealing with things you don't really even have accurate words for. Things that want you out of the way."

"What things?" Frank asks him. "And what does *bilagáana* mean?"

Frank looks at me when he asks the second question. I shrug. I don't know Navajo. Apparently when I was a kid I had a decent understanding of it because my family had some Navajo friends, but that was almost forty years ago. I picked up a few words here and there, but that was only because they were common in the Southwest.

"*Bilagáana* is what we call white people. It's not meant as a slur, it's just a word," Begay says. "As for what you're up against, *Na'iidzeeł* and your friend Eve are far more than you realize. You'd call them gods, but that's only because you can't really comprehend what they are. They're ideas personified. You call *Na'iidzeeł* Dreamer, but that's not right."

"How is that not right?" Jessica asks.

"He's not a dreamer, or even the dreamer, he is dream. He doesn't do it. He is it," Begay responds. "Even the *Diné* word for him, *Na'iidzeeł*, doesn't do him justice because he's not just the dream you have when you sleep, he's all dream."

"OK," I say. "So he's not a god."

"He is a God," Begay tells me. "You just don't understand what Gods are."

"OK," I say. "So he is a god."

"Yes. He would say he creates dreams for everyone. Others would say he was created by everyone's dreams. The only thing that's important is *Na'iidzeeł* and dreams are the same thing."

"So who is Eve?" Jessica asks.

"Your friend Eve isn't a goddess, she's a Valkyrie," Begay responds. "And a great dancer."

"A Valkyrie," Frank says. "One of those blonde warrior women the Norse were always on about?"

"Valkyries weren't warrior women. They were choosers of the slain," Begay says. "It was their job to decide which warriors killed in battle were to go fight in Ragnarök."

"Ragnarök is real?" I ask incredulously. "The world is actually going to be drowned in water?"

"In her world reality, Ragnarök is a very real thing. That's probably why she was drawn to you."

"Drawn to me?" I ask.

"She did say we needed to be at a Bedfellow's place at a certain time," Frank chimes in. "I think we got there righ before you did. You found Bedfellow first, though."

A while back I killed a certain Senator Lucius Bedfellow. His son had killed my family and Lucius used his political collateral to get his kid off a murder charge. I couldn't get to the son, so I went after the father. I found him dressed in lingerie, standing on a chair, bound and gagged with a noose around his neck. I scooted the chair and watched the noose tighten around his neck. Watched him die, really.

"How did she know I was going to be there?"

"She's sensitive to events. She probably doesn't understand it herself, but she was drawn there by her own sensitivities."

"What did you mean when you said 'She's a great dancer'?" Jessica asks him.

"I meant she's a great dancer," Begay responds with a twinkle in his eye.

"Oh. My. God," Frank stammers.

"Was it swing dancing?" Jessica asks, "I always liked swing."

I make a mental note.

"Look, not to be rude," I interject, "but what does this have to do with why you're here?"

"You need to stop *Na'iidzeeł* before he takes over everything."

"Why the hell don't you do it?" I ask Begay. "I mean, you're a God, aren't you?"

"Didn't we just go over this?" Begay asks. "You really are dense, aren't you?"

"Fine," I say. "You're not a God. Whatever you are, wouldn't *you* have a better chance of stopping him?"

"I can't," Begay says. "My powers only expand so far. Just like he's dream, I'm the spirit of my people. I'm them and they're me and your people did a mighty fine job of crushing the spirits of my people."

"Great," Frank sighs, rubbing his temples. "We spent all that effort letting this guy out and now we've got to find a way to put him back in."

Jessica gets right to the point. "Can we kill him?"

"How do you kill a dream?" Begay asks her.

"What happens if he takes over?" I ask.

"The dream world and the waking world will combine. He'll rule it all."

"So?" I ask. Seriously, how much worse could he be than some of our current leaders?

"Do you want all of your dreams to come true? Even the bad ones? That's what would happen. *Na'iidzeeł* is supposed to let dreams be, but he's hoarding them. Controlling them, like he's trying to control you." Begay says.

"How do we stop him?" I ask.

"You can't stop him. You can only take his power away. You could try to find a weapon, but you'll also need someone to wield it."

"Why can't I wield it? I'm pretty handy with weapons."

"The weapons I'm thinking of require a special person to wield them. Not everyone can pick up a god slayer and make it work."

"Right," Frank says, rolling his eyes. "Not only are there gods, there are special weapons to kill those gods and those weapons need special people to handle them. Are you sure you're not just some wandering nut case?"

"I'm crazy, kiddo, but not like that," Begay tells Frank. "None of what I've said is a lie. There are what you people would call gods and weapons to kill those gods. I doubt you'd find a weapon, let alone someone to use it, but it is a possibility. Bottom line, though, you need to stop him or everyone suffers."

"How?" Jessica asks.

"You have him inside of you," Begay says, pointing at me. "The answer is in there."

"Gee, thanks," I tell him.

"I'm sorry I can't help you more, but his world is different from my world. I can't tell you how to stop him. We got lucky once with that circle around him."

"You put that up?" I ask.

"Yes. Not everyone in your government is a total fool. I got it up just in time, too."

"Nice work," I tell him.

"*Ahéhee'.*"

"Huh?"

"Thank you," Begay says.

"Can we build another one? Another circle?" I ask him.

"Only if you can get him to sleep long enough, which is kind of doubtful."

Begay fiddles with his seat belt and stands up.

"I need to be off now. It has been a pleasure talking to you. One last thing," he says as he points at Jessica, "He's after her. That's why you get so agitated when she's not around. I'll do my best to hold off the hit squads, but you don't have much time."

"Hey," Jessica says, "Why is he after me?"

"I don't know. He just is," Begay tells her. "Mind yourself. You're very important."

Begay goes to the bathroom and vanishes. Probably flushed himself down the toilet.

"These gods are kind of getting on my nerves," I say with a sigh. "That guy managed to answer questions by raising more questions."

"Yeah," quips Fred, "but at least we know we're really, truly in the shit."

"And I'm important!" Jessica adds in, smirking.

We still have quite a bit of flight time, so we indulge in the drinks you can only get in first class: ambrosia, Tears of Heaven, 200 year old absinthe. See, I told you first class was best class.

I take some time to stare out the window. From up here, everything looks fine. Leaning back in a comfy chair with a fine drink and a beautiful woman next to me, it's hard to feel like I'm being hunted down by gods, or one god is slowly taking over everything. Begay didn't say, but I get the feeling everyone's pissed at me for doing the one thing gods can't stand anymore: I forced them to interact with little people. Dreamer alluded to it when he told me he hated hearing the endless prayers. Begay didn't exactly seem happy to see us. Eve still won't talk about herself. It's like they just flat-out don't give a shit about us and don't want to deal with us.

Still begs the question about why Dreamer left a part of himself inside of me or why he's interested in Jessica? Maybe he's some kind of rogue?

Jessica's eyes are getting heavy. I can't blame her. The drink and the morning's excitement have left me pretty wiped out, but I can't shut my mind off.

"I'm sorry to drag you back into this, Frank," I say, "It's unfair to you and it's unfair to Chet. Hell, it's unfair to her and everyone else."

Frank grins and says, "I wouldn't miss this for the world! God, it's boring in Portland. Knocking off pawn shops is hardly a challenge. I need a challenge. I need a Radula or an Anodyne to keep me sharp."

"How about a Simms building?" I ask him.

"Well, technically speaking, that was you two," he says pointing at Jessica and me. "I just, uh, covered up the evidence."

Technically speaking, he detonated a lot of explosives and turned an Albuquerque institution into a several thousand tons of rubble. The impressive part was how he managed to drop only the Simms building and leave everything mostly untouched. That's the mark of true genius. Any idiot can throw some bombs around and blow out the windows, but it takes an artist to do what Frank did to the Simms building.

"And a very nice job you did, sir!" I say, toasting him.

He raises his glass in a toast and we both echo, "To evil," and laugh out loud. Jessica stirs in her sleep and rolls toward me, one hand on my leg. I look down and can't help but chuckle. The first time I met her she stabbed a tortured Yakuza gangster in the throat, calmly wiped the knife on his shirt and watched him die before handing me my knife back. She seduced national secrets out of a guard, later poisoned that guard and his coworker and stood up to a god. Now a thought ping-ponging around my head has made me completely obsessed with her well-being and she's sacked out with her hand on my leg looking completely innocent.

Frank and I sit quietly before we both start laughing. Jessica stirs again and I put my hand on hers and she settles down again.

"God, I missed this," he tells me. "How's Jacob?"

"We had to bust him out of a Mexican prison. My old partner still had his DHS ID so we bribed the prison warden to 'transfer Jacob to us.'"

"How much did it cost?"

"About three grand," I say. "Not bad for bribing a prison warden."

"Are you going to let Jacob live it down?" he asks me.

"Oh, hell, no," I tell him. "He's a friend, I would have burned the prison to the ground to get him out, but I have every intention of reminding him at every opportunity."

"And Eve?"

"First time I saw her was a few days ago. I woke up to find my old partner and Eve had both broken into my place at the same time. Both were kind of planning on killing me. She left about a case of empty MGD cans on my floor."

"You know, no matter how often I tried to introduce her to good beer, she always went back that swill."

"To each their own," I say. "I used to have a buddy that only drank Pabst."

"Oh, dear Lord. That's terrible."

"I know, right?"

We both get a good chuckle in and the flight attendant refills our drinks. Jessica whimpers a little in her sleep. I close my eyes and can see her dreams. Something's chasing her. I leave her a shotgun and quietly back out of her dream. When I open my eyes, she's calmed down and there's a trace of a smile on her lips.

"Did you just go into her dream?" Frank asks me.

"Yeah, I seem to have developed the ability to move in and out of dreams."

"Is it cool?"

I pause for a moment, thinking it's best to keep cool about this. Oh, fuck that. "It fucking rocks," I tell him, laughing.

"What's it like?"

"It's like dreaming, only you get to watch it unfold rather than living inside it. I can control events and leave things for people." I tell him.

"Was it Dreamer in your head that let you do that?" Frank asks me, looking serious.

"I guess so. I can feel part of him there, like he's watching what's going on."

"Suck ass."

"No kidding," I tell him. "People have some strange dreams, man."

"What's the weirdest one you've seen?" Frank asks me, perking up a bit.

"A giant chicken talking to God," I tell him.

"Dude," he says, laughing, "that *means* something."

Frank pauses and sips his drink.

"What did the chicken say to God?" he finally asks me.

"I have absolutely no idea," I tell him.

"Probably trying to find out why he crossed the road."

"Who? God or the chicken?"

"Why can't it be both?" he replies, smirking.

I laugh. "Why did God cross the road?"

"To punish the non-believers on the other side?"

"Maybe there was a good barbecue joint on the other side," I tell him.

"God likes barbecue?"

"Dude," I say with a fake sigh, "Everyone likes barbecue."

"Well, except for vegans."

"They don't count."

"Yeah, screw those non meat-eating bastards."

I yawn. The excitement of the morning, the drinks, and the drone of the engines are lulling me to sleep. "Sorry," I tell Frank, "I swear I'm not bored, just running out of juice."

"You have too much blood in your alcohol stream," he tells me. His eyes are drooping a bit, too. Booze: the great equalizer. "We should all get some rest. Lord knows what Eve's got up her sleeves or how we're going to get out of this mess."

"No shit, bro. No shit."

As I drift off to sleep, I hear the captain tell us we're about an hour out of Albuquerque, cruising at some insanely high number of feet at an equally insane number of miles per hour. My sleepy brain insists that it was Captain Crunch that was feeding us information, just like he's fed us a tasty food-like substance for years.

11 | The Shadow Knows

There are shadows in my dreams, which is a really odd since it's night in most of my dreams. I very rarely dream about the sun or light or anything like that. I suspect some therapist somewhere would have a field day with my dreams.

The shadows swirl around me, at first keeping their distance, then circling closer like black sharks. Every now and then, I can feel them, taste their thoughts. Taste their thoughts? Yes. I can taste their thoughts. They're dreams come to the real world, but they're flat, incomplete. They don't belong here, so they can't manipulate the real world. They can manipulate us, though; put ideas into our heads that ping around like billiard balls.

They taste like absinthe, sharp and sweet and full of promises that will be broken into a hangover in the morning.

I can hear them when they get close enough. "Hello, hello, hello, hello. We missed you."

I should be terrified, but I'm not. I feel like they're a part of me, coming home to roost and bringing tales of what they've seen. Feeling them is like sharing the tastes and smells of a dreaming city with an old friend. My brain interprets the taste as absinthe, but if I taste closer I can sense other things. The depraved dreams of lunatic sprawled out in a flat smell like sex and copper. He spent the day hunting and raping the bad ones. They're evil and they try to hide behind the façade of beautiful women, but he knows the truth, just like he knows that his rod will drive the evil out of them and free those poor women. A frightened mother's dreams taste of bitter almonds in her black coffee. She wants her only daughter to be safe, but it's a dangerous world and she almost idly wonders if her daughter wouldn't be better off dead. A cop, unsure of who to trust, dreams of fast-food hamburgers that promise greatness only to deliver the same salty taste of something vaguely beef-like. His disappointment is palpable, but his shake tastes like rich chocolate, even though he knows it's made from something far from chocolate. Such is his life; promised one thing, delivered another, a facsimile of the real thing. He's learned to deal with disappointment.

The shadows are hypnotic to watch. They don't move like amoeba, they're more like fractals. They explode into squares, binary dreams that flow like liquid from place to place. Sometimes they dance, bursting into swirling shapes that pulse in time with the music they've stolen from sleepers. If you listen closely, the room is a cacophony of disparate musical styles. Tribal dance beats fuse with rap which weaves into steel guitar which interlaces opera that touches death metal. Listen closely and I can hear each piece, listen from a distance and it's all white noise. It's too much for my head, so I shut it off.

A voice, somewhere, says, "Good. You're learning."

"Who's there?" I ask.

"You may as well ask where you are," another voice says.

Dreams are frustrating sometimes.

"I'm on a damned plane, flying over Arizona," I say.

"Are you sure?"

I try to pull myself out of the dream, but find I can't. This is a new development. If I relax and focus, I can feel something on my leg. Jessica's hand is still there. It will work as a guide.

"Yeah," I say. "I'm sure."

"Good. Good," the voice says.

The shadows dance and cheer. Their excitement is obvious and part of me feels like I'm back in grade school and actually spelled "territory" correctly. When I was in fifth grade I got knocked out of a spelling bee on that word and it's been my nemesis ever since.

"Your body is on the plane but your mind is here," says a female voice. "The two are connected, but the connection is flexible."

"You are one of us now," growls a voice that can only belong to a professional wrestler. The shadows on the floor coalesce into the shape of a monster of man.

"We welcome you," says a woman's voice. A shadowy silhouette of a woman in a pleated skirt swirls into form.

"Who? What? What are you?" I ask.

"We are the dreams. We are Him," the myriad sing.

"You will not take this away from me," one voice screams. "This is mine." His shadow grows spiky, anger and irrational hatred spilling off it like so much dust.

This one is real and dangerous. He absolutely hates me.

Join the club, fucker.

He fades, leaving behind the ghost of his hatred. That dreamer woke up. Probably enraged.

A figure forms in front of me, solid and heavy. Slowly the details of a suit form up, white shirt underneath, dark blue tie with a moon and stars on it drift into view. Dreamer is here.

"See you soon, Steven," he says.

With that, I awake with a start. The plane is still there, solid and reassuring. Frank is sacked out, headphones on. Jessica's hand idly strokes my leg and she murmurs, "It's Ok, it was only a dream," before she falls back asleep.

Sure. Only a dream. When Dream itself shows up in your dreams, it's probably not a dream anymore.

I close my eyes and try to relax. Bad mojo is coming and I just dropped my friends into a very bad place.

I relax slightly when Captain Crunch informs us we will be landing shortly.

12 | The Land of Enchantment

Frank awoke looking slightly hung over. Jessica woke up, patted my leg and smiled before sitting up and brushing her hair out of her face.

Albuquerque International Airport is not exactly huge so we're at the baggage claim waiting for Frank's luggage within ten minutes of landing. When I check my phone, I've got a text from Jacob. He's down the street and will pick us up when we're ready. I shoot him a text and tell him where to get us. Ten minutes later he picks us up and we're heading north on I-25 toward the I-25/I-40 interchange in his 1968 four-door Chevelle. The big V8 growls like predator and you can feel the vibration from it through the seats. He's got his biker mix blasting through the speakers: Tito and Tarantula, Satriani, Love and Rockets, and the eponymous Steppenwolfe. It's too loud to talk, but that's fine. We're all run down and looking out the windows, lost in thought.

I had thought I was done with Albuquerque, but I'm glad to be back. I love this town. In the winter it turns brown and grey, but signs of spring are showing here and there and greens are popping out.

Jessica's hand finds mine I give her a squeeze. It feels … connected.

Jacob and Frank are talking non-stop in the front seat, but I can barely make out what they're saying over the wind and the music and the engine. Every now and then they laugh out loud. Jessica's eyes are distant, watching the city pass by in a blur.

I watch everything, from the cars around us to the billboards that have sprung up over the last six months. The billboards are a wealth of information. If I lived in such and such a place, I could be home in 10 minutes. That ambulance chasing lawyer is still hawking his wares. I wonder if he still wears leather pants to concerts.

Before we get on the interchange and leave I-25 for the glory of I-40, one billboard catches my eye. It's dark blue and lit up with colored lights. The lights are powerful enough that you can even see them during the bright light of day. The billboard is simple: dark blue background, a serious-looking man with greasy hair and manic eyes. Across the board is the phrase "Worship Your Dreams," with "holydreamtime.com" underneath it.

Something about the face on the billboard sets off an alarm bell in the back of my head. I can't put my finger on it, but he looks familiar.

"Hey, Frank!" I yell.

No response. The deep bass thrum of Tito and Tarantula is overpowering. In fact, I'm not sure I heard myself yell.

He turns when I tap him on the shoulder and watches while I try to talk to him. When he can't hear a word, he turns the stereo down much to Jacob's chagrin.

"What was that?" Frank asks.

"That billboard back there. What's holydreamtime.com?" I ask.

"Sounds like a local chapter of one of those dream churches. I don't know much about that one, but apparently it's one of the first," he tells me.

"Ever been to one?"

"Just the one in Portland. Scary place. Why?"

"Nothing, that guy just looked familiar."

Jacob doesn't wait long before he decides the conversation is over and cranks the music back up. It's just my thoughts and the loud music. Satriani's "Surfing With the Alien" fits the road nicely, I must say.

Once we're over the interchange, it doesn't take long to head West on I-40. The traffic, for once, is thin, and Jacob has very little interest in maintaining a sane speed. By the time we pass Coors Road, there are almost no other cars on the road.

Jessica's hand finds mine again when I sit back again. She gives it a squeeze, but keeps staring out her window.

The hideout - we need to come up with a better name than that, by the way - is on top of the west mesas, about five miles outside of town. Wilford's Suburban is parked out front, but otherwise the place looks deserted. Jacob, probably showing off, puts the big car into a drift and slides it gently next Wilford's shot-up ride. He looks back at Jessica and smiles and winks before he shuts off the engine.

After the plane and the ride in Jacob's car, the silence out here is deafening. You can hear every little thing from the slight breeze to the birds chattering to each other in the distance. My ears, so accustomed to the noise, have receded to a deep thrum.

Jessica leans forward and puts a hand on Jacob's shoulder. "Thanks for the ride, big guy. I don't think I'd trust either of these other guys to drive." He blushes. She taps me on the shoulder and adds, "This guy can't even ride a motorcycle."

Jacob looks horrified. Frank just says, "Oh, man. You're kidding, right."

I suspect I'm bright red right now.

Jacob turns toward me and in a deadly serious voice says, "Bro, I know what we're doing tomorrow. Don't fight it, man. Riding a bike is a necessary life skill, like tying your shoes or swimming."

I guess I'm busy tomorrow.

I look at Jessica and roll my eyes at her. She just smiles and pats my leg before getting out and stretching.

I step out and do the same. It's good to be, well not exactly home, but home enough, I guess.

* * * *

Inside the place is cleaned up and Eve and Wilford are sitting at the table playing poker for M&Ms. From the look of things, Eve is winning but I've seen Wilford come back from worse.

Eve gets up from the table and collects Jessica and Frank in a huge bear hug.

"I missed you guys, how have you been, what's been going on?" she asks them.

"Can't breathe," Frank manages.

Eve lets them go with a sheepish, "Sorry."

Jessica and Frank proceed to tell their stories and I head back to my old spot to put my stuff down. The place is exactly like it was before we left. I take a moment to poke around and when I walk out I find Frank standing outside his old room with a crushed look on his face.

"You okay, man," I ask him.

"Lot of memories," he says simply and looks at me. "Chet's great, but I miss Jean. I guess I hadn't realized how much until I saw this room."

I've never been good at comforting people, so I put a hand on his shoulder and say, "I'm sorry. Jean was a great guy."

Frank nods and says a quick, "Thanks. That guy out there was responsible for killing Jean, wasn't he?"

"Far as I know."

Jeans was Frank's partner, and they'd been together for a long time. They were thick as thieves and about as deeply in love with each other as two people can be. About six months ago or so, we were breaking into an old government contractor's building. Jean was outside, copying data for us. We never saw him again. Wilford's people got Jean, cut off his hands and head and left the rest of the corpse there as a message. Frank never really talked about it with me, but I understand he spent some hours crying on Eve's shoulder.

"It wasn't personal, though, it was just business, right?" Frank asks.

"Again, far as I know," I tell him.

"I'm going to kill him. You know that, right?"

"I know. If it'll help, I'll hold him down while you do it," I say.

"We should kill just kill him now."

"We can't. Not yet. We can still use him. I agree with you, but he's … different now. I've personally shot him twice and he's still alive. We've got to figure out what makes him tick before we can kill him."

Frank looks pained, but nods.

"If you need me, you know where to find me," I tell him.

He nods again, sucks in a deep breath and walks into his old room and closes the door.

Another score I need to settle with Wilford when this is all over.

13 | Burgers!

Dinner, of course, is green chile cheeseburgers and fries. Since this is New Mexico we also have Marble Oatmeal Stout and IPA, two excellent beers brewed right in downtown Albuquerque.

The sun is going down and the shadows are stretching, casting long fingers over the back yard. Jacob is grilling and wearing his "Fuck the cook" apron. He thinks it's hilarious. I find it amusing after a few beers. Frank is mixing drinks and Eve and Jessica have both been partaking of Frank's famous margaritas. Frank has, too. I made buns for the burgers because, hey, if you're not making your own buns you're only playing at grilling burgers.

Wilford and I have kicked back with beers and are watching the sunset. He's been remarkably calm for someone who was an enemy not that long ago.

"So, buddy, what's the plan?" he finally asks me.

"I'm not your buddy, pal," I respond.

"I'm not your pal, friend," he retorts.

It's all too easy to fall back into old routines. Wilford and I worked together for a long time. I found the bad guys, plotted ways to get them and then turned Wilford loose on those bad guys. He was a field operative and tore into them. We were friends once, and worked really well together. Part of me feels like I'm talking to my ex.

So, who were the bad guys? Truthfully, the bad guys were anyone that the U.S. Government decided were bad guys. In the past, the bad guys were Communists or Satanists or various other nebulous groups who were never really threats. Nowadays the bad guys are terrorists. They're the perfect nebulous group since terrorists don't have any real organization and anyone can be branded a terrorist for the most trivial of reasons.

The war on terror will never end. Mark my words on that.

"I'm not your friend, jack ass," I say, a little harshly.

"What's going on, man?" Wilford asks me.

"Not sure what you mean."

"You guys are all in way over your heads. You know it, too."

"Yeah, we're in a bit of pickle," I say. "We've pissed off some powerful people. Or, I guess, I've pissed off some powerful people."

"Gods, amirite?" he replies.

"Yeah, fuck 'em," I tell him. "Fuck 'em all."

By about this time everyone has been drinking for at least an hour. Most of us can handle our liquor, or are at least smart enough to know when to stop. Jacob can put down kegs and not even notice it, Eve could probably drink a distillery, but she's got experience. Jessica appears to have taken it slowly. Frank, however, has been downing a shot for each drink he gave Eve and Jessica. The way Eve can drop liquor that means Frank is seriously fucked up right now. And angry. He's been watching Wilford all night long and now he's staggering over gripping an ice pick so tight his knuckles are turning white.

This could get ugly. And I haven't even had my burger yet.

I get up and try to intercept him before things get ugly. Wilford may be a dick and a murderer, but he's a pretty damn good fighter. Frank won't stand a chance.

I stop right in front of him and, keeping my hands in my pockets to seem non-threatening, ask, "I don't suppose you could make me a drink, could you?"

His eyes focus briefly and he mutters, "Sure. Just need to take care of something first."

When he tries to slide past me I move to intercept him again. "What's going on, buddy?"

Frank leans around me and glares at Wilford. "He shouldn't be here."

"He is here, and we need him," I say.

"He killed Jean," Frank says.

"What's going on?" Wilford says from behind me.

Dammit. I get that he's just trying to help, but now's not the time.

"You killed Jean!" Frank shouts.

By this point, everyone has noticed what's going on and started heading over.

"Who's Jean?" Wilford ask.

"You know who he is!" Frank yells. "You cut off his head!"

"Oh, him," Wilford drawls. "Who was he, anyway?"

I turn on Wilford and hiss, "Jean was Frank's, shit, I can never remember the proper term. They were together."

Wilford leans over my shoulder and simply says, "I'm really sorry about that, but I didn't kill him."

"What?" I ask. "You showed me his laptop. It was covered in blood."

"Seriously, Steven?" Wilford tells me. "Think it through. I worked for DHS, we don't go around beheading people. Hell, we took you into custody."

He leans around me and faces Frank, "Seriously, we didn't kill him. My guys tracked his wireless signal and found his corpse. We took his laptop hoping to get some information."

Frank looks incredulous. "If you didn't do it, who did?"

"I have absolutely no idea. We started with the theory that you guys had done him in yourselves but Steven's reaction didn't bear that out."

"My reaction?" I ask.

"Yeah, when I showed you the laptop."

"You mean when your freak-ass buddies were beating on me?"

"Enhanced interrogation. I needed information. You had information. I didn't have time."

"You're a dick, you know that?" I ask him.

"Fuck you. You've done the exact same thing. You were a rogue agent, a terrorist as far as we knew. Actually, I'm still not certain you're not terrorists," he spits.

"You've tortured people?" a quiet voice says from the side. Jessica looks aghast.

"Yeah. Bad people," I sigh.

I'm not exactly proud of some of the things I've done in the past, but at the time they all seemed like good ideas. You get caught up in the moment. You need to get the job done. Whatever the reason, bad things happen. I realize this is no excuse, any more than the Nazis claiming they were just following orders, but it happened and there's nothing that can be done about it now. I take solace in the fact that I saved a lot of lives by ruining a few.

"He was never terribly good at it," Wilford says, trying to be helpful. "That's why we only let him do it a couple of times."

"Shut the fuck up Wil, you're not helping," I snap.

"Sorry, bro," he says.

"I don't get you two, you hate each other but you act like old friends," Jacob says.

"I don't hate him," Wilford says. "We just had a falling out."

"Is that what you call it?" I turn on him. He blinks like he doesn't understand why I'm pissed. "A falling out?"

"What do you call it?" he asks me.

"You murdered kids and told everyone I sent you in there to do it!" I yell.

"Ask yourself something, Steven, what are you more pissed about? The kids? Or everyone blaming you?"

Fucking Wilford Saxton. He's right and he knows it.

"What, exactly, happened between you two?" Eve asks.

"This will take a while," Wilford says.

"Let me get a beer, bro," Jacob says, heading off to the cooler.

I watch him go and desperately want to just stalk off into the night. Sure, it's desert out there, but I've lived in this area most of my life, going out in the desert would be fitting.

Frank is still holding the ice pick. "Are you sure you didn't kill Jean?" he asks.

"Yes. We don't kill people who might have useful information. Why do you think I kept this guy alive?" Wilford tells him, motioning at me. "He's DHS enemy number one. If I took him out I'd probably get a medal."

"Fuck," I curse. "He's right. He wouldn't have killed Jean. He might have tortured him and imprisoned him illegally, but Wilford wouldn't have killed him."

Stupid world. Why the hell does it always come crashing back in on you? I ran away from all of this for a reason. I stuff my hands in my pockets and stalk over the old picnic table in the yard.

It's one of those old wooden ones you used to find in parks back in the day. Jacob showed up with it one afternoon. Felt it would be great for everyone to gather around and picnic at and shoot the shit at. Its face is scarred from the pocket knives of dozens of angst-ridden or love-struck teenagers. You can learn a lot of history from it, all of it disconnected of course, but a lot of history nonetheless. I used to like to sit at this table and smoke and ponder at the messages.

This table taught me that Metallica is number 1. I also found out that Rosa is a lovely flower, the West Side Vatos own this table, Rosa gives great head, someone still hates George Bush, Rosa is a two-timing whore and Chevy is fucking awesome. I've been tempted to leave a few notes of my own for posterity: Metallica hasn't put out a good song in decades, all Gods are bastards, and I killed Congress.

A hand on my shoulder breaks my reverie. I look up and Jessica is standing there holding two beers. A glance across the yard and I see Frank and Wilford shaking hands. Wilford is all dopey grins and hand clasping. He'd kill Frank if he thought there was a good enough reason.

I gratefully accept the beer and Jessica sits down next to me.

"I'm sorry," she says. "I didn't mean to judge. It was just a shock. I've never known anyone who has actually tortured anyone."

"The rest of these guys did it the night we met," I tell her.

"I know, but that guy was different. He was a monster."

"So were the guys I worked on," I tell her. "No offense to your guy. For what he did to you, and a lot of others, he deserved to die, but the guys I worked on were absolute evil."

"Have you ever told anyone?"

"No, never. I don't like to think about them and what they did, let alone talk about it."

She puts a hand on mine and says quietly, "I'd like to hear about it sometime, if you ever want to talk."

Part of me wonders if she's some violence junkie, but a look in her eyes tells me that's not the case. Frank was right, she can take care of herself and she's hardly some innocent flower. I've seen her kick the hell out of a guy and then run a knife through his throat. She also poisoned a couple of guys that had the unfortunate luck to be in our way.

I put my other hand on hers and say, "I will. Thank you."

Jacob shows up out of the blue and plops himself down, beer in one hand and a couple of burgers on a plate in the other. "Burgers are done, guys, load up before they get cold."

He notices my hand on hers, but just shrugs it off and takes a huge bite. "Jesus, Steve, these are some fucking good buns."

"Thanks, bud," I tell him.

"Seriously, man, get some food. Everything looks better with food. And beer. Lots of beer. You know me, man, I'm gonna give it the old college try, but I don't know if I can down all those beers on my own. You two have got take one or several for the team."

"And by team, you mean you?" Jessica asks.

"Damn right, little sister," Jacob tells her and takes another huge bite out of his burger.

"Hungry?" I ask Jessica.

She nods and we both get up and grab our own food and drink. When we get back, everyone else has squatted at the table and there's only one spot on the end left right next to Eve. I offer it to Jessica and stand while I'm eating.

Wilford is sitting across from Frank and animatedly telling him some story or another. I have to admit this about Wilford, he's kind of a bastard but he can tell a story and is an expert at getting people to open up to him. Eve still looks like she wants to slug him, but Frank has apparently decided to forgive him.

"So, we go in there and find porn everywhere," Wilford is saying. "Nasty ass porn, stuff even Steven wouldn't be caught dead with. I glanced at the cover of one of these magazines and it took me a minute to even realize what I was looking at and then it dawned on me. I didn't even know you could do that with a woodchuck."

Frank laughs. Jacob just smirks and says, "Did you catch the name of the, uh, periodical?"

Even I have to chuckle at that one.

Eve takes a bite of her burger and says, "So what about you guys? What happened?"

I shrug. I really don't want to remember this.

"A mission went off-parameter," Wilford says, calmly.

"Off-parameter?" I almost yell at him. "That's what you call four dead kids 'Off-Parameter'?"

Wilford glares at me for a moment before softening. "You read the report, eh?"

"Yeah, I read the report where you blamed me for you killing a bunch of kids."

"No one killed any kids. I'd say you could ask Manfredi and Johnson," Wilford says.

"But Manfredi and Johnson are dead. Carried out in Mason jars."

Manfredi and Johnson were the backup on that mission. Most cleanup teams consist of three people. Experience has shown that three is an ideal number in terms of firepower and mobility. Too few people on a team and it doesn't have enough punch. Too many and the team rapidly loses mobility.

And, yes, Manfredi and Johnson were carried out in Mason jars. The cleanup crew was pressed for time and the house was filled with Mason jars. I only saw the pictures, but I'd never seen anything like it before and I hope to never see it again.

Wilford peers at me. "With all your intellect, all your cunning, didn't you ever stop to wonder what happened that would reduce two people something that would fit in Mason jars?"

Honestly, I guess I never had. It was one of those things that went so badly so quickly that I never really thought to sit down and question everything. One minute everything was OK, the next it went to shit and the storm dropped on my shoulders.

"You never asked me, Steven. You never asked what actually happened." Wilford looks sad, broken.

"I read the report. That was enough for me," I tell him.

"I didn't write a report. By the time I got my head back together, that report was posted and I was told that report represented the official story. That was that."

"What? You faked a report?" I ask incredulously. "You?"

"Like I said, I didn't fake anything. I just never posted a report."

"Can we get to the point?" Eve asks with a sigh.

"Yes," a voice says from behind us. "A point would be nice."

I spin and reach for a gun that I don't have. John Begay is standing behind us, still dressed in his jeans, cowboy shirt and boots. He looks at all of us a laconic expression of pure, unconditional tolerance painted across his face.

Eve sees him and her face lights up. I've only ever seen her look excited like that once before, deep under the Simms Building, holed up in an office with a secretary's corpse and talking about UFOs.

Frank waves and offers him a drink or a burger. Begay politely refuses and tells Wilford to continue his story.

Wilford looks slightly confused but nods and says, "Steven, perhaps you should start."

"What's there to say? We got word a small group plotting to blow up a car in a parking lot on the first day of school. From a terrorist's perspective it would be great. A lot of dead kids makes for a lot of fear and anger, perfect for pushing the Jihadist philosophy of tearing down everything they don't like.

"They were based out of a small house in the South Valley, intel suggested a group of four, two couples. Probably armed, definitely dangerous.

"Wilford and two other guys, Manfredi and Johnson, went in late one night. They were supposed to capture the couples, alive, and quietly get the fuck out of there. In the end, there were two dead agents, one dead bad guy, and four dead kids. This guy walked out untouched and wrote a report that said I had not mentioned the kids or the guns."

"I told you," Wilford says, "I didn't write that report."

"Whatever," I say dismissively.

"Do you want to know what happened when we got in there?"

"Not really, whatever you say it will probably just be more bullshit," I tell him.

"I'm interested in knowing what happened," Jessica says.

"I know what happened," Begay adds, "but I want to hear your side of it."

"Fuck it," I say. "Whatever. Tell the tale, Christopher Marlowe."

"First off, there were no living kids there. There were no living couples there. There were no explosives there. There was one guy sitting in a chair surrounded by all kinds of graffiti. Strange symbols all over the damn place. The whole place reeked of decay. There were body parts and blood everywhere. That's where your kids and your couples were.

"The guy in the chair glanced briefly at us and attacked.

"God he was fast, Manfredi was down before I even realized the guy was moving. He shoved me out of the way and ripped Johnson apart.

"Those guys were good, but neither of them even had time to react. He tore them apart and let me watch while he did it.

"Have you ever seen someone get dismembered?"

"No, I've never actually seen it happen," I say.

"I've done it," Eve chimes in cheerfully.

"Eve," Frank says calmly, "that was the proverbial turd in the punchbowl."

"What?" she asks, gesturing at Wilford. "He asked."

I've never seen anyone actually in the process of getting dismembered. I've seen the aftermath of it, though. We had a guy, a body builder, huge mother fucker, crazy as a shit-house rat and one mean bastard to top it all off. Anyway, he decides he's had it with America and he's going to show everyone how a master physical specimen such as himself can take over. He gets hopped up one night on some messed up meth variant and, no kidding here, rips his girlfriend's arm off.

Normally this is nothing DHS would involve itself in, but this guy wasn't too bright and starts sending letters to the local IRS talking about how he couldn't wait to kill everyone in there. He'd start with them and once everyone there had "tasted his genius," the rest of the country would follow him.

Threatening to overthrow the US Government is something the Department of Homeland Security does concern itself with. This is why we were extremely quiet when we all worked together in the past. It doesn't matter how tough Eve is, the rest of us die of lead poisoning just like everyone else does. Hell, even Eve can be taken down by enough people, and the government has a lot of disposable people.

Long story short, we found the body builder and took him down without a shot fired. When we showed him pictures of his dead ex-girlfriend and her arm he wept like a baby, crying huge crocodile tears.

Imagine the last time you tore a drumstick off a chicken, add a lot of blood and some shattered bone and you get the general idea of what a dismembered limb looks like.

So, no, I've never seen anyone actually get dismembered and I have absolutely no desire whatsoever to see it happen. Seeing the results is bad enough.

"I watched Manfredi and Johnson get ripped limb from limb right in front of my face while I was lying in a pile of dead kids."

Everyone is silent for a moment. "Why didn't you do anything to stop him?" Jessica finally asks.

"I emptied a full clip from my MP5 into him. The bullets didn't do a damned thing."

See, that right there is the terrifying thing about knowing. Not knowing is so much better. I used to sleep peacefully all night long until I started hearing stories like this. Here's another terrifying thing for you, Wilford's story is hardly unique.

"You can't kill Coco," Begay finally says. "At least not with anything you Bilagáana have available to you."

"Coco?" Jacob asks. "That fucker's real? My mom used to tell me to be good or Coco would come get me."

"You might want to watch your back," Frank quips.

"Nah, man. That's not what my mom meant when she said 'be good,'" Jacob retorts.

Knowing what little I know about his past, this is a statement best left alone.

"Who, or what, is a Coco?" Jessica asks.

"He's a traditional Northern New Mexico monster, a kind of boogey man that the Northern Latino community talks about," I tell her.

"So why would the boogeyman give a damn about terrorists or DHS agents or anything else?" she asks.

"He probably didn't," Begay says. "Everyone was just in the wrong place at the wrong time. You Bilagáana are nuts to toy with him. Even I'm smart enough to give him some leeway. He's powerful and angry. Bad combination."

Jessica glares for a moment at Wilford and then whirls on me. "Are you guys telling me the government knows the fucking boogeyman is real and they're not doing anything about it?"

"What would you have them do?" Wilford asks her.

I nod and shrug. "These things aren't common and there's fuck-all anyone can do to stop them, so official policy is contain it, cover it up, and pretend it didn't happen. Same thing with the aliens."

Eve shoves a finger at me. "I still haven't forgotten about that, you know."

Frank holds up his hands and says, "Whoa, whoa, whoa. Forgotten about what?"

"There may or may not have been a UFO under the Simms building. We don't know and she's still grumpy that I didn't waste our only key so she could look at it," I say.

Jessica is taking all this in stride. She sips her beer and laughs to herself. "There was a god down there, why the hell wouldn't there be a UFO?"

Eve points at her, glares at me and says, "See! You owe me a UFO."

"I'll see what I can do," I tell her dismissively.

"You'd better," she tells me.

"So, John, what brings you to the neighborhood?" I ask.

"Well," he says with a sly grin, "I didn't come for burgers."

14 | Dance Hall Days

John Begay eventually caved and ate a burger. He didn't want green chile on it, which is a sin in my book, but whatever. It's getting late, and the coals are dying down. It's springtime in New Mexico and the days are unpredictable and the nights get chilly fast.

He wasn't really there for a burger, he wanted a dance and he wanted to tell a story. Don't get me wrong, he dug the burger and he especially dug the bun, but, just like all gods, he had ulterior motives. Mostly he wanted the dance.

While we all sipped beers and pondered Wiford's story, we were treated to a gratuitous display of a god's power. Invisible drums beat a rhythm and hidden singers chanted a hypnotic beat. A coyote chased a road runner. The stars spun up a mandala and Eve and John danced.

I swear I haven't been hitting the peyote.

Watching John and Eve dance I get a sense of the danger we're facing. Leave it to the Great Spirit of the Southwest to cloak his message in some obscure language like movement. Things are never obvious in this part of the world. Other parts of the country you have a pretty good idea of what's about to kill you: the flood or the snake or the bear or whatever. Out here, the sun will slowly sap your life. The hot, dry air will turn you to dust if you don't watch yourself.

You learn to pay attention in this part of the world, look for the subtle clue: the spindly black leg means eating that tomato nets you a black widow at the same time.

John and Eve's dance hides a message, something most people would ignore or simply not understand. Pay a little bit of attention and you'll see it, though; either we kill Dreamer or some, others I guess, I don't know what that part of the dance means. Some others will hunt us down wherever we go. We'll end badly.

Truthfully, I don't have much of a problem with letting Dreamer run roughshod over this world. It's not like humans have done such a great fucking job with the place. Maybe letting someone else take over isn't such a bad thing.

Problem is, if we leave him alone heaven only knows what those others can throw at us. Whatever it is, rest assured, it will be bad and it's not like we could just switch side and head over to Dreamer's team; he's a solo player. That much I know from what he left in my head.

So, we're stuck between the proverbial rock and hard place. If we don't take out the Dreamer, he'll continue to warp reality. Frankly I don't have that much of a problem with that. I've never been what you would call a people person. He'll also keep coming after Jessica. That I do have a problem with.

There's something else buried in John and Eve's dance, something dangerous and erotic; like watching forces of nature coming together.

As George Takei would say, "Oohh my."

I guess all dance is just sex with more movement, so this shouldn't surprise me.

John was right, Eve dances like a gazelle. It shouldn't surprise me, she's an accomplished fighter and fighting is just like dancing only in fighting the dancers get hurt if they're not good enough.

Eve's been fighting for a very long time and she's exceptionally good at it.

Begay, it turns out, was also a very good dancer. Not surprising, either.

I wish I could describe the dance, but it was beyond anything I've ever seen. They moved like mortals can't, they went places we didn't understand. A god and a demigoddess dancing is an indescribable, surreal thing. It makes about as much sense to my tired mind as a black velvet painting of a beaver brushing its teeth with a tire iron.

When their dance is over I fight back the urge to applaud. As they walk back to the table, John Begay slowly dissolves until he's nothing but a quiet voice whispering, "Dulce."

Jacob smashes the top of his beer on the table and downs the rest in one gulp. "Did we just watch those two have sex?"

Jacob's more perceptive than some people like to believe.

"I don't know, but something strange happened," Jessica says. "Did we really just watch them dance?"

"After she got laid in the back of that truck, I always assumed she had sex like everyone else. You know, in pickup trucks behind bars," I say.

It's just a thing I do, a way of blowing off stress. I refuse to take anything seriously, no matter what it is. Life is too short to take everything seriously. When Death comes for me, I'll tell her a joke and we'll both laugh before I shuffle off to pay Charon his due.

Everyone looks at me, somewhat relieved. I've been wound too tightly, trying to wrap my head around the situation. Dreams in my head have been setting my goals for me. By cracking wise, it makes them realize I've finally come home.

Someone squeezes my hand and I see Jessica smile at me.

Eve sits down with a smile on her face. A flick of her hair and she sighs and drinks her beer. A deep-down look of relaxation crosses her face and her eyes glow like storm clouds lighting up. She has this innate ability to look like a little girl, all innocence and peace when she wants to.

There's still a flicker of energy, a taste of electricity lingering in the air when Eve slams her beer down. She's shifted from the little girl to the chooser of souls in the blink of an eye. "Was it as good for you guys as it was for me?" she asks us.

I actually have to laugh out loud at that one. "Is someone still planning on killing us all?"

Eve rolls her eyes at me. "I was otherwise occupied. We weren't exactly talking, you know?"

It looks like the bad guys are back.

"Did anyone else hear a whisper right after he left?" Frank asks.

"Yeah, I heard it," I say with a bit of a grimace, hoping I heard wrong.

"What did he say?" Frank asks. "Dolce? Sweet?"

"Dulce," Wilford says with an equal bit of grimace.

"What the hell does that mean?" Jacob asks.

"Do you think?" I ask Wilford.

"I seriously hope not," he responds.

"What? What is Dulce?" Jessica asks.

"Dulce is one of those places best left alone," I tell her. "Ever hear of Operation Paperclip?"

She shakes her head no. Not surprising, a lot of people haven't heard of Operation Paperclip.

Remember how the Soviets beat the U.S. into space with Sputnik? That was a great source of national pride for the Russians and huge black eye for the Americans. Sputnik went up in 1957 did nothing more than orbit and beep, but it was a quantum leap in terms of space travel. It was the first time a man-made object was placed in orbit and it scared the bejeezus out of everyone.

The problem is neither country's native scientists were actually responsible for the success or failure of the respective programs. As a buddy of mine is fond of saying, "Their German scientists were better than our German scientists."

"Operation Paperclip was an OSS project at the end of World War II that aimed to prevent the Soviets and the Brits from getting their hands German scientists. Our intelligence service captured Nazi scientists and spirited them to the United States where we put them to work," I tell Jessica.

"Dulce is one of the places we dropped off the less savory ones," Wilford says. "Most of them, the rocketry and aeronautics guys were sent to White Sands to work on the various rocketry and flight projects we had going on. The doctors and chemical guys were dropped off in Dulce, New Mexico and encouraged to continue their work."

"I'm almost afraid to ask, but what work were they continuing?" Jessica asks.

"The usual Nazi stuff," I say. "Freezing people to see what happens, mixing new and exciting gasses, usual crimes against humanity kind of stuff."

"We kidnapped Nazis and put them to work?" Frank asks.

"Hell, yeah," Wilford tells him. "You don't leave resources like that lying around."

"Resources?" Jessica asks.

"Resources," I say. "The Nazis may have been bastards, but they were smart bastards. Our intelligence guys went into Germany during the last days of the war and scooped up everything they could find, rockets, planes, scientists, everything."

"But they were war criminals," she says.

"Indeed," Wilford tells her, "They were bad people, but they were smart bad people and we needed them. Set them up with new lives, cars, money, wives. Whatever they wanted, as long as they would work for us."

"So what's in Dulce? Those were chemical and bio guys, not rocketry," I say.

Wilford shrugs. "Who knows, maybe they took the Thule freaks there, too."

Nazis were a varied group of nutters. While some of them worked on the war effort doing things like designing rockets and tanks, or developing exciting new toxic gasses, or trying to exterminate the Jews, others worked a more occult side of the war. The Thule Society, part of which was folded into the Nazi party, was the backbone of the occult side of Nazi philosophy.

"If the Thule followers got taken to Dulce it's possible there's some information at least we can use," I say.

"Get me into that place," Eve finally says. "If there's something there, we need it."

Jacob raises his nth beer – I lost count a while ago – and says, "Fuck, yeah! I was getting bored doing nothing!"

We all raise our drinks in toast.

We might not have a full game plan, but we're got play to make and that's better than guessing.

* * * *

It's after midnight and the air is getting downright cold before we finally decide it's time to stop drinking and people start heading off. Wilford shuffled off an hour ago. Jacob's nearly catatonic and Frank has to help him get up. Jessica gives me a slightly drunken peck on the cheek and heads inside. I watch her go and just before she goes inside she looks over her shoulder and gives me a little smile.

It's just me and Eve and the stars now.

We stare at the stars for a while.

If you watch the sky long enough you'll eventually see a shooting star. Wish on it, and you're supposed to get your wish fulfilled. It's never worked that way for me in the past, but I still wish on falling stars every time I see one.

"Eve, you still awake?" I ask.

"Yeah, why?"

"Why did you do it?"

"Do what?"

"Start this whole thing?" I ask her.

"What do you mean?"

"You never cared about Congress, did you? I mean, why would you?"

"Not really," she says with a sigh. "That was just a means to an end. Honestly, I hoped to see more chaos result from that."

"So, why?" I ask.

"I've been here for a very long time," she says. "I can't leave until the world completely falls apart. It's my mission."

"So, ignore it," I tell her. "I've ignored plenty of missions in my time."

"It doesn't work that way for me. I can't ignore my mission. My mission is really my only reason for existing and until it's complete, I can't stop."

"Sounds like quitter talk to me. Or not quitter talk. Whatever. Just do you what you want, walk away."

"I may as well ask you to quit breathing ," she says.

"Shit. That sucks," I tell her.

Eve takes a huge swig of beer and simply says, "Yup."

"So why us?"

"You're all good at what you do. That's one of my talents; I can spot people who will be useful. I choose them."

"For what?"

"The end," she says.

"So, if I'm reading you right, you chose us because we would be useful in 'the end,' whatever that is and sparked this whole mess just to force 'the end' to come sooner."

Damn. I thought I was good at manipulating people. I'm a rank amateur compared to Eve. It must come with experience.

"That pretty much sums it up. Hate me for it?"

I should be livid. I should be choking on my own rage, but I just can't find the energy to care enough. If I'm going to be pissed at anyone, I should be pissed at myself. I didn't entirely know what I was getting into, but I was in such a bad place at that time that I would have happily joined up anyway. In the end, it was better than the alternative of drinking myself to death.

"Not really," I tell her. "It's not like I didn't walk in with my eyes open. I should have suspected something was off when you told that cooked squid you didn't choose him, though."

The cooked squid was some damned kind of monster or something that was guarding the entrance to Dreamer's jail. He was one tough hombre. I fought him and pretty much lost. Eve managed to hold her own and may have been able to take him, but we didn't have the time for a prolonged fight. I wound up shooting him with a Dragon's Breath shotgun round and he went up like an inferno. When she was standing over his charred remains, Eve told him she didn't choose him. At the time, it didn't make a lick of sense. It's starting to make more now.

"He was an asshole," she says simply. "All of his kind are."

I suppress a yawn. It's only midnight, I must be getting old.

"We need some intel, you know," I tell her. "We really don't know what Dreamer's up to other than trying to take over."

"I think I may have an idea. Wanna go bust up a preacher?"

"Depends, which preacher?" I ask.

"The Very Reverend George W. Smith, head pastor of the Church of the Holy Dreamtime," she says.

"The nebbishy guy on the billboards?" I ask.

"The same."

"What makes you think he'll know anything?" I ask her.

"I've heard stories."

"Stories?"

"Stories."

"What kind of stories?" I ask.

"Stories about shadows," she says.

"Let me grab a coat," I tell her.

16 | Dreamtime

The Very Reverend George W. Smith's Church of the Holy Dreamtime has taken over one of the older churches in town and run the few remaining members off. I understand this is happening all over the country and places like this are slowly popping up south and north of the border. The Church of the Holy Dreamtime is only one of a larger group of liars and thieves capitalizing on the country's new-found God. It will only be a matter of time before Dreamtime, like all religions before it, rewrites history to support its own aims.

Smith - sorry, The Very Reverend George W. Smith - used to be a small time hustler whose best score was cheating at poker out at any of the number of casinos that dot New Mexico's landscape like acne on a teenager. He was slowly banned from each and every of them.

When Dreamer left the Simms building he almost ran over George Smith, who was not a Very Reverend at the time, but who had, at some indistinct point in the past, worked at the facility under the Simms building. Smith was there when Dreamer woke up and was so terrified he bolted with his tail between his legs. Fast forward nine years and Smith, down on his luck, is walking in front of his old place of employ when he hears screams and gunshots and generally everything going to Hell.

Smith ran into Dreamer as the God of Dreams left the Simms building and nearly shat himself on the spot. Dreamer touched George Smith's head and he became The Very Reverend George W. Smith on the spot. Rather than following his plan of rolling the homeless people downtown for petty change, The Very Reverend George W. Smith set out to Save Their Souls for the Lord High Dreamer.

I know this because Dreamer knows this. He left a part of

himself in Smith as a lark, basically because he thought it would be funny to set up a religion around himself.

Anyway, The Very Reverend George W. Smith's Church of the Holy Dreamtime boasts a congregation that numbers in the thousands. People line up to get into his church and hear his sermons. The people have heard stories about The Very Reverend George W. Smith's ability to control shadows and how those shadows will take all your worries away.

People have a lot of worries these days.

It's 2am, the time when most people worship the God of Dreams by actually dreaming. By not dreaming right now, the faithful see themselves as being on a kind of fast. In their eyes, they're denying themselves the glory of dreams and therefore glorifying the dreams.

Or something. I don't know. Religious people have always been a mystery to me.

Eve and I are at the end of a long line of people waiting to get in. All the people in front of us have the same glassy-eyed expression that's usually limited to hippies and meth users. There are men and women in suits walking up and down the line, The Very Reverend George W. Smith's minions. They're peacekeepers and enforcers all in one. Ostensibly they exist to keep people safe, but they're really little more than hired muscle. They keep the flock in line, usually through force.

"We are never going to get in there," Eve says.

"Oh, ye of little faith," I tell her.

"How do you propose we get in?"

"Well, you're pretty tough, why don't you just start shoving people out of the way?" I ask her.

"I couldn't do that, they're just looking for salvation," she responds.

"Salvation? Most of these people just want to forget their problems for a while."

"Same difference," Eve says.

While we're dickering back about getting in one of the Reverend's minions stops right next to us and holds a finger to her ear. "This one?" she asks no one in particular.

There's a beat and the minion points to me and two handlers come walking toward us. The handlers are a lovely couple with glassy, unfocused eyes and permanent smiles. They stop in front of me and squee, "We're so happy to meet you. You have been chosen!"

The message echoes up and down the line like ripples from rock in a pond. The people on either side of us turn to stare in amazement.

"Which one of us?" I ask.

"You, sir," the lady handler says, pointing at me, "you have been chosen by the Very Reverend George W. Smith to hear his message tonight."

The pair are classic clean cut, all American models of wholesomeness. He's actually wearing a sweater vest over a shirt and tie and she's got a skirt and blouse combination that could bore Gandhi. Except for their blank eyes, they could be any couple from the fifties. They are the walking definition of fresh-faced and innocent. The man is wearing a nametag that reads "Chad" and the woman's reads "Sally."

I point at Eve. "Can she come?"

"I'm sorry," Chad says. "Only the chosen are chosen."

"Well," I say, "I'm going to ignore the semantics of that argument and just say, either she comes with me or you choose someone else."

Sally looks around, clearly concerned. Probably no one has ever questioned their status as chosen and it's slowly blowing her mind.

"It's okay," I say. "If you choose someone else, it only means I wasn't the chosen. I'm sure the choosing process has been wrong before."

Chad's jaw drops and everyone around us gasps. The minion holds a finger to her ear, nods and whispers something in the Chad's ear.

"The choosing process is never wrong. It was my frail mind that failed to comprehend the majesty of The Very Reverend. Of course, both of you are chosen." Chad says, tripping over himself to appease us.

It's remarkable how easy it is to push religious lunatics around.

The minion clears a path and Chad and Sally escort us up the line and through the front door. As we walk past the people in the line we can hear the whispers. "Chosen. Chosen. Chosen." People look at us in awe as we walk. Eve is used to it and leads the way with her head held high and shoulders back.

I kind of slink through the crowd. I don't like attention.

Inside Eve and I are escorted to a pew up in the front of the church. "You have the best seats in the house," Sally whispers to us, like it's some kind of honor to be close to the Reverend.

I politely thank her and we take our seats in a private pew.

The church is your typical old-school church. Its huge altar and massive walls were designed to make you feel small in the presence of God. Places like this always make me wonder how people fell for that trick. The whole point of religious places like this is to make you feel insignificant. Insignificant people are much easier to control. The new owners of this old church have removed the traditional images of Jesus and replaced them with iconography of a man in a suit helping various people.

Come to think of it, the pictures are a more twisted version of what the Church of the Subgenius would come up with. Difference is, though, J.R. "Bob" Dobbs only wants $30, Dreamer wants you.

It's good to see Dreamer's cults are just like everyone else's. He once personally told me he didn't really care for worshippers, he found them tedious. I wonder if all the other gods who've had worshippers felt the same way about them. Gods aren't exactly my forte, but I've actually met a couple of them so I'm a step ahead of most of these folks.

People all around us are pointing and staring in awe. Maybe picking out the chosen is a rare thing, but it seemed to me to pretty scripted. I turn in the pew and ask the people behind us how often people have been chosen.

The lady behind us says she's never seen it happen before.

Okay, so I was wrong. Something about this whole situation is making my hair stand on end. Why did the Reverend pick us of all people out of the crowd? Granted, Eve's pretty tall, but that's hardly a good reason.

Eve leans toward me and whispers, "I don't like this."

"Gotta concur with you. I'm not sure coming here was such a great idea," I say.

She leans back a bit, but she's tense, ready for a fight. This is a bad combination; one tense Valkyrie and a henchman versus a whole church full of brainwashed loons. Never look at anyone and assume just because they're nuts they're not dangerous. These people are true believers and true believers are dangerous. If you doubt me, ask any Jihadist, crusader, or pill-pushing pharmaceutical rep.

The lights drop and the entire church plunges into darkness. People all around us are squirming in their seats. You can feel the tension all around us. Slowly my night vision kicks in and I can see pinpricks of light all around, flickering like little stars. A small cluster of stars at the front of the church gets brighter and starts moving. People gasp. If you watch closely enough you can make out the shape of a man, calmly striding toward the pulpit. When the stars reach the pulpit they stop and a hush falls over the church.

"Ask yourself a question 'Are you dreaming?'" a voice whispers in the darkness. "More to the point, 'Are you dreaming correctly?'"

People shuffle nervously or sit upright, backs ramrod straight as if they're trying to impress the voice.

"Am I dreaming?" the voice continues.

You can almost feel the energy in the building. There's an old saying, "Never underestimate the power of stupid people in large groups." It's true. They don't have to physically do anything to generate energy, just be there and be excited.

"I like to think so. There's a special dreamer out there. Yes, a special dreamer, better than you and I. His dreams create reality. My dreams only reflect reality," the voice intones, its intensity increasing.

"What do your dreams do? Do you dream of fame? Do you dream of fortune? Do you dream of power?

"Am I dreaming?"

I lean into Eve and feel her head meet mine. "At least he didn't start off with 'I have a dream.'"

Eve snorts quietly.

"I am his prophet, and you, you are his people," the voice booms. The lights come back up, not full, but it feels like full after the darkness.

The Very Reverend George W. Smith is a greasy bastard in a fancy pinstriped suit. He looks completely at ease except for his eyes. They're manic and full of monsters. He may well have met Dreamer, but I doubt it was a pleasant meeting for either of them.

He holds his hands over his head and yells, "We are the chosen people.

"I look around this room and I see beautiful dreams. Yes, it's true. You are beautiful dreams." Smith singles out a pretty, young woman in the audience and points directly at her. "You are a beautiful dreamer."

Two assistants appear out of nowhere and hand the young lady a letter before vanishing again. She opens it, smiles, and holds it her heart.

I've seen this game played by rock stars before. Next time you're at a concert and you see the singer point at someone in the crowd, keep an eye on who was pointed at. I'll guarantee you that person will get a visit from some escort soon enough. Next thing that person knows, they're back stage getting naked in front of some rock star's sweaty ass.

The young lady is beaming and the people around here vacillate between encouragement and jealousy. Jealcouragement? Sounds good. Anyway, I make a mental note to follow her later.

All around us, people murmur and nod.

"I have met the special dreamer. He is the God of Dreams, and he is the best dreamer the world has ever seen. He watches your dreams. He loves your dreams.

"Am I dreaming?"

Eve leans into me and whispers, "What kind of bullshit is this?"

"Dunno," I whisper back, "but it seems to be working. Look around."

Smith pauses and gazes out over his audience. His eyes are like lasers, boring into everyone, but they skip when they hit my eyes and skim over Eve's entirely. The rest of his audience is transfixed by his stare, rabbits gazing at a snake.

"When I was at my lowest, He came to me. He met me right here in this very town, not two miles from this very room. He is the one that freed this country from the tyranny of evil men. He revealed their own dark dreams to them and when they saw what their dreams were like, He set them free. Yes, it's true. He freed them from their terrible dreams of greed and control. When their dreams left, these evil men went back to the world of dreams, free of pain and fear and ready to try again! Because that's what He does; He gives you second chances. And third chances and fourth chances. That is His dream. He dreams of everyone being free.

"Am I dreaming?"

"I kind of wish he would quit asking if he's dreaming," I whisper.

"If he doesn't bump up the excitement, I'm going to sleep," Eve whispers back.

"I haven't told anyone this before," Smith says dropping his head like he's ashamed of something. "No, it's true, this is the first time I've told anyone this: I set Him free. And He set me free. Now I'm His prophet, His shepherd, here to bring you all to His Kingdom of Dreams. In His Kingdom, your dreams will be made real. In His Kingdom, your fears will be gone because your dreams will be too powerful for fear to get to you. In His Kingdom, you will find the Peace of Dream, the Freedom of Dream. You won't have to worry, you won't have to fight."

"Am I dreaming?"

Eve chuckles under her breath. She released Dreamer, not this buffoon.

"So, how do you enter His Kingdom? How indeed? Did you dream of Him? He's already called you to me. He wants me to help you get to Him. He wants you to join us on His pilgrimage. Unlike those other religions, I can promise you this: You can meet Him in this life, this world, this reality. He's waiting for you. Across the country, yes, but He's there, waiting patiently for you to come to Him and taste His immaculate dreams."

"Am I dreaming?"

Dude, shut up about the dreaming. I get that it's an important rhetorical technique to constantly remind people, but it's damned annoying when you recognize it. Maybe I'm bored, but I see what looks like a shadow gliding across the way behind Smith.

That's not good.

"I promise you, my children, to serve you as he would serve you. We must strike down the fake Gods of this world and replace them with the one, true God of Dreams. For it is dreams that make us strive to be better than we are. It is dreams that drive us, and it is dreams that make life worth living. We are the children of dreams and our Father wants us come home."

Agreement ripples through the crowd. Eve leans in and asks, "What are they agreeing to?"

Good question. It's all rhetorical nonsense, but these people are eating it up. "Maybe they're just agreeing to give away all their money," I say.

Eve stifles a laugh. A few people near us look over at us.

"Home, friends, is in that city of dreams, Washington D.C.! It's there that the God of Dreams has taken up His holy residence. It's there that we will go! We will take back this country from the foul nightmare creatures that run it. We will bring the dream that was America to fruition!"

"Someone just watched *Gladiator*," I whisper to Eve and she sniggers.

Heads are starting to turn our way, including the Very Reverend George W. Smith's. We both give guilty smiles and nod as an apology. Smith doesn't look happy, but he accepts our apologies.

Smith continues on, trying to recapture his former energy. "The God of Dreams wants you to be happy. Wants you to be free. He asks only that you follow His divine plan."

Eve laughs out loud.

Smith freezes, unaccustomed to any criticism of his holy message. He glares daggers at Eve. She bows her head slightly in mock acceptance. To his credit, Smith continues on, feathers barely ruffled.

"Now friends, here is where we differ from those other religions. They will offer you false platitudes and bury you in nonsense if you dare ask questions. I want you. Nay, I need you, to walk into our faith with eyes wide open and all questions answered.

"This pulpit isn't a one-way street. If you have questions, you may ask them now."

Well, at least he's pretending he gives a shit about what his flock thinks. In my book, that ratchets him a couple notches up from most "men of God."

The questions come hesitantly at first. Superficial things like "What's He like?" or "Is He really the King of Dreams?" and Smith answers them superficially: "Well-dressed" and "Yes!" Over time, the flock gets bolder and starts questioning why the King of Dreams isn't in Albuquerque and "How did you set Him free?" and "Will He keep His promises?"

Smith answers with the glib tongue of a born manipulator. His flock sucks up his answers with slow minds of born followers. I almost feel sorry for them. These people are just looking for meaning. Maybe they're hurt or worried or scared. When they reach out to find something to anchor them, people like The Very Reverend George W. Smith are all they find, and, for the most part, that's a good enough anchor. They'll follow him to Hell and he'll lie to them and abuse them and they'll love him for it.

Eve and I hold our snarky comments in check and take the opportunity to wait and listen. Smith expects all their money and will give them a map and a plan of how to get to Dreamer. He'd love to go himself, but his destiny is to be but a lowly guide and he will be denied salvation until he has helped all who want to visit the King of Dreams. Smith says it's his penance for all his past misdeeds and he thanks the King of Dreams every day for the opportunity to redeem himself.

I guess there is one major difference between Smith and the rest of the prophets out there fleecing the flock. Smith can actually lead these people to an actual, factual god. He'll still abuse the living hell out of them, but he's not entirely full of crap.

Eve taps me on the shoulder and whispers in my ear. "Something really stinks about this place. Let's stay and find out what the deal is with this guy."

It's always been a dream of mine to bust up a cultist, so I nod and smile.

After the service, people start shuffling out. The young lady that Smith pointed out is approached by some of the Smith's assistants and, after waffling a bit, allows herself to be escorted back to the Very Reverend's private chambers. The last assistants attempt to escort us out so they can seal the church.

"Pilgrims, the Reverend needs his rest, and so do you. It is time for all of us to visit the King of Dreams. Sleep and be peaceful," a blank-faced man tell us. According to his nametag, this is Curt. He's clean-cut and has the bright-eyed mania of a true believer.

Eve drops him with a punch and I seal the outer doors.

Well, Reverend, you've drawn the attention of the people who accidentally planted the seed for your little cult, and we'd like to know more. As Leonardo would say, "Dimmi!"

Every church has an entrance to the inner workings somewhere around the altar. Church is a lot like theatre; it's very important that what's happening on stage seem both real and magical, so the players have to appear out of nowhere, like they were always there. It also helps that you tell the audience that what they're seeing is absolute truth.

Now, I'm not saying there's no God. I've seen too many strange things to doubt the existence of an all-powerful God. Hell, one of those strange things just cold-cocked a kid named Curt. What I'm saying is this: all churches are a ruse. They use primitive theatrical techniques to keep you in thrall, keep you powerless, and take everything they can from you. Churches give you absolutely nothing in return.

You want a relationship with God, by all means, have one. Ask yourself, though, as an adult, do you really need a chaperone in that relationship?

We find the entry to the backstage area of the church beyond a hidden door next to the original altar. Between the hidden door and the darkness, Smith could come and go like a wraith. The latch is a recessed button. The door opens silently into a deserted corridor.

These people are amateurs, Eve and I have broken into much more secure locations than this.

The corridor leads to a set of old wooden stairs that snake down into the bowels of the church. Unfortunately wooden stairs tend to creak. We take it slow and easy, sticking the edges of the stairs and manage to make it down without actually waking the dead, although we may have interrupted a dream or two here or there.

The stairs lead down into an old basement. The older parts of Albuquerque are lousy with basements, and they're all the same: cramped, tight, poorly lit and generally nasty. This one has been renovated so it looks less like the set from a bad horror movie, but still maintains its charming horror roots. The basement has four rooms, including this small landing room. I couldn't tell you the exact layout, but there are doors on either side of us and a door in front of us.

We stand there staring for a bit. I have yet to have that sudden flash of inspiration the hero always gets in the movies when he escapes with his lady fair. I'm usually the guy stepping into the sun beam in the Hovitos temple and winding up with spikes through my chest. I've managed to survive this far by being only slightly ahead of death.

"Number two worked last time," Eve finally says.

Dreamer was behind door number two down in that pit below the Simms building. Given recent events and the strange thoughts pinging around in my head, I'm not sure I would say number two "worked," but it did lead us to what we were looking for.

"True. Which one's number two?"

"The middle one. Start counting on either side and you wind up with number two in the middle."

"Can't fight that logic. You wanted to look in number three, though, last time," I say.

"Only because there may have been aliens," Eve responds.

"I'm telling you, they're not that interesting."

"To you!" Eve hisses.

"Someday, we'll find you some aliens."

"I'm going to hold you to that promise."

We creep up to the closed middle door and Eve puts her ear to it. She listens for a moment and straightens up, running a hand through her blonde hair.

"Well?" I ask.

"We should wait," she says.

"Why?"

"They're busy."

"Busy?" I ask.

"Busy," she responds.

"Doing what?"

"Screwing," she says.

"Ah," I say. "It would be improper to barge in right now wouldn't it?"

"I'd be pissed if someone busted in while I was getting some," Eve says.

"I would, too. Neither of us is a skeezy fake preacher, though," I retort.

"He may be skeezy, but she sounds like she's enjoying herself."

"Gotcha. We should wait then." I find a nice patch of wall and lean against it. "Can you hear anything in the other rooms?"

Eve sneaks to the other doors and puts her ear up to each of them in turn.

"Nope. Quiet," she tells me.

I pick a door using the logic I was taught in college. "Eeny meeny miny moe."

"What are you doing?" Eve asks.

"Trying to figure out which door to open first."

"Just pick one and open it," she tells me.

"Catch a tiger by the toe if he hollers let him go eeny meeny miny moe."

I smile and pick the door on the right. It's unlocked and opens smoothly. "Ah," I say, "Well that's that then."

"What's in there?" Eve asks.

"Someone's bedroom. It's covered with posters for 90s Goth bands."

Eve leans next to me and glances around the room. "Oh God. Who still listens to Bauhaus?"

"Sally, if the name tag on the wall is any indication. I wonder if Chad's room is next door."

The opposite door does turn out to be Chad's. His room is organized to an almost pathological degree and decorated with things from Pottery Barn.

"I guess Chad and Sally aren't a couple," Eve says.

"They do seem less than compatible," I respond.

A noise slowly builds in the middle room. A woman's moan rapidly increases in volume before turning to an epic orgasmic scream.

"I guess they're done," I say.

"I guess he's better than I thought," Eve says thoughtfully.

"Wanna bust in now?"

"Yeah, why not?"

Turns out the door is unlocked and opens silently like the other ones. I swear no one bothers to secure anything anymore. Inside we find Smith and the young lady he pointed to during his sermon. They're both naked and she has a glazed look in her eyes, like she's not quite there.

Either Smith is really good, or something bad is going on here. Of course, that shadow slinking out of the bed might have something to do with it.

Smith looks at us, points at me and yells, "You!"

Me. What the hell did I do? I wonder.

Oh, yeah. That whole breaking in thing. Hey, we waited until they were done. What more does he want?

"Me?" I say.

"You," Smith replies. "I've seen you in my dreams. Who are you?"

"Hi," I say with a wave a smile. "I'm Steven and this Eve. We're wondering what the hell you're up to."

"I am getting laid!" Smith thunders.

"Well," Eve says, "actually we waited until you were done. So, you're not really getting laid right now."

"Besides," I add. "That's not what we're interested in. This little church is dedicated to a certain God and we'd like to know what he's up to."

There's a knock at the door, probably one of Smith's flunkies checking in on him.

"Piss off!" I yell. "We're busy intimidating someone."

I faintly hear a gasp and then the flap of shoes running down the hall.

Eve walks over and helps the dazed girl out of Smith's bed, ripping the covers off to wrap her up. Smith stares daggers at her, but Eve ignores him and helps the girl to a chair in the corner.

"What did you do to her?" Eve asks.

The Very Reverend George W. Smith, Pastor of the Church of the Eternal Dreamtime stands up straight and tall, squares his shoulders, looks Eve in the eye and says, "I gave her over to God."

"God?" Eve asks. "You gave her over to God? Which God?"

"There is only one God!" Smith roars.

"I can assure you," I say, "there's more than one of them."

"You should know better. There's only one that matters." Smith says with a manic gleam in his eye. "I know who you are now. He has told me."

This can't be good. There are shadows flowing around this guy and he seems to know me.

"Who are you?" Eve asks.

Smith just smiles. His grin reeks of madness and the promise of power that will never be delivered. You have to be crazy to think anyone, Gods especially, will share power. People like Smith are easily manipulated and, more importantly, easy to use to manipulate other people. I guess all religions really are the same: find a patsy and use that person to control others. Call me cynical if you will, but I've never seen a holy man who wasn't drunk on his own power. Smith fits the bill to a T.

"I'm just a humble prophet of a higher power."

"No," I say, "you're a puppet."

"Once I take care of you, I'll be a prince," Smith says.

"Good luck with that," I tell him.

There's a thunderous sound outside the door. Whoever is coming down the stairs didn't stick close to the walls, which would have been much quieter. Frankly, it would have been more dramatic if they had been silent and we just turned around and, bam, there they were. Now, we have plenty of time to get ready.

"Luck, my friend," Smith says, "is just the intersection of skill and opportunity."

Hey, that's my line.

Eve vaults to the door and locks it. There's a decent-looking bolt on the inside, probably put there so Smith can screw his parishioners in peace. She checks the lock and leans against the door. "I'll handle this, you take care of him."

There's a shadow creeping around the edges of the room. Shadows are one of Dreamer's, uh, things that he does. Fuck. I don't know how to explain this eloquently. He has shadows, living shadows that are part of him. They act as disconnected limbs and weapons and communication tools and, well, probably all sorts of things. Think of the shadows as a kind of early warning system of sorts. They're semi-autonomous things that obey his will like disconnected limbs connected over Wi-Fi. Hell, he's a God; the normal rules don't apply to him.

The shadow explodes and reconstructs itself. It looks like a fractal exploding into squares, an 8 bit Nintendo character dying by pixel degrees. No, seriously, it looks that cool.

The last time one of these things touched me, it felt like cold crawling up my body and sticking its dirty fingers in my brain. It wasn't the most pleasant experience of my life, but it was the only way the Dreamer could communicate at the time, unless you count shouting.

The thing sweeps across the walls and floor, stretching and contracting like a digital amoeba. The effect is hypnotic. When it reaches me, it spreads around me in a circle of black, but doesn't come any closer.

A voice rings in my head, a cloyingly sweet sing-song falsetto. "We missed you."

I smile. I was worried for a moment there.

"What is happening?" Smith says.

The shadow surrounds me, neither moving in, nor moving out. It seems confused, torn between attacking and protecting.

"Why are you here?" the shadow's voice sings in my head.

When I close my eyes, I can see it and see myself through whatever passes for eyes in the thing. There's adoration and fear in its mind. It thinks I'm Dreamer and can't understand why it can't come home. Its attention vacillates between a confused idea of who I am and a desire to do Smith's bidding. It wants to consume me because that's what Smith wants it to do, but it can't consume me because I'm Dreamer and it is Dreamer and it can't consume itself.

Why the hell does it think I'm Dreamer?

"Take him!" Smith shouts.

The shadow doesn't move.

The Very Reverend George W. Smith, Head Pastor of the Church of the Eternal Dreamtime has just had his power taken away in the blink of an eye. Like all Pastors whose flock has awakened, Smith is scared and angry. He's a beast now, a vicious thing deprived of its dinner. His eyes are whirling in his head, flickering back and forth between me, the shadow on the floor, Eve guarding the door, and the lost, naked girl wrapped in a blanket and sitting on a chair in the corner.

"Get them!" he screams at the girl on the chair, but she's gone bye-bye and doesn't react to him at all.

The minions have reached the door and are banging on it. I don't know how many are out there, but it sounds like a zombie invasion. The rhythmic thumping makes the room feel like we're at a Drum and Bass show.

Eve slams her fist against the door and yells "Shut up!"

The thumping stops for a minute and restarts.

The din outside the door is getting louder, all of Smith's mindless minions hammering at the old wooden door, desperate to get in and help their master. The door is solidly built and guarded by seven foot of irate Valkyrie. They're not getting in, he's not getting out.

I'm still not sure what the shadow intends to do. It may know what evil lurks in the hearts of men, but I have no idea what lurks in its heart. If it has one.

I take a tentative step forward, and the shadow moves back slightly. It won't touch me, but it won't leave me. Another step forward and the shadow flows backward. It would appear I have a shadowy moat around me. Its voice is quiet now, but there's a sense of worry coming off it. Keeping one eye on Smith, I reach out to it, trying to touch it in the dream world. The shadow welcomes my mind, but it's apprehensive, not sure of what to make of me.

"Guard the girl," I send.

A tendril reaches toward the girl in the chair and wraps around her foot. She doesn't react, and the rest of the shadow oozes across the floor. It takes up a protective circle around her and doesn't move.

Smith looks shocked and horrified. He reaches beneath his pillow and stands back up, naked as the day he was born and brandishing a long dagger.

"This ends now. No one can take Him from me. He's mine! She's mine!" he shrieks.

Maybe it's the rage, maybe it's the insanity, maybe he actually knows what he's doing, but he doesn't bother threatening me with the knife; he just charges like a rhino. He's got the knife held low and slashes at my stomach. I manage to dodge the first slash and dart in with a quick right punch to the side of his head. Smith staggers back, but recovers quickly and darts back in with a stab to my stomach.

A quick, short kick to the knee pushes him back and gives me enough time to get my own knife out.

Smith pauses briefly when he sees my knife, but comes in anyway. His knife flashes toward my face and I barely manage to put my own blade between his knife and my face.

Smith has some experience, but he's still thinking about just a knife fight. He thinks his only weapon is the knife and he's still stuck in a rut trying to cut my body or face. He's trying to for the single shot kill, not realizing there are better targets that are easier to hit.

When he slashes again, I block the strike at his elbow and smash the butt of my knife against his temple and he goes down on his ass. He wipes a trickle of blood from the side of his head.

"Just stay down, all we want is information." I tell him. "Stay down and you'll walk away from this."

Smith growls and crawls to his feet.

"What's your boss up to?" I ask him.

"You'll find out soon enough," he tells me.

I sigh and get ready. My eyes are on his shoulders. One mistake people make is trying to watch the knife. It's a small thing to see and almost impossible to keep your eyes on when it's moving. His shoulders, however, will give me a lot of information about what he's trying. When his shoulders change, the knife is coming, and you can pick it up in his shoulders before you can pick it up anywhere else.

I really wish I had my shotgun. This nonsense would be over already. Even crazies sane up fast when the shotgun appears. Unfortunately, I was too late to FedEx it with same-day delivery.

Damn. Was that this morning? It seems like a year ago.

"You could just tell us what's going on now and we'll quietly walk away from all this," I say. "Last chance, bro. Take the easy way out, please."

"I'm going to gut you and take her before your blood is cold," he snarls, pointing at Eve.

I look at Eve. She chuckles and points back at Smith.

When I turn back, Smith is surging forward, the knife drawn back and ready to strike. It's probably time to end this. I wait for him to strike and pull an old Kenpo technique out of my bag. It's Flash of Light and it's one of the few knife techniques we have before 5th Black.

Smith stabs straight in and I brush his attack aside and step in and slightly to the side to meet him. My blade goes up and under his armpit, coming out the behind his arm. Before he can react, I slash back at him, down toward his thigh to take his leg away. I keep my knife sharp and both cuts find their targets and slice deep.

Here's a thing about a cut. We've all had them, albeit probably not as deep the Reverend just got, but with a sharp enough blade you sometimes don't even notice you've cut yourself immediately. Now, get yourself all keyed up and get that old adrenaline flowing and you might not notice you've been cut in a fight until it's over. That's why it's important to pick your targets well. Cut an artery and your opponent will bleed out, but it may take a while. Cut a tendon and whatever that's attached to won't work anymore.

The cut under Smith's arm severs his Axillary Artery and the cut to his thigh is deep enough the muscle can't hold him up anymore. The cut to his armpit will kill him, the cut to the thigh makes sure he doesn't go anywhere while he's dying. He falls to his knees with a wince and a confused look on his face. The pain hasn't set in yet.

"Last chance, bud. Tell me what Dreamer's up to and I'll call an ambulance."

Smith just mutters "Fuck you" and tries to figure out why his leg won't work. He's kneeling in a pool of blood, but doesn't seem to realize it's his. His fingers are pawing at the gaping wound on his thigh, trying to keep it closed with his hands. It works about as well as you might expect, but the blood bubbling up between his fingers doesn't deter him.

"You'll never win, you know," he smiles up at me. "He's already got your number, Steven."

"How do you know my name, asshole?"

Smith's grin is back and just as vile as ever. It's the grin of every asshole that smirked when they narced you out in school. "He knows your name. He wants her and he'll get her. She'll be his, just like that bitch on the chair."

"Who, her?" I ask pointing at Eve.

"You know who," he says and sneers at me.

Jessica. Shit.

I slam the knife into the base of Smith's skull and watch the lights go out in his eyes. He's still smiling as he falls face first into the concrete floor.

With it all over, I notice the room has gone silent as the grave. The beating of fists on the old door has come to a complete stop. I turn and look at Eve and she looks just as confused as I am.

She takes a tentative step away from the door. I wipe my knife on Smith's bed sheets and move to stand next to her.

"Well," I ask her. "Now what?"

"We've got a choke point, I bet we could handle the one or two that could get through the door at a time," she responds.

"Wow," I say. "It would be like Thermopylae in the basement of cult's church."

"Exactly," she says with a gleam in her eye. "You ready?"

I nod my head.

"Three, two, one," Eve counts down.

I get ready for whatever's out there. It's just a handful of deranged cultists. How hard could it be?

If I remember my history correctly, Custer said the same thing.

Before she can unlock the door we hear a laconic clapping behind us.

We both whirl around and find the girl slumped over in the chair, head drooped and clapping slowly. Her face slowly rises to face us. Her eyes are blank, partially rolled back into her head, but she turns to face us dead on.

"Nice work," she says.

Her voice feels like silk sliding across my skin. Those two simple words filled my head with dreams of warm places. It's Dreamer's voice, intermingled with the girl's own voice in a perfect sonic harmony.

"Uh," I stammer, "Thanks."

The girl slowly, jerkily stands up. It's like watching a puppet standing up when the strings are pulled. Her head lolls around before focusing on Eve. "I owe you my thanks, my dear. Freedom has been exhilarating."

Eve nods and says, "No worries. What are you up to?"

Dreamer lurches the girl across the room, looking at things. It apparently takes effort because she drops the occasional book or tchotchke. Watching her lurch around the room is like watching a video of someone walking backward but played in reverse; it doesn't make sense to your eyes. There's something that's just so – off - about it.

"I'm taking over," Dreamer says through his puppet.

"Taking over?" I ask.

"Yes," it says.

"What do you mean, taking over?" Eve asks.

The girl's head swivels to an unnatural degree to stare at Eve. "I mean I'm taking over. Everything."

"How?" Eve asks him.

"People," Dreamer says, "They give themselves to me."

"I don't think they actually intended to literally give themselves to you," I say.

"They didn't realize it at the time, but they meant to. Like this girl," Dreamer says, running her hands up her body. "She gave herself fully to me."

"I'll bet she did," Eve says.

"Do either of you want her?" Dreamer says.

"No, thank you," Eve and I say in unison.

"Are you sure? She thinks she's quite good. She's very experienced."

Some part of me thinks it's odd that she's referring to herself in the third person. Some other part of me realizes that she's not referring to herself, he's referring to her. So, based on that, is she moving her hands up her stomach to fondle her breasts, or is he doing it for her? Is it masturbation if someone else is controlling your hands?

A small gasp escapes the girl's mouth when her hands move between her legs, but his voice doesn't quaver. "She's quite fond of you. Both of you. You could share her."

Eve just sighs and puts her back against the door.

"Sorry, not interested," I say.

"Pity. The things this girl thinks." A shudder goes through her body. "Tremendous."

"What are you doing, Dreamer?" I ask her, uh, him.

"Oh, the usual," he says, "taking over. I'm surprised you didn't see it coming. You seemed so smart."

"I'm kind of slow on the uptake," I respond.

"It's true," Eve says, "he is slow."

I look at Eve and she just shrugs. "Well, you kind of are."

"These people," Dreamer says, shaking the girl's hands in the air, "you people, you need control. You just don't realize it. This girl gave herself to me, willingly. All the people this place has given me have given themselves willingly."

Eve pushes herself from the wall and folds her arms across her chest. "I doubt that."

"No," Dreamer responds, "It's true. They gave themselves up and are happier for it."

"How can you do this?" Eve asks.

Dreamer's girl shrugs her shoulders, "It's remarkably easy. I promise them dreams."

"You're … we're supposed to leave them alone. Let them make their own decisions." Eve tells him.

"Ah, but I do let them make their own decisions. These people will follow anyone who promises them what they want to hear."

"You lie to them?" I ask.

"Have you ever known a dream that didn't lie?" Dreamer retorts.

He's got me there. Dreams may drive us, but they rarely tell the truth. When was the last time someone had a dream where they were themselves? When did you ever hear of someone dreaming of anything they could actually do? People dream of winning lotteries or being attractive or being famous or being important. Most people will never achieve any of those dreams. They may strive toward them, believing in their hearts that their dreams will come true, but those dreams never come true, do they?

I look at Eve and she looks concerned.

This leaves us in a bit of a conundrum. It would appear we toppled one government just to have it supplanted with a worse one. Maybe I should have paid attention to history; this kind of thing happens all the time. Just goes to show no good deed goes unpunished.

Actually, this whole thing feels like voting: no matter who wins, everyone loses.

"No," I say, "I've never known a dream that didn't lie."

"Could you please stop gyrating and touching yourself. Herself. Whatever. Stop it," Eve says.

"Don't you like my show?" Dreamer asks.

"No," Eve says.

"I gotta say, it's not doing much for me, either," I add.

Dreamer stops moving and clumsily brushes a lock of hair from her face. "Can't blame a girl for trying."

"You're not a girl," I tell him.

Dreamer holds her arms out and looks down. "I appear to be a girl. Perhaps you've never seen one."

"What are you, twelve?" I spit. "Grow up. What are you doing?"

The girl's eyes narrow and glow slightly. "I told you. I'm taking over. You can either join me or I'll roll over you."

Dreamer eyes Eve, "I could always use a Valkyrie slave. Trust me, you'll love it."

Eve snorts.

"And you, dear Steven, I could always use a right hand man. You killed a monster. Not a lot of people can claim that. I can always use a monster slayer."

"Tempting," I say, "but I'm not a team player. I don't like the responsibility."

"They've sent their monsters after you, haven't they?" Dreamer asks. "I still hear rumors through our grapevine. I can help you with the monsters."

"What grapevine?" I ask.

"Oh, I see I've piqued your interest. She never told you, did she? Still following the old rules, Eve? Why bother? He knows about us and the world hasn't collapsed."

Eve tenses. Old rules? What the Hell?

"No answer, Eve. Oh, well. Being clever was never your kind's greatest strength."

Eve starts forward, but stops herself. She's strong, but she's out of her league with this guy and she knows it. Besides, even if she kills the body, the brain is somewhere else.

"I'm taking over, folks. I'm done with watching. Stop me if you can. Steven, bring me the girl or I'll take her piece by piece and let you watch while I do it."

Now it's my turn to start forward. I grip my knife tighter and imagine sticking it in him. Eve's hand on my shoulder stops me.

"What?" I say, pulling myself back together. "Can't you take her on your own?"

He doesn't answer. The girl's eyes are aglow now, amber suns buried in her face. They're actually kind of hard to look at, but also impossible to look away from.

"See you soon," he tells us.

Eve and I watch in horror as the girl twists her head slowly. The bones crack and pop. As the Dreamer's light fades from her eyes she screams in agony in her own voice but her head keeps twisting. With a final agonized scream, she collapses to the floor.

"What now?" I ask after I've recovered.

"We take him out," Eve says.

"How do we take him out?" I almost shout.

"Fucked if I know. We've got a good team, get me a plan," she replies quietly. "Let's get out of here."

Outside the door we find a dozen or so minions standing quietly, watching us with blank eyes. They're armed to the teeth with a terrifying variety of weapons both home-made and manufactured. Lots of knives, axes, machetes, guns. One guy actually has a baseball with nails sticking out of it. I've never seen one of those in the wild and am tempted to snatch it.

The crowd is motionless, eyes dead and black, like someone reached inside their heads and switched their brains off.

Eve leans in and asks, "Why aren't they tearing us apart?"

"Probably because you're indestructible."

"Point taken. Why aren't they tearing you apart and trying to tear me apart?"

"I don't know," I answer.

I walk directly in front of a woman in the front. She's gripping an axe tightly in her fist and her face is a frozen mask of rage. When I wave my hand in front of her face she doesn't move a muscle.

A shadow flitters across the floor. I get a sense of manic joy from it as it dances around the feet of the frozen crowd.

"They've been switched off," I say.

"Switched off?"

"He turned their brains off. He was done with them and didn't want to expend the energy controlling them."

"How do you know?"

I point at the shadow. "That told me. We should leave before they reboot."

"Reboot?" Eve asks.

"He stopped controlling their brains, shut them off basically, but they'll remember themselves soon enough. They'll be unstable. Lost and armed to the teeth. We need to go."

17 | Could Be A Good Day

For the first time in a long time, I slept the sleep of the just.

Seriously, this is a good thing. More and more of my sleeping time has been spent in other people's dreams and, while it can be interesting, it's also surreal as hell. Think about your last dream, what you remember of it anyway. Remember that scene where the dark clouds in the distance started to light up like windows on an airplane and it turned out it was a actually a whale in a flying parade? And what about that gibbon on the tricycle with the balloons attached?

See, you think a dream is surreal when it's your dream; try it with someone else's dream sometime. The crazy shit that runs around in your head makes some sort of sense to you but it's completely alien to me.

Sleeping all night, or however long it was, without dreaming is kind of a relief. You can only watch so many dominatrixes spanking midgets before it gets old.

I awake to the faint sound of trucks on the Interstate and the quiet rattling of people in the house. These moments when I first wake up and the whole reality of the world hasn't come crashing down on my head are the finest moments of my day. I lay on my side, half awake, drifting like a reed boat cast into the ocean.

The greatest thing about first waking up? The whole day stretches out before you and you can imagine it might be a good one. Shortly, you'll realize it's shit, just like every other day. But for a little while you can imagine everything is gonna be great.

I know, I know. I'm a cynic.

Anyway, I'm lying here, enjoying the quiet and the peace when I feel a hand brush against my back and my skeleton nearly jumps out of my skin.

The last time I woke up with strangers in my room I found two people who were there to kill to me. Only the power of my scintillating personality saved me.

The hand slides down my back a bit then disappears.

When someone's in bed with you, they're going to notice you move. It's impossible to mask your movements, especially in a cheap-ass bed like mine. Still, I feel the need to be stealthy, so I very gently twist first my top and then my legs.

Ever tried to roll over in a bed without waking someone else up? Harder than it looks.

When I turn around I find Jessica's sleepy eyes looking at me.

"Sorry," she says, sleepily. "I was having nightmares."

I stare at her for a moment. This is absolutely the last person I expected to find in bed with me. Someone trying to kill me, sure, I could understand that. Hell, a boogeyman would have been less of a surprise. Coco, all big teeth and reeking breath, would have made sense.

"No worries," I tell her.

She's beautiful, you know, still drowsy, a lock of hair falling across her face, a halo of sunlight blazing in her hair.

How do women do that? How do they manage to find the perfect position where the sun lights them up just right? The sun only shines in my eyes. It doesn't illuminate me so much as blind me.

"I hope it's okay," she tell me. "Me being here."

I relax and sink into my pillow. "It's all good," I tell her. "Sorry about your nightmares."

"I almost wound up in Jacob's room," she says.

"He would have had a heart attack waking up with you."

She smiles a little at that and brushes the stray lock of hair from her face. "It would have almost been worth it."

"Sure, but you would have been stuck resuscitating him."

"Ugh, too early for that thought," she says and covers her face with the pillow.

This is a strange feeling. I was married for years before my wife was killed. I haven't woken up to anyone else in my bed for a very long time.

Jessica peeks out from the pillow. "What time is it?"

I manage to roll over and look around for a clock. I'm slow in the morning and it takes me a few minutes to remember I don't have one. There's one on my phone, but that's all the way across the room and I don't feel like getting up.

"I have no idea. Someone else is up, so it must be pretty late."

Last time I was living here, I was always the first person up. Over the years, I had developed a tendency to get up early. I never thought I would ever be a morning person, but I came to actually enjoy it. The quiet when everyone else is still asleep is the perfect way to start the day. The rest of these guys sleep like professionals. If anyone else is up, it must be late.

She sits up and stretches; eyes closed, a long, languorous stretch, arms over her head. I try hard not to stare. She's wearing a T-shirt with Morphine's "Cure For Pain" cover on it. At the same time I'm appreciating the stretch I have to chuckle a bit at this woman wearing a shirt for an album that was released when she was something like four.

Jessica's eyes open and she sees me watching. "Enjoy the show?" she asks.

Honesty is probably the best policy here. "I did, thank you."

Her eyes soften a bit. She hasn't hit me, so I'm probably safe here. When she notices me smiling, she cocks her head and asks, "What?"

"I'm sorry," I say. "I was just remembering seeing those guys play here in town back in '98. It was a great show."

"I would've loved to see them play live," she says.

"Mark Sandman died in '99, not long after we saw them play here. You would have been, what, nine or so?"

"Ten," she tells me.

"They were pretty amazing," I say. "Dana Colley, their sax guy, did a solo where he played two saxophones at the same time."

It's times like this when our age differences stagger me.

We stare at each other for a few minutes before she finally says, "I wasn't kidding when I said I missed you."

"I kept your photo on my fridge," I tell her.

She blushes and says, "I hope no one else saw it."

"Just Eve."

"Oh, God," she says, collapsing back into the bed and covering her face.

When she moves her hands we watch each other for a minute again before she tentatively stretches a hand toward my face. Her face leans in to mine and I lean into hers. Just before our lips make that first scared touch there's a knock at the door.

Jacob doesn't even wait for answer, he just busts in with a happy, "Good morning! You got a package, Hoss."

He doesn't even break stride when he sees Jessica and I leaning into each other.

"Hey, Jess. Good morning to you, too. Package is on the table, bro."

Without another word he turns and walks off, leaving the door wide open.

Jessica and I look at each other and start laughing.

"I guess it's morning," she says and hops out of bed with a sigh.

Fucking Jacob.

I watch her walk to the door in her Morphine shirt and tattered boxer shorts. She smiles again when she catches me watching her. "See you in a bit."

"See you in a bit," I tell her.

When the door closes I lean back in the bed and stare at the ceiling for a spell. This is something I leaned to do when I was a kid. I can get lost in the ridges and valleys of almost any ceiling. I imagine it as looking down at another world from high above. With enough concentration, I can see the mountains and passes and the occasional lake.

It's very Zen of me.

A few minutes of that and my head is back together again. I find a shirt and a cigarette and go on my epic morning quest for coffee.

18 | Reprioritize Your Actionable Items Matrix

It doesn't take long to figure out it's nearly ten. Fortunately there's still some coffee left. Without coffee life is not worth living. Make note of that ye mighty and despair.

I grab my package, some coffee, and a smoke and head outside.

I set everything down on the bench and enjoy my coffee and cigarette. The morning is still a bit crisp and the sky, as usual, is cloudless. It's a nice morning and I'd love to spend it reading or playing games or, well, whatever. My package seems intact. I was honestly kind of worried about that. I've sent weapons through the mail before and nothing has ever happened, but I was a little worried that the time I sent some exotic pistol through the mail would be the one time Wilford Brimley would open the package and decide I was some kind of criminal mastermind.

The guns are still inside, still neatly wrapped in their bubble wrap. When I unwrap them, I spend a few minutes admiring their design. A lot of people freak out when they see a gun and can't fathom how it can be a work of art. Sure guns are dangerous, and they're all scary and weapon-y, but that doesn't mean a firearm can't be a work of art. If you want to appreciate a firearm, you need to appreciate it as it is: a gun. It's not a classical art form, it's specialized and rarified and you have to appreciate a weapon for what it's capable of doing.

I know, I know. Gun porn. What can I say? I like guns.

I hadn't had much of a chance yesterday to examine the thumper, I was too busy hoping one didn't blow a large hole in me. It's sleek, matte black and angular. Frankly, it looks like something out of a dystopian sci-fi movie. It has no markings and no obvious way to load it. Hell, the trigger is just a pad. The thing has no moving parts that I can see.

It's one of those things that just doesn't look quite right, like something other than humans designed it.

When I pick it up, it's lighter than it looks. Carbon fiber, maybe? I don't know. It fits my hand well. Guns. Easy to pick up, hard to put down.

There's no one around, the nearest neighbors are quite a ways away. Sighting down the barrel, I discover another strange thing: no sights. The top of the barrel is perfectly smooth. Fuck it. I assume my shooter's stance, put a finger on the trigger pad and gently push. And not a damned thing happens.

"Nice gun," a voice tells me.

I turn around and find Jacob staring at me.

"Thanks. Found it in Mexico," I tell him.

"Usually the Mexicans aren't known for their guns. Mind if I check it out?"

"Be my guest."

Jacob carefully takes the gun up and goes through the same motions I did. He notices the same things I did: no moving parts, no way to load it, no sights.

"Either you're pulling my leg and this is a toy you spray painted or you've got yourself some crazy-ass gun here, bro."

"I assure you it's not a toy. I don't know what it fires, but it blew big holes in things."

He sets it down and we both stare at it. It's hypnotic, almost like touching something that shouldn't exist.

"Don't know, man, but it looks pretty evil. Can I try it?"

I nod and he gently picks up the gun like it's the Holy Grail. Like all experienced gun guys, he treats it as a weapon: finger off the trigger pad, barrel pointed down range. "It's light," he says pointing it out into the desert.

"Yeah, but it'll blow a hole in you big enough to drive a truck through," I tell him.

"What is it?"

"I don't know. I've never come across one before."

Jacob looks down the barrel. "How do you aim this thing?"

"Again, no idea. The guys who had it were wearing glasses, maybe that's part of it," I say.

"What guys?"

"The guys who tried to put holes in us. Jessica and me. They blew the snot out of her bar," I say.

"She had a bar?"

"On the beach."

"Damn, you can pick 'em," he tells me with a grin.

I decide to let the comment go. I'm not embarrassed, but I know these guys and they will never let up.

"Are you still in contact with Mr. Smith?" I ask.

Mr. Smith – not his real name – is a local dealer in pedestrian and exotic weapons. He's the guy you go to when you need to put holes in things.

"Oh, yeah. I had just finished a run for him when those Federales nabbed me."

"Shit," I say. "Are you still on good terms?"

"Yup. It was a payment run. I finished it and never sold him out, he should be fine."

"He might have come across one of those," I say, motioning to the gun.

"I'll see what I can do," Jacob says, gently setting the thumper down. "In the meantime, you still need to learn to ride."

"Oh, come on, man. We've got important things to do today. We've got to arm up, figure out what's in Dulce, figure out how to get in there, we've got a god to kill, another group of gods who will kill us if we don't kill the first god. I'm kind of booked."

"Well, we've still got an arsenal in the garage," he says.

"Still got the other problems to deal with," I tell him.

"Do you know how to break into a building?"

"No. Frank and Wilford will probably handle that."

"Can you do anything about the gods?" he asks.

"No, not really."

"So, what are you planning on doing today? Overseeing?"

"Well, I…" I stammer.

"See, you're free today, bro."

I really don't want to do this right now, but I don't have an excuse.

"This is part of living, man," Jacob says. "You need to learn to ride a bike if you want to call yourself a man."

"Well, if my manhood is on the line, I guess I'd better learn."

Jacob slaps me on the back and it nearly knocks me over.

"Right on! I've got a bike coming for you in a bit. A buddy of mine is delivering one later."

***

A few hours later Jacob's buddy, a swarthy-looking fellow covered in various colorful tats ranging from your typical frat-boy tribal to an intricate Quetzalcoatl swallowing a man, arrives in a beat up Dodge Ram truck. The truck is towing a trailer with a shiny, new Harley on it.

The Harley is dark blue and adorned with all the expected chrome parts. To tell you the truth, I've never been a huge fan of Harleys. I always figured when I learned to ride, it would be on a Ducati or some other sport bike. This Harley is hypnotic. It's like a muscle car on two wheels.

I'm starting to see the allure of this bike. I watched "Sons of Anarchy" like all good Americans, but until now I could never see myself in the role of a biker. This bike looks like the open road on a sunny day, a taste of freedom with loud pipes in the back.

"Bucky!" Jacob cries and the two bikers hug in that way that only bikers can hug. It's a strangely manly hug. I honestly don't know how they do it.

"Jacob, my brother, you're looking well for a former guest of the Federales," Bucky says.

Jacob grins. "Yeah, well, smash a couple guys and the rest will leave you alone," he says.

"Prison, man. Fucking same everywhere you go," Bucky says.

"Fuckin' A, bro," Jacob responds.

Bucky catches me looking at the bike and gives me a quirky look, like he can't quite see the likes of me on Harley. "Beauty, ain't she?"

"She is, indeed," I respond, kind of dreamily. "She is, indeed."

"So, Jacob, who's the lucky lady that gets this baby?" Bucky asks.

Lady?

"Well, bud ..." Jacob says.

"Ooooh. Cute bike. Can I have it when you're done?" a voice asks from behind me.

When I turn around, Jessica is eyeing the bike with a glint in her eyes.

Cute bike?

"Cutie-pie," Bucky tells Jessica, "I believe this is for you, 2014 Harley-Davidson Superlow. The color even matches your eyes."

"I didn't order a bike, but it is pretty," she tells him.

"Who's this for, bro? Where's the luck lady?" Bucky asks Jacob.

"It's not exactly for a lady," Jacob tells him. Pointing at me he continues, "It's for him."

Bucky looks stunned for a moment and then starts laughing so hard he has to sit down in the gravel.

"Jacob," I ask, "did you get me a girl's bike?"

Jacob looks concerned for a moment and then grins like an ape before finally settling on a serious expression. "It's like this, man: you can't learn on a Hog, it's just too much bike."

"You could have gotten a Yamaha or something," I tell him.

Jacob gives me the look. Everyone can give the look. It's the look you give someone when they've just said something insanely, unbelievably, complete, irrevocably stupid. "Dude," he sighs.

I'm kind of surprised he didn't smack me.

"Sorry, man," I say. "You're right. This may be a girl's bike, but it's at least a real bike."

He grins and slaps my shoulder. "All good, bro. You have to buy your next bike, though. And from her look, you may have to fight her for this one," he tells me hooking a thumb Jessica's way.

Part of me is pissed, but, on the other hand, it is a motorcycle. It may be a girl's bike, but it's one more motorcycle than I started out with this morning, so it can't be all bad. Right?

A quick look around reveals Jacob trying hard not to laugh, Bucky wiping tears from his eyes, and Jessica chuckling quietly. Fuck it, right? It's hardly the first time I've been laughed at.

"Let's get started, then," I tell Jacob.

He claps me on the back and he, Bucky, and I pull my new ride off the trailer.

   ***

Learning to ride isn't as hard as I expected. Brake with the right, clutch with the left, shift with my feet, try hard to keep the bike upright. It's like a big bicycle that weighs a lot more and goes a hell of a lot faster.

The Superlow is, no kidding, super low. It's almost too easy to get both feet on the ground, but that's kind of a saving grace since I can easily keep the bike from falling over. Well, maybe not easily, but I manage.

Jacob drills me all morning. Start, stop, when to hit the front brakes, when to hit the back, how to gently twist the throttle, how to shift, how to turn, what to do when you feel the bike going out from under you, and so on and so forth.

By lunch time I can proudly say I can ride a motorcycle. I may not be able to sit down anymore, but I can ride a motorcycle. Jacob asks if I want to hit the bar, playfully calls me a pussy when I decline, and tears out down the street.

As I'm going in, Jessica asks if she take it for a spin. I toss her the keys and watch as she hits the throttle and spins the bike around, laying a circle of rubber on the driveway before righting herself and tearing ass down the street.

Well, I was feeling good about myself.

Oh, well. Baby steps.

The terrible feeling in my gut when she leaves is getting better, but it's still there, and the confrontation with Dreamer last night didn't exactly leave me with warm fuzzies. I have to keep reminding myself she can take care of herself.

Inside Eve, Wilford, and Frank are pouring over documents on kitchen table and arguing about something.

"You're insane," I hear Frank say. "You can't just walk into a place like this. They'll kill you!"

"Trust me on this one, there is no sneaky way," Wilford responds.

Eve snorts and says, "We've gotten into tighter places."

"Not like this," Wilford says. "Places like this are staffed by fanatics."

"Okay, if they're fanatics how are we going to just waltz in there without getting noticed?" Eve asks.

"Simple," Wilford says. "We watch for a couple of days, find some people that look like us, lump them and steal their IDs. Then we just go right in through the front gates."

"What?" Eve asks, incredulous.

"Seriously. All we need is to look similar to someone who works there and security will breeze us through. Once inside, no one will say anything because they've all been taught their entire careers to keep to themselves."

They're looking at maps, presumably of the Dulce installation.

"Where did you guys find maps?" I ask.

"Internet," Frank tells me offhandedly, peering at one of the maps.

"Someone posted the layout of the whole place," Eve says.

"Are you sure you want to trust something you found on the Internet?" I ask. "How do you know this isn't total bullshit?"

"Someone from the installation posted these," Wilford says.

"Fanatics, eh?" I respond.

"Always some disgruntled guy out there," he says with a grin. "Last week I would have been turning the guy in, now I'm tempted to buy him a beer if I meet him."

"Come on," I say. "This is classic misinformation. We did the exact same thing ourselves, just not on this scale."

"Sure, we planted misinformation and I'm sure some guys in DOD have spent their entire careers putting out misinformation about Area 51 and Cheyenne Mountain, but this is different," Wilford says.

"Different how?" I ask him.

"Everyone knows about Area 51 and lots of people have heard of Cheyenne Mountain. No one knows squat about this place," he replies. "Most people don't even know it exists. Even the UFO loons mostly think the place is bogus."

I hate to admit it, but he's got a point.

"We need some on-site intel," I say, deciding whether or not I want to try sitting down. My butt is still numb, so I think I'll keep standing for now.

"I'm free tomorrow," Eve says.

"Any hotels up there, or are we going camping?" Frank asks.

"Dulce's what, a couple thousand people? Gotta be some kind of hotel or something around there," I say.

"It would raise eyebrows if all of us went up there at the same time. We'll need to split up," Wilford says thoughtfully. "Come to think of it, I could go for some camping."

He looks around at us. "Who's in?" he asks, completely seriously. "Come on! Camping out under the stars, drinking hot cocoa."

"Eating bugs," I chime in. "Hoping you don't get eaten by wolves."

"It's roughing it!" Frank says.

"My idea of roughing it is no Wi-Fi," I tell him. "I'm getting a hotel."

"I'll go camping," Frank says.

"If he's in, I'm in," Eve says.

The rumble of loud pipes lets everyone know either Jessica or Jacob has come back. My bet is on Jessica, Jacob can spend days at a bar.

Sure enough, she walks in a minute later, all but bouncing and trying to untangle her hair.

"I'm serious," she says, tossing me the keys, "I want that bike when you're done with it."

I toss the keys back to her and tell her it's all hers. She does a little dance and notices everyone else standing around the table.

"What's up?" Jessica asks.

"Oh, nothing," Eve says.

"Yeah," Frank adds, "we're just trying to figure out how to break into that place in Dulce."

"Oh, anything I can help with?"

"Can you thump someone?" Wilford asks.

"Thump someone?" Jessica asks.

"She can throw a beat down," Frank says.

Eve nods. "I've seen her do it."

"Great!" Wilford says. "I'm getting a plan."

"Care to share it?" Eve asks.

"When it's fully formed, I would love to."

I leave them to it to figure out how to infiltrate the base in Dulce. Frank can get into most places and Wilford can probably get into the rest. If it's possible to break into the base there, those two can figure it out.

I have to admit, Wilford's fitting in well, especially considering Frank was planning on gutting him last night. Something still doesn't feel right, though, like my Spidey-senses are tingling or something. It's probably nothing, just lingering paranoia from all the times he tried to kill me last year. Hell, apparently most of D.H.S., our former employer, is completely out of their heads so it's not like he'll have any back up.

On the other hand, I have personally shot him in the head twice and he's still here.

Time for a smoke and a step back from the problem.

* * * *

Jacob gets back a couple hours later with some good news. We can meet Mr. Smith tomorrow morning at 8am since one of Smith's appointments cancelled. I don't know who schedules a meeting with an arms dealer at 8am and then cancels, but it turned out to be a good thing for us.

A little history for those who are joining the party late. Mr. Smith, no I don't know his first name, is a local arms dealer who provided us with some exotic potions and my shotgun last time we met him. We had to knock off a drug dealer to get the cash to buy all that stuff, but he did have everything we needed. Smith's former military, but I have no idea which branch or, for that matter, which country. He looks like the modern Brawny man and lives in the mountains outside of Albuquerque.

Jacob has worked with him in the past, probably running guns down into Mexico or wherever people run guns to these days. That's important because you can't find Smith in the phone book, if you show up and he doesn't know you, his house will probably kill you, bury you, and sue your relatives for trespassing. When Jacob and I met him last year, he let Jacob know from the get go that if I got out of line Jacob would be responsible for killing me. If you need exotic weapons, though, Smith is the guy to go to. I'm hoping he'll be able to identify the thump gun I pulled off that, well, whatever the fuck it was down in Mexico.

I'm also hoping he'll have a SPAS-12 lying around somewhere. It's not that exotic, and I could probably get one from a gun store, but I prefer the anonymity that comes from paying Smith. Plus, his reputation is important to people in his business so he's less likely to sell some rusty piece of crap.

One problem with Smith: he's a cash only operation. You also don't get a receipt or a money-back guarantee, but that's less of an issue than the cash thing.

See, way back when, when the U.S. was first getting into the amazingly successful "War on Drugs," the feds decided it would be a good idea to remove $1000 bills from circulation. Guess why. Go head, guess. $1000 bills were never very common, but they were removed from circulation because it was felt by the fine folks that run our country that removing large denomination bills it would make it too difficult traffic the large sums of money drug dealers tend to make.

Seriously.

Now if you want to buy a nice Baume and Mercier or Cartier watch and pay cash for it you need to carry one hundred and twenty $100 bills with you rather than carrying twelve $1000 bills with you. Or, you know, use a card.

But using a credit card causes a whole new set of problems. Large purchases are tracked diligently. If you've never dropped twelve grand on a watch and you suddenly do, someone will notice and start sniffing around. Because, obviously, if you can suddenly afford something like that you're up to no good.

If you try to make a large cash withdrawal from a bank that will be noted and tracked as well. Basically, anyone running around with large amount of cash is guilty of something, probably buying or selling drugs, in the eyes of the State. Use a card, debit or credit, to make a large purchase and that gets noticed, too. Trust me on this one, as soon as the Feds know you exist, they'll find something to charge you with just as a way to get closer and closer to that delightful drug money.

Here's why. The State, be it Federal or local State government, can legally seize anything that might have been used to support the sale or transportation of illicit drugs and anything that might have been purchased using money from illicit drug sales.

In most drug cases it's usually assumed that everything a defendant owns either supported drug trafficking or was purchased with funds from illicit drug sales. Think about that for a moment. Just let it swirl around in your head. They can seize everything a person owns. That's why drugs will never be legal.

Why bother making money when you can just take everything a citizen owns based on the flimsiest of reasoning?

The drug war was never about protecting people from drugs, it was all about a way for government to get in on that sweet, sweet drug money without actually having to resort to the dastardly parts of selling drugs.

Well, except for the CIA. Those guys love selling drugs in ghettos and then busting the same people they just sold drugs to.

So, circling back around; dealing with large sums of cash is tricky. I can hit every ATM in New Mexico and not get more than

$200 a day. This was done to make it harder for the citizen to move around freely and anonymously. Now, if you want to go on walkabout, you'll need a card so your government can track your purchases and, therefore, you.

Bottom line is I need to get hold of a large chunk of cash in a short time without raising any eyebrows. Can't go and just withdraw it. Can't go to an ATM. Last time we needed a large infusion of cash, we knocked off some drug dealers and stole their money. That probably won't work again because all the big time dealers are either busted or blowing their money on other kinds of drugs.

Fortunately, I learned to be prepared.

There are storage rental places all over town. Hell, all over the country. People have too much crap today. But I digress.

These places take a minimal amount of information and let you store your stuff indefinitely, with no questions as long as the rent is paid on time. If the authorities come sniffing around, the owners will happily cut your lock off and let them in, but otherwise the owners couldn't care less about what you're storing.

I rented one a while back, down off San Mateo and used to regularly drop bits of cash in there every now and then. The payment came from an account in a fake name and was automatically billed every month. Why didn't I take it when I left? You never know when you'll be in Albuquerque and need some cash.

I hope it's still there.

19 | Money Money Money Money Money

It's early evening and Wilford and Frank have headed out to get supplies. Jacob's sacked out watching T.V. Eve is off doing whatever it is that Eve does when she's not here. The more I learn about her, the more I'm convinced I don't want to know what she's up to.

Jessica's in the kitchen, reading a magazine and looking bored.

"Want to go grab some cash?" I ask her.

She looks up and says, "I don't know. There's a fascinating article in here about upcoming indie movies."

"Looking forward to the next movie about how everything is wrong?"

"Always," she tells me. "I love slow, whiny movies."

"Me," I tell her, "I always go for explosions, but whatever floats your boat."

She leans forward and puts her head in her hands. "Any good movies with explosions playing right now?"

"Not that I'm aware of, but there is a stack of cash out there with my name on it. There's a good steak house out there, too."

"Are you asking me out on a date?" she asks with a slight twinkle in her eyes.

Am I? Sure, why not?

"Yeah. Large stack of cash and dinner. Isn't that how it usually goes? I've been out of the dating scene for a while."

Jessica laughs and says, "Let me get changed. Can we take the bike?"

"Sure," I tell her. "You can even drive if you want."

"Yay! But you're driving, you need the practice," she tells me as she heads off to change. "Stay here. I'll be right back."

I grab a bottle of water out of the fridge and hang out, waiting. This is a perfect chance to go over the next few days. Tomorrow I'm hoping to find out about a gun or two. The day after that, we'll start trying to break into a facility so classified most people don't even know it exists. We've got at least one god that wants us dead, another that wants Jessica for some reason or another, a demi-goddess who's trying to start Ragnarök, and some indestructible assassins with heavy-hitting hardware.

It sounds easier in my head.

I'm almost done with my water when Jessica comes bouncing back into the room. She's wearing a short, flared skirt and tights, a motorcycle jacket and some boots. The ensemble manages to look tough and soft at the same time. I'll never understand how women manage to do that.

She stands there staring at me. It takes me a moment to figure out what's going on.

"You look great, nice outfit" I tell her. Kind of out of practice here.

"What? This old thing?" she replies.

Ah, the age-old predate dance of compliments. It's been a while since I've been on an actual, factual date, but it's slowly coming back to me.

"It's awesome," I tell her.

She does look pretty damned awesome.

She smiles and twirls, the final part of the dance. "Let's roll," she says.

I grab the keys to the bike and climb on. Jessica slides on behind me, arms wrapped around my waist. She gives me a quick kiss on the back of my head and says, "Hit it."

Slowly, carefully, we pull out and onto the freeway

* * * *

I-40 is still busy, but slowing down. A couple of hours ago it would have been wall to wall soccer moms in SUVs, teens in hopped up Civics, and extremely manly men in lifted 4x4s with American flag decals on the back. Now the soccer moms are all at practice getting loaded on Xanax, the kids are at home and it's down to just the 4x4s.

We roll down the freeway, wind in our hair, and me hoping the other drivers haven't been drinking too much just yet. Jessica's just loving life. Hell, I'm loving life. We could grab my cash and hit the road, disappear into the night.

Sure. And get hunted down by angry gods.

Eastbound 40 is straight and open and would be the perfect place to open this bike up and see what it could do, but the cops are out in force tonight and you absolutely do not fuck with the Albuquerque Police Department.

We fly over the interchange and head north on I-25, get off on Menaul, head north on San Mateo and, bam, we're there. Now I just hope the cash is still there.

The cool thing about places like this is no one wants to know what you're up to. The less they know the happier they are. You periodically hear about meth labs being run in these places, but that's more extreme than hiding some cash. The problem with meth is you can smell the shit being cooked miles away. Cash doesn't smell like anything. I wouldn't be surprised if half these lockers were stocked with cash. In most major cities places like this are filled with money or dead hookers, but Burqueños hide their dead hookers on the mesa. It's tradition. Or something.

By the way, Burqueños is a term some hipster douchebag came up with and it sort of stuck. Now everyone refers to Albuquerque's nearly million people as Burqueños. Personally, I hate the term, but it's easier to say than Albuquerqueans.

The storage rental place is a typical hunk of concrete and metal sheeting. This area is hardly an industrial wasteland, although Radula is right down the street. Fancy that. Last time I was in this area of town, Frank, Eve, and I were breaking into Radula, a mostly defunct contractor facility, to steal information about a black project. That project was the research Jessica's dad was working on, the one that ultimately drove him off the rails and into the waiting arms of madness. Turned out he was trying to figure out how to turn a sleeping god into a weapon, the same god that trounced D.C. and killed **Congress for shits and giggles. The same god that's haunting my dreams and wants Jessica. Where her dad failed to weaponize a god, we succeeded. Of course, like all biological weapons, this one got completely out of control with a quickness**.

It wasn't far from here that Jean was killed. Head and hands cut off by some unknown entity. I had always assumed it was Wilford and his gang of miscreants, but he swears, and I believe him, that he found Jean like that and just used the knowledge to get information out of me.

Which begs the question; who did kill Jean? It's possible it was just random event and Jean was in the wrong place at the wrong time, but the chances of that are so astronomical they're not worth considering. It would be like winning the lottery and surviving a lightning strike on the same day. There must be a third party out there somewhere.

But why stop with Jean, why not go for all of us?

Damn. When did life get so fucking weird?

A tap at my shoulder brings me back to reality. Jessica's standing there watching me.

"You okay?" she asks.

"Yeah, sure. Sorry," I say, pointing to the southeast. "Radula's right over there."

She stares down the street, probably with different memories than I have. I still don't know what happened to her dad, other than being hooked on heroin and kicked out onto the streets over a postcard he sent to her. The postcard was accidentally delivered to a Yakuza guy out in Las Vegas. He and his buddies hunted her down, beat her and threatened to rape her to get to her dad. It was a lost cause on their part; her dad's brain was toast by the time they found her.

We found her naked and strapped to a table covered with sushi. The rest, as they say, is history.

Jessica's brow is knit, her smile gone and eyes brimming with tears. I take her hands and she grips mine tightly before rushing into me and wrapping her arms around me and sobbing. It's easy to forget sometimes that extremely bad things have happened to her. She's tough, but no one's invincible. I hold her and stroke her hair and mumble the sweet things you're supposed to tell people to make them feel better.

It will be okay. You'll be fine. Everything is okay.

But it's not okay and it will never be okay. The supposed good guys, the ones who were charged with watching over us and taking care of us did nothing more than fuck us. They made laws to protect us and then decided they were above those laws.

When Jessica's tears dry up and she slowly pulls away, I look into her eyes, still puffy from crying. "I'm so sorry," I tell her. "I'm sorry you got drug into this. I'm sorry for everything that happened to you because of all this. I'm sorry there's a god out there that has a personal interest in you. I'm sorry about your dad. I'm sorry about your bar."

She brightens and wipes her eyes when I say that last bit and a little hint of a smile plays across her face. "I never liked that bar that much anyway."

She gives me a peck on the cheek and says, "Let's get some money so you can buy me dinner."

✳ ✳ ✳ ✳

My storage unit is number 42, a little joke that still brings a smile to my face. My lock is still in place and it looks like only a few people tried to pick it. The lock is a Sargent & Greenleaf Environment padlock, a $110 hunk of nearly indestructible steel alloy. It's a good lock, with a highly pick resistant cylinder, but no lock is completely safe from a good thief. Fortunately, no one made a serious effort at getting in because all it takes is time and any lock will spill its secrets. Locks are merely an inconvenience for experienced thieves.

I keep the key handy because I suck at picking locks.

Inside, nothing has been moved or touched. There's the usual half inch of dust that covers everything in this town every spring, but no footprints or any other signs that anyone has been in since I shut this place and locked late last year.

Here's a pro tip for you, free of charge. Keep a bug out kit somewhere safe, a place you can get to it when you need to. Even if you think you'll never, ever need it, keep one anyway. If you want to get away from everything, and do it quickly you need a few things: clothes, weapons, a wad of cash, and, most importantly, a change of identity.

You might think you'll never need to get away, but there is absolutely no guarantee that's the case. I knew a guy one, real stand-up fellow who kept his nose clean and never bothered anyone. One day there's a clerical error at the court and he suddenly finds he's got a warrant out for his arrest. Turns out some dipshit at the courthouse transposed his record for speeding with a guy who was wanted for violent assault.

Sure, sure, sure. Innocent until proven guilty, right? Wrong. This is America and I guarantee you are guilty until proven innocent. The court system will figure out the error, right? Wrong again. Once they've got you for something, your ass is hosed until you can prove they've got the wrong guy. This guy I knew wound up in jail for a few years before his lawyer finally convinced the court they had the wrong dude and my buddy got sprung.

Problem is, by the time they let him out, his life was shot to shit. His wife left him. He had no job, and every job he applied for he got turned down on. Seems his background check revealed he was in jail for violent assault because the courthouse never got around to clearing his records. A lawsuit against the courts takes a long time and, when you have no money and nowhere to go, you simply don't have time.

They found him dead in an alley. His throat was slit because he had pissed off some high level gang member while he was in prison.

So, next time someone tells you if you've done nothing wrong you have nothing to fear, punch 'em in the jaw. You have everything to fear. After I heard what happened to that guy, I decided if the cops ever come sniffing around my place I'd just bolt and take care of the problem my own way. Hence, this place.

My storage unit holds only a single black duffle bag, covered with dust and the odd cobweb. Jessica seems less than impressed. "This is it?" she asks incredulously.

"All I need," I tell her, unzipping the bag. "Not what you expected?"

"I guess not," she tells me. "I watch too much T.V."

As I start pulling things out, her attitude slowly changes. The clothes are uninteresting. Save for my leather jacket, they're just jeans and shirts. The two pistols and extra magazine raise her eyebrows.

"What are those?" she asks, eyeing the small guns.

"Detonics .45s. They're a cut down version of the classic 1911. The usual .45 caliber pistol."

"Forty five? You mean that gun you always see in movies?"

"The same. That's a Colt model 1911, the Detonics uses a similar frame, just smaller, but fires the same bullets and is easier to conceal."

"Can I see one?" she asks me.

I hand her one and a couple of magazines. "Enjoy. It probably needs a cleaning, but they're good guns."

"Why two?"

"What?" I ask.

"Why two guns?"

"Too many John Woo movies," I tell her.

"John Woo movies always used nine-millimeters," she says.

Wow. How did I find her? How many women have not only seen John Woo movies but can ID the guns in them?

"This is nice," she says, test aiming at the wall.

"Consider it a gift," I tell her.

"You still owe me a shotgun," she says with a sly grin.

"Tomorrow," I tell her and go back to pulling things out of my bag. A couple of knives, smallish Cold Steel daggers. I toss one to Jessica and she snatches it out of the air, examines it briefly and clips it behind her back. My fake identity wallet comes next, complete with driver's license and various and sundry other cards: library card, Costco card, a Furr's buffet card with a couple of marks on it.

Jessica squats down next to me and I hand her the wallet.

"Your fake identity was actually Richard Flaire?" she asks. "No one made the connection?"

"People see what they want to see," I tell her. "Besides, how many people remember 'The Nature Boy' Ric Flair these days? Ah, here we go."

At the bottom of the bag is what I was looking for; ninety thousand dollars in neatly wrapped hundreds, five thousand in fifties and another five thousand in twenties. The pile of cash takes up some serious space. That's nine hundred one hundred dollar bills, a hundred fifties, and two hundred and fifty twenties.

Jessica whistles as I keep pulling cash out.

About six months ago, after we let the Dreamer out and blew up the Simms building, Eve handed us all cashier's checks for ten million dollars. Having that kind of money in a bank is a very different experience from seeing a hundred thousand in cash right in front of you.

I throw the money, the extra knife, my jacket, and the fake ID back in the bag and leave the rest of the clothes on the floor. I won't need this place again.

"Ready for dinner?" I ask.

20 | Date Night

The High Noon Restaurant and Saloon is a kind of touristy steak house in Old Town Albuquerque. Hell, Old Town is a pretty touristy spot, so it stands to reason anything there would be touristy, too. It has wonderful steaks, though, and a plentiful supply of good tequila. Normally, I prefer scotch with my steak, but good tequila is acceptable, too.

The place is listed as romantic on various websites, for whatever that's worth to you.

Parking is an utter nightmare. I think this whole part of town operates on the same philosophy as trendy night clubs: if you can't get in it must be because it's so amazingly awesome that everyone you'd want to hang out with is already inside and waiting for you. In Old Town's case, it's just because nobody bothered to think through how a lot of tourists were going to park in one general place.

Fortunately, we're on a motorcycle. Bikes don't have as many problems in traffic as cars do, so we can weave around cars and find the motorcycle parking places that no one else gets to use. A handful of tourists throw us some dirty looks, but no one cares what tourists think, we just want you to drop some cash and get the hell out of our city. At least it's not Balloon Fiesta. I've never seen it personally, but I've heard Old Town is completely impenetrable during Balloon Fiesta.

Old Town is down around Central and Rio Grande part of town, an older part of Albuquerque that has been through its ups and downs. Currently it's in an upswing, so there's a fairly nice mix of people. I was here when the gangs tried to take over. City government realized that gang activity was cutting into city revenue and sicced its own street gang on the problem. The Albuquerque Police Department took care of the problem and now Old Town is relatively safe for tourists to come spend money on rocks, Dia De

Los Muertos figures, and obscenely shaped candies.

The place is a buzz of activity, a short ton of people wandering around in shirts adorned with Balloons and "oohing" and "aahing" at chile ristras and wondering out loud what's up with all the skeletons and skulls. The gaily painted bones are *Dia De Los Muertos*, or Day of the Dead, figures that are popular in Mexican culture. *Dia De Los Muertos* is a celebration of the dead, people you've lost and missed and want to remember. The days run from October 31 to November 2 and people make *ofrendas* to honor the dead. Frankly, the Mexicans have a much healthier view of death than most Americans. The skulls and skeleton figurines have been around for centuries and there has always been a small clique of people who enjoyed them as art and collected them. Recently they've become trendy so the price has gone up and the quality has gone down.

I'm hoping they don't turn into the next howling coyotes. I've always liked *Dia De Los Muertos* figures and would hate to see them co-opted.

We don't have a reservation, so we have to spend some time at the bar before we can get a seat. Being as this is The High Noon Restaurant and Saloon they've got a good bar. We're surrounded by people wearing touristy gear, but at least they're leaving us alone. I order us a couple shots of *Chamucos Añejo* and settle in to watch the madness.

"*Salud*," I say and we clink our drinks together.

Jessica sniffs her drink, wrinkles her nose a bit, and says, "I've got to admit, I've never been a huge fan of tequila. The only time I ever had the stuff it took me a week to get over it."

"This is the good stuff," I tell her. "A good tequila *añejo* is a different experience from the basic Cuervo most people drink. Just sip it."

She braces herself and sips, expecting the normal punch in the gut that you get from cheap tequila. A look of pleasant surprise fills her face when it goes down smoothly.

"Okay, that's actually good," she says examining the glass.

Tequila is like every other liquor out there; there's good stuff and there's rotgut. Most people only experience the highly questionable stuff you can find in any supermarket, but there's as much difference between cheap tequila and good tequila as there is between store brand scotch and Ardbeg Uigeadail. Seriously, try the good stuff sometime. You might actually find you like tequila when tequila isn't actively trying to kill you.

"There's nothing like good tequila," I tell her. "Of course, there's nothing like bad tequila, too. Except maybe Mad Dog."

"Ugh," she cringes. "Mad Dog."

"Bitten by the Dog, I take it?"

"At a party in high school. Terrible stuff. You?"

"I've been bitten by the Dog and hit by the Train a few times," I sigh.

"I cannot imagine you drinking Night Train."

"Yeah, well, the song was pretty popular at the time."

"Just because Guns 'N' Roses sings about it, it doesn't make it a good thing to try," she laughs.

"Well, in my defense, I was, uh. Well, actually, I don't have a defense."

That gets me another laugh. It's nice to see her laugh. She has a beautiful laugh and her smile is radiant. It's going to take a while to get our table, so we spend some time talking about ourselves, sharing stories about her growing up in L.A. and running with her white girl gang and me growing up in New Mexico, hiking around the country side looking for buried treasure and UFOs.

Turns out, she grew up reading Wonder Woman comics and wanting to change the world. I grew up reading Batman and wanting to destroy it. She likes hard science fiction, classic punk rock and old-school rap. She hated school, but did really well math. Loved geometry, hated algebra. It took me some time, but I finally grew to like Algebra – mostly because my granddad insisted. I did so-so at geometry. I could conceptualize the figures, but had problems with proofs.

And, as an added bonus, she loves old John Woo movies: *The Killer, Hard Boiled, A Better Tomorrow,* some of the classics of Hong Kong cinema. We were united in our tolerance of *Hard Target*, both of us felt it could have been a great movie if Van Damme hadn't been given an edit. She thought *Face/Off* was terrible, I thought it was OK.

The hour wait time for a table flies by in a blur of good tequila and conversation, and both of us are slightly tipsy and hungry as hell when we the hostess finally calls us. Holding hands and kind of leaning on each other we make it to the table, still giggling about

Travolta and Cage chewing the scenery as each other's characters. We just manage to get steaks and assorted accoutrements ordered when my phone buzzes and I see a text message from Frank.

Where are you?

While I'm thinking about what to say, Jessica's phone buzzes.

"Eve," she says. "She wants to know where I am."

"Mine's from Frank," I say.

"Looks like mom and dad are wondering what's up," she says with a smirk.

"How do you want to play this?" I ask her.

"You know they'll never let it go if we tell them where we are," she says.

"Screw 'em," I say.

"Yeah, screw 'em," she says and starts tapping away on her phone.

I send a text back to Frank.

Dinner

Know where Jessica is?

Yes

There's a pause while Frank processes this. I suspect he was expecting a more direct answer, but I did technically answer him correctly. Plus, and maybe this is just the tequila talking, but he's not my fucking boss.

With you?

Yes

Everything OK?

Yes

Just checking. Have fun!

So, maybe he's not trying to check up on me. I look over at Jessica and she's quietly laughing with her hand over her mouth.

"What?" I ask her.

She holds up a finger for one moment and starts tapping away madly on her phone.

My phone buzzes and it's Frank again.

Are you on a date?

"Frank wants to know if we're on a date," I say.

"Eve just asked if we were having sex," she responds.

"Ah, Eve, so subtle. What'd you tell her?"

Jessica looks at me for a moment, bites her lip and says, "I told her, 'the night is young.'"

I smile and go back to my conversation with Frank.

Nunya

Nunya?

Nunya business

Duuude. Carry on my wayward son.

Roger that

"Frank just asked if we were on a date," I tell her.

"Well," she says with a chuckle, "I don't know what you call it when you take a girl out for drinks and steak, but I call it a date."

"A date it is!" I say and raise a glass. She toasts me with a smile and twinkle in her eye. Our eyes meet for a long moment, interrupted by our waitress bringing food. Food is good, but it could have waited a minute, damn it.

Being something of a beef traditionalist, I got a ribeye with potatoes. She got the brown sugar cured beef tenderloin with mushroom enchiladas. We spend the rest of dinner feeding each other bites of food. It's terribly romantic and impossibly cute.

* * * *

If the dinner and drinking dragged me down a bit, the company and the after dinner coffee picked me back again. You can see the stars and hear the laughter of drunken tourists in the back ground.

"I'm kind of cold," Jessica tells me.

"I happen to have a jacket," I tell her, digging through my duffle bag. "It's been in storage for a bit, but it's still relatively clean and is guaranteed to keep dragons at bay."

"Why, thank you brave knight," she says with a laugh.

My old jacket is big on her, but she looks terribly cute in it. She steps toward me and my arms go around her. We stand there, in the parking lot in the back of Old Town, and stare at each other for a while.

"Thanks for dinner," she whispers.

"Thanks for the company," I whisper back.

There it is again, that tense moment right before that first kiss. It's both the best and worst moment in the world. This is the point where time stretches and possibilities are endless.

Slowly, tentatively, we close in on each other. Just as our lips brush, we hear the click of a switchblade and quiet chuckle.

Jessica tenses up, leans her forehead on my forehead and mutters, "Oh, God dammit."

The guy with the switchblade is still hiding in the shadows, probably trying to intimidate us into giving up without having to actually put himself in any danger.

"You know, pal," I say to the figure in the shadows, "we were kind of having a moment here."

"Yeah," Jessica adds. "Can you fuck off for a little while."

I'm guessing from the silence that wasn't the response the guy expected. I can see him shake his head and he mutters, "*Pinche cabron.*"

"You interrupt us and I'm the asshole?" I say to him.

"Seriously, just go somewhere else. There's a whole bunch of tourists over there, go harass them," Jessica says.

The figure brandishes his knife and the moonlight glints off it. The blade is about six inches long and polished. I suppose this is supposed to be menacing, but it really just looks pathetic. Why do people still use switchblades? They're terrible fighting knives and there's really no better way of saying, "I don't know shit," than to threaten someone with a switchblade.

"I'll take the bag, asshole," a voice says from the dark shadows next to my bike.

"I like this bag," I say.

"I wasn't asking," the kid says, stepping out of the shadows. He's young, maybe nineteen or twenty, but already covered with jailhouse tats including the ubiquitous teardrop tattoo next to his right eye. He probably thinks it makes him look tough, but most people don't realize the teardrop tattoo symbolizes someone who bitched out in prison. The teardrop means he's crying because a man died in prison, and in a way it's probably true.

"Take a hike, nutsack," I tell him.

"Give me the bag, pussy, and we don't have to rape this fine bitch," the kid says.

When he mentions rape, Jessica tenses up.

"Who's we?" I ask. "You got a mouse in your pocket?"

"We, *pendejo*, are me and those guys behind you," the kid says.

I swear, I thought this part of town was clean. I am totally going to write a strongly worded letter to someone about this. The two guys behind us are big gangy types, tatted up and none too bright looking. Of course, when you're hired muscle, brains are less important than brawn and these guys have their brawn part down pat. They're both north of six foot tall and built like small trucks. The baseball bats in their beefy hands only add to the allure.

"Last chance, bro," I say. "Walk away."

"Fuck you and fuck her. Give me the bag," the kid says, stepping close to us.

Jessica's arms slowly slide off me and she steps back slightly. Her eyes are wide, but not scared, and locked on the kid. He has absolutely no idea what he's just unleashed.

Since she's got the kid, I turn to the big guys. They both look me up and down and grin. Easy pickings, right fellows?

Here's the thing about big guys in a fight. Sure, they're strong, and they may even be experienced, but they're used to using their size to scare their opponents into just quitting. I'm not quitting and I've fought bigger so I'm hardly intimidated.

I hear a few thumps behind me and surprised squawk. Sounds like Jessica's done.

"Well, guys, shall we get this over with?" I ask. "I'm kind of on a timetable, here."

The guy on the left moves first, a big, horizontal swing of the bat. Easy enough to duck under the swing and step to my left. This does two things: Obviously, I avoid getting hit, but it also gets me closer to the guy and puts his bulk between me and the other meathead.

I put a solid kick into the side of his knee and am rewarded with a satisfying crunch.

I don't care how tough you are, a kick to the side of the knee is debilitating. Once that joint gets stressed or broken, your leg is useless. The guy's knee collapses and he falls, slamming his knee into the pavement. It must hurt like hell because his eyes go wide and he screams. I grab a couple of fistfuls of his hair and drive my knee into his face and follow it with another to the back of his head. He hits the ground like a sack of potatoes.

Out of the corner of my eye, I see Jessica get up and head toward the last guy and, damn, does she look pissed. He turns toward her just in time for her foot to find his balls. He doubles over and she punches him in the back of the head.

He collapses in a heap and, without missing a beat, Jessica's got her knife in her and murder in her eyes. Before I know it she's on top of the kid with a knife at his throat. His nose is broken and his face is covered with blood and snot.

At least she didn't pull a gun.

"You still want to rape me, little boy?" she asks him.

All he manages is a whimper.

"What's wrong?" she asks him. "Afraid? I'm going to carve your eyes out, you little shit."

"Whoa," I say, putting a hand on her shoulder. "You beat this guy down in a parking lot, no one will give a shit. You kill him, we'll have troubles."

"Are you going to rape anyone else?" she asks the kid, knife in his eye.

"No," he blubbers.

"Sorry, what?" she asks. "Couldn't hear you."

"No," the kid shouts, before he goes back to sobbing.

"If I see you again, I'm taking your balls home with me. Understand?" Jessica growls.

The kid looks at me, pleading with his eyes.

"Don't look at me, pal. You brought this on yourself. If it comes down to it, I'll hold you down while she castrates you," I tell him.

"Understand me?" Jessica asks again.

The kid nods furiously, desperate to get away from her.

As she gets up, she drops a heel in his crotch for good measure. The kid curls on his side and sobs, huge tears sliding down his face. I imagine when he woke up this morning thinking he was on top of the world. He and his buddies were going to make some cash, maybe rape someone, blow the cash on drugs and alcohol. It would be epic.

Now he just got his ass kicked by the girl he threatened to rape and his buddies are laid out on the pavement. I'd almost feel sorry for him if he wasn't such a worthless shit.

Speaking of buddies, one of the big guys is slowly getting to his feet. The other guy, and not to toot my own horn here; the guy I took down, is still flat out.

"We should probably go soon," I tell Jessica.

She's still in full-on pissed-off mode. Time in Mexico may have cooled her, but her temper is still something even the gods should be wary of. Hell hath no fury and all that.

"Seriously, we need to be somewhere else before the cops show up," I say.

She whirls on me. "I'm not done yet," she snarls.

She's not threatening me. Yet. But if I don't get us out of here she's going to cut this guy to shreds and set fire to the pieces.

"Dude," I yell to the big guy. "Get the fuck out of here."

He holds up his hands, placating. I suspect he'd like to beat down this crazy woman who just kicked his ass, but he's still smart enough to realize he's playing with fire.

"It's all good, man, it's all good," he says, backing away slowly. "I'm just going to walk away from this…"

It's beginning to look like this may work out. Well, at least until his chest explodes.

Jessica and I look at each other, each kind of wondering how the other managed to make this guy explode. I shrug my shoulders and she raises her eyebrows. It wasn't either one of us.

"Oh, shit," Jessica says.

As the guy with the missing chest collapses to his knees, I see what she was seeing: two guys in suits and glasses. The one on the left is holding a long black pistol, aimed right at the piece of meat that just hit the pavement.

They apparently don't want us dead or they would have shot one or both of us, but the warning is clear. If these guys will blow a hole in a complete stranger they won't hesitate to nuke us, too if we start getting too uppity.

So much for date night.

21 | Not These Guys Again

So far no one has moved. The hitters just stand there watching us, motionless as wax statues. As soon as they decide to go after us, they'll turn this place into a war zone. While I have no great love of tourists, I certainly don't want to see some family from Minnesota detonated because they were too close to me.

"We need to split," Jessica says.

"Get the bike, meet me around by the restaurant," I tell her. "I'll see if I can buy you some time."

"Keys?" she says.

I hand her the keys and she slowly backs to the bike. The guys don't move a muscle when she gets on. I wonder where the third guy is.

"You are wasting time that could best be used to bring the King of Dreams to heel," a voice says.

The voice belongs to something vaguely man-shaped in a black cloak with a hood that slid out of the shadows. I can't see a face, there's just solid black inside the hood. I would have expected at least some glowing red eyes or something, but there's nothing, just inky black that may or may not go on forever. I have to stifle a laugh.

Think through the scenario here: You've got a beautiful young woman, a not completely unattractive guy, two messed up gang-bangers, one corpse missing his chest and something in a black cloak standing in a parking lot in Old Town. Part of me wants to laugh out loud at the absurdity of the situation. All we need now is some clowns and maybe a bear riding a tiny motorcycle and we'll have an authentic New Mexico Hoedown. Throw in some "Yakety Sax" and you've got the makings for a great comedy show.

"Who the fuck are you?" I ask, pulling my pistol and pointing it at him.

"Are you going to shoot me with that?" the thing asks.

"I'm thinking about it," I tell him.

"You're going to shoot me with a banana?" it asks.

Motherfucker. My gun is a banana.

"Dammit, I really liked that gun," I say.

"I've still got one," Jessica says. She's slowly moved to stand right next to me.

"Your weapons are of no consequence."

"Okay, so I'll ask again. Who. The. Fuck. Are. You?" I ask.

"I am everything that goes bump in the darkness. All those unseen things your imagination runs wild with. Every fear of the unknown you've ever had. Every dark thought you've ever imagined."

"You're Nancy Grace?" Sorry. Couldn't resist.

"I don't know who that is," the thing says.

"Trust me, you're better off. So you're, what, fear in a cloak?"

"I am eternal waking nightmares," it says.

"Ooh, scary," Jessica snarks.

"And kind of melodramatic," I add.

Then comes what is commonly referred to as a "pregnant pause," that extremely long, uncomfortable time where everyone is waiting for someone else to say whatever it is that everyone seems to think needs saying.

"Sorry," I say. "The whole cloak thing is very scary and, seriously, I'm incredibly intimidated. I just use humor to mask my quivering innards."

"Are you innards really quivering?" Jessica asks me.

"Sure. Why not?" I respond.

"Enough," the thing says in a voice that's a deep basso boom. Windows shatter and car alarms sound off. "You will stop him or she will pay the price. I will rape her and rend the flesh from her bones and let you watch while I do it. You will spend the rest of your extremely long, miserable, life reliving every cut, every blood curdling scream. Forever. In time you will learn to say my name with respect."

Fucking gods. It would probably do it, too. If I've figured out anything recently it's that these guys don't give two tugs of a dead dog's dick about us. I still don't know what they're up to, and may never know, but they're certainly not interested in humans at all.

By my best guess, the thing in front of me is Fear.

"Okay, okay," I say, placatingly. "We're on it. Any hints on how we can do that?"

"He is dreams," Fear says.

Gee, thanks.

"Uh. Can you expand that thought?" Jessica asks.

"This is your responsibility," it tells us.

"So, you don't know, either?" I ask.

"Don't try my patience, child," Fear says.

There's another one of those pregnant pauses and a small part of me wonders if we're going to get shredded here and now. I'm strangely aloof about it. I really don't want to watch Jessica get tortured to death, but I'm honestly neither here nor there about my own death.

"Oh, my god," Jessica says. "You don't know how to stop him, do you? You're not going to kill us because you need us to fix a problem."

Fear points at her and says, "I would feel nothing shredding you. You mean nothing."

"Hurt her and you lose me," I say.

I immediately get a vision of Jessica bound to a table, open to the world, raped by demons and screaming as her skin is carved off in long sheaths by doctor in black latex. She's crying and there's blood everywhere. As soon as all her skin is gone, it immediately grows back and the scene starts all over again. An eternity of being flayed alive and raped by monsters.

Shit. I hate these guys.

A glance at Jessica tells me she got the same vision. She's ash gray, eyes filled with a terrified rage.

"Fine," I say. "Answer me two questions, at least."

I get no response, just that empty black visage. Not big on communication, apparently. Maybe this is some kind of tacit agreement.

"Okay," I say, waiting for some kind of answer. Still no response. "Why do you want Dreamer taken out?"

"He has broken the law," Fear says simply.

Now, I'll admit, I'm no expert on, well, whatever these things are, but I suspect I get exactly two questions. If I ask what law I'll get a useless answer like "our law" or "Archimedes' Law of

Chondrite Kumquats." So, I can waste my final question and get an answer that makes absolutely zero sense, or I can come up with a new question.

The hit men, those jolly fellows in the dapper suits with advanced weaponry are still motionless. Fear has not moved.

"Who are those guys?" I ask, pointing at the hitters.

"Minions, created from raw matter. I'm surprised you ask."

What? "Why?" I ask.

"Your people have modified one of you into one of them," Fear says.

What the fuck?

I look at the hitters, still as stone statues. I've shot these guys and they pop back up like malevolent Weebles. Cut them and they don't bleed. As far as I can tell, they're indestructible and unstoppable, but not too bright. What they lack in smarts, though, they more than make up for in tenacity. Point them at a target and they'll keep after it. The three after us in Mexico happily got into a fire fight with cartel members just to get us. We only got away because we had a motorcycle and they had feet. Plus they had to deal with a whack of pissed of cartel members with AKs.

It's easy to see why someone would want to make more of these guys: an army of indestructible soldiers would make anyone stand up and take notice. For safety's sake, you'd modify someone and probably not tell them. A prototype would need to be someone you could trust, someone you could keep an easy eye on, someone already on payroll.

Oh, shit.

Someone just like Wilford Saxton.

We've either got an ace in the hole or a big trouble brewing.

"You've got a deal," I say. "We'll take out Dreamer."

"Don't disappoint me, Steven or you will both pay the price."

"I don't doubt you for a moment," I say. "Can we go now?"

Fear doesn't answer, just disappears in a poof of black smoky tendrils. The hitters come back to life, glance at us, turn and disappear into the night. And, just like that, the parking lot is empty again. Apparently no one noticed the strange goings-on. Jessica is shaking, whether from rage or terror I can't tell. Her color hasn't come back, yet. Her normal tannish color is a light gray.

When I put a hand on Jessica's shoulder she nearly tears it off before she realizes who I am. "I'm sorry," she mumbles before collapsing into me.

I wrap an arm around her and contemplate exactly how boned we really are. Dammit, I had a nice evening, nearly got a kiss and these fuckers had to ruin it all. Personally, I have nothing against Dreamer. Sure, he lied to me and wrecked a government and may be slowly taking over everything, but he was mostly nice to me. If I had a nickel for everyone who's lied to me and then wrecked a government, I'd be pretty rich. I'm fed up with these gods, or whatever they are. I'll happily take out Dreamer, but I'm not stopping there.

I'm going after all these guys. One way or another, they're all going to pay for this.

"We've got to go, sweetie," I tell Jessica.

She smiles up at me and hands the keys back to me. "You drive, okay."

Fortunately my bag was right where we left it.

22 | We Are So Boned

I've had run-ins with the cops in the past. When I was in college, my roommate took off one night hootin' and hollerin' and tore out of the driveway, spraying gravel and dust all over the damned place. He worked the night shift, about 10pm to 6am or thereabouts. Our neighbor, an immensely fat woman who claimed to be a witch, hated us; probably because we regularly pulled stunts like tearing ass out of the driveway late at night. We never did find out her real name, so we took to calling her Bavmorda. She found us especially loathsome when her multiple attempts at casting various dark curses at us failed to do anything but increase the amount of roaches in our yard. Since our apartment was attached to her apartment, all she managed to do was increase her own roach load.

Finally, Bavmorda decided to use police magic to harass us after regular magic failed to bring us to our knees before her awesome might. So, after my roommate took off to work kicking up a racket, Bavmorda, dread witch of Portales, New Mexico, called the police and reported a rape in progress. Being as Portales is a town of about twelve thousand people, it only took the local PD about 15 minutes to show up in force in front of my apartment where my girlfriend at the time and I were holding hands and looking at the stars.

The first cop that got out of her car sized up the scene in a matter of moments and decided, all visual evidence to the contrary, that I was in the middle of violently raping the girl I was holding hands with. She was moments away from smashing my head in with her club when another cop, who happened to live around the corner from me, stopped her and took control of the situation. Once everyone calmed down and we explained that my roomie had just gotten excited about going to work, all was well. The lady cop explained she would be keeping her eyes on me, though.

Bottom line, if I hadn't known the cop that lived around the corner from me, I would have been brained and arrested before I knew what the hell was happening. The police are a force unto themselves, like the weather wearing black uniforms and bad attitudes.

Scary as the cops can be, they're nothing compared to the various gods that have been popping up in my life lately.

Go ahead, have a run in with Fear and tell me I'm wrong. I'm not one hundred percent certain what these, uh, things are. I don't know if they're manifestations or attributes or actual, factual gods, but they're scary as Hell and twice as dangerous. Eve could snap me like a twig and she's not even fully one of them. Begay could probably cause the land to rise up and swallow me whole. Fear could lay me out and fill my head with every terror I've ever felt and, probably, a few novel ones to boot. Dreamer, over the course a short handful of months, has spawned a whole new religion and nearly toppled the entire country.

Here's the problem, I don't have a clue what any of them really want. Fear wants me to stop Dreamer. Begay, aside from wanting to "dance" with Eve is a mystery. Dreamer is apparently up to something bad that has managed to piss off Fear. And Eve. Fuck. If I believe Begay, Eve is trying to kick off Ragnarök. She's trying to bring about the Norse version of the end of the world and wants me, and probably Jessica, Frank, and Jacob, to fight it. Fight what? Fucking Jörmungandr? I'm not Thor and I'm sure as shit not throwing down with the goddamned Midgard Serpent.

Light thoughts for a motorcycle ride back to home base. I don't know how much I can trust Eve at this point, but she's the best chance I've got. Devil you know and all that, right?

The night air is helping clear my head. Jessica's arms are wrapped tight around me and she's pressed up next to my back tightly, like she's terrified and I'm a teddy bear. It's kind of amazing how quickly she can go from enraged murderess to scared girl. It's kind of scary, too.

The Chinese have a saying; "May you live in interesting times." Actually, it's more of a curse than a saying, but whatever. Maybe one of Bavmorda's multiple spells finally hit me lo these many years later.

＊＊＊＊

The lights are still on at Carfax Abbey when we ride up.

The name's not official, but I've started calling home base Carfax Abbey in my mind. At first I hadn't realized where it came from but I finally remembered it was Dracula's London residence. The name lends a certain respectability to the place.

"Sorry the evening went to hell," I tell Jessica when the bike finally stops shaking the pillars of Heaven.

"Not your fault," she tells me with a sad smile. "Besides, it's not every night a girl gets to eat a good steak, nearly get kissed, get in a fight with low-life gang-bangers, and meet the embodiment of fear."

"Well," I tell her. "When you put it like that, it actually sounds better than most of my first dates."

She gives me a quick peck on the cheek, grabs my hand and says, "Come on. You know these guys are going to grill us, so let's get it over with."

Turns out she was right.

＊＊＊＊

After five minutes of everyone talking at once we finally manage to get them to stop talking long enough to hear two final questions: Frank's "When are you getting married?" and Jacob's "Did you fuck?"

"I plead the Fifth," I say.

The questions immediately start back up again, louder than before. I love these people but I swear it's like working with kids sometimes. Kids with guns and big chips on their shoulders, but kids nonetheless.

"Everyone shut up and leave them alone," Eve say in that voice that she gets when she wants to be heard.

It works. I think the neighbors heard her and they're nearly a mile away. Everyone goes silent and Eve takes a moment to look around the room and give everyone *the look*. *The look* is a combination of a glare and a glimmer in her gray eyes. It's a look that nonverbally says she'll do terrible things to you and enjoy every second of it. Think about the look your mom gave you when she caught you taking cookies out of the jar just before dinner and add seven feet of angry Valkyrie to it. *The look* been known to bring

Marine Corp drill sergeants to their knees. Frank starts to say something, but *the look* stops him.

"Now," Eve says, "What happened? Did you fuck?"

Aiyah.

"We ran into Fear," I say.

"That's why you didn't have sex?" Jacob asks. "I get it, man, performance anxiety is a bitch."

"No," Jessica says. "Fear personified."

"Huh," Jacob responds. "I didn't know women got performance anxiety."

"Jacob, shut up," Eve tells him. "What do you mean, Fear?"

"Big guy, back cloak, minions, no face," Jessica says.

"I wondered when she'd show up," Eve mutters.

"We also beat up some gang bangers," Jessica says with a smile. "And drank tequila."

"Eve," I say. "What do you know about Fear?"

"Hold up," Jacob says, hands in the air. "Fear's a girl?"

"In a manner of speaking," Eve says.

"Come on!" I say. "No more 'In a manner of speaking' or 'You don't need to know.' What the hell is happening. Who, or what, is Fear?"

"Fear is an embodiment of sorts. Queen of Fears. Kind of like your friend is the King of Dreams or Begay is the Spirit of the Southwest," Eve says with a sigh.

"Gods?" Wilford asks.

"Sure, why not?" Eve tells him. "Listen, it's really complicated and there are no words that adequately describe them. Read up on Shinto sometime and you'll get a better idea of what you're up against. Think of them as embodiments of things, dreams, fears, love, war. The most important thing to remember is they're extremely dangerous."

"So why is Fear here? Is she going to Cliff's?" Frank asks.

In case you're wondering, Cliff's is an amusement park in Albuquerque.

"She's here because she's checking up on me," Eve says.

"Checking on you?" Jessica asks.

"Fear ordered the hit on you," Eve says, pointing at me. "All of you actually. I talked her down to just Steven."

"Why?" I ask.

"These things, these embodiments, they don't really intermingle and they tend to leave humans alone. They find you somewhat distasteful. I'm distasteful to them for a whole other set of reasons. Anyway, from what I've gathered, Dreamer is trying to rule the humans and, at the same time, expand his own power, which is a serious no-no among these folks," Eve tells us.

"Because they think we need to choose for ourselves?" Frank asks.

"No, they don't care about you that much. Mostly it's because they don't feel you're worthy of their interaction or guidance, let alone their rule. In their eyes it would be like you ruling a bunch monkeys.

"The power part is a whole other problem. They've spent millennia working out their various roles and balancing power. They don't handle change very well and the idea of a shift in power is terrifying to them. Almost as bad as dealing with humans."

"Even John?" I ask.

"Especially John," she replies.

"Damn. I kind of liked him," I tell her.

"Oh, he likes you, too. You're like a beloved pet hamster to him. When you die, he'll tearfully bury you in a cigar box out back," Eve says with a smirk.

"Fucking gods," Wilford hisses. "What about you, Eve? What's your game?"

"Trying to keep you guys alive. That's all," she says.

"What about Ragnarök?" I ask her. "Begay said you were trying to spark it."

She falls silent and glowers at me. This is one of those very uncomfortable silences. Ever go to the gym and taunt the body builders? I always loved doing that. Wait 'til one of those spandex –clad buffoons is in full squat with four hundred pounds of iron on his shoulders, walk by and quietly mutter, "Fat ass." Trying to push Eve's buttons is roughly the same idea, except she's a hell of lot more dangerous. Body builders are tough but usually not very good fighters, Eve's indestructible and an incredible fighter to boot.

"Eve?" I ask, taunting the polar bear.

"I want out. And that's my only way out," she says with a sigh. "But it's more complicated than you think to kick off the end of the world."

"Christians have been trying for two millennia and haven't pulled it off yet," Frank says, patting her shoulder. "And there are a lot more of them than there are of you."

Eve puts her hand on his and smiles. "Thank you, Frank," she says with genuine gratitude. "You don't know how much that means."

"This has been, bar none, the most bizarre evening of my life," Jessica says, slumping into a chair and rubbing her temples.

It's easy to forget that Jessica is kind of the odd person out in our group. Well, Wilford, too, but for different reasons. Jessica may have helped us release Dreamer, but she did it to find out what happened to her dad. She wanted to hurt the people that hurt her dad, but the rest of us actively wanted to kill everyone in Congress. We all had our reasons, but in the final analysis, a general feeling of "fuck the world" was pretty prevalent.

Wilford was thrust into us. He actively opposed us when we were trying to kill off Congress, but has discovered he needed us, at least for the time being.

After killing off Congress, we didn't really care what happened. I think, deep down in places we don't like to talk about in polite company, we were all hoping for an apocalypse. The end of the world didn't quite come, but at least it was fun watching everyone in Congress getting ripped to shreds.

Pity they're all being replaced by other jackasses as we speak.

Maybe it takes more to crush a civilization than you would think. There's a theory that there are a number of pillars that hold up society. The exact number depends on who you talk to, but it's at least a few. Generally you'll see government, business, family, and religion touted. Occasionally someone will wax philosophical about art and entertainment, but those are kind of superfluous. Actually, I'd argue that business is kind of superfluous, too, but that's just me.

So, let's suppose that we've got government, religion, and family propping up society. We took out a large portion of government and government is still standing. Granted, we took out the part of government that no one really likes, anyway, so maybe that has something to do with it.

Dreamer's apparently going after government agencies. If he managed to infiltrate DHS, it's a sure bet he's going after the rest, too.

Dreamer's churches are apparently getting more and more popular, too. That's not unsurprising. It's hard to get people to throw money at you to glorify invisible gods when there's an actual factual god running around possessing people and killing Congress critters.

Family's about all that's left untouched.

Everyone falls silent, lost in their thoughts. Jessica's still rubbing her temples. Frank's standing next to Eve, her hand still on his. Wilford's scowling, almost like the gravity of the situation just completely dawned on him. Jacob just grins and lights a cigar.

"Let's put our cards on the table," I say. "We've got a God of Fear."

"Goddess," Jessica says.

"Sorry," I reply. "We've got a Goddess of Fear who wants us dead because we released the God of Dreams. We don't know either one's ultimate goal, but if we don't kill one, the other will kill us. Of course, we'll probably all get killed trying to kill Dreamer anyway."

"On top of that," Frank chimes in, "we've got a completely unknown player in John Begay, a wild card in one Wilford Saxton, and what's left of every police force in the nation pretty unhappy with us."

"Thank you, Frank, for making things seem that much better," I say.

"My pleasure," he says with a bow.

Eve leans back in her chair, crosses her arms and sighs. "I'm sorry I got you all into this. You all are the best group I've ever worked with."

"How many other groups have you worked with?" Jacob asks.

"Lots. I've been around a long time," she replies.

"How long?" I ask.

"A man should never ask a lady her age," Eve says with a slight smile.

"Okay," Jessica pipes up. "I'll ask it. How long?"

Eve glowers for a moment before cracking a smile. "A little over 1200 years."

"Girl, you look good for your age," Frank says.

"I never would have pegged your age at over 600," Wilford adds.

Eve shoots him a glare, but even she has to admit it was kind of funny. Eve and Wilford are arguably the two most dangerous people in this town right now, unless there's some other Lovecraftian horror floating around that I'm unaware of. It's nice to see they're finally starting to get along.

The fact that they're getting along both encourages and frightens me. It's encouraging because we need both of them to crack this nut. It's terrifying because there are now two dangerous beings in my life and that doesn't count Jessica when she's pissed off.

"So," Jessica says, breaking the slightly jovial mood. "Anyone got a plan of attack here?"

"Jacob and I have an appointment tomorrow morning," I say. "After that, I say we head to Dulce, break in, find whatever Begay thinks is there that can stop Dreamer, then go to D.C. and stomp on him."

"You know," Frank says. "I don't really have that much of a problem with what he's doing. He wants to run the country, let him. He can't be any worse than any of the other idiots we've had running the joint."

"I agree with you," I say. "I'd be happy to let him run this country, Hell, this world, if it didn't mean Fear was going to come gunning for us. Unfortunately it looks like Dreamer is looking to enslave the country, not rule it. We're between the proverbial rock and hard place. From what we've seen he's dangerous."

"What have you seen?" Jacob asks.

Eve grimaces. "Last night we saw him possess a woman and make her snap her own neck."

"Most of DHS are zombies right now," Wilford adds. "Whatever will they had is gone. They stand around and stare at things."

"How is that different from normal operations over there?" I ask.

"Those churches of his are apparently popping up all over the place," Frank says. "It wouldn't surprise me in the slightest if there's some brainwashing going on. Maybe he's got priests, like that Smith guy, all over the place. I'll bet his priests are true believers and they're helping to mold the flock. It's got to be hard to remote control that many people, so he'd need some help."

"That's pretty much how most churches work," I say. "Why should his be any different?"

"Well," Eve says, "I doubt we'd be able to root out all the churches out there. After we killed Smith, I wouldn't be surprised in the slightest if the rest of them start dropping off the map. When religions go underground that's when they really get dangerous. That's when you start getting martyrs."

"Yeah," Jessica adds, "Let's not forget, Dreamer can probably set those churches up far faster than we can take them out."

"So what's the solution?" Jacob asks.

"Well," I mumble, thinking out loud. "If we can't take care of the churches, I say we go after the head. Kill Dreamer and everything will be hunky dory."

"How, exactly, do your propose to kill the god of Dreams?" Wilford asks with a deep sigh. "Go to the gun store and get a god-killer?"

"We may already have a god killer," I tell him. "That gun I brought back packed a serious punch."

"That may be true, but it doesn't work," Jacob says.

"It works. I saw it blow apart my bar," Jessica tells him.

"I have no doubt it works," I say. "We just don't know how to use it. I've got an appointment tomorrow morning with a guy that might know something, though."

"Who's that?" Frank asks.

"Mr. Smith," Jacob tells him.

When Frank looks confused, Jacob continues. "Mr. Smith is an arms dealer. He's probably seen everything anyone has ever turned into a weapon."

"Does he sell guns, too? Because I seem to have misplaced a very fine Italian shotgun," Jessica quips.

"He does," I tell her, "and I'll look for another SPAS-12 for you."

She brightens at that.

23 | Smith, Mr. Smith

Mr. Smith is our local acquirer and purveyor of high and low-end weaponry. At least that's how he describes himself. In his mind, this sounds much more impressive than the more plebian "arms dealer." Smith associates the term arms dealer with little people selling cheap, rusty weapons to both sides of the conflict in some east African shit hole. A purveyor, however, provides discriminating customers with only the finest in implements designed to drastically shorten lifespans.

Smith's a quiet, unassuming looking fellow with a neatly trimmed beard and a penchant for flannel shirts. Actually, he kind of resembles the new Brawny man.

Before you ask, no I don't know his first name and I assume his last name is fake. He always insists on cash for any business transaction. Usually fairly large chunks of cash. Last time I met him I dropped fifty grand on some poison and my shotgun. Kind guy that he is, Smith threw in some shotgun shells completely *gratis*. The shotgun could probably have been found cheaper, but the even the seediest of gun shops won't sell you poison, let alone some artisanal Japanese poison.

That's the price you pay for quality and selection.

Smith's house is at the edge of nowhere up in the Sandia mountains, far away from the prying eyes of people who would be less than accepting of Mr. Smith's preponderance of lethal hardware. We had to borrow Wilford's Suburban to get up since nothing short of a four wheel drive will make it.

Jacob and I arrive at Smith's estate almost exactly on time. Too early and bad things happen. Too late and he'll just ignore you. Truthfully, it's best to be as close to on-time as absolutely possible. We're a couple of minutes early and, following protocol, we wait.

At 8:00am on the dot Smith appears on his porch and waits

patiently for us. Jacob gives me a quick grin and says, "Ready, bro?"

"Let's get 'er done," I tell him.

We both step out of the Suburban and walk up to greet the master of the domain.

"Gentlemen," Smith says when we get within earshot. "It is a pleasure to see you again."

"How have you been, Hoss?" Jacob asks.

"Business has been booming, thanks to the late unpleasantness," Smith says with a smile.

Talking to Mr. Smith is like this; he'll use the most circuitous language possible at all times. It's probably added security on his part on the off chance that someone decides to record him or blackmail him. You'd have to be made of crazy to try to blackmail this guy but the world is full of absolute idiots looking to make a buck and one can never be too careful.

I have this sneaking suspicion that Mr. Smith knows we were at least partially responsible for the "late unpleasantness." He's not stupid and the fact that a couple of guys walk in one day asking for a shotgun and some poison and a couple of days later all hell breaks loose had to at least piqued his interest.

"A pleasure to meet you again, too," he says, addressing me.

"Good day," I tell him. "Thank you for shotgun and shells. They were very effective."

"Excellent. That was a beautiful shotgun. I'm glad it's proved useful to you."

We all stand and stare at each other for a bit, none of us quite sure how much to trust the other. On the one hand, Smith sold us poison, which is undoubtedly multiple kinds of felonies. On the other, we bought it and used it, which is also frowned upon. Something tells me, though, that Smith has even less love of the rule of law than we do.

Fortunately, Jacob is adept at breaking awkward silences with even more awkward statements.

"You know what would go good with us standing around and staring at each other?" Jacob asks with a huge grin. "Scotch. Got any?"

Remember, it's 8:00am.

Smith actually laughs out loud and claps Jacob on the shoulder. "Same old Jacob. Of course, I have Scotch. Even out here we're not entirely uncivilized. Now, come in gentlemen and let's see what we have to discuss."

* * * *

Normally, I have an aversion to drinking even fine Scotch during the wee hours of the morning, but some business requires you suck up your aversions and down some Scotch. At least Smith's Scotch is the good stuff and it pairs nicely with the aftertaste of the Golden Pride breakfast burritos we had on the way over. That and the requisite small talk help to take the edge off the earlier tension.

"Now, gentlemen," Smith asks, leaning back in his chair and crossing his legs. "What can I do for you today?"

"We're mostly in need of information," I tell him. "I have an, uh, exotic, weapon that has recently come into my possession. I was hoping you might know something about it."

"An exotic weapon?" Smith asks.

"Well, exotic to me. I've never seen one before at any rate." I tell him.

"It's a noodle scratcher," Jacob adds. "In all my years of distributing firearms, I've never seen anything like it."

"Interesting. If Jacob has never come across one, this must be an unusual weapon. Shall we retire to more private surroundings?" Smith asks, rising out of his seat and gesturing toward a bookshelf on the far wall.

As we found out last time we were here, the bookshelf is fake, a cover for a doorway to a hidden room full of various weapons. It's probably just one of many hidden rooms in this place. Last time we saw a room filled with everything from small arms to rocket propelled grenade launchers and vials of poison. I wouldn't be the least bit surprised if Smith's house harbors even more powerful weapons.

The door slides silently open and reveals Smith' armory, a brightly lit place with dozens of weapons from the mundane to the exotic hanging on pegs. In the center of the room is small table. I feel like a kid in a candy store, but I'm fond of guns. I fired my first gun when I was four and spent the rest of my formative years growing up regularly shooting various firearms.

Inside, Smith closes the door and gestures to a table in the middle of the room.

"So, gentlemen," Smith says. "How may I be of service?"

"Well, I've got the exotic for you to take a look at, but I could also use a SPAS-12 if you happen to have one," I tell him.

"SPAS-12. Italian shotgun, semi-auto or pump. Made popular in *The Terminator*, if I recall. Nice weapon. There are better shotguns, though. What's so special about the SPAS-12?" Smith asks me.

"I kind of lost one and promised I'd replace it," I tell him sheepishly.

"How do you lose a shotgun?"

"Well, I was in Mexico and it fell out of my hand," I say.

"Whoa, hold up, Hoss," Jacob says. "Was that lost shotgun Jess's?"

"Yes."

"He needs a SPAS-12 for his girlfriend," Jacob tells Smith. They both get a chuckle out it. Jerks.

"Your girlfriend has good taste in shotguns," Smith tells me.

Part of me wishes they would quit calling her my girlfriend. Another part likes it.

"She's pretty impressive," I say.

"I'm fresh out of SPAS-12s," Smith tells me. "They're getting harder and harder to come by. I do, however, have something that might actually be better."

"Okay, I'm interested. What do you have?"

Smith walks to the side of the room and pulls what I thought was an assault rifle off the wall.

"Meet the successor to the SPAS-12, the Franchi SPAS-15," Smith says, formally handing the weapon to me with a slight bow.

I instinctively bow back. Too much time spent in the martial arts, I guess, and take the gun in both hands. It's big and looks like an M-16 with a pump at the front end.

"Very nice," I tell him. "I'll take it if you're willing to part with it."

"You realize this weapon is illegal in this country, right?"

"That's the least of my concerns," I mumble.

Jacob, being Jacob, absolutely cannot resist the temptation. "Dude, do you have a bow to put on it?"

Smith just stares at him before politely saying, "No."

"What do you want for it?" I ask.

"Ten thousand should cover it. I had to bribe no small amount of officials to get this in. I will, of course, throw in a few more magazines and a full range of whatever shells you want."

Say what you will about Smith, he's into customer service.

"No problem," I tell him. "Now, about the other thing."

Smith brightens. "Yes, shall we see this exotic weapon of yours?"

I put the case on the table and open it. The matte black gun is in stark contrast to the rest of the brightly lit room. It kind of looks like all the light in the room is falling into it, sucked into the guts of this strange weapon.

Smith's eyes get very wide and he takes a step back from the table.

"Where did you get that?" he says, his voice a shaky whisper.

"Found it in a bar in Mexico," I tell him. "What can you tell me about it?"

"Well, for starters, you're not supposed to have it."

"Yeah, the guys that had it seemed less than happy to let it go," I tell him.

"You don't understand. You're not even supposed to know this thing exists, let alone be carrying one around town."

"What is it?" Jacob asks.

"It is bad news. And it opens doors better left closed. If I were you, I'd toss it at a cop and run like hell. Let Albuquerque PD deal with the consequences of having this thing."

"How bad could it be?" I ask. "It doesn't even work."

"It works just fine. You just can't fire it."

"Can we cut with the cryptic? What is this thing?" I say. "I realize in your business secrecy is paramount, but you're the only one I know of that can tell me what I've got here."

Smith sighs and rubs the bridge of his nose. "You've heard of Mjolnir, right?"

"Thor's hammer? Of course."

"The gods have always had weapons, sometimes they used those weapons themselves, and sometimes they imparted weapons to their followers." Smith says.

"Sure. Magic hammers, enchanted bows, stuff like that," Jacob says.

"You don't honestly think that the weapons of the gods wouldn't evolve over time, do you? If humans aren't still fighting wars with sharp sticks why would the gods keep using them?"

"You're telling me this thing was made for a god? By who?" I ask.

"Well, this wasn't made for a god, it was made for a follower, but otherwise you're right on the money. As for who made it, I can make a few educated guesses, but I doubt you'll find out for certain. May I pick it up? I've never seen one in person."

"Be my guest," I say.

Smith picks the gun up reverently, like it's a sacred object. I guess it kind of is. A weapon made to help god project power.

"How does it work?" I ask.

"I'm not 100 percent certain, but I believe the power source is the user of the weapon. It focuses the energy they generate somehow," Smith says vacantly. The gun is completely absorbing him.

"Who can fire this?" Jacob asks.

"Servants," Smith says simply. "Assassins. I don't know much about them, but they're apparently pretty tough to kill. I've heard they regenerate themselves."

Smith stops and stares at me for a long moment, searching my eyes. "I would happily give you every gun I own for this," he tells me completely deadpan. "At the same time, I would give you everything I own to get this thing as far away from me as possible. Mark my words, gentlemen, this thing is very bad to have around. Whoever owns it will move Heaven and Earth to get it back."

Smith reverently puts the gun back in its case. His face is a mask of confused emotions, terrified to hold it, devastated to let it go. I can see the fight inside of him. It takes an active effort for him to close the lid and his eyes are closed as he latches it shut.

"Thank you," he tells me without opening his eyes.

"Uh. You're welcome," I tell him.

"I will never forget this moment, gentlemen. I've always wanted to see one of these. Did you ever get to see it fired?"

"Yeah," I say. "A couple of times."

"What was it like?" Smith asks in a voice filled with awe.

"It took a few moments to charge up but it fired an explosive ball. One shot took out most of a bar. Another one blew a car in half." I tell him.

"Amazing. So much power in such a small package. I would

have loved to seen it fired."

"I would have preferred it wasn't fired at me."

"Guys," Jacob says. "Time."

"Thank you, Jacob," Smith says, returning to his stoic self. "Gentlemen, it has been an honor. If you will wait a moment, I'll get you your extra magazines and shells."

"What do we owe you for today?" I ask.

"For what you have shown me today, you owe me nothing. You have given me a gift I always dreamt of, but never thought I would receive. Today, I have actually touched a weapon of the gods. I won't forget that. Let me get your shells."

Smith hands me a tactical bag filled with shotgun shells and extra magazines for the SPAS-15 and escorts us out. When I heft the new shotgun a small part of me is disappointed in it. Sure, it's probably a superior shotgun, but it lacks the traditional charm of its predecessor. The SPAS-12 looked like a shotgun, the SPAS-15 looks like an assault rifle, almost like something from a movie set in the near future. Call me old school, but I liked it when shotguns looked like shotguns.

I hope Jessica likes it.

As we're leaving a thought hits me and I turn to Smith.

"Mr. Smith, can I ask you a personal question?"

"Of course, but I can't guarantee I'll answer it," he says.

Fair enough.

"Why did you get into this business? Dealing in weapons is some pretty dangerous stuff."

"I like guns," he says simply.

"So do I," I reply. "But I don't deal them."

"Have you ever read van Vogt's *The Weapon Shops Of Isher*?"

"Yeah," I say.

"That's why I do it," Smith tells me.

My respect for Smith goes up a notch.

"Mr. Smith," I say. "It's been a pleasure doing business with you and I'm looking forward to doing it again sometime."

"The pleasure, sir, has been all mine, I assure you."

With a handshake, we part ways.

As we're driving off Jacob asks, "What was that fisher thing he was talking about?"

"Huh?" I ask. I was staring out the window lost in thought and didn't understand what he was asking about.

"Fisher. He asked you'd read something about fisher."

"Oh, that. Isher. *The Weapon Shops of Isher.* It's a book by A.E. van Vogt. Part of the story concerns these shops that sell guns to everyone but the government. Powerful weapons. Powerful enough to keep the government from completely walking over people."

"What did he mean when he said that's why he does it?"

"In the book the government is pretty corrupt, but the shops don't try to stop that. The general feeling is everyone got the government they deserved. So the shops sell guns to anyone who wants one and the government is powerless to stop them. The guns are almost magical in how powerful they are, but they can only be used in self-defense."

"Okay," Jacob says.

"The motto of the shops is 'The right to purchase weapons is the right to be free.'"

Jacob nods his head sagely and simply says, "Fuckin' A, man. Fuckin' A."

After a moment of silence, Jacob says, "So, what are you going to do with the money you saved?"

I honestly hadn't thought about that yet.

"I don't know," I tell him. "Maybe I'll look for a supercar."

24 | My Idea of Roughing It...

Dulce is a tiny town in north central New Mexico. It's a sleepy little wide spot in the road right on the border between New Mexico and Colorado. It takes up roughly 12 square miles. As of the 2010 census the population was slightly less than 3000 cheerful people and ten grumps.

This, of course, is the official census and it fails to take into account the more migrant population of aliens. The aliens are bad at filling out census forms, though, so no one is really at fault.

Dulce is the Holy Grail of the UFO hunting community due to the ramblings of an Albuquerque businessman named Paul Bennewitz who, in the late 1970s, decided he was intercepting electronic communications from aliens. He was convinced these communications came from nearby, some secret location. Somehow or another Bennewitz settled on Archuleta Mesa in Dulce, New Mexico and the rest is history.

Bennewitz and others have since claimed the Dulce base has been the site of all manner of nefarious things. He claims the aliens took over the base, forcing the government to send in Delta Force soldiers. The various firefights between aliens and Delta Force soldiers led to a truce between the humans and aliens. The truce led to cooperation and now the secret base is where aliens and humans are conspiring to genetically engineer strange alien-human hybrids for purposes too sinister to imagine.

How Bennewitz stumbled upon Dulce is one of life's great mysteries. It's rather unfortunate that he did, though, because there is a very secret location in Dulce, but not one dedicated to creating alien-human hybrids. The alien-human hybrids are being created in Texas.

What is happening at Dulce is every bit as strange as alien-human hybrids, though Scully and Mulder are less likely to be interested.

Back in the 1940s, after the Germans had been largely defeated, the Allies recognized the enormous potential of the Nazi sciences. Nazi scientists were responsible America's early space program. A lot of our fighter jets were based on their early designs. The B-2 bomber is a direct descendent of the Horton Ho 229, the first jet-powered flying wing design. The list of technology pilfered from the Nazis is spectacular.

Those are just the savory technologies, though.

The Nazis were a great example of what can happen when you have some really smart people who completely lack ethics. In addition to their skills at designing things that flew really fast and exploded really well, the Nazis performed enormous amounts of human experiments, made some exceptionally nasty gases and took the first steps toward ripping apart space and time.

It's the space/time thing that should scare the hell out of you. Every culture throughout history has worked tirelessly to find new and exciting ways to exterminate other cultures they didn't agree with. Most cultures figure out novel ways to take care of their enemies. Lots of groups have dreamed of time travel. The Nazis very nearly made that dream reality and that would have changed the history of the world in some spectacularly bad ways.

Like I said, they were exceptional scientists. Don't worry; admitting they had some smart people on the Nazi payroll doesn't make you a Nazi.

So, while the airplane and rocket Nazis headed to America to spend the rest of their lives at Area 51 or White Sands, the really dangerous guys – the biological and chemical guys and the space rippers – got sent to Dulce.

For over thirty years the Dulce base remained completely off the radar of anyone in the United States except for the staff that moved there and never left and the Nazis who were condemned to spend the rest of their lives in that place. The scientists were given free rein to carry on their work, unfettered by such trivialities as war, political pressure, or ethics.

They built some amazing things. They may have been vicious bastards, but they were clever vicious bastards.

I know all this because I stumbled across an after-action report by an agent that had to investigate a suicide of a scientist with some impressive security credentials and an extremely murky past. No one, it seemed, could identify where this guy came from or what he had been doing for decades. He got paid by the U.S. Government but there was no record of his activities. He was one of those guys so deep down the rabbit hole that people had forgotten he even existed.

So, anyway, he offs himself. Hanging as I recall. Anyway, in the process of trying to find out who he was, an agent of agency I worked with before I got shuffled to DHS stumbled across a whopper of a story. It seemed our scientist had been working at Dulce his whole career and, in what could have been a monstrous security breach, had written down everything he had seen.

The investigating agent said he found mountains of data, ranging from notes on weathered pieces of yellowing paper to a laptop with an external drive. Our scientist had been methodically copying down everything he had seen and done, everyone he had worked with, everything he could find because he felt, to put it in his own words, "The United States has entered into an agreement with the greatest monsters history has produced and, in so doing, has violated its sacred trust with those that it has sworn to protect and serve."

He was in the process of scanning old data into the system when he came across something that was simply too much for him. Maybe he had written it down in a drunken stupor, or maybe it didn't matter so much at the time. The sheet was a neatly typed dissertation on how the Nazi movement was slowly gaining hold out at Dulce. Over the top someone, probably our rogue scientist, had hastily scrawled, "We have made beautiful monsters and they will be our undoing."

Then he hung himself.

The agent in charge of the investigation was Wilford Saxton. At the time he seemed nonplussed about the whole thing. According to him, the dead scientist was just another bad apple pruned from the tree before it could infect the other apples. "It's just fortunate," he told me, "that the good guys got to the stash before the media could spread it all over the place."

A couple of weeks later, Wilford's tune changed. He said it had to have been some elaborate hoax perpetrated by a loon with way too much time on his hands. When I tried to convince him that the guy had actually worked for the government, I couldn't produce any evidence. All tracks that said the government had ever had this scientist on its payroll were gone. Poof. He never existed.

I figured out later that Wilford's memory about the event had been altered. Again, poof. No one wiped my memory because no one ever knew I read his after action report. The only reason I saw it was because he dropped it off for a proof-read before filing it.

Still, rumors abounded even in the secure halls of the intelligence community about the dastardly deeds being played out somewhere in New Mexico. You never heard about these things because we're pretty tight-lipped with outsiders. Also, none of us knew for sure what was really going on and everyone was terrified of breaking the code of silence anyway.

So, that's what I know about the Dulce Base at Archuleta Mesa. Nothing concrete, but definitely nothing good.

＊ ＊ ＊ ＊

Right now we're split into two groups: Eve and I are posing as a newlywed couple touring New Mexico. Everyone else is out in the hills, camping in the sparse forest and trying to find a way in. We have a couple of external options, neither well mapped and neither confirmed. Apparently there are two entrances to the base, both old mines. Eve and I are looking inside the town to find anyone who might know something. We're kind of hoping that Eve's presence will focus everyone's attention inside. It's not every day that a seven foot tall woman goes wandering around this tiny little town.

Jessica was apoplectic about having to go camping with the guys.

On the upside, we get a hotel. On the downside, I have to share a room with Eve. On the real downside, we have to act like newlyweds on a budget.

Yes, it's uncomfortable, but not as uncomfortable as camping out in the hills. I have a bed (that I have to share with Eve because requesting a two bed room would raise too many questions and the rug terrifies me), a T.V. (that only has shows in Spanish), and a bathroom (with day-glo mold patches). I think the room might kill me before whatever's buried in the hills will.

Small towns like this are natural secrecy barriers. This isn't a tourist trap and people here don't really like outsiders. Still, rumors abound.

In order to keep the teams working together it's decided that we will all meet up for a picnic. It's an opportunity to swap information and lets Eve and I bring supplies to the poor schmucks wandering the hillside looking for a hidden entrance.

"So far, zip," Jacob says by way of a greeting.

"There's simply too much area for us to simple stumble across something," Frank adds.

Jessica just gives me a hug and Eve a glare.

"We're looking but these people absolutely refuse to talk," I say. "We'll keep at it. There's got to be a town drunk or loony running around somewhere."

"Try the bars," Wilford says. "People at bars love to talk."

"There are only a few bars, and the music is terrible," Eve tells him.

"Yeah," I add, "and they only have shitty American beers."

Frank rolls his eyes. "Sweethearts, we're sleeping in tents in the ass-end of nowhere, you can handle some Country and Western music and Coors."

"You haven't heard the Country and Western music they play in there," I tell him. "It will make your ears bleed."

"All Country and Western music makes my ears bleed," Jessica says.

"Anyway, we're looking," Eve says. "Worse comes to worst, there's only a couple thousand people in this town, we can always just start beating people."

"Have you guys seen anything at all that looks promising?" I ask.

"Not a damned thing," Jessica says, sliding over next to me. "Just miles of brush."

"We could wander around out here for decades and not find a thing," Wilford says.

"There's nothing on the paper maps, Google Maps doesn't work out here. We've got GPS, but no data. I can tell you our exact latitude and longitude but there's no way to tie that to anything in the real world," Wilford tells us. "You two have got to get us some decent intel."

"I told you," I tell him. "We're working on it. We'll hit the bar and the casino tonight. If we can't figure this out by tomorrow we'll have to switch in-town teams or people will start talking."

"You guys want some food and decent beer?" Eve asks.

25 | …Is No Room Service

The bar in question is the Wildhorse Casino and Hotel. It's a run-of-the-mill casino on Native American land meaning it's cheaply opulent and populated by people who see slot machines as a viable career option. It's depressing in ways you usually only see in Academy Award winning movies about cancer patients and people with mental problems.

There are other bars in town, real shitholes with authentic wooden floors and authentic passed-out drunks, but those turned out to be a wash. Eve and I had originally decided any refugees from the base would be laying low in the shitholes and the casino would be mostly for tourists.

If you've never been in one of these Native American casinos it's worth your time to try it out at some point. You've got to admire the moxie of these guys. Gambling is illegal in most of the United States, save Nevada and New Jersey, so the tribes look up at one point and say, "You know what? Our land is technically a sovereign nation, so our laws trump U.S. Federal law."

Yay for gambling, fireworks, and tax-free cigarettes. Yay for freedom.

The government tried in vain for a while to find a way to stop the spread of the casinos, but couldn't find a way to legally stop the tribes from putting them up and proceeding to fleece everyone they could find.

This just goes to show, the Native American tribes play the long game. Early American settlers took their land, the tribes found a way to get back.

The Wildhorse Casino is your prototypical reservation casino, over appointed and tacky. Las Vegas would be proud. It's early evening and the place is sparsely populated. The hotel here only has forty rooms or so, but there's maybe a dozen people in the place.

Most of them are at the bar, nursing whatever passes for problems.

For the most part, they're just your generic tourists wearing T-Shirts with Apache sayings or "Visit Amazing Dulce, NM" emblazoned on them. Even the tourists who aren't trying to look like tourists look like tourists. Pro tip folks, when you want to blend and look like the locals, find out what the locals dress like. In a place like Dulce, NM the average person isn't going to be wearing golf slacks and designer shirts.

Coincidentally, Eve and I are dressed exactly like tourists trying to look like we're not tourists. Yes, I'm wearing tan golf slacks and a blue polo shirt with an image of crossed golf clubs on the chest. It was a struggle to not beat myself up. Eve's in similar attire, just switch the slacks for a skirt and girly up the colors a bit: tan skirt, pink polo. She was nonplussed by the wardrobe.

We look just like everyone else in this shitty little casino, except for one guy in the corner.

He looks like he could be a local: faded jeans, a rumpled western shirt and cowboy boots. The only thing completely off is his beat up baseball hat with RAND emblazoned across it.

What's so special about RAND? They're a think tank that's rumored to have dug the first tunnels of the base out here. Also, who the hell wears a RAND hat anywhere, let alone in a casino in Dulce?

He's a scruffy looking fellow with a beard, unwashed hair, and eyes that you could get a contact crazy from. He's mechanically pulling the arm on a slot machine with a glowering alien face on it. I take the machine to his left and Eve settles into the one on his right. For a few minutes, we all play the nickel slot machines.

Scruffy glares at me when I hit a minor jackpot. Yay! I just won 1000 credits! That $50 is going to change my life. I'm tempted to cash out, but decide to push my luck. Scruffy isn't doing well and it's a comfort to the wretched to have companions in distress.

Eve hits her own jackpot and Scruffy turns to glare at her, too. He's about to say something, but stops dead in his tracks when he gets a look at her. Eve just smiles at him and turns back to the slot machine.

The Scruffster turns to me and whispers, "Did you see her?"

I give him my best innocent expression and say, "Who, her?"

"Yeah, man. She's a giant," Scruffy whispers.

"Yes," I say completely deadpan. "That's my wife."

All the blood drains out of Scruffy's face and he starts to apologize profusely. Unfortunately for him, he's been drinking all night and starts babbling and staring at Eve. Eventually, the apologies start flying at Eve who looks at him for a moment and then looks over him at me and asks, "Is this guy okay, sweetie?"

She's adopted a slight accent, but nothing you could really put your finger on. If I were pressed to listen to her accent and guess where she's from, I'd say somewhere in Northern or Eastern Europe.

"I think so, he's just been drinking," I tell her.

"I am so sorry," Scruffy slurs.

Eve stands up and Scruffy's eyes go wide. When she stands next to me and puts an arm around me, Scruffy nearly loses it. I should have been prepared for his next question, but it takes me completely off guard.

"Do you two, you know, have sex?" he asks wide-eyed.

I have no response to that.

"We fuck like bears," Eve says, completely deadpan and with a slight but undefinable accent. "He is daddy bear, I am momma bear."

"Yes," I say. "Bears."

"Then we hibernate," Eve adds.

"My God," Scruffy whispers.

"What is RAND?" Eve asks.

"Huh?" Scruff stammers. "What?" Oh, the hat."

He takes off the hat and tries to hand it to her, but he's so drunk and nervous he drops it on the floor. When he reaches down to grab, he nearly falls off the stool. While I steady him, Eve reaches down and grabs the hat and examines it closely.

"What is RAND?" she asks him again.

"It stands for Research ANd Development. They're a think tank. I used to do some work for them around here," Scruffy says.

Looks like we found the right guy.

"What is a think tank?" Eve asks him.

"It's, uh. It's hard to explain. Basically they figure out solutions to problems and advise governments," Scruff says.

"You get paid to think?" Eve asks.

"Kind of. It's more like solving complicated problems,"

"Ah!" Eve says, "Like Rubik cube."

"A little more complicated than that. I'm Devon, by the way," Scruff says.

"Jackson," I say, shaking his hand. "Mama bear here is Brunhilde."

"That's, uh, a beautiful name, Brunhilde," Devon says, shaking her hand.

Eve beams at him and nearly crushes his hand when she shakes it.

"So," Devon asks, "what are you two doing in this wide spot in the road?"

"Passing through," I tell him. "We're touring the Southwest and got kind of lost. We're heading up to Silverton. Thank God these people had the Internet. What about you?"

"That's a long story," Devon says.

"We buy you a drink, you tell story, yes?" Eve asks.

"You got yourself a bargain, ma'am," Devon says.

Devon's already three sheets to the wind, but Eve helps him to a table and I get us drinks. Quality booze is in short supply here, but they did have a bottle of drinkable scotch. Since I just hit a jackpot, the bartender doesn't even blink when I try to buy the whole bottle. She doesn't need to know I won a whopping fifty bucks, she just needs to see a couple of Franklins and she happily slides a bottle of Speyburn and three glasses across the table.

Yes. I did just pay $200 for a $30 bottle of Scotch.

Devon perks up when he sees me show up with Dulce's finest scotch and three glasses.

"That must have cost a pretty penny," he says.

"Too much, but I've been winning all night, so it's all good," I tell him, pouring us all glasses.

"Is all good, sweetheart. It is tradition in old country to celebrate stories with good alcohol," Eve says, downing her glass in a single gulp. "Good alcohol means good stories, as grandma used to say."

"Where's the old country?" Devon asks.

"Finland. Finest country on Earth. Even the Russians are afraid of us. Simo is long dead, but still they fear Finland and rightfully so, yes?"

"Simo?" Devon asks.

I furiously motion to him to not ask, but it's too late. Eve launches into the story of Simo Häyhä.

"Bah. This country," she says and punches me in the arm. My arm immediately goes numb. "Simo Häyhä was Finnish farmer when the hated Russians invaded in 1939. Over the space of 100 days during the Winter War, Simo sent over five hundred Russians back to Hell."

"How did a farmer kill over 500 Russian Soldiers?" Devon asks.

"Simo was greatest sniper in history. He killed them all with an unmodified rifle and iron sights."

"No shit?" Devon asks.

"No shit," I tell him. "Simo's a folk hero in Finland."

"Russians are still afraid of him!" Eve yells and downs another glass.

"Where did you find her?"

"Finland," I say. "Although, to be more technical, she found me."

"What do you mean?"

"I had let my mouth run a little too loud and was in a fight with three guys. Well, okay, I was getting my ass kicked by three guys. I got in a few good licks, dropped one of them, but the other two were busy beating holy Hell out of me. One guy had me from behind and the other guy was just about to brain me with a 2x4. It was one of those moments when your life flashes in front of your face and you think, well, crap, I wish I had deleted all that porn I downloaded."

"You have porn?" Eve asks.

"Of course, dear," I tell her, patting her arm.

"I wish to see the porn," she says. "Is the porn here?"

"No, baby, it's at home."

"Oh," she says simply and downs another glass.

"Anyway," I say. "This guy was just about to brain me when he just goes flying and Brunhilde is standing there looking extremely pissed. The guy behind me went from holding me to hiding behind me instantly. I elbowed him in the jaw and she threw him through a window. We've been together ever since."

"I like man who is not afraid to fight and is not afraid of woman's help," Eve tells him.

Devon looks awed.

"I'd wish you guys luck, but I think you can take care of yourselves," Devon says.

"Truth," Eve says and pours him another drink. "Now, what work did you think about?"

"Oh, I wasn't one of the thinkers, really. I just supervised some digging out in the hills," Devon says.

"Mining?" I ask.

"No, there's more out there than mines," Devon says.

I can tell he wants to talk. Everyone wants to talk. Come on, pal. Drink up.

"Like what?" Eve asks.

"There was, uh, is, some government stuff out there," Devon says.

"Oh, come on!" I tell him. "There's nothing out there. Look, pal, just because we bought you a drink doesn't mean you get to fill our stupid tourist heads with some bullshit. Come on, sweetie. Let's grab our bottle and get out of here."

Devon's hand is on my arm in a flash.

"No, seriously, there are things out there. There are things out there you don't want to know about," he says.

Part of me feels bad about manipulating an obvious alcoholic with booze, but not enough to actually stop.

"What kind of things? We looked this place up on the Internet when we got here and found all kinds of nonsense about aliens and crap like that. I look around this town and I can tell you 100% there are no aliens around here."

"They're really well hidden. And it's not just aliens," Devon says, staring at his glass.

Eve thoughtfully fills it back up for him and Devon sighs and drinks it down. Welcome to the art of the con where we don't make anyone do anything they don't want to do anyway.

"What else?" Eve asks.

Devon freezes. If he's like anyone else who knows government secrets he's been coached over and over again to keep his mouth shut, but he also desperately wants to tell his secrets. The trick is to convince him we're harmless.

"It's alright if he doesn't want to talk, sweetie," I say. "We're leaving tomorrow anyway."

A little light comes on in Devon's eyes. Here's his chance to spill some secrets to a couple of people who won't believe him anyway.

"I … can't," Devon stumbles.

"Why? Is it secret?" I whisper, leaning in close to him and looking around.

"Yes," he says.

Eve takes the hint and leans in close, too. "What do you mean, secret?"

"It means he'll be killed if he tells us," I whisper to her. "We'll be killed if we hear it."

"It's not like that," Devon says.

"No, no." Eve says. "I have been watching X-Files. I know how bad secrets are. Don't want to know."

She leans back in her seat and studiously ignores us.

I start to lean back, too and Devon stops me. "Everything you've heard is true. Bad things out there. Best to get out of this town. When you leave, take Dulce Rock Drive. Take the last right turn before it turns south. Follow the dirt road up the side of the mesa until it stops."

"Won't they shoot us?" I ask.

"It's not like that. There's no guard house, no guards. Just a door. This place is pretty much shut down and so secret it couldn't afford to have an external presence. Everyone lives inside. They will live the rest of their lives inside."

Devon gets up and looks around nervously.

"I was never here," Devon says. "You never met me."

With that, Devon glances at the bottle and high tails it out of the casino.

"Well, Brunhilde, it looks like we've narrowed the search area," I tell Eve.

"Yes we did, Jackson, yes we did," she tells me.

We toast and I look around at the tacky décor and sigh.

"What's wrong?" Eve asks.

"We should have stayed here," I tell her. "I bet this place has room service."

26 | Hi, Can We Tell You About Our Lord And Savior, Cthulhu?

We met up with everyone else first thing in the morning and headed up the road in Wilford's Suburban. It took some scratching around in the dirt, but Jacob finally found the door under a bunch of tumbleweeds.

"Odd," I say. "After all the horror stories I've heard about this place, I would have expected guards or at least some No Trespassing signs."

"They don't want to call attention to this place," Frank says.

"Besides," Wilford add, "guards have a nasty habit of talking. You know what they say, two people can keep a secret if one of them is dead."

Frank is looking around, peering into the scrub brush like he sees the Predator off in the distance. "They know we're here. Mark my words. They're watching us right now."

Jessica looks around. "How can you tell?"

"Two cameras on the ridge up there, sensors on the ground there, there, and there," Frank says, pointing around.

"So where are they?" Eve asks.

"Probably inside," I say. "With guns."

"Pointed at us," Wilford says, slapping me on the shoulder. "Good times, right buddy?"

"Yeah, good times. Frank, what's it going to take to get through that door?"

"Not much. It's just a padlock."

"This stinks," Eve says. "How do we know that jackass at the bar wasn't setting us up?"

"Good point," I say.

"So, what do we do now?" Jessica asks. "Go in or take off?"

"I say we go in. We can die here or get torn apart by an angry god later," I say.

"I'm going in," Eve says. "I hope there really are aliens in there. I always wanted to see one."

"I've got nothing else going on," Wilford says.

"Let me get that door unlocked," Frank says, pulling one of his trademark electric saws.

With practiced precision, Frank cuts the lock off the door and gently pushes it. The door quietly opens on well-maintained hinges. Inside is a long hallway lit by bare bulbs covered with wire mesh strung down the hallway. There's no one waiting inside, but nowhere to hide if they decide to open up on us.

The hall looks like a walkway to an industrial wasteland.

The hallway continues into the heart of the mesa and the light is dim enough that we can't see the end. It's bare concrete with a red wainscoting. Immediately inside are four holes, probably where a sign was posted at some point in the past. Think about the most boring hallway you've ever experienced and you've got a good idea of what we're looking at.

That right there is the problem. A place like this, with cameras and sensors outside, should have big guys with guns waiting for us. As soon as we opened the door, we should have been greeted with steely eyes and laser sights, but there's nothing there.

We're all wearing simple body armor, stitched together from a miracle fabric we stole from a company out near Vegas last year. I don't know what the technical name for the stuff is, but it's pretty awesome. When you're wearing it, it hangs and moves like thick canvas. As soon as something hits it hard enough the material stiffens to spread the impact out. It was apparently designed for infiltration guys who needed to look normal, but still require protection.

For a beat no one moves. We're all convinced the forces of darkness are going to come tearing down the hall guns blazing. After a moment, I realize we're the forces of darkness and take a tentative step inside.

Nothing happens.

There's no movement, no sound save a faint buzz from the lights. If there's an end to the world, it's probably down this hall.

I tentatively move forward, trying desperately to be silent. I'm not sure why I'm trying to be quiet since I'm pretty sure the cameras outside have already warned anyone inside that they have visitors. Maybe it's just my paranoid nature.

I should have put Wilford or Eve in front, they're bullet-proof, but I don't trust Wilford that much and I need Eve behind us in case we need to break the door down to get out.

This would be a perfect place for an ambush and a stupid place to die. Jessica steps in behind me, the barrel of her SPAS-15 looks like the open end of a trash can and I decide it's best to hug the wall in case that damned thing goes off.

One by one, everyone steps in and Jessica as I keep slowly pushing forward. When Frank comes in last, he quietly shuts the door.

"Keep pushing forward," Eve's voice says in my earpiece. "Let's not get trapped in this hallway."

Jessica's hand touches my shoulder and she says, "If someone comes up, drop and I'll open with Painless here."

"Painless?"

"Yeah, that's what Jesse Ventura named his gun in *Predator*."

"You named your gun?" I ask.

"Sure, you guys name your dicks all the time, why can't a girl name her gun?"

"Mighty Thor and I take offense at that statement," I respond.

"Get a room, you two," Jacob's voice says through my earpiece.

"We keep trying," Jessica says. "But some people insist on taking the hotel room and leaving me camping in the brush."

"Quiet everyone," Wilford says. "Let's get through this hallway before the bad guys come running."

"Don't you mean the good guys?" Eve asks.

"I'm not sure whoever's here actually qualifies as 'The Good Guys,'" I say.

"Maybe they're the worse guys," Frank quips.

"Yeah, them. Let's get out of here before they come calling," Wilford says.

Wilford's slipping into his attack mode, trying to take control because it's what he's used to doing. I've never gone into a situation with him, but I've seen videos he and his group took during an attack. He's ruthlessly efficient and extremely attentive to miniscule details.

I slow down and wave him forward. Trust or no trust, he's the best bet for point man.

We press forward quietly, but we pick up speed when it looks like no one is coming. The hallway runs straight and narrow for what seems like an eternity, dipping slowly into the side of the mesa. We don't see any cameras or other sensors, just the eternal gray highway.

The hallway terminates – after five minutes of tense walking – at a plain set of industrial stairs. It's here that we see the first signs of government habitation, a sign warning trespassers of dire consequences that will befall them if they don't immediately stop and surrender.

It's a strange place for a sign.

Over the years, I've seen a lot of warnings at a lot of government installations, but never one like this. Usually, the US Government is more proactive, they'll warn you off miles away from the place they'll shoot for entering. This sign is well within the secure area.

Wilford stares at it with a furrowed brow, probably thinking the exact same thing I am.

"We're not in Kansas anymore," he says to no one in particular.

The stairs seem to go on forever, too. Whoever built this entrance hated people. Maybe this is some kind of tiered security; by the time you get through the hall and to the bottom of the stairs, you're too tired to actually fight anyone. My legs are sore by the time we hit the bottom. Jacob's a delightful shade of gray. Frank is slightly winded. Wilford just shrugs it off and keeps moving. Jessica and Eve look like they could do it a hundred more times. Must be nice to be young. Or a Demi-Goddess. Demi-God. Whatever.

At the bottom of the stairs is a simple sign with a set of arrows pointing different directions. Left is the infirmary. Right are the guest quarters. Straight ahead are the elevators and bathrooms. Science A is down and to the left, Science B is down and to the right.

Beneath the direction sign is a smaller sign identifying this facility as a restricted area with a whole series of notes about obscure laws that we're breaking by simply reading the sign.

"Is it just me, or is this place smaller than I would have

guessed?" Jacob notes.

"We haven't seen the whole thing," I say. "Plus, smaller places have fewer people. Fewer people means less talk."

"Is there a visitor's center or anything?" Jessica asks.

"Doesn't appear to be," Wilford says.

"At the risk of sounding negative, that's not very neighborly," Frank adds.

Eve is staring at the signs intently, probably trying to discern where the important places are.

This whole place feels empty. It's definitely not government standard protocol to let people barge into a secure location and not, at the very least, question their motives. It may feel abandoned, but it doesn't look abandoned. Everything is neat and tidy. The air conditioner is still running smoothly. There's none of the broken down look that comes with abandoned places.

The ceiling is dotted with black domes. Each one is more than likely filled with a camera. Each camera is doubtless watching us standing around scratching our asses.

"Got a plan, Eve?" Frank asks.

"That way," she says, pointing to the left.

"The infirmary?" Jacob asks. "Not feeling well?"

"They'll have records of anyone who's ever walked into this place," I say. "Places like this, first thing you do when you work here is get a checkup."

"Good point," Wilford says. "If they bothered keeping records."

27 | HIPAA Violations Galore

Frank may not be the best hacker in the world, but he was in a relationship with a damned good one for a long time. His partner, Jean, was killed last year while Frank, Eve, and I were breaking into a secure contractor facility. We got jumped by Wilford's guys. Eve carried Frank out, killing at least a few DHS goons on the way, and I got captured and subjected to Wilford's idea of enhanced interrogation, which largely consisted of getting locked in cage and beaten by guys who could slip between worlds. There would be a poof of air and then, wham, a punch to the head. The guy who hit me would disappear again.

Good times.

During the interrogation Wilford showed me Jean's laptop, covered with blood and intimated he'd whacked Jean. Turned out Jean was beheaded and behanded, but it wasn't Wilford or his guys. We still don't know who actually did the deed.

Jean would have had this computer singing show tunes by now. He was that good of a hacker. Frank has picked up some of Jean's tricks. Not many, mind you, since Frank hacks buildings, but enough to cut through the light security on this system. In a few minutes, he managed to call up all the medical records, including scans of original hard files from the 40s. Surprisingly, there aren't that many people in the system, less than a hundred to cover over sixty years of operation.

The medical records stopped in 2010. After that, there's not a damned piece of information about anything or anyone coming through here. That was four years ago, and the last record was for a Mr. Devon Sheffield.

"Look familiar?" Eve asks, pointing at the picture of Sheffield.

Mr. Sheffield, listed as an intelligence officer, is the same guy we met last night.

"Yeah," I say. "Now I'm really worried."

Jessica is peering over my shoulder at the picture. "Who's that guy?" she asks.

"We met him last night and tried to pump him for information," Eve says. "He's the guy that told us about the entrance up there."

"Looks like he was pumping you for information," Wilford says dryly.

I start to shoot him a look, but realize he's right. We should have been more careful. That's the problem with the spy game, it's difficult to tell who's spying on who at any given point.

"Thing is," I tell him. "He never asked us anything important."

"At least nothing you realized was important," Wilford tells us. "Look, Steven, I shouldn't have to remind of you this, but your picture was all over the news for a fairly long time. Your hair is a bit longer, but otherwise you look the same. Eve's picture was out there, too, and it's kind of hard to claim you're a different seven foot tall woman. That guy was up to something and you suave spies fell right into his trap."

It's at this moment that I really begin to feel like a total dork. He's absolutely correct and I've got a sinking feeling in my stomach that we were played here. Some small part of me, the part I don't like to admit I even have, tells me whoever is running this place has been one step ahead of us the whole time. They probably planted that guy in town as soon as we showed up in town.

"He knows something, though, and he managed to lure us all here," Wilford continues.

"Yeah, but why?" Frank asks.

"That's the million dollar question," I say. "Whatever's going on, though, that computer has fake data. There's no way this place operated for decades with less than 100 people."

"Could be they didn't digitize everyone," Frank says.

"Possible, but this still smells funny. Some of the records are obviously scans, but I'd expect a lot more people for that amount of time," I tell him. "This whole place stinks to high Heaven of something bad."

The lights are still on, the air unit is still quietly humming and the place is otherwise silent as a tomb. Somehow, that makes it worse. They, whoever they are, know we're here. Hell, they lured us in. Yet, there's no one around.

This whole place is slowly driving me nuts. It's like a form of torture. You know something terrible is about to happen, you can feel it coming, but there's no obvious evidence of it. Maybe that's the point of the place; let you think everything is safe and then drop the boom when you least expect it.

Maybe I'm just getting jumpy.

"Let's get a look around, there's got to be something here," Eve says. "If we split up, we can cover more area."

"Sounds like a plan," I say.

"Frank, Jacob, you're with me," Eve says. "We'll check out Science A, you three hit Science B."

"You got it, boss," I tell her.

"Be careful, guys, we don't know what's going on and it's a little nervous making," Eve tells us.

Jacob pulls out his .44 Automag and checks the cylinder for a round. The gun is a pistol, but it fires rifle rounds that make big holes in everything they hit. "You know what cautious fellows we are," he says with a grin.

I do a quick check of my sawed-off buddy and my Detonics. The bizarre thump gun is hooked to my lower back; I'm hoping to find out more about it here. Wilford pulls an MP5 out of somewhere and Jessica racks a round into her SPAS. The sound of the shotgun is almost thunderous in this quiet place.

"Let's roll out, buddy," Wilford says, clapping me on the shoulder.

* * * *

Science B is on the opposite side of the hallway we came in through, a door at the end of an extremely uninteresting hallway. Jessica's on point since she can flood a hallway with more lead than either Wilford or I can. At the door she stands guard, shotgun at the ready as I cautiously reach for the knob. A small part of me thinks this would a perfect place to lay a trap. Electrify the knob or put a bomb in the door and that would end our excursion quickly and effectively.

I'm getting jumpy. Who in their right mind would actually wonder if a doorknob is electrified? Take a deep breath, pull it together. Once I relax, once I realize the place is trying to drive me over the edge, it makes it easier to fight the edginess that's slowly been building in me ever since we walked in here.

There's more to it than just getting jumpy about this strange place. I feel like there's static in my head, confusing my thoughts, making me edgy.

The knob isn't electrified and the only thing that happens when I try to turn it is I find out it's locked.

"Wilford," I ask, "would you mind doing the honors?"

I can't pick locks for beans, but Wilford's an experienced infiltrator. It takes him all of five seconds with a lock picking kit. He steps back into position, MP5 pointed at the door as I reach in turn the knob.

The door swings quietly open and reveals a small science lab. There's nothing really out of the ordinary, just white walls, microscopes, a couple of computers, and some unidentifiable equipment in the corner quietly blinking to itself.

The place is spotless, sterile, and completely devoid of anything interesting.

"Eve," I say, "You guys finding anything?"

"Nothing," her voice comes back through my earpiece. "We've got an empty lab complete with some microscopes."

"Same here," I tell her.

"Meet back in front of the stairs," she tells me.

"Roger that, we're going to check the guest quarters and meet up with you at the stairs."

＊ ＊ ＊ ＊

Eve's team is waiting for us when we get back to the stairs. Everyone's starting to look pensive. This place feels wrong, but I can't put my finger on why. You'd think we'd all be excited that no one has shot us, but we're all just getting more and more nervous.

It's the boom dropping thing. Every time I look around a corner or turn around or look in an empty room, I'm convinced something is waiting for me. At first, I imagined a single person who would sound an alarm as soon I poked my head into a room. Soon it became a lone guard, then a group of guards, then an alien. Then it just got weird.

On a lark, we checked the guest quarters. They were fairly nicely appointed, for government guest quarters. The mattresses were reasonably thick, the doors were solid, and the listening devices hidden in the lights were state-of-the-art. Well, they were cutting-edge back in the mid-90s. Now they're kind of quaint but they probably still work.

Other than that, there was absolutely nothing outstanding about the rooms. Clean sheets, fluffed pillows, Bible in the dresser.

"What is going on here?" Frank asks.

"Whatever it is, it must be down those elevators," Jessica says.

"I think this whole floor is just a show," Wilford tells us. "This level is designed to look important, but nothing really happens here. I used to see it all the time with bad guys who wanted to stay hidden. We won't find a damned thing up here."

"Think the elevators work?" Jacob asks. "I didn't see any other stairs anywhere."

"I don't see why not," I tell him. "Everything else up here is oiled and smooth, the elevators should be, too."

28 | Going Down

The elevators are industrial sized, built to handle huge scientific equipment like, uh, cars. Honestly, I'm not sure what they were planning on hauling up and down in this elevator, but it's huge. The sofa in the corner is a nice touch, though, even if it only takes a few seconds to go to the next floor. There are other buttons on the elevator; places lower than the next level down. There are three sublevels marked on the elevator, all marked storage, but it looks like you need a key to get to them.

The keyhole looks a little strange, like some specialized key from the not too distant future. I can't help but be a bit disappointed. A place a like this, you'd expect at least some kind of card reader or retinal scanner, but the tech seems primitive.

I point at the keyhole and ask Wilford, "Can you pick that?"

"Not with the tools I've got," he replies. "I didn't plan on running into a custom lock."

We all have guns drawn and pointed at the door when the elevator stops. This would be the perfect place to shoot us all down in a hail storm of hot lead.

I've always wanted say "a hail storm of hot lead." It's so film noir.

The elevator gives us a happy ding and the doors slide quietly open. Outside is an empty hallway with a simple sign on the wall. Offices and labs are to the left, quarters and mess hall are to the right. I take one side of the door and Wilford takes the other. We lean out and look down the hall.

"Clear," Wilford whispers.

"Empty," I say.

"What the fuck is going on here?" Jacob asks. "This place is driving me to drink. I mean more than usual."

"Let's check it out," Eve says, pointing to the left. "You guys go that way, we'll go this way."

"Can we check out the mess hall?" Jacob asks.

"Okay. Steven, you guys go that way, we'll go this way," Eve says, pointing her fingers in different directions.

This level shows more signs of life, there's trash in the trash cans and the place is generally not perfectly spotless. Not dirty, mind you, just lived in. Someone has been here, and been here recently.

The lock on the office door is more advanced than the ones upstairs, but Wilford takes the numeric keypad in stride. I'm not sure how he does it, but he manages to open the door after three tries. The office is neat, but someone was here not too long ago. There's a nearly full cup of coffee and a single folder on the desk and someone has been doing a crossword on the computer. Above the desk is a bank of monitors, each displaying a room upstairs that we were in a few minutes ago.

Again, there's that feeling that whoever we're up against has been one step ahead the whole time.

We should get the hell out of here. This is such an obvious trap. Of course, if we leave now we're back where we started: gods gunning for us. Stay here and we might get whacked, but we might find a solution. Go back out and we will definitely get slaughtered.

"Well, at least we know where the cameras were being fed to," Wilford says.

Jessica sticks her finger in the coffee on the desk. "Still warm," she says.

"Where are these guys?" I ask. This is getting exasperating. I feel like a dog chasing its tail. Whoever, or whatever, we're looking for is a ghost silently gliding down abandoned corridors, probably sniggering at us the whole way.

I sit down at the computer and start digging around. Whoever was here didn't lock it which makes hacking the thing much easier. After a minute of checking the Start menu of this old XP box (apparently they didn't get the memo to upgrade), I stumble across a program that looks promising.

When I call it up, I get the full record of everyone who has ever worked here or come through here. I was right, the list is far, far bigger than the one upstairs. Actually, far bigger even than it should be. There must 20,000 records in this list.

Each record shows time in and time out, full name, some kind of identifier, gender, and a simple column called status with U, C, or M in it.

Scrolling through, I find Wilford's name.

"Hey, Wil," I say, "you're in the computer."

He peers over my shoulder and squints at the data.

"Recognize the dates?" I ask.

"Yeah, right after that mission. What does 'U' mean?"

"No clue, but you're one of only handful with 'U'," I tell him. "Most everyone has 'C', there are only a couple with 'M'."

"This is fucked," he tells me and goes back to looking around.

Wilford picks up the folder and starts looking through it. Each time he flips the pages his eyes get a little bigger.

"What?" Jessica asks him.

"These guys have been stalking you for some time now," he says, holding the folder out to me.

Inside the folder I find pictures of us going into Radula, pictures at the Crossroads motel, pictures of us getting off the plane a couple days ago. There's a picture of Eve and me standing in line outside of The Very Reverend George W. Smith's Holy Dreamtime. It was while Chad and Sally were trying to get us inside. My head is circled and there's an arrow pointing at Eve.

"What does that text say?" I ask, peering at the photo.

Jessica and Wilford look closely at the text. "Kill him," Jessica says. "Take her."

"Who do you think 'the girl' is?" Wilford asks.

"What?" I ask.

"Down here at the bottom, it says 'find the girl,'" Wilford says.

"Can I see that?" I ask.

Wilford hands me the folder and wanders off to search other part of the room.

The folder is full of pictures of all of us. The text is a complete log of our activities over the past few days. There are pictures of my house from this winter. Someone has been watching us, taking meticulous notes on everything we've been up to. They tracked us in Mexico, on the plane, all over Albuquerque, even out to Smith's place.

Smith would be livid if he knew.

"I think I found out who the 'the girl' is," I say holding up the folder. Inside is a picture of Jessica opening up her bar in Mexico.

"You worked at a bar in Mexico?" Wilford asks.

"Owned a bar in Mexico," Jessica tells him, distractedly staring at the picture.

"Awesome," Wilford tells her. "I always wanted to do that."

"It's not all it's cracked up to be," she tells him.

While they look around the room I finish looking through the folder.

"Motherfucker," I whisper.

"What?" Wilford asks.

"Whoever these guys are, they killed Jean. They were going to go after everyone that night but your people showed up," I say.

"Does it say why?" Jessica asks.

"No, it's just an after-action report. It only says the mission was scrubbed before it could be completed. Subject one was neutralized and recovered, which doesn't sound too good, remaining subjects were let go after government intervention interrupted the mission. Two subjects, including the girl, escaped on a motorcycle and their trail was lost. Attempts to reconnect with the subjects were abandoned after the subjects failed to return to primary residence."

"Looks like spending time at the Crossroads was a good idea after all," Jessica says.

"Oh, God. You guys hid out at the Crossroads?" Wilford says, completely shocked. "How many crack whores did you displace?"

"A couple," I tell him. "Why were these guys after us?"

"They were after you," a voice says, "because you discovered her."

We all spin around, looking for the source, but the room is empty. Must be a hidden speaker around here somewhere. Hopefully it's two-way.

"Who are you?" Jessica asks.

"I'm your only hope of getting out of this place alive," the voice tells us. "You can find me in Lab 1, it's around the corner from you."

We all look at each other, trying to decide just how bad a move it is to follow instructions from disembodied voice. If you've ever watched a horror movie you know it's always a bad idea to follow any advice you get from voices on speakers.

"Time is of the essence, children. They'll tire of their little game shortly and come to see you. I assure you, you don't want that.

Lab 1 is right around the corner, just like our personal assistant told us it would be. A camera outside the door tracks us as we walk up and the door clicks open just as I reach for the handle.

Beyond this door is a promise of answers, but I don't move an inch. It seems every time I get answers lately, it just leads to more questions and more problems. I thought I had everything under control. You know how it goes: release a God, destroy a large portion of government, and retire to a nice A-Frame cabin in the woods to watch the world collapse. Of course, one morning you wake up to a gun in your face and a goddess who was supposed to kill you but decided to turn on other gods instead. One thing leads to another and the next thing you know you're stuck in some fucked up lab under a mountain in the ass-end of New Mexico. Seriously, it's enough to make me want to blast the door open and fill the room on the other side with lead.

Jessica sighs and gently pushes me aside before opening the door with the barrel of her shotgun. Wilford snorts, that little laugh he gets when he finds something amusing, but not outright funny. I'm not a small guy, right around 6 foot tall, and watching all 5' 7" of Jessica push me out of the way must look a little strange. To be fair, though, I've seen her fight and have no great desire to tangle with her. She's also got a large shotgun.

The door swings wide and Jessica gasps and raises her gun to her shoulder, finger on the trigger. Seeing her react like that Wilford and I both raise our guns and step into the door way.

"Motherfucker," is about all I can come up with.

"That's not a good sign," Wilford says.

I put a hand on Jessica's shoulder and she shoots me a glare over her shoulder.

"We need him," I say softly. "He has answers, and maybe a solution. We need him."

Her eyes soften and the gun lowers.

Inside the room is a blonde man with piercing blue eyes in his early 30s wearing a lab coat over a freshly pressed dress shirt. He's got a dark red silk tie and his hair is perfectly combed. His expression conveys an amazing intellect, no small amount of disdain for us, and a general feeling of boredom, like whatever threat we provided was completely beneath his threshold of things to worry about today.

The real worrisome thing, though, is the red flag with the white circle and black swastika hanging behind his desk.

"My name is Werner," the man says with no trace of an accent. "Welcome to the most dangerous place on Earth."

29 | Finally Some Answers

Werner waves us inside and asks me to shut the door. Something about him warns me from lipping off about being a doorman.

"What did you mean when you said they were after us because we found Jessica?" I ask as I close the door.

"There are connections in the world that you haven't taken the time to discover," Werner tells me. "She is special. More so than you. More so than your giantess. More so than the God of Dreams. They were never meant to meet. To get them together would be disastrous. We planned on taking her and keeping her here."

"Killing us in the process, right?" I ask.

"Of course. Your trajectory was sending you toward something that was best left alone. He knew about her, saw her in her father's mind. As a god himself, he had to know what she was and what she meant. In some ways, it would have been better for everyone if she had died on that table. Anyway, what's done is done. Sit, please. We don't have much time," Werner says.

I have absolutely no way to process what I just heard. It explains a lot of things, sure, but it's so surreal and he said it so matter of fact that it was like getting hit in the face with brick dipped in absinthe.

My eyes keep darting back and forth between the flag and the man. It must show in my eyes because Werner sighs and motions to the three chairs neatly laid out in front of his black oak desk.

"The flag is a reminder of past failures," Werner says. "The problem with the Reich was never one of determination, it was always a problem of putting principle ahead of practicality. They focused on their doctrine of racial purity rather than their abilities. They had the most technologically advanced army in the world and a group of dedicated soldiers and they threw the whole thing away because they insisted on listening to that fool's rambling about the Jews."

At least the flag on the wall makes sense. Sure, it's reprehensible, but it makes sense. It's tangible.

"So, you're not a Nazi?" Jessica asks.

"Oh, I believe in a great many of the things that made the *Nationalsozialistische Deutsche Arbeiterpartei* what it was. Most of the people here believe the same way. Except the monsters downstairs, but what can you do about monsters, yes?"

"How can you say the Nazis weren't monsters?" Wilford asks.

"Mr. Saxton, how can you, of all people, call someone else a monster?"

"What do you mean?" Wilford asks him.

"You were my greatest creation. A human *monster* put together with parts of other *monsters*," Werner tells him. "When they brought you to me, you were all but dead, torn apart by that despicable thing. I put you back together, boy. I made you what you are."

Wilford sits in stunned silence.

"What, exactly, is it that you do here, Werner?" I ask.

"We are trying to save this race," Werner says.

"What, the white race?" Jessica spits at him.

"The human race," Werner says patiently. "We're trying to save the human race from things that would destroy it."

"What would destroy it?" Jessica asks.

"All manner of things are out to destroy our race, Miss Hayha. Aliens want to settle here. Gods want to rule us, monsters want to destroy us. The governments of the world lack the stomach to do what is necessary to protect our species. We're here, madam, to prevent those things from getting their way. We have eyes everywhere. We have an army downstairs and we are prepared to do what must be done to take care of this world."

"How," Wilford whispers, eyes focused on the floor tiles at his feet. "How are you going about saving the race?"

"It's complicated," Werner says.

"Simplify it for us dummies," I tell him.

"We are remaking humans, piece by despicable piece. We are removing the effluvia that are clogging up our gene pool. We are strengthening the species by merging traits. The aliens are a pathetic race, weak and faltering, but they can withstand the rigors of space travel," Werner tells us.

"Who are you removing?" Jessica asks quietly.

"The weak races," Werner says with a sad smile. "The ones who cannot stand on their own, who reproduce like rats, who refuse to become members of the whole."

"You're no different than the Nazis," I tell him. "You may not be as overt about it, but you're just like them."

"Perhaps," Werner muses. "We are different from the National Socialists in one very important area, though."

"What's that?" Wilford asks.

"Where they failed, we will succeed. We are patient. We are thorough. We finish what we started."

With no warning, Werner draws a small air gun and shoots Wilford square in the chest. The action takes me completely off guard, but Jessica has her shotgun in his face before he can react. Werner calmly sets the pistol on the desk and raises his hands.

To her credit, Jessica has the presence of mind to not pull the trigger. Her eyes are hard, though, the same dangerous look she gave the guy in the parking lot when she threatened to castrate him.

"What did you do?" she hisses, shoving the barrel in Werner's face.

Wilford's face turns ash gray before becoming bright red. Not the bright red of someone with a high fever or even a bad sunburn. He's the color of a stop sign or a fire engine. It's an unnatural hue on a person and looks cartoonish and terrifying at the same time. His whole body tenses and drool pours out of this mouth. Eyes roll back in his head and a silent scream emerges from his open mouth.

"What did you do?" I yell.

Werner doesn't immediately answer so I kick his desk as hard as I can, sliding the mahogany beast into his gut and trapping him between it and his Nazi memorabilia. I've got a pretty serious kick when I put my back into it, but it doesn't really do anything to him other than surprise him and knock the wind out of him.

"What did you do to him?" I yell again.

Werner sucks in a breath and wheezes, "I finished what I started. I finished him."

Wilford is slowly relaxing and his color shifts back from bright red to his normal pale pinkish hue. His breathing is returning to normal.

"He one of them now. A hand of the gods without the tedium of needing gods," Werner says with a smile. "He is completely indestructible. He was our first engineered Übermensch. Not Hitler's pathetic blonde Aryan master race, Nietzsche's true Übermensch, a man with no need of gods. We have created others since then, but he was my first success, even if I did not get to finish my work. I do not like to leave business unfinished."

Wilford is breathing deeply, eyes blinking and looking around.

"What the fuck have you done?" Jessica asks.

"I have finished what I started. Stage one created impressive results, modified from data we gathered from your friend here. He is stage two. The first stage two. He will survive the change and emerge a new god."

"Stage two? What the fuck is stage two?" I ask.

"He will set the world free," Werner says with an awed look in his eyes.

Wilford's hands fumble around and finally manage to pluck the dart out of his chest and toss it on the floor. "Why are there three of you?" he asks Werner.

"Patience, my son. Your body is learning to be better than you have ever imagined."

This is like watching a chrysalis hatching. Wilford walked in here basically unstoppable. Kind of a dick, but basically unstoppable. Now I have no idea what he's becoming, but it sounds like he's going to be even more dangerous than before, probably indestructible. And probably still kind of a dick to boot.

Jessica is torn between watching Wilford recover and shooting Werner, and I can't say I'm in much of a different boat. Although, honestly, I'm leaning more toward shooting Werner; Wilford seems to be coming together nicely.

"How you feeling, buddy?" I ask Wilford.

"Better. There's only two of him now," he tells me, head in hands.

"Hold it together, pal."

Werner is watching, fascinated. "Normally by now the subjects have fallen apart."

"Fallen apart?" Jessica asks.

"The other subjects could not handle the change. They

disintegrated from the inside out. It was fascinating to watch even if it was frustrating. He will survive, though. He must survive."

"Were you planning on telling him that?" she asks.

"Of course not. Science requires the subject not influence the outcome."

Wilford is standing now. His legs are shaking, but he's learning to overcome whatever's happening to him. There's a faint glow coming off his skin and his eyes are on fire, like he's got a high fever. He staggers but catches himself on the back of a chair. He's looking around the room like he's seeing the world for the first time.

"How did you figure out how to do this?" I ask.

"We captured something, a god's hired muscle and reverse engineered it. The biology was mostly compatible and it only took minor tweaking with alien DNA to start the process," Werner says.

"Are you planning on doing this with everyone?" Jessica asks.

"Oh, my, no. Most people will have to be content with simple alien DNA. They'll be more resilient, but hardly on the level of our friend here."

"Separate classes of people, then. Some better than others, literally and figuratively," Wilford says quietly. "Hardly an American ideal."

"This is not only America, Mr. Saxton. This is the world and the sad fact of the world is most people need someone to lead them. People like you, Mr. Saxton," Werner tells him, "People like me. We will remake the world for the strong and intelligent and sweep aside the lesser races before they overrun everything."

"No," Wilford says simply.

Say what you will about Wilford Saxton, that he's a dick sometimes, that he has done some horrible things in his life. But he believes in his country and the ideals that drive it. You could never accuse him of being a racist. Sure, he's an ass, but he's an equal-opportunity ass.

"I won't help you," Wilford tells Werner, "because I think you are full of shit."

"You don't know what you're giving up," Werner says, pushing the desk away from him.

Jessica reacts to the movement by pointing the shotgun at his crotch and smiling.

"I'm giving up a life of regrets and self-hatred," Wilford tells him.

"We made you a god!" Werner yells.

"Gods make their own decisions," Wilford says quietly.

"This is your last chance, Mr. Saxton. We brought you here so you could take your rightful place at my side. I created you, I can destroy you."

"How do you kill a god?" I ask.

Okay, so I've got ulterior motives, sue me. Hopefully I can get this guy to talk before Jessica blows a hole in him or Wilford tears him apart.

"The same way I put him together. We have tools," Werner says, eyes narrowing.

"Are these tools here? In this place?" I ask. "Like the bell?"

"Yes, Die Glocke is downstairs. We stole it from the Argentinians some years back."

Good enough for me. Jessica and Wilford can pop this asshole at their leisure.

Let me explain a little about Die Glocke. Most people haven't heard of it and those who have generally dismiss it as myth or the product of late World War II Nazi propaganda. Die Glocke, German for "The Bell," was an experiment that didn't work. It was supposed to be an antigravity device but it never worked for that. What it did do, though was nothing short of miraculous. The damned thing tore apart reality. It didn't take the Nazis long to figure out how to fine tune it to manipulate reality.

I'm willing to bet a machine that can alter reality can kill a god.

"Mr. Saxton, my patience is wearing thin," Werner declares menacingly.

Wilford doesn't respond, just calmly pulls a pistol and shoots Werner square in the chest. As Werner slides down the wall, leaving a trail of blood all over his swastika, his hand flops against the desk stopping his fall. I can't see what he does or how he does it, but suddenly the lights go red and an alarm sounds.

"They're coming for you, Mr. Saxton," Werner whispers. He coughs, spraying blood all over his desk. "You and your little friends, too."

I have a feeling Werner's army won't stop with us.

30 | Hell Breaks Loose

The alarm stops and the silence feels heavy, like the air before the thunderheads explode. The light is still red, that same red you see when backup generators kick on in movies, even though normal emergency lighting is white. The red is intimidating and makes the shadows hard to penetrate. Distantly I hear the happy ding of the elevator arriving and all hell breaks loose. Over my earpiece I hear Jacob bellow and Eve let loose with crazy war scream and then the sound of gunfire reports down the halls.

My earpiece suddenly fills with distorted chatter.

"Wha ... that?"

"Don ... know."

"Ugly ... stard."

"There ... comin ... shoot!"

"Steve ... get .. edy ... your ... way."

"Jacob, umph, ... over ... there ... out."

There's a thumping sound in the hallway almost like someone wearing two different shoes, boots on one foot and dress shoes on the others. It's a thump flap thump kind of sound, punctuated by piercing screech.

Jessica kicks the door shut and backs away rapidly. We all know the door won't hold, but it's better than nothing. With one hand, Wilford flips the huge desk over and motions us to get behind it.

I'm not sure what's coming down the hall, but it doesn't sound good and it feels like whole bunch of problems are heading our way. That keening screech is like a thousand cats screeching into vuvuzelas. It's a high pitched vibration that sets my teeth on edge and makes me pine for the relative silence of a Ministry concert.

"Eve, are you there?" Jessica is asking into her mike.

"Here they come," Wilford says, ducking behind the desk.

"Eve, come in," Jessica continues.

I put a hand on her shoulder and try to get her to duck behind the desk before the shit really hits the fan and am rewarded with a withering glare for my troubles.

"They're coming," I say. "We need to get to cover."

"Eve could be in trouble," she tells me.

"Eve *is* in trouble," I tell her. "But Eve can take care of herself. Do you really want to be standing here they knock down the door?"

As if on cue, the thump flap stops and all is silent for a moment. I can hear my heart beat. I can hear Jessica's worried breathing and Wilford calmly checking his weapon.

My heart nearly stops when I see the door handle move.

"Is it locked?" I hiss.

"I hope so," Jessica says.

"My guess is yes," Wilford says. "I just hope they don't know the door code."

The door handle is all the way down now. If it's unlocked all it will take is a gentle push and whatever's out there will waltz in. There's a thump outside the door and everyone jumps.

Thankfully, the door holds. It was locked.

I breathe a sigh of relief.

"Don't get too comfy, bud," Wilford says. "We still have to get through whatever's out there before we can call ourselves safe."

Something slams against the door, hard enough to shake the whole door frame.

"What the fuck is out there?" Jessica asks, creeping backwards toward the overturned desk.

"Whatever it is, it's strong," Wilford says. "How do we want to play this?"

"We've got your MP5, her SPAS-15, my sawed off. I've got a pistol, nine rounds and a knife. Anything else you guys brought to the party?" I ask.

I've also got the strange black gun strapped to my back behind my jacket, but there's no reason to mention that right now.

"I've got a .45 and knife," Jessica says.

"Pair of nines, a couple of knives, a grenade," Wilford says calmly.

"Where the hell are you carrying a grenade and how did you find one?" Jessica asks.

"Right jacket pocket," Wilford says stoically. "Got it a Grenades R Us."

"Jackass," Jessica mumbles.

"*C'est moi,*" Wilford says. He's moving into position behind the desk, his SMG pointed at the door.

Another loud slam and the door shakes again. The door holds, but the keening wail starts up again. The sound is burrowing into my brain like a Ceti Eel, making it hard to concentrate and focus on the task at hand.

The next slam splinters the door and Jessica grabs me and tries to pull me behind the desk. Thirty seconds ago she glared at me for trying to do the same thing. I pause long enough to drag Werner's corpse in front of the door and dive behind the huge desk just as the first part of the door fails completely and an arm pushes through the hole.

The red lights make it hard to make out details but the arm looks misshapen and strong, a warty appendage that's probably attached to something equally disturbing. The arm feels around, trying to find the door handle. A single shot from Wilford's gun and the arm darts back through the hole.

"We've got a choke point," Wilford says. "Let's exploit it. Wait until the door totally falls apart and unload everything we've got."

"I'm ready," Jessica says.

"I'm good," I add.

Another hand works its way through the hole and almost finds the handle before Wilford shoots it.

After the hand pulls out there's a respite, like they're trying to figure out another way in. It doesn't last long before the pounding starts again. Pieces of the door are flying off now and it won't be long before what little shield we have is gone.

I had thought Werner's corpse propped against the door would slow them down but didn't realize they'd just go through the door rather than opening it.

I'm feeling a little unarmed here. A sawed-off shotgun and a .45 sounds like an arsenal when you're facing one person. There's an army out there and I've got a whopping nine shots before I need to reload.

The door finally drops and we get our first look at the enemy.

"The master race has arrived," I say.

31 | The Master Race

I get a brief look at the things at the door before they surge forward, shoving and stepping over each other to get at us. They deftly hop over Werner's corpse, completely ignoring it. Jessica and Wilford open up and the red light is punctuated with flashes of white light, muzzle flashes from Wilford's controlled bursts and the room lighting effect of Jessica's cannon.

The things are hunched and knobby and covered with rippling muscles. No hair, only a stiff bristle that sprouts from their bodies in uneven patches. Think pale, white apes with scattered black dish scrubbers and you've got a good idea. Glowing red eyes zero in on us.

They're not bullet proof, though. Wilford's 9mm rounds rip into the apes and Jessica's 12 gauge rounds punch big holes in them. One makes it through the wall of lead and nearly gets to us but a close-range blast from Mjolnir pushes it back across the room.

They're not stupid, either. After the first wave the creatures stop mindlessly attacking and hold back just outside the door.

"You can't win," a voice says. "You're trapped and outnumbered. I have plenty of soldiers to throw at you and they'll all happily charge in until you're out of ammunition. Then they will gleefully rend you limb from limb."

"Good luck," I yell. "We're armed to the teeth and crazy as shit house rats."

"It doesn't have to end this way, children," the voice says. "You could join us. There could be a place for you in the New World Order."

New World Order. I hate that phrase. Every two-bit, tin-horn despot has been screaming about the New World Order since time began. The implication is that their idea of how the world should be trumps the will of everyone who actually has to live in the world.

It's the conspiracy world's Holy Grail, the idea that there's some underground group secretly trying to rule the world.

It's all nonsense, of course. The people who have the power to rule the world already rule the world. The people who want to rule the world have to have the power to take over from the people already ruling the world. These things usually don't happen behind the scenes for very long because the people in power have a vested interest in staying in power and have an almost preternatural ability to sniff out threats.

Why do you think the U.S. Government tolerates the militias running around the country? They're not a threat. Never have been never will be.

Of course, these guys have an army of mutated ape things, so who knows? Maybe they can successfully wrench control of the world from its current rulers.

"Last chance to back off," Wilford says. "You can still walk away from this."

"I'd honestly prefer to shoot them all," Jessica quips.

"I'm with her on this one," I say.

"Perhaps we can discuss this, yes?" the voice says.

"I thought we were discussing this," I say. "What's your definition of discussing?"

"Face to face, my son," the voice says. "Discussion requires face to face communication."

I look at Jessica and Wilford, hoping one of them has a better plan than spitefully getting ripped apart by mutants. They both shrug.

Thanks guys.

"Okay," I say. "We'll hold fire if you'll hold the apes off."

"We have an accord," the voice says.

The man who steps around door way is perfect. I don't know how else to describe him. He is the perfect balance of speed and power. He's the perfect size to be a threat but not so big you think he'll be slow. His blonde hair is perfect. His light gray suit is perfect. Everything is perfectly in place from his perfect power tie to his wingtip shoes.

This is the kind of person that no matter who you are, no matter what you do, no matter how you dress, you'll always feel like you're not quite good enough to be in his presence. Sure, you'll keep trying, desperate to win his approval, but you'll never get there. I'm a straight man and I'm kind of developing a crush here. Wilford's appraising him and Jessica's jaw is almost on the floor.

He is everything the Nazis ever tried to create and failed miserably at. Apparently the addition of alien genetics to the Aryan ideal has actually succeeded in creating something that, at the very least, looks like superman.

I hate him already.

When he notices Werner's corpse on the floor, the man frowns slightly and says, "Dear Werner, I told you this was a bad idea."

"Nice suit," I tell him. "Brooks Brothers?"

"The suit is custom, but thank you nonetheless," he says.

"What's the play here?" I ask.

"You surrender and join us," he tells me.

"We're not really team players," Jessica says.

"That is not important," the man says. "There is no option other than joining us."

"Resistance is futile?" Wilford asks. "Surely you could come up with something better than that."

The man cocks his head to the side like he doesn't quite get what Wilford is talking about. Hell, perhaps he doesn't. Maybe they don't get Star Trek reruns down here. His head stays to the side for a moment before he realizes he doesn't have an answer and snaps back up.

He appraises us and apparently we pass muster. While he's looking us up and down, I reach behind my back and pull my Detonics. Damn, I hope I remembered to cock it.

"You, Mr. Saxton, will be useful as a template for a new soldier. You have skills we can use to train our troops," the man says, pointing at Wilford.

His finger moves to me. "You have tactical skills and a moral flexibility that will come in handy. Miss Hayha will make excellent breeding stock in lieu of her original role in this world."

"Wait, these guys get to train troops and I'm what? A hole and a womb?" Jessica says, sounding pissed.

"What I am offering you is to become the mother of a new race. A race that will fix the world," the man says solemnly.

"Not interested," Jessica says.

"Your cooperation is not strictly necessary," the man responds.

"Yeah," I say. "I'm going to have to agree with her. Now, correct me if I'm wrong, comrades, but I think I can safely speak for all of us when I say, go eat a bowl of dicks."

I wait patiently for the guy to get hung up on the strange idiom. When he tilts his head to the side, I pull the Detonics up and shoot him in the face.

A .45 caliber round is a heavy, slow round that transmits its power directly into the target, often without going all the way through a person. A bullet may not seem like it could be heavy, but trust me, they can. My hollow point bullets weight about 15 grams each and travel at right around 1000 feet per second. That's a lot of force concentrated into a small area.

The bullet finds its mark and the man's head snaps back and he collapses in a heap.

Everything stops. The apes freeze in their tracks and Wilford claps me on the back.

The man immediately stands back up like he's got strings attached to him. Without a word he points at us and the apes explode through the doorway with fire in their eyes. Jessica doesn't hesitate and her hand cannon rips through the first wave like the apes are butter made of meat. Wilford opens up almost immediately after her and I pick up the strays.

I don't know how many we go through, each taking turns reloading while the other two fire. Needless to say, it doesn't take long before we start to run low on ammunition. Jessica is especially in a bad way since shotgun shells are so damned huge. Fortunately, Mr. Perfect runs out of soldiers before we run out of bullets and we wind up in an uneasy sort of truce; he can't get us and we can't get through him.

Ducked back behind the huge desk we discuss our options.

"I say we charge him," Wilford says.

"Go for it," Jessica says. "We'll back you up."

"I might have an idea," I say.

"You're going to charge him," Jessica says.

I shoot her a look.

She just shrugs and says, "Well, someone needs to charge him."

"Why don't you charge him?" Wilford asks.

"You're taller," she says. "And probably bullet proof."

"Let's focus, kids," I say.

Wilford takes a moment to peek his head over the desk. "He's still watching us."

"How many rounds do you have left?" Jessica asks Wilford.

"Um, about five if I'm not mistaken. You?"

"Looks like three or four. I've got a couple magazines for my pistol, six rounds each," she replies.

I pull the black pistol out my jacket and hand it to Wilford. "Try this," I tell him.

Every time I've touched this gun it's done absolutely nothing, but something tells me he'll have better luck. The guy who I stole this from was a minion of Fear, you could shoot him and he'd immediately heal. Cut him and he'll shrug it off. Sound like anyone else you know? Wilford may be artificial, but all signs are pointing to some similarity.

When he touches the gun, it immediately starts humming.

"Careful," I tell him. "It puts big holes in things."

The strange gun chirps happily, like it's excited and ready to destroy something.

Wilford grins and leans over the desk taking aim at the perfect man. The man must not recognize the weapon because he just cocks his head to the side again and stares at Wilford, completely unconcerned.

The thump gun is humming full bore now. A cheerful ping and the weapon is ready. Jessica and I, already familiar with what the gun can do immediately drop behind the desk. Wilford fires and the explosion is almost immediately followed by the sound of splats.

When I poke my head over the desk there are parts of the perfect man scattered across the hallway and Wilford is staring at the gun grinning like an idiot.

"Steven, I don't say this very often, but thank you very much," he tells me.

"Glad you like it," I tell him. "Shall we get out of here?"

Jessica is peering over the desk, somehow managing to look both bemused and disgusted at the same time. "Gross."

"Let's roll," I tell them and step around the desk.

Damn, what a mess.

Did you know when someone dies their body completely relaxes? Sure, of course. Everyone knows that. It's a stupid question, pay it no mind. Well, your bowels and bladder are controlled by muscles and guess what happens when those muscles relax.

The room is filled with blood, dead apes, pieces of the formerly perfect man, and various bodily effluvia. It reeks to high heaven of bodies and gunpowder. The floor is slick and I nearly slip. This is the damnable thing about gun fights and death. In the movies it's all clean, maybe the odd blood splat on the wall, but the result of a real firefight is decidedly more disgusting. The coppery smell of blood, the reek of torn organs and emptied bowels mixes with the burnt gunpowder. Put the sight and the smell together and you've got a recipe for never wanting to eat again.

Wilford is used to this, I'm somewhat prepped for it, but it takes Jessica by surprise. To her credit, she manages to avoid puking, but she's pretty ashy by the time we get out of the room.

Down the hall, a firefight is raging among Eve's team and another set of apes. As we watch one of the apes flies out the door and smashes against the wall. That's what I like about Eve; she's very hands-on.

Wilford doesn't wait, just calmly aims the black gun at a group of apes and fires. The apes explode in blast of spiky fur and blood.

A few moments later, Mr. Perfect's perfect twin comes flying out of the room with an angry Valkyrie stalking out behind him. He hits the wall and bounces off, but immediately comes up swinging. His punches are a blur, but Eve casually blocks them and hits him so hard he bounces off the wall and back into her waiting fist.

"You piece of shit!" I hear her yell before she casually snaps his neck and tosses him down the hall.

She brushes a stray lock of hair out of her face and takes a look around. Apparently she hadn't noticed the ape juice all over the place because she does a double take and jumps a little. She finally turns around and notices us, gives us a little wave and walks down the hall to find the limp body of the perfect man she tossed away.

A second later Frank pokes his head out the door, looks around at the blood and guts and says simply, "Hi guys, what's up?"

"Oh, nothing," Jessica says. "How 'bout you?"

A loud "Mother fucker!" echoes out of the room just before Jacob strides out, eyes wide at the carnage surrounding him.

"Got any more of those guns?" Jacob asks.

"Sorry, only one we've got and only he can fire it," I tell him.

"It's got some kind of genetic trigger lock and he's one of a very few people who has the key."

"Dammit," Jacob curses, "I knew those bastards would find a way to take guns away from civilians."

"This is a little more complex than a simple trigger lock," Wilford tells him. "I can feel this gun, deep in my head. It talks to me, tells me what it sees and how best to kill it. It's alive. It's amazing."

"Seriously?" I ask him. "It's talking to you?"

"Boys and their guns," Jessica sighs.

"No, really, I can feel it in my head," Wilford says. His brow furrows like he's listening to something he doesn't quite care to understand. "Steven, this is a god killer."

"Groovy, man," I tell him. I've got bigger worries than Wilford and his happy pistol.

Eve is still rifling around the corpse of the perfect man, digging through the pockets of his suit. She's obviously looking for something, but I'll be damned if I can figure out what it is.

"What are these things?" Frank asks, kicking a large chunk of one of the apes.

"Some kind of soldier they were working on here," I tell him. "Didn't you guys have a scientist?"

"A what?" Jacob asks.

"A scientist. Our room had a scientist who was waiting for us," I tell him. "Well, waiting for Wilford. Actually, now that I think of it, I suspect Jessica and I may have been extra baggage. Oh, well. He told us they were working on reengineering the human race here. They wanted to, how did he put it? Wipe away the trash?"

"Removing the effluvia," Jessica says.

"Yeah, that was it. Effluvia. Remove the effluvia that were clogging up the pipes. Or something. Those perfect looking guys were the new master race; the apes were some sort of soldier. I suspect they were going to use the perfect guys as the carrot and the apes as the stick."

"Sick fucks," Frank says. "I hate people who think they're better than everyone else."

Eve comes strutting down the hall a few moments dangling a set of keys. "Anyone interested in seeing the basement?"

32 | Underground. Again.

The key is a flat piece of metal with no teeth, just grooves on the side that control the lock mechanism. Considering what we now know about the place, the little piece of plain metal seems downright pedestrian. The keychain even has lucky rabbit's foot on it, like you could hop in your hot-rodded Model-T and head down the malt shop for sock hop. Even the rest of the elevator has that old-school vibe that you only see in government installations that haven't been upgraded in decades.

Of course, this place is built into the side of a mesa and was highly classified to boot, so maybe they just never got a chance to upgrade the security.

The aging elevator rumbles to a stop with a deeply satisfied groan a few moments after we start down. One of us, not that I'm naming any names (cough, Eve, cough) felt it was best to start at the top and work our way down. I felt we should go all the way down and work our way up. Seven foot of still keyed up Valkyrie convinced me of the error in my logic.

The doors open and the two guards who were waiting for us with guns drawn immediately open fire. Naturally, we'd planned on this. Eve is standing in front, the rest of us are ducked around the sides of the elevator.

Sound familiar? It's worked in the past so why the hell not use it again?

The guards are armed with MP5s, clones of the one Wilford is carrying. They're standard-issue close quarter submachine guns designed by Heckler & Koch. It can fire 900 9mm rounds per minute at a muzzle velocity right around 400 meter per second.

In short, it can put a whole lot of lead in the air in a very short amount of time.

Like all people, the guards focus on the primary threat: the large woman standing right in front of them, and open fire. Eve is a strong woman, but the hail of bullets still pushes her against the back wall of the elevator where she slumps in heap. She plays possum really well and the guards are almost convinced she's dead. One of them fires one last shot into her chest just to be sure before one of them calls, "All clear."

At that point Wilford and I pop out and drop them.

Don't feel too sorry for them, they should have realized something was up when the bullets hitting Eve didn't throw up the usual spray of blood. Amateurs.

So much for the quiet approach.

We're in a straight white hallway with traditional DOD signs scattered around the walls. The signs point the way to absolutely everything you could possibly want: bathrooms, break rooms, labs 1-10, labs 11-20, mimeograph room, telephones, etc. That's one thing you've got to love about government installations; they may be a huge pain in the ass to get into, but once you're inside there's a map on every corner and more signs than you can shake a stick at.

A map on the wall displays the layout of the complete installation. This floor is laid out in straight line connecting two large areas marked storage. Off the main line are things like offices, quarters, mess halls, labs and so on. The two floors below are laid out basically the same way, but offices and quarters give way to maintenance and storage the further down you go. The two floors above us are marked as decoys. I'd wondered about that. I'll bet the top two floors were for whatever government functionaries showed up. Show them the top floors, tell them everything else is dangerous, get to keep your funding. Places like this live and die by their funding.

Here are the first real signs of life, but the place is still deserted. I'd expect more than just guards to be here. Where are the scientists, the secretaries, the bureaucrats?

There are surprisingly few guards down here, none of them exactly on the ball. That's the problem with advanced security systems: it's too easy to become reliant on them. These guys have probably spent all their time letting the perfect men and those advanced ape guys protect this place and have become completely complacent.

At the end of the hall is set of double doors with "No

Uncleared Access" written across them in giant letters. Since we stopped being quiet, Wilford uses the thump gun and the doors explode inward. After the debris settles Eve steps through and stops dead in her tracks.

When I peak around I can see why. Rows and rows of tanks fill the large room, each of which contains one of the apes at some stage of growth. Some of the apes are nearly full grown, some are babies. The big ones are pretty terrifying. I didn't get much of a look at them earlier but they're monsters on a "made by a mad scientist" scale. The babies are surprisingly cute, but their big eyes are empty and there's something so off, so alien about them that even the young ones are the stuff of nightmares. You can imagine one of the babies playfully crawling into your lap and gleefully eating your face.

The tanks are big, eight feet tall and four feet across at least and filled with some viscous, greenish liquid. Bubbles gently trickle up from grates in the floor of each tank. Looking at the liquid, even behind the glass of the tank, makes me feel dirty. There are tubes everywhere, wrapping around the tanks and snaking across the floor. It seriously looks like something out of monster movie.

The room has grate floors, decorated in 50s industrial décor, grays and pale greens. Under the grates you can see the subfloor which looks like it may have been carved out rock. There are lots of tubes, cables, and occasional flashing lights. The signs warn of disastrous consequences if strict adherence to procedure is not observed. Overhead, the lights are hanging circles covered with chicken wire, spilling rings of sickly pale light on the floor.

On each of the tanks is a red flag with a white circle and swastika in the center. It looks like our German friends have taken over.

"I totally did Nazi that coming," I mutter.

"Did you just make a Nazi pun?" Jessica asks me.

"What? Me? No way," I tell her.

"You are so going to Hell," she says and brushes past me.

"How many tubes do you think there are?" Franks asks as he steps inside.

"Thousands," Eve says. "And probably more on other levels."

"What do you want us to do, boss?" Jacob asks, looking slightly unnerved at being around these things.

"Do you have anything in your bag of tricks that will take out the room?" Eve asks him.

"This room is at least a couple hundred feet on a side, it would take thousands of pounds of high explosive to take this place out," he tells her. "Maybe if we can collapse the whole place."

"While I agree these things are dangerous, killing them all is mission creep," Wilford says. "We're here to find a weapon to kill a god, remember?"

"He has a point," I say, staring at the tube in front of me. The ape thing inside is young, probably still being accelerated into adulthood. Its large eyes are watching me emotionlessly.

Have you ever been around a sociopath? I mean a true, honest-to-God, sociopath. There's something terrifying about them. A true sociopath has no concept that other people really exist and have feelings and emotions. Sociopaths are like human lizards, soulless and unnerving.

That's how it feels to look into the eyes of this baby ape floating a vat of liquid. It doesn't care that I'm watching. It doesn't care if I live or die. I can still see the traces of humanity, fading from the edges of this thing. It's then that it hits me; these things were at least partially made from humans.

"He has a point, this is mission creep. But these things need to go," I say.

"Why?" Wilford asks.

"They're made from people," I say. "People and something else, but they're made from people."

"What? Like some kind of monstrous Soylent?" Frank asks.

"Well, to be fair, regular Soylent was pretty monstrous, but basically, yeah," I tell him. "Look at them. They're intended to be the soldiers for some kind of New World Order; they'll roll over everyone and won't feel a damned thing when they do."

"You didn't give a damn when you started your own little New World Order," Wilford says with a hint of an edge in his voice.

He has a point, I guess. We were all so pissed at the world we gleefully loosed a horror on the world, thinking it would only do the one thing we wanted to see done. Dreamer killed Congress, but mostly because he felt like it would be fun. From there he branched out, started taking over.

That's the problem with biological weapons; they tend to have a mind of their own.

"I had a beef with Congress," I tell him.

"A beef?" Wilford almost shouts. "You had a beef? You don't unleash gods on people you have a 'beef' with."

"Fine!" I shout back, "I hated them and wanted them dead. They fucked over the country all their putrid little lives. I celebrated when Congress was killed. Saved the video and watched it over and over while I ate popcorn and laughed!

"These guys," I tell him, motioning to the apes around us, "will destroy everything. You, me, them. Wipe it clean and replace it with a world ruled by those perfect assholes. You got your answers, and you didn't even have to go to D.C. You know what they did to you. You and I, we're just meat to the people that set this place up."

"We're less than meat to the gods that want us dead," Wilford replies. "These things are bad, I'll grant you that, but there is a more immediate concern."

"We're here right fucking now," I yell.

"Send someone else in. Blow the lid off this place," he says calmly.

"Sure, let the U.S. Government know what's going on down here. Do you think they'll just burn it and call it good?"

"No," he says. "I can't, but we still need to worry about a god."

"Two gods," Jessica says.

"Right, two gods. That we know of."

"Guys," Frank motions, "The tubes under the floor are all going the same direction. Maybe we can kill all of these things in one fell swoop."

"Right, then," Eve says. "Let's kick this place over and get back on task."

The hoses on the floor congregate into a single large hose at some sort of the nexus point about thirty feet away. That large hose is as big around as a man's torso and made of some kind of dull gray metal. Part of me wonders what's inside of the hose, the rest of me really doesn't entirely want to know.

The hoses do, in fact, meet in the center of the room. They're all patched into some kind of thrumming machinery, a humongous metal canister that sinks through the floor. When I look down, I can see the whole canister descending into the lower levels.

"I think we need to go the bottom," I say.

Out of the corner of my eye, I see a shadow silently glide over the tubes. The ape inside reaches its hands out, but the shadow is gone before the ape can get it.

I feel my hear sink. We were so close.

"I think you are at the bottom," a voice says. "The nice thing about being at the bottom is there is nowhere else to fall to."

I turn around and find an older gentleman in a freshly pressed suit calmly staring at us. The suit is deep blue, almost black, with fine stripes. His shirt is so white it hurts your teeth to look at it. But the tie is the amazing thing. Black as night in North Korea and dotted with pinpricks of light that flicker in and out like stars in the heavens.

He's got a cane in his right hand, but he's not leaning on it. I get the feeling it's a prop since he's holding it so casually. Jauntily. If that's a word, he's holding it jauntily.

His hair is slightly gray around the temples, but a deep ebony black everywhere else and perfectly coifed. Not a hair is out of place, as if each strand was personally terrified of what would happen if it got out line.

If the perfect men radiated a cruel, unforgiving kind of light, this man exudes a calming darkness. Unfortunately, it's the kind of calming darkness you only get when you've fallen down the well and given up. He's been called many things in his long existence: Morpheus, Nodens, Bormanus, Muludaianinis, The Sandman.

I prefer to call him Dreamer.

33 | When Dreams Have Come

Dreamer hasn't come alone. He's got at least a dozen armed guards, decked head to toe in black. Each is wearing a balaclava and only their eyes are visible, tinted glowing black by Dreamer's touch. They've each got an MP5 pointed at us, the laser sights painting little red dots on chests and heads. Well, Jacob's, Frank's, and, presumably, my chest and head. No one is aiming at Eve, probably warned that bullets won't harm her. No one is aiming at Jessica. No one is aiming at Wilford, either, because he's nowhere to be found.

The bastard slunk off and disappeared.

There's one guy in front, standing guard over Dreamer with a feverish intensity. Interestingly, his eyes are normal brown, but they dance with the madness that you usually only see in the guy who lives behind the 7-11 and thinks the ants are his friends. This guy hasn't been touched, at least not directly, and he's under no overt control other than religious fervor.

"Hello, Steven," Dreamer says with the calm you only get from extremely long life. "Hello, Eve. So nice of you to clear out the rabble down here."

"Hi, buddy," I say. "How's it hanging?"

"Ah, Steven, always joking," he tells me with a huge smile. "It is hanging low and lazy, thank you for asking."

This isn't exactly how I'd planned on having this play out. I had really expected to find something in here to kill this guy and get everyone off our asses for a while. The absolute last thing I expected to encounter in this place was the God of Dreams and his entourage of brain dead gunslingers.

A sudden sound makes everyone jump. Something just went crashing down hole around the canister.

"Sorry," Jacob says. "I'm kind of clumsy."

"Not a problem, I assure you," Dreamer says, dismissing his ungainliness with a casual wave.

He gestures to his guard to lower their weapons and steps up to me. He puts his hands on my shoulders and squeezes gently. "Steven. You did everything I expected of you. I knew I could trust you to complete the tasks I set before you. I knew I had chosen well when I chose you."

Dreamer's eyes settle on Jessica and glitter with stars. Literally. In fact, come to think of it, those may be actual stars in his eyes. He is a god, after all.

"Thank you for bringing her, Steven," he says, eyes locked on Jessica.

"No one brought me, asshole," Jessica tells him calmly.

"You're cute when you're naïve," Dreamer tells her. "Everything was part of my plan. I nudged you along and you all did exactly what I wanted."

"What did you want?" Frank asks him.

"What everyone wants, god and human alike. I want control. I'm tired of hiding out in the shadows with the rest of these fools. We were meant to rule you, not shy away from you."

"Won't Begay stop you?" I ask.

"Not in slightest, Bilagáana. We hatched this plan together," John says, stepping out from behind the armed guards.

"You son of a bitch," Eve hisses at him. "I can't believe I danced with you."

"Is that what the kids are calling it?" I ask.

I simply could not resist, I mean the joke was hanging right there in front of me, how could I not go for it? Eve shoots me a look, but doesn't say a word.

"What's the deal with brown eyes over there?" I ask, pointing at the guy with normal eyes.

"This is Sergeant John Ketch," Dreamer says with a faint smile.

"Is he some kind of action hero? With a name like that, he should be," Frank says.

"Sergeant Ketch is quite capable, I assure you. He is everything Steven was supposed to be, brave, strong, loyal. The good Sergeant is a true believer, the first of many to make the journey to me. Unfortunately, they will have to wait a while so I can finish my plans. No matter, though. My churches are churning out true believers at a simply phenomenal rate."

"That's why you set up churches," Eve says with acid in her voice.

"My dear, that's the only reason people set up churches. Churches are a mechanism to create and maintain power, plain and simple. People go to churches not to be saved, but to be told what to do. It's actually for the best. Most people are simply not good at making choices, so it's best someone handles decision making for them."

"And the fact that your preachers get to have sex with the parishioners, what's that? A job perk?" I ask. "Your boy in Albuquerque was certainly busy going to town."

"Indeed he was, and thank you, by the way, for waiting for them to finish. That showed a lot of class," Dreamer says. "That man, George W. Smith, was one of the first minds I touched. He was a scientist working in that cell where they kept me. He had been preparing for my coming for quite some time. It was a pity to see him die, but I must admit I enjoyed the fight.

"I also enjoyed letting you think you understood my motives and my history with Mr. Smith, letting you think you could read my mind. All I had to do was plant thoughts and you did exactly what I told you to do.

"But, to answer your question, yes. My preachers can feel free to use the parishioners however they deem fit. That's really the point of having parishioners, isn't it?"

"So, what's the plan here?" I ask.

"Ah, yes. The plan. Well, the plan is simple. I need an army and this place was building one. Those apes are easy to control, but I couldn't take them over as long as their caretakers were still alive. The caretakers are gone, which freed me to take their army. Now, Steven, are you with me or against me?"

"What do you think?" I ask.

"I think you like power. I think you would make an excellent second in command."

I have to admit, there's a certain allure to it.

"Of course," he says, gesturing at Jessica, "she's going to be mine. I hope this won't become some kind of strange love triangle between us all. That wouldn't do at all."

I sigh. Even if the stakes didn't include Jessica, I just couldn't sell out the whole world to another despot. "I'm sorry, I can't join you."

"I'm sorry to hear that. I hope it's not just because of her."

"I'm … it's … it's not that simple, but, yes, it's partially because of her. Also, I'm not sure the world needs another dictator."

"You realize you can't stop me, right," Dreamer says, stepping close to me. This close, I can smell him. He smells of cinnamon and stardust. "This is your last chance, Steven. Join me. Join me or I will take her by force, and bend your will until you beg to join me."

"We're not exactly a soft target, you know," I say, not backing down an inch. "You may be a God, but we've got a Valkyrie."

"A Valkyrie!" he says, stepping back and smiling. "She's a demigoddess at best. Allow me to show you a trick."

With a snap of his fingers, Eve's eyes turn ebony black and her features go slack.

"She lives by rules, Steven. Demigods and demigoddesses exist to serve us. She's even easier to take over than you will be."

Shit. Shit. Shit. Outgunned, out maneuvered, out manned. Our ace in the hole just turned. This whole mission just went to shit in a few short minutes.

"Final chance, Steven," Dreamer says.

I shake my head, no.

"Take them," Dreamer says.

Jacob leaps forward, a huge shining knife in his meaty fist. The attack is completely unexpected and he takes out two of the guards before anyone knows what happened. As he spins around to take a third, Ketch calmly shoots Jacob in the stomach.

Jacob's knife clatters to the floor as he sinks to his knees. Frank charge out and grabs Jacob before he can fall. "Son of a bitch, you didn't have to shoot him!" Frank yells at Ketch.

"Let this be an object lesson, Steven. The first test for you. Join me and I'll see to it he gets stitched up. Otherwise, he can die in a pool of his own blood in a dank cell."

Dreamer motions to three of the guards. "Take her to her quarters, prepare her. I'll be along shortly. Eve, take care of my lieutenant."

The guards grab Jessica. She kicks up quite a fuss, breaking the first guy's nose before the other two completely overwhelm her. As they drag her off, I yell, "I'll get you out!"

"I've got this," she yells back. "Save Eve."

I look at Eve and wonder just how in the hell I'm going to save her. The last thing I remember is Eve's fist coming at me before everything goes black.

* * * *

When I come to, my head hurts like nothing I've ever felt before. I'm in a bare cell somewhere in the installation. There are stone walls on three sides around me and rusting bars in front. The floor and ceiling are smooth stone.

This place was carved straight into the mesa. Even if I had a jackhammer, it would take me a decade to go through the solid rock to the outside world.

Bastards couldn't even give me a bench to sit on or toilet.

I slowly stagger to my feet and check the bars. Completely solid. I was kind of hoping the rust had eaten through the bars, but lady luck does not seem to be with me right now. A quick, final glance around tells me there is no way out of this cell except through the currently locked door.

Outside the door, I have four guards. Three regular slaves of the Dreamer and one Valkyrie with black eyes.

"Hey, Eve," I hiss. "Open the door."

Her dark eyes swing toward me, but there's no recognition or spirit in them. She's just a puppet.

"Hey, guys," I yell toward the three guards. "I need to take a leak. What does a guy have to do to take a leak around here?"

No response.

Shit.

How can they be so checked out? It's like they're asleep or something.

Shit.

How could I be so dumb?

Don't answer that.

Eve's sleeping and dreaming. I've never tried to get into her dreams, but how different could it possibly be? She's a demigoddess. That means at least part human, right? I mean, I never really studied mythology, but I seem to remember demigods and demigoddesses were half human, half god. If that human part is in there, it must dream.

I sit cross-legged in the middle of my cell. Above me is a spider descending on a tiny thread. Normally, I'm petrified of spiders, but I'm more scared of dying alone and forgotten. My eyes close. As my brain starts to slow down, I reach out for any minds around me. There are four in this room, and they feel like stars in the night sky. Three of them are tiny, insignificant kinds of things. The other, though, that one is spectacular. Eve glows like the full moon.

It takes an active effort, but my mind finally finds a way into hers.

34 | Eve

Eve's mind is a jumble of emotions both alien and pedestrian. She controls herself with a will of steel and, externally, she's solid. Inside is a mixture of images, a pastiche of hundreds of competing visions like a wall of monitors each playing a different YouTube video. Human dreams are singular things. You dream of the time you fought the Empire and won. You dream of the home run, or fighting ninjas, or the green pants with no one inside of them, or the son you'll never see again. You dream one dream at a time.

Eve dreams thousands of dreams at a time. Some of her dreams are memories; visions so fantastic they defy imagination. She dreams of things I'll never see with my own eyes; gods charging down from the clouds on lightning bolts and toasting to the end of the world. She also dreams of everyday things like eating a hot dog in a mall and watching the sun set over some frigid ocean up north. If there was ever a doubt in my mind that she's something other than human, being inside her head makes it very plain that she is more than I am. More than I'll ever be.

The sheer array of what she keeps in her head at any given time is absolutely stunning. More stunning, and speaking to his power, is just how easily Dreamer took her over. It took him absolutely no effort to completely seize control of Eve. A small part of my brain, the part that's not completely overwhelmed by Eve's thoughts, wonders what Dreamer's mind looks like. Probably so far beyond anything I can understand it would just look like a single 10-sided die sitting on a slice of pizza.

I have plenty of time here. Dream-time exists on a completely different scale than real-time. When I was a kid I used to wake up to the radio. A song would play and I would wake up, usually after hearing the song in my dreams for what felt like hours. In reality, the song was only a few minutes long and turned out to be some bubble gum pop crap that passed for music in the late 80s.

Yes, the late 80s. The 1980s. That wonderfully decadent decade that brought us neon colors and Oingo Boingo albums.

Great. Now "Dead Man's Party" is going to be stuck in my head for another few years. Oh, well, since it's in my head and I'm in Eve's head, she'll get to relish it, too.

Off in the distance, or whatever passes for distance in Eve's head, is a solitary dream lying hidden away, protected, but neglected. As I focus on it, it grows more real until it feels like I can touch it. It wraps around me and, with a pop!, I fall into it.

In her dream, Eve is in the remains of a battlefield in some part of the Midwest. I'm sure the wingnuts out here were pleased as punch that the end of the world came in their backyard. There are bodies everywhere and not all of them human. When I look into the distance I can see the ruins of a once mighty city, its elegant, organic structure smashed and broken. Black smoke from an unseen fire drifts lazily into an already soot gray sky.

With all the destruction and bodies it takes me a moment to realize I'm in the suburbs outside of some future city. Across the street is a strip mall with a nail salon, a comic book store, and a day-old bakery. I'm standing on the sidewalk that wraps around a park.

The park is toast, plain and simple.

The slide is bent in two and the play structures are melted, pieces of the cheap plastic dripping down like stalagmites. Or stalactites. Whatever.

In the center of the park, sitting on a Merry-Go-Round that's missing about half of its pie piece panels sits Eve. She's wearing red leather and metal armor, her long blonde hair twisted into pig tails that manage to look menacing instead of cute. A discarded helmet, shield, sword, and several guns lie on the ground, haphazardly strewn around the Merry-Go-Round. It looks like she has something in her lap, but I can't make it out from here.

Closer to the Merry-Go-Round I can see Eve's armor is pitted and torn. She's covered with blood and her left arm is resting delicately on whatever is in her lap. Eve is grinning like a maniac and there's a touch of madness in her gray eyes. When she looks at me I feel a small pang of worry that she'll hop up and rip me in half for transgressing into her dreams, but she just waves and motions me over.

The thing in her lap turns out to be the body a dead warrior. Whatever killed him tore him up pretty good before it finished him off. Eve's left arm looks strange, and her right arm is distractedly stroking the warrior's hair.

"Push me," she says as I get within earshot.

"Push you?" I ask.

"Yes, push me. Make this thing work."

"What happened here, Eve?"

"You like stories, don't you? Push me and I'll tell you a story, Steven."

"You're freaking me out," I say,

I know I should stop walking toward her, some kind of sixth sense tingling that this is a bad place and I'm not supposed to be here. The colors are all desert colors, reds, tans and other varying shades of browns. This is the Midwest, it's supposed to be green here.

"Come on," she tells me. "Push me."

I take a tentative step forward and the ground doesn't fall out from under my feet.

"You're just feeling the remnants of me when I get keyed up and fight," Eve tells me. "It's meant to make people think twice before attacking me."

The closer I get the more the unease intensifies. Each step forward causes my heart to beat faster and my brow to sweat. Every time my foot hits the ground, I get a little more panicked. I need to get out of here, but I can't get out of here until I've talked her out of this dream.

When I'm close enough, she reaches out her hand and I take it. A simple up and down shake and the panic disappears.

"What is that feeling?" I ask her, wiping my brow on my shirt.

"It's a way I have of keeping people so scared they won't approach me. It's always easier to fight when the opponent is scared," she says with sly grin.

"It works. I'm not even here looking for trouble, and I felt like turning tail and running for all I'm worth."

"That's the point," she tells me. "Are you going to push me or not?'

"Which arm did you break?" I ask her, feeling snarky.

She holds up her left arm and winces when it moves. I've seen this woman get shot, point blank, and shrug off the bullets. She's borderline indestructible and something managed to break her arm so badly that a shard of bone is sticking out of her forearm. Now I feel like a total ass for asking that snarky question.

With a sigh, I push the Merry-Go-Round and she slowly floats away. The Merry-Go-Round creaks something fierce and goes tick, tick, tick, thunk every half turn, climbing a little and then suddenly dropping down. Eve smiles at me as she passes and, for the first time since I've known her, she looks innocent and happy. She has that look that people get when the weight of the world is finally lifted from their shoulders.

We spend a quiet eternity of me slowly pushing her around in circles and her smiling about it. The only sound is the creaks and ticks and thunks of the Merry-Go-Round.

Now that I think of it, this place is dead silent. No birds chirping. No bugs clattering for sex with lady bugs. There's not even a breeze. The whole world is dead, save the two of us.

"You owe me a story, you know," I tell her when she passes again.

"Keep pushing and I'll tell you a story."

When she passes again a furrow has crossed her brow.

"I'm not sure you'd call how I came to be being born, exactly, but it will work for our purposes. I was born in the early 800s. I'm an answer to the final question of this world. It was always my role to prowl the battlefields of the world looking for recruits. We call it choosing."

"You choose the dead?" I ask her.

"And the living. I get to decide who will live in a given conflict. I also get to choose the dead, recruit them into fighting this battle."

"What is this battle?" I ask, curiosity getting the best of me. Sure, I've got problems back in the real world, but it's not often you get Eve to open up about anything.

"It's the end of the world," she tells me, gazing at the body on her lap.

"Isn't there supposed to be a giant snake that kills Thor?"

"You shouldn't take your myths so literally. This is the final battle between those who want to keep the world running and those who want to dismantle it and build something new."

"Which side were you on?"

"The winning side," she tells me.

"How many of your people survived?"

"Me."

"Any others?"

"Just me," she sighs.

We wait and listen to the tick, tick, tick, thunk that pierces the silence.

"Eve?" I ask.

"Yes."

"Begay told me I needed Jessica more than she needed me. What did he mean by that?"

Eve is silent as the Merry-go-round completes a couple of turns and I'm wondering if she heard me when she finally says, "How many times has she saved your life?"

"A couple, why?"

"How many times have you saved hers?"

"Probably about the same. Well, at least once that I can think of right off hand."

"You were supposed to be here," Eve says as she comes around me again. "You were supposed to fight in this battle."

"Sorry to disappoint," I tell her.

"It means you didn't die in a battle," she says simply. "You have to die in a battle to fight this fight."

"Who's the dude?"

"The dude? Oh. Him. He's Abdul al Azhred. We were lovers once, a long time ago. He died saving me."

"al Azhred? The guy that wrote the *Necronomicon*?"

"A myth. There is no *Necronomicon*," she tells me while she strokes his hair. "He was a mystic, to be sure, and a great lover. He fought well and, because of his actions, the battle was won."

"Speaking of battles, there's one brewing back in reality and I could really use your help."

"What makes you think this isn't real?"

"Well, uh. It's a dream. You're dreaming, that's how I can get in here," I stammer.

It is just a dream, right?

"All this time with his fingers in your brain and you still haven't figured out that dreams and reality aren't that far apart," Eve tells me with a sad smile. "The two of them can come together sometimes and make magical things happen."

"Okay," I tell her, "the part of reality where I'm trapped in a cage and you're a zombie puppet needs your help. Jacob's been shot, Frank's trying his damnedest to keep him alive, Jessica's been captured, and Wilford fucked off to do God only knows what."

Eve strokes Abdul's hair one final time before her gray eyes flash and darken.

"Ready to wake up?" she asks.

"Ready to kick ass and take names?" I respond.

I feel myself being flung out of her mind, falling backwards through whatever passes for space in her head before waking up in my dank cell with a spider crawling over my face. Normally, I'd smash the damned thing, but for some reason I feel it's better to gently pick it up and put down so it can go find some food, or whatever it is that spiders look for; bugs, safe places, the souls of the innocent.

Outside the cell, Eve's eyes go from coal black to angry gray, the color of storm clouds before the downpour starts. She shakes her head a few times sending that blonde mane of hers flinging around her face.

One of the guards notices her and walks over to check on her, not realizing what he's walking into. She's a full head and half taller than him. As he cranes his eyes up to look a blur smashes him. Even unarmed she's a force to be reckoned with and crushes the side of his face with a single fist.

The other two wise up and try to work together to take her down. One circles left, the other right, encircling her. She waits patiently for them to get into position, eyes closed, body relaxed. When they stop she breathes deeply and exhales slowly. The guards have their guns trained on her, unsure of what to do against this giant that just dropped their partner with a single blow.

Apparently they haven't gotten the memo about that whole bullet-proof thing she's got going on.

There follows that interminable moment before the first blow is thrown or the first trigger is pulled. Eve's eyes open and before either guard can react the Valkyrie has disarmed both of them, kicked one across the room and has the other by the throat. His legs are pirouetting a couple of feet off the ground while he tries to break her iron grip on his throat.

A single squeeze and the man goes limp in her hand. Eve's eyes peer into his dead face, searching for some spark that only she knows about. I guess she didn't find it because she sighs and drops the corpse unceremoniously on the ground.

Standing in front of the bars of my cage she says, "How do you keep getting yourself into these situations?"

"I keep following you around," I tell her.

"Well, that doesn't sound too bright."

"I'm a slow learner."

Eve effortlessly tears the door off the cell and tosses it aside before grabbing me and embracing me in a huge bear hug.

"Thank you for pulling me out of his dream," she says.

"Can't breathe," I reply.

"What's that?"

"Can't breathe."

"Sorry," she says and drops me.

I wind up on my ass back in my cell.

Eve's hand is over her face and she's making a choking kind of sound. At first I think she's crying, but it become obvious pretty quickly that she's laughing.

Part of me is pissed. Jessica's been kidnapped, Jacob's been shot, Wilford's been turned into god only knows what, we've got the master race trying to rewrite the world and Dreamer getting ready to take over. But even I have to admit there's something so remarkably off about the whole situation that all you really can do is laugh. Before long, we're both huddled up together laughing our asses off in the middle of my cell.

"Thanks for tearing the door off this cell," I tell her when the laughter finally subsides.

"Don't mention it," she tells me. "That's two doors I've destroyed for you."

"I'll buy you a six pack when we're done. Good beer, not that swill you usually drink."

"I like what I like, but I'll take you up on the offer," she tells me. "Let's get this done. I'm thirsty."

"What's the plan, boss?"

"Grab some weapons, kill everything that moves that's not one of ours," she says.

The guards had MP5 SMGs, spare magazines, knives, body

armor, everything we need. I miss my knife and my shotgun, though.

35 | Feeling Stabby

The plan entails killing a bunch of mutant apes and one God of Dreams, freeing our comrades, figuring out what Wilford is up to, and rescuing the damsel in distress. It's real hero stuff and would make a great movie someday. No one would believe a word of it, but who cares? I guarantee it would be a summer blockbuster.

Eve takes the apes because Dreamer can probably control her again just as easily as he did the first time. That leaves me with Dreamer and one question that keeps pinging around in my head: how do you kill a dream? I guess I could send him a snarky rejection letter, but that just seems so petty.

Of course, one problem trumps how to kill him and this how to find him. He's here somewhere, I can feel him, but I can't lock up on his position, only that it's lower than I am.

His troops are still patrolling, but they're not exactly on the ball tonight. Dreamer's running a lot of guys and it's clearly taking a bit of a toll on him. Every now and then one of his soldiers will walk into a wall or trip over a pipe. It's no wonder he wants the apes; they're probably easier to control.

Just because the guys didn't bring their A-game doesn't mean they're not dangerous. They travel in packs of three, all armed and all wearing body armor. Wilford's gun would make short work of them, but he's not here, so I do my best to avoid the patrols.

The walls are thick and there's not much echo. That means I can't hear a damned thing until the patrols are almost on top of me, so I have to take my time, sneaking from hole to hole, shadow to shadow.

It's not easy, but the place is dark and that helps. I don't know much about the layout of this facility, which doesn't help, but at least there are maps all over the damn place. As near as I can tell, there's a set of stairs not too far from me. There are also signs that

Wilford's been here. There are pieces of a patrol all over the place and no brass on the ground. I'll bet when he hit them he did it from behind and it happened so fast none of them had a chance to return fire.

The concrete around the ambushed patrol is soaked with blood and other things best left unstated. Chunky things and pieces that resemble parts of bodies are on the floor and sliding down the walls. This didn't happen long ago and it would appear he's heading in the same direction I am.

My cell was on the second sub level and there are stairs going up and down. Up would be the smart way to go, just get away from all this crap and run away.

Sure, and spend every waking moment for the rest of my life regretting the decision to run away with my tail tucked between my legs.

I head downstairs slowly, muzzle of my MP5 leading the way, just like I was taught in combat training. At the bottom of the stairs I nudge the door open with my gun and take a peek. So far, so good.

The warehouse at the lower level still houses a whole mess of gestating apes. The green glow from the tubes is all that illuminates the area. Apparently at the bottom no one really needs to see anything. Instead of a hole in the floor, there's a large machine making a huffle-puffing sound. It's a terrifying sound that whispers stories about the end of the world.

At the end of the rows of apes stands a single man, wearing black BDUs and body armor. Ketch. Of course the believer would out think the rest of his zombie compatriots.

His MP5 is aimed directly at me and I have no doubt he's a better shot than I am. Oh, well, throw enough lead in a general direction and it's bound to hit something.

He doesn't flinch when I raise my gun and aim it down the row at him.

"I figured I'd find you down here," he says. "You computer pukes are always sneaking around in the dark. What's the matter? Afraid to stand and fight?"

"Not in the slightest," I tell him. "Are we going to throw down our weapons and fight like real men?"

"Of course not," he says and opens fire.

As soon as he starts talking I know he's going to shoot. Ketch may be an ass, but he's not an idiot. I had my finger on the trigger and dove to the side shooting an instant before he dove to the other side his gun barking fire and lead.

Turns out the ape cylinders aren't bullet-proof. Each of us had about 30 rounds in our clips and more than a handful of those 60 rounds tore into those glass walls. The glass shatters and the green liquid pours out in streams and sheets. At least a few of the apes were hit, too. Those little 9mm rounds ripped right through the delicate skin of the incomplete monsters and their blood mixed with the liquid and turned the whole room into some kind of science fiction abattoir.

The smell is revolting and the apes that weren't hit directly are dancing the funky chicken in their tubes as their life-sustaining liquid pours out over the floor.

Ketch isn't done, though. Another blast of rounds shatters the tube next to me and all I can do is duck back and hope for the best. My clip is almost empty and my spare got lost somewhere when I dove to the side.

"You missed me, you missed me, now you've got to kiss me!" I yell.

A trace of bullets explodes just above my head and I know school yard taunts aren't going to work.

The room is big, a couple hundred feet on a side and densely packed with test tube apes. This would normally give me some protection, but the tubes are clear and I have no doubt Ketch will see me running through them.

Staying low, I crawl away from the action, deeper into the primate forest. If I can flank him, I may be able to pull something off, otherwise he's going to light me up like a fire cracker and piss on my corpse. Well, I don't know for certain about the corpse-pissing thing, but he seems like the kind of guy who would do that.

The clear tubes turn out to be useful to me, too, and I catch a bit of motion in the distance. He's moving slowly, but he's moving upright and it's doing a wonderful job of giving away his position.

It takes time, but I finally manage to flank around and sneak up behind his back. His full body armor makes for a difficult shot. Can't go for center mass since his armor will protect him. All I've got is the shot to the back of the head and I've never been much of a marksman.

Line up the shot, breathe out, pull the trigger.

Click.

Shit. I'm empty and Ketch heard the click. With a growl he spins around and opens fire again. My only hope is to fall back and pray I don't take a round to the head as I'm falling.

Luckily, his shots go high. Unluckily, I'm on the ground with an empty weapon. Ketch ejects his empty magazine and starts walking straight at me as he slams another magazine in place. His fingers release bolt and I find myself staring down the barrel of a fully loaded gun.

I roll for all I'm worth, hoping I can make it out of his immediate line of sight. Bullets tear up the floor where I was and ricochet about the room.

A moving target is harder to hit. I get up and sprint away and to the side of him while bullets shatter the glass on the tubes as I pass. My gun is useless now, so I drop it and keep moving, changing direction as randomly as I can.

Running fast it dawns on me just how quiet the room got. I wonder if he's out of ammo.

Cautiously, I peek around the tube I'm hiding behind and get rewarded with a volley of bullets. The glass shatters and I get to experience the heady smell of ape juice close up. In addition to reeking to high Heaven of nameless terrors, the stuff is slicker than snot on a greased doorknob.

Scrabbling for purchase I just barely manage to get out of the way before Ketch unleashes another volley that spills more crap on the floor. Fortunately, for me, Ketch doesn't realize just how slick the stuff is and when he tries to go tearing off after me he slips and falls backward into the muck. He lands with a solid oomph and his gun slides away into the ape forest.

Funny thing about falling: it doesn't matter how much armor you're wearing it hurts. In fact, *jiu jitsu* was developed by samurai who realized punching a guy in armor would just hurt your hand, but throwing a guy in armor would knock the wind right out of him.

Ketch lands hard, testament to just how unexpected the fall was. He strikes me as the type who knows how to fall, but even the best of us can be surprised sometimes. I'd love to dart forward and drop an elbow on him, WWE-style, but moving quickly over that green goo is a good way to wind up flat on my back next to him.

I creep forward, stepping carefully until I'm right next to Ketch. Knife in hand, I plan to just drop to one knee and ram the blade into his throat. Before I can finish him, his hand reaches out and pulls my leg out from under me. I manage to twist during the fall but it's still a case of floor meet face. I catch myself before I land but my hands immediately slide out from under me when they hit the slick stuff on the floor and I face plant into the nasty stuff.

Without thinking, I plant a kick into Ketch's side and we both go sliding apart. Apparently this surface will not suffice for fighting. Ketch winds up at one edge of the goo spill and I wind up at the other. He looks a little more graceful getting up, but we both manage to get to our feet.

Guns gone and covered in goop, we face off with knives drawn.

"You know you're going to lose this one, right?" Ketch asks me with a sadistic grin. "I can't wait to cut you up. Ever feel a knife enter a body?"

"Yeah, it's not all that spectacular," I shoot back. "You should try getting laid sometime. You know, with a real woman and everything."

"When you're out of the way and we take over, I'll have every woman I want."

"Honestly, more than one is too much work."

"That bitch you brought in has you pussy whipped," he spits at me.

I know this game. He's trying to get my dander up, get me so pissed I'll do something stupid and give him a clean shot. It's the same game I tried with him earlier. Just like it didn't work with him, it's not working with me.

"Are we going to stand here all night acting tough or are you going to move so I can get this done and get some sleep?" I ask him.

"You're going to have to go through me, son."

"Fine by me," I tell him and start walking toward him.

The trick to winning a fight is to do the last thing your opponent expects. Ketch is a big, bad military guy, ready to take on anything, so it kind of throws him for a loop when his opponent just casually walks right at him.

He's strong, he's smart, and worst of all, he's experienced. That doesn't mean he's ready for anything though. The United States military has only recently started training its recruits in how to fight hand-to-hand and they're still hamstrung by the fact that they have to come up with something effective that can be taught to anyone in a minimal amount of time. Don't get me wrong, what they're teaching recruits these days is nothing to trifle with, but the lack of training time for most of these guys means they're linear and kind of predictable.

As I get closer, Ketch drops into a stable base, ready to move, but he's leaning forward and that tells me he's going to press the attack and not be ready to defend.

Back when I was studying Kenjutsu, I overheard one of the students talking about how the Karate guys at the dojo would punch over and over again. He was used to a sword where a single, solid strike is a fight ender. Kicking and punching don't work that way, you usually have to hit someone a lot before they go down. A knife is kind of in between. You can end a fight decisively with a single strike, but it's best to not rely on it.

Ketch is relaxed, knife in his forward hand, back leg ready to push off and get that magical single strike that will put me down for good. When I see him lean back slightly I realize he's getting ready to strike and just keep casually walking toward him. As soon as I enter his sphere of influence, that dangerous area where you can touch someone, first his back leg tenses to push his body forward, then the hips pick up the movement and send it to his shoulder, down his arm, and his hand shoots forward like a snake.

All I see is a blur of black steel, but I had started dodging as soon as I saw his weight shift. His right arm misses my throat by mere inches, but it's enough and it puts me on his dead side. Using my left hand, I push his knife hand away, bring my knife inside his defenses and slash at the side of his throat. It's not a deep wound, but it's probably enough. Just be safe, I keep moving until I'm behind him, grab his hair, pull his head back and jam my knife into his windpipe.

It's unlikely that he can stab me from here, but it's still possible, so I give the knife a quick twist, yank it out and give Ketch a good solid shove. He stumbles forward, gurgling and holding his throat. I'll hand this to the guy, he's tough. He manages to stay on his feet long enough to turn around and give me one last glare before he falls to his knees.

"Sorry, bro," I tell him. "You totally telegraphed that move."

His front completely soaked with blood, Ketch falls face first onto the ground and lies still.

Time to finish this.

36 | Dreamer. Again.

I got turned around during the fight and it takes me a minute to figure out where the doors are. I swear it would be so nice if people would put Exit signs in the ape factories of the world. Common decency is just a lost cause these days.

Outside the door is another plain hallway, illuminated by flickering fluorescent lights.

I don't know what it is about flickering fluorescents but they always weird me out. They remind me of the end of something. I think it stems from watching the death of the five & dimes when I was a kid. For the most part, places like TG&Y were out of business when I was growing up, but there was that one downtown that refused to go quietly into that dark night. I'd go in looking for model kits and the lights were always flickering. The owner said he couldn't afford new ones. The last time I went in, all the lights were doing flickering on and off. The place closed a week later, just before I got my allowance and could buy that Romulan Bird of Prey.

I think, when the end of the world comes, we won't have any questions about it coming. The sun will flicker on an off and we'll all know that it's time to pack our bags and look for work somewhere else.

There are several doors running down the hallway that connects my ape warehouse with whatever lies at the other end. The map in the middle is somewhat vague about what's behind the doors; they're all just listed as Special Purpose rooms. The warehouses at either end of the hallway are listed as just Storage. Whoever made these maps must have been feeling pretty lazy.

There is one standout, though, that wasn't on the maps upstairs. In the middle of the hallway, opposite the elevator, is a stairwell. The elevators plainly showed this as the lowest level and the upper level maps definitely didn't show any stairs.

Down that road, madness lies. And it's madness to be here so, ipso facto, I need to take the stairs. Or something. I like to give myself rational sounding reasons to justify the bad decisions I make. I didn't get drunk and punch a priest, I helped him understand humility. I didn't kill a senator, I moved a chair. I need to go downstairs and fight a god because it would be wrong not to do it.

The stairs are right where the map said they'd be and, unlike everything else in this place, they don't look well maintained. They have been opened recently, though, the scuff marks on the floor are proof of that.

A small voice tells me this is a bad idea. Dreamer is down there. Jessica's down there, too. I don't know how I know this, but I know it. It's like the lady or the tiger, only to get to the lady, I need to go through the tiger.

Save for a knife that's sticky with Ketch's blood, I'm unarmed. I don't know if a gun would do much good against the God of Dreams, but I'd certainly feel better if I had Mjolnir handy.

Shit.

Oh, well. Fuck it, right? What else do I have going on tonight? It's time, as Mac Bolan used to say, to live large.

The thought of my imminent death puts a smile on my face and a spring in my step and I take the stairs two at a time. At the bottom I kick open the door and yell, "Honey, I'm home!"

No one responds.

I find myself in front of two doors, both labelled "Private: Shipping." Behind one of these is Jessica, behind the other is the God of Dreams who is doing nothing more than trying to realize his own dream for once. Honestly, I don't care what he does. He could rule the world with an iron fist, crush all dissenters, tear the tags off every mattress on the planet and it wouldn't mean a damned thing to me. Hell, his enemies could whack me and I wouldn't care.

I'm not a happy person.

But either he goes or the few friends I have in the world go and it's simple math; one life, however godlike it may be, for five. I'll choose the five every time. Besides, it's not like I've got a ton of friends. Even if the numbers were even, I'd choose friends.

I use the best scientific mechanism I can to choose which door to open. In the end, it's not a complicated choice.

"Eeney meenie, miney, moe…"

The door on the left it is.

I open the door and nudge it with my shoe but there's nothing inside but darkness and stars. It feels like looking into infinity or standing on the precipice of the universe. In the middle of the room, wearing a tuxedo with no tie is the Dreamer. He's both right next to me and a brazillion miles away.

I've never really looked at him closely before. I only ever saw him as an older guy with impeccable taste in clothes, but he's so much more. His eyes are a sparkling amber, almost like flames dancing in a camp fire. His tux, which is perfectly tailored, is a smaller version of this room with stars twinkling on and off.

"Steven, so nice to see you," he says. "I'd love to stay and chat, but I do have a date."

"Sorry, buddy, I'm not here to talk, and I'd appreciate you missing that date."

"Miss out on the great Waltz? I think not. You may be my second, but I wouldn't pass up this dance for anything."

"I can't let you do this," I tell him.

"Do what? The young lady?"

"Take over."

"What do you care who rules this country? As I recall, you were rather discontented with the previous management. Have you considered that you might just be averse to authority?" Dreamer asks.

"I'm allergic to authority, not averse to it," I tell him.

"Well, your people are sometimes bright; perhaps someone has made a pill or something you could take."

He claps me on the shoulder and brushes past me, heading for the door that looks so anomalous against the star field in the room. Before he can get all the way past me, I shoot my arm out and stop him.

"I really need you to stop what you're doing," I tell him. "If you don't, I die, she dies, everyone dies."

"And how, pray tell, will all of you die?"

"One of your buddies, Fear, I guess, has a hit out on you. If I don't take you out, she takes us all out."

"Nonsense, my boy," Dreamer says with a smile. "You're with me now, perfectly safe. Now, please excuse me, I have a young lady to woo."

"That's the other thing, I don't think she's all that into you."

"You said this wouldn't get weird, Steven."

"Actually, I said nothing of the sort. You said that, not me."

"Well, nonetheless, I'm going and you can either move or be moved," he tells me. His amber eyes are squinting and I can almost feel his anger building.

This is probably not the wisest thing I've ever done. I've gone out of my way to piss people off before, but never a god. Still, it's all for the greater good, right? Or is that just I'm coming up with a flimsy justification again?

Maybe I should just be honest. I'm doing this for myself, because I don't want to see Jessica with someone else.

The knife in my hand lashes out without warning like the strike of a bullet shrimp. It's that perfect attack that a guy, if he's lucky, will see maybe twice in his lifetime. The point is almost in Dreamer's throat when he simply disappears and I hit nothing but air.

He reappears behind me and simply swats me across the room. Yes, it hurt. At least I manage to roll when I hit the ground and come up facing him. Whatever patience Dreamer had with me is gone now and his eyes are filled with the rage you only get from scorned gods.

"You dare try to kill me?" he roars.

The shadows are there now, moving about like black amoebae. You can only see them when the stars wink out in a blob-like pattern and reappear as the things move on. Their voices fill my head in a sing-song cacophony, a dozen songs all playing at once and none of them good.

Dreamer just watches as the shadows swirl about my body, spiraling closer but never quite entering touching me. I can sense their confusion. Just like with Smith in his pathetic little lunatic asylum, the shadows think I'm the Dreamer. Or at least close enough to being him that it doesn't make any difference.

"They won't attack," I tell him. "They think I'm you."

"No matter," he says.

In the blink of an eye, he's inches from me, only he's not himself anymore. He's switched to full-on nightmare mode and has reappeared as a white faceless thing. No eyes, just a pair of glowing amber dots, no nose, no mouth, yet it reeks of terror and power.

I barely manage to stop the haymaker he throws, but the second strike catches me directly in the stomach and I double over. I can feel him standing over me, getting ready to deliver the killing blow. Can't dodge because I can barely move, so I try my best to short circuit him a bit. I bring the edge of my hand straight up into his nuts and put every bit of force into it I can. The strike is a fight-ender on a human. That much power concentrated into the edge of my hand and directed at the groin will usually stop even the toughest guy in his tracks.

It has zero effect on Dreamer who calmly reaches down, grabs me by the neck and lifts me up with one hand. Slowly strangling to death, I stare into his eyes. This is it, I guess. The final enchilada, the last drop of whisky, the last steak.

His eyes are enraged, their dark amber color swirling with specks of pure hated. As my vision starts to dim it hits me; that's the way in. No matter what he changes into, his eyes remain the same.

I focus on those eyes, let myself be drawn into them, boldly go into his dream world. Just before I rush into his eyes I catch a glimpse of Wilford in the doorway. After that, it's just cold gray of nothingness, a flash of light, a burst of color and I'm in his head.

37 | Bad to Worse

I'm in a desolate landscape, flat, dull gray as far as the eye can see. This is place of potential, not actual. Unlike jumping into Eve's head where I wound up in one of her dreams, this is jumping into a whole land of dreams with no clear beginning and no clear end. Just like your dreams and mine, this place is nowhere and everywhere.

I can feel this world around me in a way I can't in the real world. The place fairly buzzes, like it wants to become. I reach out to part of the ground and feel it in my head, wrap my brain around it and make it my own. A pair of fuzzy dice forms from the gray nothingness. They're hot pink and furry and each side and opposite side add up to seven, just like they should. They feel real, but things often feel real in dreams.

There's a faint sensation of choking, a pressure around my throat and it's hard to breathe. No matter. Oxygen is for suckers and I just created a pair of fuzzy dice out of nothingness. I can create air out the nothingness here if I need to.

This would be a perfect place to be forever. People like to say stupid things like "If you can imagine it, you can become it." In the real world, that's bullshit. You can imagine all you want, but without effort you'll never become anything but a pathetic loser sitting on a shitty couch and complaining about whatever sack of shit is President these days. If all you do is imagine, you'll never accomplish a damned thing.

Here, however, it's a completely different story. I can imagine anything and it becomes real. Fuzzy dice are just the start. A cabin, a stream, a pine tree, freedom from everyone and everything. Here I can be and have everything I want.

But it will never be real. At least not in any meaningful sense of the word.

This place is would provide endless entertainment, but it would be nothing and mean nothing in the long run. It's the location equivalent of Cheetos and chocolate milk: fun for a while, but it would drag me down in the long run and I'd be reduced to making snarky comments on this world's Internet. This place is the shitty couch and if I stay here, I'll be the pathetic loser.

I close my eyes and reach out, feeling for Dreamer.

I find him, everywhere and nowhere. He is the place. I'm in his dreams, but his dreams are more than our dreams. His dreams build worlds and shatter cities. His dreams are very much the stuff of everyone else's dreams.

"You are this place, aren't you?" I ask out loud. "You don't just enjoy dreaming, you're not just a god of dreams, you are dreams."

I hear clapping behind me and Dreamer's voice says, "Very good, Steven. You figured it out all by yourself."

A gold star appears in the sky in front of me.

"Jackass," I mutter under my breath.

"You'll have to excuse me," the voice says, "I couldn't resist."

"It was pretty funny."

"See, we're not all that different, you and I."

"You have better fashion sense than I do," I say.

"It comes with the job. There are certain, how shall I put this, contractual obligations."

"Do you get casual Fridays?"

The voice laughs out loud at that. "Days are a little different for me than for you."

"You always struck me as a night owl."

"Night owl? Aren't most owls nocturnal?"

"It's a figure of speech, it means someone who enjoys the night more than the day."

"Most people sleep at night. Their dreams are my food and my power. I create the raw materials and they fill them for me. Think of how a plant turns sunlight into energy and you'll have a pretty good idea of what I do."

"What happens when you're gone?" I ask.

"Is that why you're here, Steven? To kill me?"

"Fun as this conversation is, yes. In the real world, you're choking me to death and about to take my girl. In the real world, if I don't take you out my few remaining friends will be killed."

"I told you," Dreamer says, "stay with me and I'll protect you. You could be my number one guy."

"You'd still take her, wouldn't you?"

"Of course. She was destined to be mine. You still have absolutely no idea what she is, do you?"

"What do you mean?" I ask.

"I shouldn't be surprised. She has no idea of what she is, why should you? I suspect your boss has an idea, but Eve isn't given to talk, is she?"

"Not so much, no. So, what's so special about Jessica?"

"Other than her looks?"

"And personality, too. What's so special about her? Why am I drawn to her?"

"She looks good in tight shirts. Isn't that reason enough for you humans?"

"Normally, yes, but this is more than a schoolboy crush. It's different, somehow."

"It hurts to be away from her, yes?" Dreamer asks.

"Yeah. I get antsy and extremely protective. I nearly started a fight with a TSA agent a couple days ago over her."

"You would hardly be the first person who wanted to start a fight with a TSA agent."

"There is that, but I came damned close to doing punching a guy over a picture."

"So, shall we play a guessing game about what she is? I'll give you three guesses. If you can guess correctly I'll give you another gold star."

"Any hints?" I ask.

"Of course not. This is reality, not school."

"Let's see. She's smart, impetuous, prone to fits of rage, beautiful, dangerous. She's Nature."

A sad trombone plays somewhere in the distance.

"No," Dreamer says, "try again. You have two more."

What would prompt a god of dreams to be attracted to a human woman? It can't be looks, he doesn't seem the type and besides, beautiful women are a dime a dozen. Why would John Begay say I need her more than she needs me? For that matter, was Begay lying? He was in cahoots with Dreamer, so I don't completely trust him anyway.

Jessica is unpredictable, but in a generally good way. Strong-willed, but reckless.

"She's Chaos." I say.

The sad trombone plays again.

"No. I know Chaos. I assure you they're different people. Chaos is quite stunning, but extremely tedious to be around," Dreamer says.

I have to admit, I hate things like this. Why the hell can't he just tell me?

Wait a minute. Smart, impetuous, beautiful, dangerous, strong-willed, reckless.

"She's Reality," I say.

Another gold start appears in the sky and I hear clapping drifting over the gray landscape.

"A minor correction, though. She's potential reality. Dreams and reality are always intertwined, my boy. As you figured out, without reality a dream is wasted energy. How did you put it? Sitting on a shitty couch."

"You read my mind?" I ask.

"You're in my realm, son, I don't have to read anything."

"Potential reality? Why potential reality?" I ask.

"The real world, as you so naively call it, will exist on its own with no help from me. But, by combining dreams and reality, you can make something magical."

"So, why am I so drawn to her?" I ask.

"Aside from her looks?"

"God, let it go. Yes. Aside from her looks."

"You're attracted to her because dreams always want to be reality. I left something inside your head, boy. Once I've gotten it back, she'll be just another woman who looks good in tight clothes. As you pointed out, they're a dime a dozen. This one just happens to be mine. Now, about that part of me."

If he can read my mind that part that he left behind lets me read his, and I get a vision of what he intends to do. He owns this land, lock, stock, and barrel, but he wants more. Like all potentates, he wants more power.

"You're going to consume her, aren't you? Replace her with yourself."

"Of course."

"I can't let you do that," I say.

"Well, Steven, I don't think you can stop me," Dreamer says, suddenly appearing in front of me. His suit is immaculate, as usual, and he's casually leaning on a cane like some kind of English aristocrat.

"Let's find out," I say, and throw the fastest punch I've ever thrown.

Dreamer deftly blocks and the fight is on.

38 | Tyson vs. Holyfield

Throwing a punch at a god while he was in his own realm was not the smartest thing I've ever done, but in my defense, it seemed like a really good idea at the time.

Dreamer is probably on the order of thousands of years old and is quite adept defending himself against his many enemies. He dodges my punch like he has all the time in the world and doesn't even bother to counter strike. Just waits patiently for my next attack.

Thunder slowly rumbles across the sky. It's a strange sound, though. More like a drawn out thump, a smooth sound that slowly rises rather than the random cacophony of thunder that builds and only grumpily dies off.

No rain, though and the smooth thunder seems to last an eternity.

Dreamer smiles and draws a sword out of his cane. I should have figured he'd have sword-cane. It just seems so him.

The sword flashes and I feel blood on my cheek. I barely saw him move, just a flicker and then my cheek was cut. He stands there, calmly watching me, and I know I am horribly outclassed. I've fought people better than me before and managed to survive, but he's not just better than I am, he's worlds beyond me.

I need a weapon. If I go hand-to-sword with this guy he'll cut me to ribbons without even breaking whatever passes for sweat in gods. Keeping an eye on him, I think hard and feel the world around me. It responds immediately and a katana forms in front of me.

Dreamer seems to be using an old European style of fencing, so a katana's not the best bet in the world, but it's really all I know how to use. At least it has the advantage of being fast and it's heavy enough he'll have trouble blocking it. I could conjure up a Chinese broad sword or a rapier, but I have no idea how to fence.

I am so fucked right now, it's not even funny.

"You could accept defeat right now. I'll make it quick and let the rest of your friends live. You could die to save them."

"No, thanks. I'll take my chances."

"And die in the process."

"I'd rather die on my feet than live on my knees."

I try to find the stillness I was taught to look for when fighting. When your mind is still, you're faster, stronger.

In a smooth motion I step forward and raise the sword up, in the next step I slash down in a classic kasagiri strike. Done correctly, the sword slashes down rapidly and cuts the opponent from left collar bone through to the right hip. The first few inches of the sword tip are supposed to cut though the ribs, sternum, heart, lungs. It's a killing strike.

My sword is heavier than Dreamer's and I'm using two hands so he can't block the strike. My kasagiri is nearly flawless and it flows like water. It must be this place because I could never do them that well in the real world.

Dreamer simply steps to the side and my blade misses him completely. The follow-through of my strike leaves me vulnerable to his blade, but I'm faster here and manage to twist and push his lighter blade away with my katana before he can run me through the neck.

After the block, my blade is pointing down and I'm inside his defenses. Rather than wasting the time to bring my sword to bear I just send a kick at his knee. Again he just moves. He is amazingly fast and hasn't even started using his flickering yet. Maybe the flickering doesn't work here.

After he dodges my kick he puts a fist in my face. I stagger back, but manage to maintain my footing.

"A very well executed strike, Steven. A lesser opponent would be dead right now," Dreamer says.

In a blur, he launches forward and the tip of his sword races toward me. I barley mange to twist and avoid taking his sword in my chest, but it still slices the outside of my arm. Mushin, no mind, takes over and I twist my sword sideways and thrust the point at him. He dodges, but this time the tip catches him and leaves a small, bloody rip in his formerly perfect suit.

I give him a small bow and start circling, looking for an entry. I know he's fast and skilled, better than I am by far. On the plus side, though, I just cut a god and that's pretty damned cool.

Here's a pro tip for you. Almost everyone you fight will be better than you at something. If you always approach the fight from a position of honorable fighting, you'll get creamed. In boxing, there are rules, designed to make sure the better fighter wins. Sure, the rules get broken, heads get butted, ears get bitten, but mostly boxing and MMA are rules-oriented sports.

In a fight, especially a sword fight, there is no such thing as a dirty move, there's only survival. Real fighting encourages the head-butt and the ear bite. It also smiles favorably on fingers in eyes, strikes to throats and kicks to knees.

He doesn't wait for me to find an opening, just swats my sword out his way with the tip of his own sword and lunges forward. I twist at the last second and get nothing more than a nasty cut on my chest. It burns like fire and bleeds like hell, but it won't kill me.

That's if anything can actually kill me in this place.

I continue my twist around and let it drive the hilt into the side of his head. I make contact and am busy mentally patting myself on the back when his side kick to my ribs nearly collapses my right lung.

We both immediately back off, me holding my side and him shaking the cobwebs out of his head.

Together, we continue the dance, each taking little pieces of each other but never quite managing to land that killing strike that would finish the fight. His hits, though, draw a little more blood. Every cut slows me down, makes me weaker, and the blood loss is taking its toll on me.

Finally, too slow to react, he slides the tip of his sword clean through my stomach. Strangely, it doesn't hurt that much, only a sensation of extreme cold and the shock – and relief – that it's finally over.

The light starts getting brighter and I know I'm about to pass out. I just hope he finishes it quickly.

Good bye, friends. Good bye, Jessica. I'm sorry I couldn't

save you. I'm sorry I wasn't good enough.

"It's a pity you wouldn't join me. You would have enjoyed what I plan to do to this world. When I force myself over Reality, this whole planet will be mine."

His voice sounds like it's a million miles away and I can barely hear him over the thrumming in my ears.

I manage to hold my head up and look him in the eye one last time. "Eat a dick," is all I manage to say.

"Good bye, Steven," he says and starts to move away from me.

Why isn't he finishing it?

There's thunder, actual thunder roaring exploding across the land now and Dreamer's eyes are lit up in rage as we slide further and further apart. A force is pushing me, roughly, away from him and he's screaming in pain and anger.

I can't figure out what's going on here. Maybe he took my advice and ate a dick.

My body hurts and something is pushing the air out my lungs, probably broken ribs or cuts or something I don't even remember getting hit with.

Dreamer is dissolving now. Breaking into pieces of dreams that fly in all directions. No matter which way they scatter, they all arc back to me and slam into my body. Is this some kind of crazy super attack, pummeling me with pieces of himself just to be a dick?

The pressure builds and I feel myself being thrust out of his land and back into reality. For a moment, time stands still and I get a good look at Dreamer's arm holding me off the ground, anger in his amber eyes, a strange line in the air like something just flew fast enough to ripple the air around us, and a bulge pushing out Dreamer's left side.

Time speed up and an explosion rips Dreamer in half and pushes me across the room, knocking the wind out of me. The two pieces of the former God of Dreams fall to the ground. All around me, shadows slide out of hiding and slither toward me. They feel different now, not so alien, just more parts of me like fingers or toes.

To my left, Wilford still has his thump gun aimed the remains of Dreamer.

Wilford grins, a huge, toothy grin full of vengeance and says, "Told you it was a god killer."

39 | Meet the New Boss

The star field that was in the room is gone now and all that's left is a simple space about fifty feet on each side. It's got shelves full of old wooden crates against the back wall and lots of posters. Some of the posters are warnings in English and German about safe handling procedures. Some of them are aging posters of naked women.

This used to be some kind of receiving center, storage or some kind of staging room for shipping materials. Whenever this place switched over to making mutant apes, they must have stopped shipping anything out.

I wonder how they got stuff down here.

"Nice shooting, Tex," I tell Wilford as he helps me to my feet.

"Yeah, it's tough to hit a static target with an explosive round," he replies.

"Well, when you're trying hit one target and miss another, it is. Anyway, thank you. He had me. Here and in the dream realm, he had me. If it hadn't been for you, I'd be dead, Jessica would be subsumed. He would have won."

"Subsumed?" he asks.

"She's Potential Reality, kind of like an engine of creation, he intended to overtake her and make our world his world."

"Yeah, but subsumed?"

"He wanted to absorb her."

"You know, I liked this world better when it was just terrorists," Wilford says with a sneer.

"I know, right? Find 'em, shoot 'em, done deal."

"A guy could kill an awful lot of bad guys with this gun. I could make a lot of bad things just go away."

"Don't forget the wound healing and probably immortality," I tell him as I clap him on the shoulder. "How are we doing?"

"I got most of their patrols, bombs are planted. That duffel bag full of explosives Jacob kicked down the well really helped. I think we're ready to bust this place up."

"Nice work. Where is everyone?" I ask.

"I saw Frank dragging Jacob to the elevator earlier. Not sure where Eve is, but I found a lot of broken guys. Necks snapped, heads crushed. I think she might be a trifle pissed. Haven't seen your girl, though."

My girl. That's kind of hard to wrap my head around. If she is who Dreamer said she is should I stay away? I think I may be him now, but I'm not sure. Also, am I him, or did I just inherit his mantle, or did I just imagine the whole thing?

This is getting too hard to deal with. I want to shoot something.

"She's next door, I think." I tell him.

"Go get her, I'm going to start making sure this place collapses."

We shake briefly and he heads up the stairs and I head next door.

* * * *

The room they had Jessica in is almost identical to the one I found Dreamer in. His had more art, but otherwise they're carbon copies. This one, however, has an extra cargo door cut into the side. That must be how things got moved around here. I'd always heard crazy rumors about an extensive tunnel system between this place and other places. The most common rumor was an underground railroad out to Area 51. Like most rumors, maybe that one had a grain of truth to it.

The room is mostly empty, save for the three guys knocked out on the floor and a couple of broken chairs. In the middle of the room is a simple wooden table that was probably made sometime in the 1950s. The table is extremely sturdily built, like someone used an entire tree to manufacture the thing.

Sitting on the table, wearing a tight black dress with inlaid gems that sparkle like stars and matching heels, is Jessica. She's calmly kicking her feet back and forth, holding her wrist, and looking around at the guys she laid out.

"Took you long enough," she says with a grin when she sees me.

"Sorry, had a run in with Ketch and had to fight a god."

"It's always some excuse with you, isn't it?"

"As excuses go, you've got to admit fighting a god is a pretty good reason to be late. What happened to your wrist?"

"I sprained it punching one of those assholes. The little guy over there," she says pointing at a guy whose right leg is bent backwards. "He looked like a wuss but had a jaw of iron."

I take her sprained wrist and give it a quick kiss. "Looks like you got the better of him in the long run."

She steps next to me and puts her arms around my neck. My arms find the small of her back and pull her close.

"Told you I could take care of myself," she tells me.

I look at the guys lying scattered around the room and can't help but agree with her. They probably thought there was no way this little girl was going to stop them. Just like those guys in the parking lot back in Albuquerque, they found out the hard way not to underestimate her.

"Nice dress," I say.

"What, this old thing? Had it for years."

"Just out of curiosity, how did you manage to take those guys out in that dress?"

"Oh, that. They had me undress and took my clothes. While they were busy gawking I kicked some ass. Then I put on the dress."

We stare at each other for a few minutes before our faces start drawing closer together. Just as our lips touch, there's a thunderous explosion and the walls and ceiling shake. Plaster and concrete dust lazily drift down over us.

"God dammit!" Jessica all but yells. "Who do I have to fuck up to get a kiss around here?"

"Fucking Wilford," I hiss. "He's blowing the place early, trying to bury us down here. We need to bolt and fast."

That said, I grab her and kiss her while the floor rumbles beneath our feet. Sometimes you just have to force that first kiss, especially when the world seems absolutely convinced that it just ain't gonna happen. Her arms tighten around my neck as she snuggles in closer and kisses back.

You know you've found a keeper when the world is all but collapsing and she kisses you back.

We break when another explosion rumbles and parts of the ceiling start actively dropping.

"Much as I'd like to continue, I'd also like to kiss you again sometime," she says. "Preferably soon."

"Yeah, we'd better get out of here unless we want to move in permanently."

Another explosion rocks the walls and there's a sound of something large hitting the door. When I open it, I find an extremely large piece of ceiling blocking out path.

"Fuck," Jessica hisses.

"Yeah," is all I can manage to come up with.

I put my shoulder into the debris and shove as hard as I can. Jessica joins me. Together, we manage to move it all of not an inch.

"Must be more debris on the other side," I say.

"Think that might be a way out?" she asks, pointing at the big cargo door.

"I sure as hell hope it is. Aside from the company, this room kind of sucks."

The door slides open easily enough and, indeed, there is a tunnel on the other side. There's a few foot drop, but there is a tunnel. Thank the gods, which may or may not include me at this point.

The tunnel isn't a railway tunnel, just a dirt floor that heads in the general direction of up. I'll take up right now. In fact, up seems downright perfect to me. I hop down into the tunnel floor and help Jessica down. The ceiling doesn't look too stable and parts of it are falling down. I have no idea how far this tunnel goes, but I've got a sinking feeling it's too far.

"Can you run in those shoes?" I ask pointing to her black heels.

"No, not even close and this floor is rocky enough that I'll shred my feet if I take them off. We could, however, take this motorcycle."

Holy shit. There is a motorcycle parked next to the door, a nice new BMW touring bike that someone left here recently. I'll lay you dollars to donuts that this bike once belonged to the biggest asshole in the universe, Devon Sheffield, wearer of RAND hats and drinker of free Scotch. This is probably how he got around without being too obvious.

The keys are in it and everything.

"You feel like driving?" I ask Jessica.

She holds up her wrist and shakes her head.

Shit. Well, at least I've ridden a bike before now. I throw a leg over the bike and settle in. I feel Jessica slide in behind me and her arms wrap around my waist.

When I turn the key, the bike gently roars to life. I take a minute to familiarize myself with the layout. So far everything looks normal.

There's a tap on my shoulder and Jessica leans forward and says, "Can we go now?"

Fuck it. Drop it into gear, hit the throttle and the bike darts up the tunnel. Jessica clenches my stomach and holds on for dear life.

I'm not terribly good at riding, but manage to dodge the huge piles of debris. By some remarkable twist of fate, none of the falling stuff brains us. I'd like to say the trip is was uneventful, but it's absolutely terrifying. Dodge one rock and another falls in front you. Dodge that one and there's a huge pile of debris on the ground.

It's a thrill ride that would be awesome if it was anyone but me doing it. Watch someone else deftly maneuvering a purloined motorcycle through falling rocks with a beautiful girl on the back and it's amazing entertainment. Try doing it for real sometime, though. Jessica's fingers are digging troughs in my skin and I'm in a near panic state. I'm absolutely convinced the next rock is going to brain me or smash her or I'm going to miscalculate a turn or dodge too sharply and lay the bike down.

Add in the fact that I'm not a very good biker and you have a recipe for disaster. For once, though, lady luck is on my side. The tunnel ends and the sky is covered with stars. There's a tap on my shoulder and I see Jessica pointing at a clearing.

Looks like as good a place as any to stop.

40 | What I Don't Know About Being A God Could Fill A Warehouse

We park the bike in the clearing and take a look around. It's quiet out here, the kind of quiet you only get in the wilderness. Jessica stands next to me, hand in mine, head leaning on my shoulder. This side of the mesa faces the town and you can see a few dots of light moving around. The casino is still lit up like some pathetic version of Las Vegas.

If you listen closely, you can hear secondary explosions deep under the mesa.

"I hope everyone got out okay," I whisper.

"I hope all those apes got fried," she says.

"I hope Devon Sheffield is pinned under half of ton of rubble."

"Who?"

"That guy that tricked Eve and I into here."

"Oh, him," she says. "He'll get his."

There's a rustling in the brush and Wilford pops through into the clearing. He's standing tall and proud, like he used to whenever he took down some group of terrorists or another. He's got that look that says he just saved the world and can't believe no one cares.

"Hi, Wil," I call out to him.

He stops dead in his tracks. When he sees us his body goes briefly white. No, literally white, like a complete lack of pigment. White like paper white. Some people look like they've seen a ghost, he briefly looks like a ghost. The shocked look passes quickly and something that approximates relief floods his features.

"Thank God, you guys made it out. The charges had faulty timers. They must have gotten screwed up when they fell or something," he responds.

I'll admit I'm no expert on Jacob. We've hung out, drank beers, fought, shot guns, but for all that I really couldn't say I know the man. Unless that's all there is to him. Some people live their lives right out in the open and have very little in the way of sub surface strata. It doesn't mean they're stupid or shallow, it just means that everything you need to know is right out there for the taking.

One thing I do know for certain about Jacob: he wouldn't have kicked those explosives down the shaft if he thought it would detonate them or damage them.

"Good to know," I say. "I was worried you had detonated everything early so you could bury us down there. How funny is that?"

His body flashes white again. What the hell else have they done to him to make his color literally change like that?

"That's messed up, man. You know I'd never do that to you," he says with a nervous laugh.

Wilford's hand is slowly inching toward his gun. The gun I gave him. The gun that blew a god in half. If he manages to skin that smoke wagon, I could be in trouble. He's a hell of a shot and he completely lacks compunction when it comes to killing. Put a gun in his hand, and the man becomes a machine.

I can feel shadows out there in the brush, silently slinking around. In the long run, after I figure out what I am, I may be tougher than him, but it will take me some time to sort out what I can and cannot do. If I had Dreamer's skill set, I could pop over there and disarm him before he even knew what happened, but I don't have that skill set and I'm not sure if I ever will.

I can control the shadows, though. I don't know what I can do with them, but I can feel them out there.

"Are you planning on shooting us?" I ask Wilford.

"Thinking about it," he finally confesses.

"What the fuck, man? Why would you do that?" I ask him.

Jessica has quietly moved away from me, probably trying to find a position to attack him from. I hate to break it to her but she wouldn't get two steps before he burned her down. Add that dress and those shoes and there is no way in hell she can get anywhere near him.

I put a hand on her shoulder and she stops moving.

"You're the bad guys," he says simply.

"And you're what, the hero?" Jessica asks him.

"I have more power than you can imagine. I can feel it coursing through me. Whatever they shot me up with has changed me for the better," he tells her. "So, yeah, I'm going to be the hero. You guys nearly toppled a government. There are people out there hurting right now and I'm going to help them. Those people you put in danger? I'm going to save them.

"I'm going to hunt down all the monsters we couldn't take out before."

"Quick question: does that include us?" I ask.

Wilford blinks for a moment. This clearly isn't going as easily as he planned. I'm sure in his mind he had a completely different scenario built up. Show up, rattle off something witty, blast us, and disappear feeling heroic. I guess it turned out to be harder to shoot a friend than he thought.

"Yeah," he finally says. "Yeah, it does."

In a small part of my mind, I send one of my shadows on a mission with a simple parameter: Find Eve and bring her back. It shoots off like black blur.

"You know, pal," I tell him, feeling around in my jacket for a cigarette. Ah, there's one. Light it up, look dramatic. Be Constantine. "You know, buddy, that's the first time I've ever heard one of the good guys monologue. Did you practice that or was it completely extemporaneous?"

"You're an asshole, you know that?" Wilford tells me. "But you're a fun asshole. I'm going to miss you."

With that, a whole mess of things start happening all at once.

Shadows snake up Wilford's legs, running some kind of automated defense routine. Wilford draws his gun before the shadows can take his head, but my minions are already having some effect on him. His aim, normally laser straight, is off. Jessica drops to the ground and rolls off. Somewhere in the distance, I hear something crashing through the brush. I hope it's Eve but I'll settle for a bear.

I just stand there like an idiot while my former friend fires at me. I may as well have my thumb up my ass for all the good I'm doing here. If I'm going to be the new God of Dreams, I should probably step up my game somewhat. Luckily, though, Wilford's shot goes wild and a tree behind me explodes.

I know that gun takes a moment to recharge, so I calmly exhale the smoke I had been holding in, making it look like I wasn't at all concerned when, in reality, I had stopped breathing. My shadows wrap around him and his hands go to his eyes, trying to pull the things off his face.

Then, without warning, he simply stops moving and his body glows red for a moment. When it fades back to normal, all my shadows have disappeared. It was a strange sensation feeling them die and it kind of rocks me on my heels. I'm not sure I can describe exactly how it felt. It wasn't a physical pain so much as a mental pain. Think back to your first break up with a girlfriend or boyfriend and how your heart ached. That's what it felt like.

He opens his eyes just as his gun gives a quite ping to let him know it's ready to be fired. In a flash, the gun is pointed directly at me and that barrel sure looks big.

It figures. I just took out a bunch of Nazis, killed Ketch, fought a god and walked away to tell about it, and just got a first kiss. Now I'm going to buy it at the hands of a former buddy with delusions of grandeur.

Wilford's a professional. He doesn't bore me with tedious speeches, or threats, or gloating. Just a simple, "Goodbye, Steven."

I must have earned up some good karma somewhere, though, because before he can shoot me, Eve hits him in the back of the head hard enough to knock him about fifteen feet. It's a blow that would kill a mortal, but Wilford's not mortal anymore. Probably not even human. The irony of a guy who can change colors and get shot without getting killed calling me a monster is not lost on me.

He's down for just a moment before he's back on his feet, pointing the gun all around him. His eyes go dark and he frowns. He's got me on one side and Eve on the other. He might be able to get one of us, but the other will be on him like white on rice before the gun recharges.

"You can still walk away from this," I tell him.

"Fuck that," Eve snarls. "I told him I'd pull his spine out through his nose. I'd kind of like to see if I can actually do it."

"The first person that moves get blown in half," Wilford whispers.

"Immediately after that you get to smell your own spine," Eve hisses at him.

This is a real mess. At least Jessica had the smarts to get out of the way.

When I glance down to check on her, she's gone. There's just a pair of shoes and a trail where someone rolled away. I guess while everyone else was preoccupied, she decided to take matters into her own hands. Well, hand, anyway.

"If I kill you first," Wilford tells Eve, "it won't take much to take care of them. She's just a girl and he doesn't know what he is anymore."

Wilford turns on Eve and raises the gun. She's tough, but I have a feeling that damned weapon may do her in. There's a sinking feeling in my gut, like someone got a wild hair up their ass and decided to make another season of "Arrested Development."

He doesn't quite finish the turn before a pistol barks and Wil's head snaps to the side. Another two shots immediately follow, pushing him over. As I watch, the small wounds in the side of his head heal up.

"I know these won't kill you, but they don't feel good and all I need to do is distract you long enough for these two to take care of you," Jessica says quietly.

She's standing off to the side, holding a Detonics pistol in one hand. The little .45 kicks like a .45, so shooting in one handed is no mean feat. Her dress is dusty and torn and there are pieces of tumbleweed and scrub brush stuck all over her. Somehow or another she managed to get a twig tangled in her raven locks. I could have sworn she was unarmed when we were kissing. She must have had that little gun hidden somewhere in that tight dress of hers. Seriously, I'd love to know how women do that.

Wil looks around at the three of us and decides the odds aren't in his favor. With an angry glare he holsters the gun and turns to face me. "This isn't over, you know. I'll find all of you sometime. I'll make it my goal in life to find all of you."

"Any reason we can't kill him right now?" Eve asks.

"We might get him, but he'll get at least one of us," I say. "Bad odds. I say we let him go. We'll cross paths again."

"You're damned right, we'll meet again," Wilford tells us. "This is far from over."

"What's your beef?" Jessica asks him.

"I've spent my life protecting this country. My forefathers spent their lives protecting this county. The three of you and those other two guys nearly destroyed it. My country! You want a reason? Here's your reason: I'm good and you're bad. That's the only reason I need."

"I don't feel bad," I say. "I mean I don't feel great, but I don't think I feel bad."

"Always a joke with you, isn't it Steven? Anything to ease the tension, to avoid having to face facts."

"What can I say, I'm an ass?" I reply.

"Now what?" Jessica asks, still steadily aiming the gun at Wil's head.

"Now he walks away," I say. "There's nothing else we can do right now. He walks away."

"Steven, you could end all this right now." Wil smirks, "All you need is a pair of balls, but you're unwilling to make sacrifices."

"I'm not averse to sacrifices Wil. This just isn't a good one. Why don't you beat it before she shoots your again and she rips your spine out?"

I can see the anger build up in Wil's eyes. He's as pissed as I've ever seen him before. There is absolute rage in his eyes, but he cowboys up, turns, and stalks off into the darkness. I keep my eye on him for as long as I can. Once he disappears I exhale a sigh of relief. I'll have to meet him again sometime, but I'm so tired right now I can barely think.

41 | Like Moths to a Flame

"*Yá'át'ééh, Bilagáana.* I told you I'd help you out and you went and became *Na'iidzeeł* anyway," a voice says behind us.

John Begay has a habit of showing up and insulting me. I don't think it's anything personal; it's just the way he is.

"What do those words even mean?" Jessica asks him as she points her gun at his head.

"*Yá'át'ééh* is a greeting. *Bilagáana* is a Navajo word for white folk. Kind of like gringo, but harder to pronounce. Not sure about the other," I tell her.

"*Na'iidzeeł* is a dream. It can be either good or bad, but it's a dream you have while you're sleeping. Your man here is in charge of those things now." Begay tells her. "Put down the gun, child. I'm not here to hurt anyone and your bullets won't do a damned thing to me anyway."

She lowers her weapon, but still looks wary of him. It's probably a safe bet to stay wary of this guy. I'm tired, but still fuming that he betrayed us, helped orchestrate this whole scheme. It was because of Begay that we came up here in the first place. Because of that, we nearly lost everything.

"Is your buddy Fear floating around here somewhere, too?" I ask.

"No, she's busy tonight, but she was in on it, too."

"So, why are you here? Come to betray me some more?" Eve asks him. "Gods above, I can't believe I danced with you like that."

"I didn't betray you, I distracted him for you. Let him think I was on his side," Begay tells her.

"You'll have to excuse me if I don't exactly trust you," I tell him.

"Welcome to your new world, *Na'iidzeeł.* If I've done nothing else, I've taught you that you can't trust any of us. We're all in it for ourselves."

"So, if you're all in it for yourselves, how come you and Fear were working together?" I ask.

"She had her reasons, I had mine. It just happened that it worked well for us to keep you moving this way."

"What were your reasons?" Jessica asks him.

"My reasons were my own," he tells her.

"So I'm in charge of dreams, now? What does that even mean? Is there a book or something I should be reading?" I ask.

"Like I said, welcome to your new world. You were born once with no idea what you needed to do, you've just been reborn with the exact same information."

"Thanks, asshole."

"It happens to everyone, *Na'iidzeeł*. You're not so special that you get a pass. Do you think you're the first human to do this? It doesn't happen often, but it has happened and will happen again. You get to learn on your own, just like everyone else.

"One word of advice, though: watch your step."

With that he blends back in the world and is gone.

I'm bone tired, like my soul is exhausted. The world swirls and my legs give out. I have a vision of sorts, sensation of watching myself fall and rushing toward a collapsed figure on the ground. My vision is strange and seems to come from the ground. Others are rushing forward, too, and I can see through them as well. Together we surge forward, desperate to protect the fallen figure, but another is in the way, a woman with black hair, who has beaten us there and is cradling the figure.

We can't stop her, but she feels safe, so we slow down and creep forward. She's protecting the figure, and starts slightly when we crawl out of the grass, but relaxes and turns back the figure on the ground, holding him on her lap.

We take up a protective position around the figure and the one with black hair. We're not as strong as we will be, but we will gladly sacrifice ourselves to save them.

There are energies rushing around, things happening that we can see but seem to be invisible to the others. The one with the black hair shivers when a bolt of energy passes through her and into the figure on the ground, but she doesn't see it or the maelstrom of purple and gold energies swirling around her. She glimpses it out of the corner of her eye, but chalks it up to being tired and stressed.

She has potential, this one, but it is up to her to recognize it. No one can force her to where she needs to go, but she is driven. This one will be fine.

42 | Time To Go

I wake up with a strange taste in my mouth, my head in Jessica's lap, and her fingers in my hair. She smiles when she sees my eyes open and, I must say I've never seen anything more amazing than that smile. It's a lie that it takes fewer muscles to smile than it does to frown; frowning actually takes fewer muscles than smiling. Her smile, though, makes excellent use of the extra muscles and the complicated movement of rearranging lips and eyes conveys a sense of relief, of joy, of love.

She leans down and plants a gentle kiss on my lips and I realize I'm in that perfect place that everyone seeks.

Unfortunately, perfection is fleeting. You only get it by the moment, the first taste of a great meal, the first sip of an excellent scotch, waking up in a beautiful woman's lap. You need to enjoy it while it lasts because I guarantee you something will find a way to drive it away from you eventually.

In our case, it's the sound of sirens echoing from the town below. It would appear that blowing up half the mesa didn't go unnoticed. This is probably the most excitement to hit Dulce in the sleepy little town's long life.

I sit up and feel Jessica's hand on my back, gently maintaining contact and keeping me from falling. Flashing lights are racing toward us. Every cop and firefighter down there just got the opportunity they've all been secretly craving. They're probably all thinking it's high time they got the chance to take care of problems the way they should be taken care of.

"Where are Frank and Jacob?" I ask, suddenly remembering I'm not the only person in the world.

"Back that way a bit," Eve says. "They're safe."

"We need to get out of here. Those guys are going to be keyed up to hell and back. They're probably thinking all the stories about the aliens in there are true and the invasion has started," I say.

As we watch, other points of light start tearing around the streets, the big 4x4s of regular people who are heading out to take care of the problem. Those folks are probably armed to the teeth and ready to shoot everything that moves.

Jessica and Eve help me to my feet. My legs are still rubbery, but they're rapidly getting better. By the time we get moving, I'm feeling stable. My shadows are already speeding forward, checking the ground for traps, making sure the way is safe.

When we find the place where Frank was taking care of Jacob there's only a small blood stain on the ground.

"Where'd they go?" Jessica asks.

"Jacob was pretty bad off, they didn't walk out of here," Eve tells her. "Maybe they moved to a better hiding place."

We search the area but there are no tracks leading off, no torn up pieces of scrub brush. My shadows spread out in a wave but find no traces of Frank or Jacob. Nothing. Not a god damned thing. It's like they just vanished.

"Hey! Look at this," Jessica yells.

Carved into a large rock is a simple message:

Safe,

John.

"What the Hell?" I ask.

"John's trying to atone," Eve says with a little smile. "He'll never admit he was wrong, but he feels bad. He'll take care of them."

"Huh, I thought he was Navajo," I say. "This is Apache turf. The two don't always get along."

"Steven," Eve tells me like I'm a child, "he's the spirit of this whole part of the world. He's much more than a single tribe."

"Gotcha," I tell her. "I keep forgetting."

"We need to vanish, too," Jessica says. "This place is going to be crawling with cops soon."

"We've got a motorcycle back there," I say, "but we can't get all three of us on there."

"Don't worry about me," Eve says. "I'll be long gone before anyone gets here."

Eve's gray eyes are lit up, alive with the thrill of the evening. She's a warrior and the action and excitement are what she lives for.

In the end, she'll wind up on a broken merry-go-round with a shattered arm and cradling the corpse of a fallen lover, but she'll survive and she'll happily go into oblivion knowing she won.

"Good luck," is all I can manage to say.

Eve steps in close and takes Jessica and me in a huge bear hug, crushing us together. Good lord, she's strong.

"Good luck to you, too," she says before dropping us. "I'll find you later."

Was that a tear in her eye, or a trick of the light?

She doesn't wait around, just darts off into the night, long legs carrying her smoothly across the rough terrain.

The bike is right where we left it, but there's no clear path down the side of the mesa. I tell Jessica to hold on and hit it. My shadows show me a path and I watch our descent through my eyes and theirs.

I'm getting better at this riding thing. Maybe the escape from falling mountain run we did earlier was enough to kick my trust in myself into gear. It's a tricky ride down the side of the mesa and there's no clear trail to follow. My shadows float ahead, finding the easiest routes, picking the best lines and reporting back.

Amazingly, I don't ride us off the edge of a cliff or into a tree and we make it into town without being spotted.

We stop at a convenience store to get a wrap bandage for Jessica's wrist and see if we can find a long sleeve shirt or something to keep her warm on the ride. The place is bright and clean and Sly and the Family Stone's "Stand" is playing over the radio. It's another one of those perfect, if kind of strange, moments. There's a small stack of sweatshirts in the back, emblazoned with a logo for Dulce, NM, that almost makes the place look like it might be fun to visit. Next to those is rack with the ubiquitous Baja shirts that you can find all over the Southwest. She chooses a black and purple Baja that almost matches her dress.

Luckily there are also some thick wool socks left over from winter. Her shoes wouldn't have been spectacularly warm, but it's a moot point since they're up the mesa somewhere.

The clock on the wall reads 5:30, so we must have been underground longer than I thought. I wonder how long I was out after Eve clobbered me. It was morning when we went in, so we were underground for about 20 some odd hours. She must have smashed me pretty hard. No wonder my head still hurts.

At least we buried those bastards. I hope their ghosts gets stuck down there with the ghosts of everyone they tortured.

I guess I hadn't thought about it, but we must look a fright. I'm cut up, her dress is torn, we're both covered with dust and debris, and she still has a twig in her hair. If we had been smart, we would have cleaned up in the bathrooms, but I guess the damage was done the second we walked in. When I drop the bandage and the Baja and socks on the counter the clerk stares at us like we just walked out of a horror movie.

"Rough sex," Jessica says simply as I pay.

The clerk nods and asks if we want our receipt.

Back at the bike, I wrap her wrist and she puts on the Baja and socks. We both stand there in the middle of the parking lot and stare at each other.

She manages to make a Baja sweatshirt, a torn dress, and a pair of brown wool socks look cute. For all the shit we've been through over the past couple of days, she keeps her glow going. It must have something do with being Potential Reality, whatever the hell that means.

"Where to now, cowboy?" she asks.

"Where do you want to go?"

"Out of this place."

"My place is a couple of hours north of here, Albuquerque's a few hours south of here."

"I think my legs would freeze before we got there."

"Chama's about half an hour east of here. They've got hotels and a Wal-Mart."

She steps up close to me and plants a kiss. "I think I can handle half an hour if I can snuggle up to you. You know, to keep warm."

"I think something can be arranged," I tell her as I give her a quick kiss.

Freshly minted romance is always so sickening when you're on the outside, but, like I say, live those few perfect moments that you get because they don't last forever.

43 | With Great Power Comes Great Responsibility To Abuse That Power

We hit Chama just as the sun was coming up and found a hotel with a decent bathtub and, more importantly, a warm bed. The hotel was shaped like a long wooden cabin with a bunch of rooms. It was dead silent at night save for the odd semi rumbling down the road and the stars were absolutely amazing. The little town was a nice place to hide out in for a few days while we tried to figure what to do with each other and the world around us.

We wore clothes from Wal-Mart, ate in little diners, and discussed the future.

The explosion and collapse of a large chunk of the mesa in Dulce attracted international media attention and suddenly everyone in the world descended on that sleepy little town. The locals were all too happy to have the attention and made up some amazing stories about Men In Black, aliens, and how UFOs regularly abducted people.

Nazis never made it into their stories and no one wove tales about mutant apes.

Lying in bed one morning, watching the news and drinking coffee, we saw an interview with a guy who claimed he could communicate with the aliens through his email. The aliens, he said, insisted on using AOL accounts because they were more secure because the UDP packets were triple encrypted with SSL, PPTP, and, IPSec.

Don't worry if that sentence doesn't make any sense because I know computers fairly well and it doesn't make a lick of sense to me, either. It sounded like someone had managed to pick up a beginner's book of computer security and got lost shortly after the table of contents. Total nonsense.

The media, having fun with this guy, decided to let him prattle on for a bit before shutting him down with a happy "Thank you for that amazing tale!"

The interview, in and of itself, was an unremarkable puff piece. What was going on in the background was interesting, though. Standing in the crowd, calmly watching the circus, was one of the new Aryan supermen.

"Shit," I said. "I was hoping all those guys were dead."

"Don't worry about it," Jessica told me. "He's on his own and they can't make more of them."

"I hope not, those guys seemed like they were bad news waiting to happen."

I still don't know for sure where all the scientists and assorted staff of the base were, but I have a sickening suspicion. The place looked pretty self-sustaining, so I'll be they got everything working and killed everyone or turned them into apes. Maybe the C in status stood for Converted or Changed. Maybe a few got converted to those perfect men, but I'm betting most everyone found themselves floating in a vat of green goo or used as spare parts. Werner didn't exactly seem to be above such things.

* * * *

John Begay was as good as his word and his people saved Jacob's life. They spirited them away and hid them out in some small community that most people have never even heard of. Hell, I've lived out here most of my life and I've never heard of it. It has a hospital, of sorts, though, and that's ultimately what saved Jacob from the bullet in his gut.

From what I gathered, everyone felt Jacob was hilarious and Frank was pretty dour. Between the two of them they regaled the small Apache community with all kinds of tales of hacking buildings and running guns. I would imagine the story of Dreamer came up. I would also imagine no one found it in the least bit disturbing. One of the tribes around here had to have had some experience with Dreamer at some point in the past or no one would have written that book I found in Durango. The book didn't seem particularly warm about him.

It took Jacob a few weeks of recuperation before he was

capable of getting around on his own and another couple of weeks before he was ready to leave. In the end, he healed up just fine, which is damned lucky with a gut shot. He's a tough old bastard and has probably used the story of getting shot by a religious zealot to get free drinks.

I was as good as my word, too, and saw Frank safely back to the loving arms of Chet.

Chet almost forgave me for keeping Frank away as long as I did, but caught himself and told me he'd kick my ass if I ever showed up on their doorstep again. Then he gave me a big hug. Then he gave Jessica a big hug. Then he threatened both of us. Then he hugged us again.

I don't know what the big deal was. I said I'd get him back in a few days and got him back in five weeks instead. The important point was that I got Frank back.

"Your guy is a little excitable," Jessica told Frank, which just made Chet hug her again.

We wound up staying for dinner at Chet's insistence. Chet's an amazing cook. I'd never had anemone and lobster in a cream sauce, but it was pretty amazeballs. He also made fresh bread. From scratch. I love fresh bread made from scratch.

Jessica and I kicked around Seattle for a few days, but found it too damned cold and wet to be much of a vacation.

* * * *

I've still got a few contacts in the spook game and they feed me information every now and then. Some people in that industry know all about the terrors that lurk around the country and they're extremely worried that Wilford Saxton is actively changing the rules. Eventually, they think, the monsters will bite back and there won't be an effective cover up.

Wilford has been quietly taking out monsters all over the country. The first was, predictably, Coco. The boogeyman of northern New Mexico Latino lore was found with its limbs blown off and its corpse dumped in a parking lot in Cuba, NM. At first, everyone thought it was just a bear that had mysteriously come into contact with some C4, but closer examination showed something far different.

The official word was it was some sort of mutant bear. Mutated by what, no one ever bothered to answer. The official word never explained why the arms, legs, and torso were all found in different parts of the parking lot, either. I heard someone mention something to the effect of an electrical discharge, stray lightning or some such nonsense.

It makes sense that Wilford would go after the very creature that ultimately caused him to be the thing he is now.

Most people bought the cover up story about the bear and the lightning. It's always easier to just accept a story and let cognitive dissonance take over than to accept the fact that there are very dangerous things out there.

Wilford will keep hunting and he won't be quiet about it. It always rubbed him the wrong way that there was nothing we could do about the monsters out there. I tried to explain to him once that the U.S. security apparatus was not equipped to deal with things like Coco and he should try Ghostbusters instead.

After finding out that the boogeyman is very real, panic will overtake this country. Suddenly every parent who's ever told their kid the boogeyman was coming for bad kids will worry that the boogeyman is coming for them instead. There will be hearings and inquiries and whole new army of people who claim they can take care of your monster problem. They'll get shredded the first time they find one of the monsters.

Dreamer killing Congress shook some people up, but even a few months later people were beginning to doubt what they had seen. There aren't many monsters out there but the mere knowledge of such things will drive a bunch of people over the edge. It was easy for most people to dismiss Dreamer as a figment or a one-off problem. I think this is because Dreamer, as a god, was hard to wrap your head around. Also, the fact that he killed Congress made him seem like he might actually be a good guy. No one will think the monsters are good guys.

That's how this country works; good guys and bad guys. Dreamer kills corrupt politicians and he's a good guy. No one ever stopped to think why or what he hoped to accomplish. People agreed with his outcome so he was one of the good guys.

Wilford Saxton will be seen as a good guy, too. A mighty new superhero that's saving us from the things that go bump in the night. They don't know him like I do, though. He'll kill monsters because he wants to. He doesn't give two tugs of a dead dog's dick about the people.

Personally, I think we deserve a better class of hero.

I'm sure I'll have to meet him again. He's all but said he's gunning for me. I just hope my skills are up to speed when we do meet again.

* * * *

In time I slowly figured out what Dreamer had been up to. In a flash of insight, I discovered how to take someone over and the experience was eye-opening.

We were in Durango one day when some damned idiot tourist from Florida ran a red light and nearly plowed into woman with a baby carriage. Downtown Durango is no place to be in a hurry. It's filled to the brim with people walking around without paying any attention whatsoever to where they're going.

Most of them are probably stoned, but, hey, it's legal in Colorado.

Anyway, this old guy, who was probably stoned also, was in a hurry to get where he was going and gunned his big truck through the light. Right in front of him was a young couple (who also wasn't paying attention) pushing a stroller. I felt myself jump forward without moving and the next thing I knew I was inside his head slamming on the breaks and inside my own head watching the whole thing happening.

It took an enormous effort just to move that guy's foot down on the brake pedal. The truck stopped and I popped back out this guy's head and watched him shake his head wondering what the hell just happened. The young couple flipped him off and he gunned his engine at them, but at least crisis was averted.

My best guess is this: Dreamer wanted control and he started by trying to take over as many government institutions as possible. He tagged DHS first because it's a young organization and hasn't built up the same level of paranoia as the CIA or the NSA. It made them easier to control, but even his powers had limits.

In the end, he settled for just addling those guys, dropping them into that perpetual half-sleep that you get when you haven't actually slept for a length of time. Turns out, that was an incredibly easy task. The human brain needs deep sleep, dream-level sleep, to keep functioning. The brain loves it, actually, and all it takes is boredom to make you want to sleep.

Doubt me? Set an alarm clock so it will never let you hit dream sleep and see how you're doing in a week. Then remember most of those people hadn't been in dream sleep for months. I'm amazed none of them completely lost it and gunned down a convent or something.

So, how did he do it? Well, he was the God of Dreams, and he simply denied them dreams. No dreams, no dream-level sleep. It must have been a waking nightmare.

Problem was he still needed an army to take over with. No matter how tough he was, he was no match for the combined power of the whole country. Controlling the army was right out the window. My guess was his max number to control at once hovered around a couple dozen or so. We humans generate a lot of interference, even if we don't recognize it, and the more minds you're trying to control, the harder the task becomes.

At some point, somehow or another, he got wind of what was going on in Dulce. Maybe he jumped into someone's dreams or maybe someone simply spilled the beans to him. My gut says Begay told him, probably for reasons completely unrelated to anything Dreamer himself wanted. The end result was he found his army. The Perfect Men and the other scientists and guards would have been a problem, but the apes would have been a Godsend. The apes had no real will of their own. Give them a command and they'd carry it out, even if it meant throwing themselves into a hail of bullets.

My best guess put about 15,000 of the beasts in the mesa with machinery to easily make more. Not a huge army, but he didn't need one to start with.

Dreamer couldn't control the Perfect Men, their will was just too strong. I suspect he wouldn't have been able to control Wilford, either, since Wilford is essentially a Perfect Man 2.0. So, Dreamer and John Begay cooked up a scheme to draw us in. An honest-to-God Valkyrie and a near complete hit man of the Gods would make short work of the installation. Plus it would get him Jessica and, possibly, me. Frank and Jacob would probably have been of or turned into more apes.

We fell for it, hook line and sinker, and did his dirty work for him.

The strain of controlling his little cadre and his inability to sense

Wilford were the only things that stopped him. I still wake up at night, feeling his hand around my throat and seeing his sword in my stomach. He beat me, and it was only his arrogance and his complete confidence in himself that did him in.

Those nights, Jessica calmly puts a hand on my chest and I slowly drift back off.

* * * *

We're still not entirely certain what she is. Potential Reality is a pretty nebulous term, but she's learning that she can do things, make things real if there's a possibility that they can become real. I know, I know: confusing. Think about it this way: over time a mountain can rise up and be eroded by wind and rain. On a long enough time line, if it can happen, it will happen. What she does is hurry those things along.

She can accelerate or change potential reality and she does it all on her own. I can show her things that people dream about and, sometimes, she can make them happen. I feed her ideas and energy and she changes the world. She doesn't entirely need my help, though. She can change things all on her own and all by herself although without fuel her powers are more limited.

I don't think she can do people, though, just things. Leastwise, that's what she claims. Near as I can tell, she hasn't altered me. I've always had ripped abs and been incredibly well-endowed.

On that trip into Durango we were hoping to find some kind of explanation of what we were supposed to be doing. There's book store, the Southwest Book Trader, over on the corner of 5th St and 2nd Ave. Or 2nd St and 5th Ave, I forget which. Go to the south end of Main where it turns east, you can't miss it. This bookstore is one of the few genuinely magical places on Earth. If a book has been written, it is in that shop. Note: this does not mean it will be easy to find that book, it just means any book that has ever been written is in that shop.

The Southwest Book Trader deals in more than just books, but the selection of books is what will always set it apart from any other bookstore on this planet. The books are piled on top of each other and in front of each other and you just know a spark in the store would start a conflagration that could be seen from space.

This is the place I found the book that mentioned Dreamer.

Alas, even though I was hoping to find "So, You're a God.

Now What?" or "The Beginner's Guide to Godness," I couldn't find a lick of information about what to do now. After a full day of searching, during which Jessica wandered off to the sandwich shop next door and later to the make your own wine place, I never found a single word about what it means to be a God of Dreams. I guess I'll have to write my own and secret it into the book store someday.

Or maybe not. If I have to figure it out on my own, so does the next guy. Or girl.

Until then, I hop through dreams and bring back neat things for Jessica to make real and suck energy out the dream world to fuel her powers. I'm learning to control my shadows and how to use them effectively. They're always out there, constantly feeding me information. They're like having eyes and ears everywhere; my own personal spy agency. The sensation of looking and hearing so much nearly overloaded my poor, human brain, but I've learned to adapt and compartmentalize information.

I'm also training, constantly. I get the feeling it won't always be a relaxing time. I know Wilford's still gunning for me, Begay may still be after me, there's a Perfect Man still on the loose with unknown intentions, and who knows how many of those Dreamtime churches are still lurking out there.

That's not all, though. Somewhere, out there, a storm is brewing. I can see it in every dream I enter. Something is extremely displeased and I'm going to come face to face with it one of these days.

Acknowledgments and Final Thoughts

No matter how hard I try, I can't write a book on my own. I had a small but talented team of beta readers who kept me realistic and focused. Thanks to RobRoy McCandless for the enormous amount of editing work and pointing out of things that didn't work. Also thanks to Steve VonDeneen for reminding me that bullets don't ping off bullet-proof glass, they make little spider webs where the first layer of glass breaks but the rest of the layers stay unbroken. And thanks to my wife for her time and energy and keeping me focused.

Rob's a writer, too, and his first book "Tears of Heaven" came out about the same time as "Henchmen." It's a good read and you can find it on Amazon and a few other places. Steve writes, too, but it's mostly purchase orders and things like that.

I always intended Henchmen to be just the first book of a short series, so Steven and the gang will be back.

www.ingramcontent.com/pod-product-compliance
Lightning Source LLC
Chambersburg PA
CBHW061553170626
46811CB00001B/187